CAIT
LONDON

A STRANGER'S
TOUCH

AVON

An Imprint of HarperCollins*Publishers*

This is a work of fiction. Names, characters, places, and incidents are products of the author's imagination or are used fictitiously and are not to be construed as real. Any resemblance to actual events, locales, organizations, or persons, living or dead, is entirely coincidental.

AVON BOOKS
An Imprint of HarperCollins*Publishers*
10 East 53rd Street
New York, New York 10022-5299

Copyright 2008 by Lois Kleinsasser
ISBN: 978-0-06-114051-8
www.avonromance.com

First Avon Books paperback printing: April 2008

Avon Trademark Reg. U.S. Pat. Off. and in Other Countries, Marca Registrada, Hecho en U.S.A.
HarperCollins is a registered trademark of HarperCollins Publishers.

Printed in the U.S.A.

10 9 8 7 6 5 4 3 2 1

A Stranger's Touch is the second of the *Psychic Sisters* trilogy, though the central theme began simmering in my mind years ago. We began with Claire, the empath, in *At the Edge*, and now it is Tempest's turn.

As we enter the Aisling triplets' lives, legends, and unique psychic danger, I am grateful for Lucia Macro, my editor at Avon Books, for her enthusiasm, confidence, and hard work to bring these very special sisters' stories to life.

———————————

Prologue

"DANIEL? ARE YOU OUT THERE?"

Greer Aisling wrapped her arms around herself and stared out at the dark waves of the Pacific Ocean. The Northwest's salt-scented air blended with the earthy scents of her garden. She and her husband had sat here, watching their daughters play for hours—until they were four years old, and then, suddenly, she was a widow.

Since Daniel Bartel's death, she'd tried to talk with him, but no one in her family had ever communicated or acted as a medium for the dead.

Just as the waves grew and crested beyond the shoreline, anger rose in Greer. She worked to control her anger, to push it down. Her daughters were not only linked to each other and to her by their birth, but all of them were connected by psychic talent. Right now the triplets' delicate psychic antennae could pick up any nuance of her emotions, and she had to be careful.

As she had often done during stressful times, Greer spoke to Daniel as if he were alive. "The Blair Institute of Parapsychology actually used child abuse and neglect as an excuse to come into my home. They used the law to take my children while I was away working . . . just because they couldn't get access to my daughters any other way. They just had to know the psychic endowment, the limits and abilities of my children, because I am a professional psychic . . . for some damned study."

While their mother was away, working to solve the case of a missing boy, the ten-year-old Aisling-Bartel triplets had been taken from their home and the care of their guardian and housekeeper. Until that horrible day, their home and social life had been very protected, sometimes with other children or adults with psychic abilities, or tutors who were carefully selected. But at the Blair Institute, the triplets of a world-famous psychic were researched for two whole days and nights before they were recovered by their furious mother.

The institute's doctors, psychologists, and parapsychologists had done their dirty work well, testing the ten-year-old Bartel triplets. Now, just days after that horrible two-day experience, Greer's daughters knew just how different they were, each with an individual sixth sense, and yet, each linked to the other.

Firstborn by three minutes, Leona shared Greer's ability to foresee the future.

Claire, as an empath exposed to others' emotions and physical sensations and the "baby" of the triplets, had suffered the most when tested.

Tempest, the middle-born, had been a terror to the researchers. Ready to take any challenge and a fighter by nature, Tempest could hold any object in her naked hands and know its history. When she was outside their home, gloves protected her hands, and every object within their home had been thoroughly researched by Greer's own extrasensory perceptions.

"I'll protect them as long as I can, Daniel. I'll work from home until they are grown and can safely protect themselves. But something happened to them when they were three, and our sailboat overturned.

Somehow, they became more receptive near large natural bodies of water, as if it is a portal for them, opening them to other extrasensories. I've tested them . . . they are very vulnerable by water, connecting with it somehow, and that leaves them unprotected. They can never live by the ocean, or any large natural body of water without me. And I have to live here, by the ocean, because it gives me strength. I need every bit of my psychic gifts possible to protect them."

Greer pushed down a cry, torn from her heart, born from the knowledge that each of the triplets' lives would be difficult. "And they can never live too close, because their senses would be too connected, too intertwined."

She lifted her face to the damp air. "Tempest blames herself for the boat's overturning and tossing them into the ocean. She was only a child, playing too close to the edge when that wave hit us."

She closed her eyes and shook her head, fighting the fear for her children's future. Then warm trickling energy ran up her nape. Greer turned to the triplets watching her from the shadows of the doorway.

With hair the same shade of dark red as her own, hair that could catch fire in the sun, and with the same dark earthy green eyes and pale skin, they seemed so alike, yet they were so different.

Tempest walked slowly to Greer. With a rebellious, restless, and impulsive spirit, she might have been the one most affected by the sailboat accident. The link with her father was perhaps just that fraction deeper than Claire's or Leona's, though Daniel Bartel had loved all his daughters.

Tempest took her mother's hand, and the warm connection became stronger; talk wasn't necessary, the sensations flowing between them. Then Tempest spoke quietly, "Make Dad come back, Mom. I want to talk to him. I want to tell him that I'm sorry I broke my arm that day he was hurrying home to us—when he died."

Her fierce young face and body strained toward the ocean, willing her father to step from it.

"I can't do that, honey. I've explained that—"

"I will. Someday, I'll talk to him. I'll tell him I'm sorry," Tempest promised fiercely.

Even as Greer drew her middle-born's small body protectively to her, she knew that Tempest would always seek the impossible, to reach her father beyond the limitations of life.

One

_____

"BINGO. . . . MAYBE. IF I HOLD THAT BROOCH IN MY HANDS,
I'll know if it's the original."

Tempest Storm tapped her finger on the antiquities'
magazine photograph. The Viking brooch seemed definitely larger, weightier, and more masculine than the
wolf's-head design she had created from her mother's
and sister's description. The replicas she'd created for
her sisters held softer, curving Celtic designs around
the central piece. In the photograph, the original's
ornate, interwoven designs bordered barely visible angular lines that spoke more to Viking characters.

If read correctly, the original's marred inscription
could lead to understanding the dreams circling her
clairvoyant family.

Tempest traced the photograph's brooch, lying upon
black velvet. At a hefty-looking six inches across and
four inches at the widest, the brooch was worn and
pitted, imperfectly cast and reflective of the ninth-
century craft. The evenly-spaced round indentations
circling the brooch probably had held semiprecious
stones. In the center, the semiraised wolf's head, fitting

her family's description, stared back at her. The back's photograph showed the typical sturdy, curved pin used to secure the brooch to garments.

Inside her large New Mexico studio, the air-conditioning keeping the desert's heat at bay seemed to still. Tempest's senses locked onto that photograph; she held a magnifying glass to it and read the small print aloud: "For Display Only. Not for sale by the anonymous owner, but an excellent representation of ninth-century Norseman craftsmanship. While bronze was the usual during this period, this piece is of de-based silver. Characters circling the brooch are too worn and marred to read. Owner is seeking like pieces of the period, and may be contacted via e-mail."

Her heart racing with excitement, Tempest hurried to circle the e-mail address. She took a moment to steady herself and breathed deeply as she looked out her window. Everything seemed the same in her remote studio-home near Santa Fe: The saguaro cactus cast late-afternoon shadows on the sweeping dry land-scape, and clumps of creosote brush periodically of-fered a touch of greenery. The first of July's heat shimmered beyond Tempest's cool mauve stucco home and studio. In a few hours, sunset would lay a pink cast over the sand.

In a few hours, she could be headed to wherever the original brooch was, and she could actually hold it.

In a few hours, she could hold the brooch in her naked hands and know everything—use every drop of her intuitive sixth sense to absorb what her family needed to know.

Because something connected to that brooch was definitely after her family, and it wasn't sweet.

She had to be very careful now, not an easy task con-sidering her excitement; one wrong move, and she could lose the chance to hold the brooch, to know its past.

Tempest turned her back on the desert scenery and studied the latest sculpture for her next showing. Small, gently priced, and stylized, the piece was something for her favorite Santa Fe gallery. Tempest ran her bare fingertip over the leggy woman who stood poised, one foot on a round stonelike base, the other lifted to the next step. In a dress pressed against her body, she looked over her shoulder as if afraid, her hair flowing behind her, depicting flight. The idea for the sculpture, cast in bronze, had come from Tempest's own emotions, ones that had haunted her every minute since she could remember.

But then, there were certain things she could never escape—like who she really was—a psychic "freak" who could hold an object in her hands and feel its past.

She studied her bare hands, extending them into the sunlight from the studio window. Here, in the privacy of her studio, where she had been very careful to choose her materials and suppliers, was the only place she allowed her hands to touch anything—without protective gloves. They were ordinary hands, strong and practical for a sculptor. But without her protective gloves, Tempest was at the mercy of the evil and the past of those who had touched the object before her.

Tempest flexed her fingers, studying the short, practical nails, and a fresh wave of guilt hit her. "I never should have done what he wanted. I fell for his lies. I thought I loved Brice, but he was using me—rather my naked hands—to scam money, then calling me a 'freak' to his friends. And now he wants me back? I don't think so."

Those two years had been the darkest of her life; she'd always hated and denied her psychic ability. But for him—because she was only twenty and thought she'd loved him, she'd acted the fool.

Tempest held her breath, rocked on her heels, and tucked her shamed past behind her. She had a job to do.

Her initial contact with the brooch's owner must be casual, not too eager. Antiquity collectors could be paranoid, eccentric, and unwilling to share; some of them hoarded their collections away from the world. Some of them were like worms. One wrong word, and this one could slip underground, hoarding the brooch in a private, thermal-controlled room—it could take forever to dig him out and get the brooch.

"And get that brooch," she whispered firmly, a promise she'd made a year and a half ago.

Tempest's hunting experience told her that she was locked on to the right trail and, bracing herself to be cautious with her approach, she murmured, "Okay, Mr. Anonymous, let's do this. I've been hunting for this same brooch—if it is the real one—for over a year and a half, since my mother and sister started dreaming about it. It looks a little different than their descriptions, but then psychics can only come so close to the real thing, and then it can dodge anywhere."

She turned suddenly, and her footsteps echoed in the airy studio. She passed the table where her sculpture of a fairy, peering down into a leafy pond, met her own reflection in a mirror. Tempest paused and placed her hand on another piece: The three women stood with their hands held, their backs to each other. Their faces resembled each other, but their hairstyles were different. One woman's hair was shoulder-length and turned under in a smooth bob as Leona's would look. Claire's was long and flowing, and Tempest turned the statue to a third woman, one shorter, with a more compact, athletic body, and short, spiked hair—a presentation of herself. Intended for a Christmas gift for her mother, the statue depicted the Aisling-Bartel triplets, their hands linked. Tempest sat at her computer and prepared herself to write Mr. Anonymous, owner of the brooch. She couldn't express too much interest; she couldn't appear too anxious to see the brooch and hold it.

She smoothed the replica brooch like those she had created for her mother and sisters, intended to be a protective family link, a good-luck charm. "I have to hold the real one . . . to know why it is so important. Two clairvoyants, Mom and Leona, can't be dreaming about the same thing without reason."

Tempest's fingers hovered over the computer's keyboard, then she rubbed her hands together. She glanced at her wristwatch, a large face displaying multiple time zones, bound by Celtic designs on leather. "It's five now, let's see how long it takes to answer this, then I'll know an approximate time zone."

She tapped in a careful e-mail: "Must see original for a perfect match, but I believe I have something that may interest you. Would like to set an appointment. Will bring photographs for your inspection. T.S."

Experienced in Viking antiquities and dealing with collectors for the past year and a half, Tempest understood that anonymity—neither male, nor female—and a casual touch was everything in a hunt like this.

She hit the e-mail Send button, folded her arms, and leaned back in her chair. As she waited for a response, the waterfall she had created of stone-shaped brass holding small green river stones rippled soothingly. Filtered sunlight from the window danced across the copper spines of a multimetal iguana resting on top of her computer screen.

Minutes ticked by, a lizard peered at her through her window, and nothing appeared on the screen. Restless now, and anxious to be headed toward the brooch, Tempest rose and paced her studio. She glanced at her red Miata convertible; she wanted to hop in it and ride down the sandy road leading to her studio, hit the highway, and head wherever that brooch was waiting. But her impulsive nature could work against her now; she'd waited too long to make this contact. It was no time to appear to eager, or the "worm" could disappear forever.

In a few minutes, she rechecked her e-mail to find no response.

Tempest sat down to watch her incoming e-mail and suddenly her message jumped onto the screen—with an answer. "Sorry, T.S. You understand that with a piece like this, intact and in perfect condition, I prefer no personal contact. Please send photographs of your items. If they interest me, are documented, dated by an expert, and with proof of purchase, I may be interested."

"'Documented','" Tempest muttered. "I'll give you documents."

She flipped through the magazine, found a biography on a noted antiquities expert, listed the appropriate credentials as her own in her e-mail, then attached a deliberately blurred photograph of the wolf's-head brooch she had crafted. After studying and hunting Viking antiquities for a year and a half, Tempest considered her expertise to be sufficient. She added that she had verified the date and had proof of purchase and sent the message.

She scanned the sender's e-mail and tapped in the code to trace it. It had bounced around a bit through the Internet nest, and she pinpointed necessary details. "Same time zone. I could be there in a day, two at the most."

Tempest breathed slowly, trying to force herself to be patient. The screen blinked at her, and suddenly that odd tingle at her nape told her that Claire, the youngest of the Aisling triplets was calling. Tempest continued watching her computer screen—her heart pulsing to the beat of the cursor. She reached for the telephone before it actually rang. "Claire, I'm tied up now."

Claire's soft, soothing voice held amusement. "You're onto something."

That damn cursor kept blinking, taunting her. "Could be. How's married life out in Montana?"

"We're fine. I was just setting the table, and I thought of you. Don't try to distract me, Tempest. What are you doing?"

"Waiting. I just sent a query to the owner of a ninth-century brooch. Looks like the real deal . . . the characters around the wolf's head are definitely angular, like Viking characters, but they're too worn to give any true sense of what they are. This guy is cautious. Real collectors, especially the private ones, are like that."

Tempest stared at the simple new message that had just popped up on her screen: "I'm interested. Attached are more photos of the brooch. Please send matching photos of your items."

She let out a low whistle. "He took the bait."

"He?" Claire asked cautiously.

"I have no idea of he-she, but there are photos attached. Talk with you later."

Tempest hung up the telephone and set to work downloading the collector's photos. The brooch was inside a glass cage, resting on a black velvet bed. Taken from different angles, the bold shape, the worn Viking inscriptions circling it, all seemed the same as the magazine's photograph.

Another tingle signaled a different sister, and before the telephone rang, Tempest answered: "Hi, Leona. Claire called you?"

"She's excited for you. You think that with our DNA and as a triplet, just three minutes older than you, that I wouldn't know you were up to something?" Leona asked briskly. "What is it?"

"Just maybe what I've been hunting for—"

"The brooch? Where?"

"Let me work on this, okay? I want that thing in my hot little hands as soon as possible. It's in my time zone, according to the e-mails. Talk with you later."

Tempest hurried to enlarge the computer photos and print them. She traced the ancient brooch in the photographs with her fingertip. "All I have to do is to hold you, and then I'll know."

She sat back in her chair and smoothed her large cuff bracelet; she traced the angular Viking characters within the swirling Celtic design. She rocked slightly as she thought about hunting for the brooch, somehow connected to whatever was happening to her family, including an unprovoked attack on Claire. Hating her, a simple man had suddenly run amok in April, and Tempest's gifted hands had traced his unreasonable rage back to his computer.

For the last year and a half, the Aisling-Bartels, all psychics of diverse abilities, had been restless, their senses prickling. The triplets' mother, Greer Aisling, and Leona Chablis, a sister, had similar dreams of a Viking chieftain who wore the brooch at his left shoulder.

Tempest tapped the original brooch's photographs with her fingertip. "And you are going to tell me why after I hold you—why a peaceful man would suddenly go off the deep end and attack my sister, Claire, then kill himself."

She frowned as she thought of racing to Claire after her attack, of seeing her sister bruised and shaken.

Tempest sat back and watched the screen for a minute before digitally enlarging the images. In a glass case and resting on a pedestal, the brooch seemed to be in a living room.

Beyond the glass case was a view of a large patio with loungers and plants. Several hot-air balloons seemed to be hovering a distance beyond a spacious window. The time stamp on the three of the photos said they had been taken early that spring, a morning haze softening the tall buildings in the background. The time stamp of a fourth photo, an enlargement of the fierce wolf's head snarling in profile, had been taken just a few days ago, but the shadowy detail of the room was the same—a credenza in the background, a jade globe on a pedestal, a clear shot of the patio's loungers and plants beyond. Tempest clicked back to the picture of the balloons. One of the balloons bore a huge orchid flag—

"Bingo. The Orchids," Tempest whispered tensely as she recognized a prominent balloonist family. "Now it's just a matter of where you were on the second of April."

She clicked to the Orchids Web site and traced the flying date. "Okay, so you were in Albuquerque. The question is where."

She enlarged the photo; the images were indistinct, but recognizable—the round pale face was definitely a gigantic clock on a shorter building. "Okay, now we're getting there. The picture of the dome is straight across from wherever this place is, and the clock is down and to the left of it. I know where you are. Well, almost."

Tempest dialed a top real estate agent in Albuquerque who was also a collector of Tempest's small pieces. After a few leading pleasantries she said, "Lulu, I need a favor."

Two

—

WHILE THE PACIFIC OCEAN BEAT AGAINST THE SHORELINE near her home, and the storm worsened, Greer Aisling lay very still, the shards of her nightmare wrapped around her.

She could still smell the smoke of the fires burning the Celts' crude homes. She could still hear the groans of the wounded and dying, the frightened cries of the children, the loud boasts of the Viking raiders.

Out of the darkness, a Viking longship sailed toward her, red sails billowing in the wind. Red—the color of blood.

"Aisling," Greer whispered to the night, calling her ancestor out of the smoke and battle. "Aisling, help me. Tell me what I need to know."

The Celt seer's tangled long red hair burned brightly amid the gray smoke and Greer saw herself moving toward Aisling, her ancestor. "Hello, Mother," she whispered. "Please help me."

Green eyes like Greer's own and like those of the triplets were sad, brimming with tears. "Blood of my blood, you came to me twice before—once when you were young and could not accept what you were, and once when you wanted to talk with your husband one last time. I could give you no peace before, and I cannot now. I cannot take away what I am, what has come down to you, that which no one else can see or feel. Like you and your daughters, I did not want this thing—to see the fates, to know what is inside the hearts and minds of others, to heal with a touch, to feel the pain of others."

She turned to two warriors, fighting amid the smoke, their swords flashing, the sound of metal ringing in the air. "Your daughter, Tempest, holds more of the Viking blood than her sisters, and you're worried for her. She must take this journey, this is her quest—leave it to her."

"She's too impulsive, too combative, too emotional—"

"A fierce warrior, is she, your middle child?" Aisling smiled softly and looked at the tall Viking striding toward her, his eyes pinning her. "Look at him swagger. He thinks he would rule me, but I think not. Your daughter has his blood, his need to hunt and to conquer. Leave her to her work, and don't interfere. Let her bring home the prize to you—she needs to do this. She feels she must make amends."

The Viking chieftain towered over them both. As though he didn't see Greer, he caught Aisling's arm, turning her to him. "You're mine, woman. You belong to me."

"We shall see who rules who, Viking." Then Aisling's pale face turned to Greer; she placed her hand upon the large brooch at his shoulder, as if it were a sign. Her fingers circled the angular Viking characters around a wolf's head. "It holds the answers you seek."

The smoke wrapped around Aisling and her Viking, and the vision faded away.

Greer awoke fully, jackknifing upright to hold her arms around her knees. She reached for the replica Tempest had created from her description, the Celtic swirls replacing the angular Viking characters; she held it tight against her chest. "Keep her safe."

* * *

In Albuquerque, Tempest stood inside Sebastian Tower's locked guest bathroom. She quickly drew her backpack from under the cleaning pushcart and removed her own clothing from it. Tempest stripped the maid's uniform she'd been wearing to work her way through the party guests and stuffed it back into her backpack. The uniform had not been difficult to "borrow" from the laundry service's racks at the Sebastian's delivery door. The pushcart held what she needed, and Tempest quickly went to work. She quickly dressed in her own clothing, a formfitting sweater, snug pants, her belt, and smooth-soled climbing shoes.

Thanks to Lulu, who thought Tempest might be interested in leasing an apartment at the Sebastian, she was well versed in the building's layout and security systems. The privacy of Sebastian's residents was well guarded, their keycards meticulously checked and changed frequently, and the identity of the penthouse resident on the twelfth floor was a well-kept secret.

The penthouse could only be reached by a private stairway, used as a fire escape, and an elevator, both loaded with security cameras. However, none of the patios had security cameras or alarm systems, and that vulnerability interested Tempest. On the downside, an ex-Marine named Hatchet, who was all shoulders and without a neck, ran the building's highly trained security force. As a competitive real estate agent who needed access to show vacancies to potential buyers, Lulu had tangled with Hatchet through the years and knew him to be invincible to every "sob story" and any trick. From the window of her hotel opposite the Sebastian Towers, Tempest had observed Hatchet; he looked as thorough and dangerous as Lulu's description.

Inside the exclusive apartment's guest bathroom nearest the patio, Tempest listened to the party in the living room and slid on her backpack. At midnight, the party on the eleventh floor was loud and in high gear. Engaged in celebrating the Fourth of July, the guests had barely noticed her and the maid's cleaning cart she'd pushed inside the bathroom. Her gloves would have instantly marked her and her description easily remembered; however, a maid's rubber gloves weren't noted at all. She didn't want the brooch's owner to know she was prowling in the vicinity; it would be difficult to explain why she needed her naked hands on that brooch. It would be more difficult to shield her psychic reaction. A simpler approach was an in-and-out job, a private "feel," and there was only one way to get that.

Tempest removed her gear from the cleaning cart, tugged on the safety harness, attached it to the nylon climbing rope, and looped the coiled rope over her arm. Experienced in climbing and rappelling, she tugged the rope's connection to the small grappling hook and found it secure.

In the bathroom mirror, Tempest noted her reflection; it was that of a burglar, grim and determined. She pushed down her sense of guilt with a murmur of justification. "Okay, it's been three days. The owner of the brooch isn't responding, and I can't wait any longer. I'm just going to have to go see for myself. This way, I'll be in and out, no damage done, and I'll know if that brooch is the one I'm hunting."

In the three days since Tempest had arrived in the city, she'd studied the apparently unoccupied penthouse from her hotel. Her casual telephone queries had gotten her nothing on the identity of the resident. She was certain that whoever owned it wasn't in residence—leaving an excellent time to get to the brooch. However, since no one was in residence, and since Hatchet was a definite problem, Tempest had decided there was only one way to the penthouse—and that was up to the unsecured patio.

She tugged on her own tight, supple leather gloves and locked on to her mission: If she held that brooch in her hands, she would know its authenticity.

Tempest held her breath as she cautiously opened a door leading to the patio. The small enclosure was lined with potted trees, just tall enough to hide her five-foot-six body. At the near corner of the brick-enclosed patio, a tree stood in the shadows, and above it was the penthouse.

Tempest moved into the shadows of that tree; she crouched and gaged the throw of her grappling hook up to the penthouse's brick enclosure.

The silent vibration mode of her cell phone signaled a call from Claire, but the tingle at Tempest's nape had already warned her. Instead of answering, Tempest scanned the shadows above her as she planned her route up the brick wall.

From her hotel window purposefully opposite the Sebastian, Tempest had studied Albuquerque's night lights as they hit the side of the building. The climbing lines couldn't be seen from below, blocked by the apartment's patio. In her black sweater and tight pants, her body would fall into a line of shadow as she worked her way up to the penthouse.

As a safety precaution, she secured one hook onto the apartment's sturdy gear for the retractable sunshade. Heavy-duty and securely mounted, the ironwork would hold well, but just the same, Tempest tested it with all her strength. Then, cautiously, she attached the safety gear to her body and edged out onto the brick ledge.

She began swinging the line with the grappling hook, then released it. It sailed high, snagged the patio's brick enclosure, and fell, unattached. Tempest held her breath, re-coiled the line, and swung again.

This time, the hook caught. Tempest tested the line to the hook, and then the safety line attached to the shade's gear. Assured that each line would hold, she eased out onto the edge of the enclosure's bricks and began climbing.

One wrong move and—Tempest concentrated on hand over hand; in flexible shoes, her toes found each tiny ledge between the bricks, and then she reached the penthouse's patio enclosure. Breathing hard, she hiked her body up and over until she dropped to the Italian slate tiles of the penthouse's patio. Taking care, she leaned over the side and hauled up her safety line from the sunshade.

She unhooked her safety harness and placed her gear behind a potted tree. On the street twelve stories below, traffic was light, and the sounds of the party were growing louder, perfect cover for what she needed to do. She waited for a small crowd on the sidewalk to pass, a burst of firecrackers causing them to laugh and run.

Tempest shivered, leaned close to the penthouse's sliding doors, and listened.

She removed her belt, took the large Celtic-style buckle, and used the prong to trip the lock. She eased open the French door, tensed, and listened as she surveyed the darkened penthouse.

Inside, the glass case was lit, and her senses spiked, her heart racing. She was just within feet of what could be the original Viking brooch!

Tempest stepped inside the penthouse. She waited for alarms, but none sounded. She moved cautiously toward the display case—

The slight noise behind her caused her to pivot.

A tall man stood, outlined by a colorful rocket burst in the night air. They were illegal in the city, but right now, she wasn't exactly legal herself. He shrugged free of her lines, dropped them to the floor, and the door closed with a chilling click. The penthouse's soft lights instantly flooded the room, and Tempest heard her own voice— "You!"

Marcus Greystone was just as she remembered him from last October—tall, sleek, and dark. In a designer suit, he'd looked as if he'd been cut from stone, and just dangerous-looking enough to challenge her after a successful Santa Fe showing.

She'd been riding high, filled with praises, her bank account stuffed with sales, and enjoying champagne a little too much.

"Hello, Tempest. I've been waiting for you. I took the liberty of collecting your lines and grappling hook, because you're not using them again tonight. Miss me?" he said in a deep, raspy, too-soft voice that reminded her of when he'd made love to her.

A storm of memories wrapped around Tempest: His body had been hard and long and just as hungry for her as she'd been for him. He'd been perfect to top off her success at the showing, and—and now he was here!

"Wait—waiting for me?" she managed unevenly. In his bare feet and wearing only tight-fitting jeans, Marcus still looked just as dangerous—and determined, by the set of that hard jaw and those piercing, icy eyes.

Tempest's mind flicked back to when she'd first seen him up close. As an artist, she'd first noted the pewter shade of his eyes, the black iris surrounded by bronze flecks. She'd been warned about Marcus, that he was very selective in his affairs. She knew that he'd been divorced and didn't like marriage, and that he wasn't apt to be "caught." Mr. Marcus Greystone, heir and owner of Greystone Investments, had looked sexy, steel-hard, emotionally impenetrable, and the kind who wouldn't cling later. He was exactly what Tempest had wanted that night, an equal opponent in a clean, neatly ended match that wouldn't leave scars.

Marcus picked up a squat glass and drank deeply, before placing it aside. The click of glass against the quartz tabletop echoed in the penthouse and chilled Tempest's body. She braced herself as Marcus slowly walked toward her; she remembered that walk, graceful, determined, a predator on the hunt as he came toward her at the showing.

She'd met him in the same way—on equal terms, and now he was here, watching her with those unflickering gray eyes. The heat that had once settled in those hard lips had changed from sexual to fury. In Santa Fe, he'd seemed cool and hard, but now he looked tough and furious. "What did you expect me to do, Ms. Storm? Chase all over the countryside hunting for you—after you ran out?" he asked tightly.

She'd gripped those wide shoulders and dug in her nails as he'd tasted her body, biting gently, tasting her—Tempest forced a swallow down her dry throat and, despite the icy sense that she'd been tracked and caught in a trap, she managed a cool, "How nice to see you again, Marcus."

His brief smile was tight and cold, a predator who knew he had his prize in hand. "Yes. How nice. I found you immediately, you know—just days after you ran off so rudely."

She hadn't just run away—she'd flown, terrified. After only a few hours in his arms, she'd been certain that Marcus Greystone was the kind of man who could devour everything she was, and she couldn't let that happen again.

She forced herself to appear calm and unconcerned as Marcus came close to her. Her head just reached his shoulders, the height difference as intimidating as his narrowed expression, those icy eyes taking in her face. His tone was clinical, assessing her. "Same slanted green eyes—earthy, mysterious—witch's eyes . . . same rich dark red hair, cut short enough for a boy—but I guess that accentuates those eyes, doesn't it? Same—"

His gaze rested on her lips. "Same—"

Marcus tugged her into his arms too quickly for Tempest to resist, and his lips were hard upon hers before he released her. "Same lush, exotic taste—same scent, same silky pale skin. I remember the way your body felt—strong, agile, soft in all the right places. You haven't changed at all, my little pirate."

"You're not going to be sweet about this, are you?" Tempest managed as she backed up a step. His taste remained on her lips, in her body; memories sprang to life, the way he'd cupped her breast, that primitive demand to match her own. She'd wanted to devour him and had found herself caught in her own hungry trap.

"A one-night stand with a woman who ran out on me? No, probably not. But then, I've just watched you risk your life to get here, and that's probably got me a little on edge."

"You watched me? How?"

Marcus leaned back against the quartz countertop of a credenza. Though his posture was casual, those big lean hands gripped it tightly, the knuckles showing through. "I have my own security camera, one of them facing any access to my patio—you missed it. Since I wouldn't want to spy on my neighbors, I've only used that surveillance in the past three days— when I discovered that you were staying in the hotel across from my place. I knew you were good, but I didn't know just how good you were—when you wanted something."

His look slowly down, then up her body, caused her to shiver. "I told security that I was expecting a woman . . . friend, someone who might tell some story to come up here when I wasn't home. You could have had a key to the elevator, but security may have had the wrong idea about your occupation."

"A hooker, you mean? And by security, you mean Hatchet?"

"So you've done your homework." When Marcus shrugged, Tempest glanced at the glass case, the brooch gleaming beneath the soft light. "You planned this. You deliberately set a trap."

"Uh-huh. And you fell for it. I knew when I didn't answer, that you'd be coming. You're not the kind to wait long, if you want something."

"And the photographs were taken deliberately, to identify this place."

He hadn't moved, and Tempest gauged the distance across the sunken living room, up the steps to the foyer to the penthouse's front door. Marcus's deep voice rasped dangerously across her skin, chilling it as he said, "It's locked, sweetheart. Special locks, I'm afraid. The patio door, too, and even if you could manage the locks, I'm not about to let you go just yet. You're a class-A burglar, Tempest. But then, you do everything well, don't you?"

Designed to ignite her memory of their one night together, his remark was effective. She'd dived into Marcus, their lovemaking startling her in its intensity, arousing her to feverish heights again and again. Even in her passion, her uncommon hunger shocked her because she'd never experienced it before. It was when she wanted more that she knew she had to escape—she couldn't get emotionally or sexually tangled again. "You went to a lot of effort just to see me, Marcus. You could have taken an easier route and contacted me."

"True."

She understood perfectly; Marcus had planned well, gotten what he wanted, and he was savoring the moment. All he had to do was to turn her in. "What do you want?"

"You," he answered simply. "Time with you. For a time."

"Or? You'll turn me in?"

He smiled again, that cold got-you predator's smile, and warning prickles ran up Tempest's nape.

"I don't usually lose what I intend to keep—for a while," he stated slowly. "And now I've got you. It was important for you to come to me, don't you see? Especially after your—early departure that morning. I really, really wanted you to come to me, Tempest. How discourteous of me—I've forgotten my manners. Would you like something to drink after your . . . little climb?"

Beneath his smooth courtesy, Marcus's voice was tight and angry.

"Water would be nice." At October's showing, she'd been a little intoxicated, but in control of herself. She'd known what she was doing when, from across the room, Marcus had lifted that champagne glass in a very private toast to her. She'd known that she'd wanted him—a little personal celebration that she'd never allowed herself.

Marcus Greystone would have been a catch for any woman: wealthy, a polished businessman heading a corporation. With a sleek, dark, and dangerous look that challenged women, he'd just purchased her *Predator* sculpture—a hawk in flight, wings outspread, talons opened to snatch prey.

The bronze metal had somehow personified the man's colors and texture; that sleek dark brown hair was touched with just a shade of red, and she'd remembered gripping the thick crisp texture in her fists as—

Tempest closed her eyes for a moment. She knew now why that sculpture would appeal to Marcus, one predator recognizing another. She braced herself to be casual as he turned to open a hidden refrigerator and reach inside.

She had just backed up a few steps toward the front door, when Marcus straightened and smiled coldly.

He twisted the lid of bottled water and tossed it her. "Catch. And that outfit looks great on you, by the way. The belt buckle is a nice piece of work—yours, I imagine. The design is Celtic. A tribute to your family—Greer Aisling is your mother, right? You're one of the famous Aisling-Bartel triplets?"

She'd taken Storm as a last name to place distance between herself and her family, and perhaps her past. Stunned that he would make the connection, Tempest stared at him as Marcus continued, "Oh, come on, Tempest. Let's get beyond this. You researched me, didn't you? You know about me, that I stepped into my father's shoes, running Greystone Investments. I teethed on researching acquisitions. If I want something, I'm going to check it out thoroughly. That would be you—sweetheart."

That night she'd asked about him and later, curious about her one-night lover, she'd briefly researched his life. "Your main company focuses on boating. Why are you here in the Southwest?"

Marcus's anger simmered as he looked at her; he was angry at her and at himself, because he couldn't forget her. "You. I'm here because you seem to like to stay away from water. Too bad, because I could have coupled waiting for you with work. It's always a pleasure to leave the corporate offices in Chicago."

He glanced at the bottle gripped tightly in her hand. "The lid is opened for you. You might find that a little difficult with your gloves on—but then, you always wear gloves, don't you? Long hot pink ones with that snazzy little black dress—and black silk ones when you make love—or was that just black with me, and different colors for different men?"

"Tell me what you know of my family—or think you know." In the penthouse's soft lights, her eyes seemed dark gold now, not the green that Marcus remembered. He'd have to remember that trait, how Tempest's eyes changed from that earthy green to amber when she was angry. Maybe that was why he was first drawn to her—her obvious passion for her work implied passion for other things. Later, the way she made love— almost with a primitive, but sensual hunger, diving into him, taking and giving, had proven him right.

Now, Tempest wanted to know what he knew, and then she'd probably try to use it against him. Marcus had waited months for this question, planned how he would answer it as he watched Tempest's expression. As a man experienced in business deals, he knew when the advantage was his—and he was going to take his time answering her question. "I know you want that brooch bad enough to chase all over the country for it—and into Canada. I contacted some of the collectors you had questioned. You just didn't contact the right one. I did. But they all said you were determined—almost obsessed—to get it. The question is why. Why, Tempest?"

Her fists curled at her side, her body tensed as if she would attack him. "I asked you what you think you know of my family."

Marcus smiled and walked into the kitchen, aware that Tempest was right behind him. Some dark part of him wanted her to attack him—because he was more than ready.

Her finger jabbed his back. "Hey, I asked you a question."

"Take it easy, Tempest." He turned slowly and icy gray eyes stared down at her. He was so close that she could see the sun-bleached tips of his lashes and brows, the texture of his skin, his jaw darkened by the stubble yet beneath the skin.

She remembered that roughness against her breasts. She remembered his scent, the subtle one beneath the expensive aftershave—dark, brooding, elusive, dangerous. A swift hot wave of sensual energy pulsed through her, startling her momentarily, but then she fought back to the basic here and now: Marcus had designed a very careful trap, and he knew he had her.

Marcus studied her face. "Interesting. You're steaming nicely and your eyes just turned to gold. . . . Does the Blair Institute for Parapsychology ring a bell?"

The Blair Institute of Parapsychology. The name rippled cold and ugly within her, a living nightmare from twenty-two years ago spilled over her again. *Hold this, Tempest. Tell me its history. . . . What about this?*

At ten years old, she'd held the knife of a murderer, felt the evil of its deceased owner surging through her, She'd held the cooking pot of a frontier woman, who mourned her family, left in Ohio, and a baby who had died along the way. She'd held the toy truck of a boy who knew he wouldn't live long. The next layer had been his grief-stricken mother. And when Tempest could stand no more, she held her palms tightly together, until they returned her gloves—and then the medical tests began, the electrodes measuring her vital signs.

A triplet who missed her sisters, their terrified sensations reaching out to her, tangling and connecting with her own senses, Tempest had begun to fight.

She'd destroyed an entire set of machines monitoring her before they could stop her—small and agile, she'd been under and over, slashing at everything in her path, determined to free her sisters.

Tempest looked at Marcus and coolly lied, "No, I'm afraid I don't know what you're talking about. I've never heard of this Blair-thing."

His "Don't you?" was dangerously mild. He nodded to the sunken conversation area of the living room. "Take a look."

Tempest moved slowly down the steps into the conversation area, the leather couches formed a square around the low, gleaming table. A few books on Viking antiquities were stacked on the table beside a fat file folder. She bent to flip it open and found the newspaper clipping about the triplets.

> Greer Aisling, a world-famous psychic, residing in an undisclosed location on the Northwest coast, has filed kidnapping and other charges against the Blair Institute for Parapsychology. Aisling, a widow, had been called into work with a Canadian police force to find a missing boy. Her triplets, aged ten years old, had been left in the Aisling estate under the care of their long-term guardian and housekeeper.
>
> Reportedly, Ms. Aisling had refused the institute's efforts to test the home-schooled children, whose last name is different from hers. On the suspected charge of abuse and without the mother's knowledge and consent, the triplets had been extracted from their home. They were placed in the care of the Blair Institute Child Studies Program for testing.
>
> The children are back now in the care of their mother, who has already filed several lawsuits and promises more. Observers note that the triplets seem to be well cared for and strangely gifted.

There were other clippings about Greer Aisling, a powerful psychic residing "on the Northwest coast." Two computer printouts listed the marriages of Claire Bartel to Paul Brown and Leona Bartel to Joel Chablis. Another clipping advertised Timeless Vintage, Leona's clothing shop in Lexington, Kentucky.

Tempest traced the Timeless ad with her fingertip, then focused on the words, "Claire's Bags." The one-of-a-kind handbags were handcrafted by her sister,

Claire, just remarried to Neil Olafson and living in Montana. Shaken by so much information collected about her family, Tempest asked quietly, "Just how did you track me, Marcus?"

"Give me some credit. I make my living by details. Changing your last name from Bartel to Storm didn't take you off the map. Your mother had been on television not long after we met—retrieving a girl from some cult or another, responsible for reuniting her with her parents. I had the film clip enlarged—and her unique pin perfectly matched the one you wore that night. Amazing that Greer Aisling, famous psychic, the woman who has written books about psychic experience, endorsing it as an alternate and supplemental means to finding missing people, would have a pin that matched my one-night stand's. Greer had also changed her name from Bartel, taking an unusual one, Aisling."

He knew too much, but not everything. As a widow with unusual five-year-old triplets who required special tutors and care, Greer had reached the end of her funds. She had desperately needed an income—and she'd had a very special talent. To protect her children, Greer had changed from her married name, Bartel, to Aisling. The family's unique ancestry was a well-kept secret, but Aisling had been the name of her ancestor, a Celtic seer.

"You had no right to research my family. For a little matter of bruised pride, you've gone too far, Marcus." Furious, and uncertain of how to handle him now—because he knew too much, and she was in a trap he'd set—Tempest could have attacked him.

Cautious of her own mood and impulsive nature, she slowly drank the bottled water, then walked up out of the sunken conversation area toward the glass case. He had no right—

So that she wouldn't appear too interested in the brooch,

Tempest moved around the luxurious penthouse—always aware of where Marcus stood, watching her. Everything in the penthouse was sleek, minimal, and without apparent sentimental value, a cool blend of masculine browns to light creams.

"Make yourself at home, Tempest," Marcus invited softly.

"Thanks. Where's my hawk?"

"*Predator?* Why, in my bedroom, of course. Where I can lie in bed, look at it, and think of you. It's just a little memento of our one-night stand."

She turned to him and fought the fearful, or was it sexual tremble that ran deep inside her? Her body recognizing his? "We both knew what we were doing."

"Did we?"

"Oh, lay off."

Tempest tossed the bottle of water back to him; Marcus caught it and placed it on the credenza. "Why should I? When I've got you so neatly tied up?"

"I'm really sorry about your dented ego. But I wasn't staying around. That's not my thing."

Marcus leveled a stare at her. "You're staying around this time, or you're not getting close to the brooch you apparently want."

She walked toward the case and stared down at it. Beneath the specially tinted glass, the eyes of the wolf stared back at her—the impressions circling the brooch were definitely angular, suggesting a Viking alphabet.

The size of the case, the reflection of light on glass, and the tinting marred a better look. "Okay, Marcus. I've had enough of cat and mouse. What hoop do I have to go through to get a good look at this thing?"

"You were impatient then, too. It took me a while to notice that you'd never taken your gloves off, but you had changed them. Interesting. I've never made love to a woman who wore gloves while making love. Then I decided that maybe you were shy, maybe embarrassed by scars from your work, and then—in the heat of the moment—it didn't really matter. I've wondered what it would feel like to have your hands actually—"

She turned to him and put her hands on her hips. "No way am I doing that."

He shrugged, the soft light moving over his broad shoulders and chest as he moved toward her. "Your choice, sweetheart. But that one is a fake. You didn't think the real one would be here, did you? It's tucked away in a vault."

Tempest wished her ability ran to Claire's, that of sensing emotions and "reading" people. As an empath, Claire would have known in a heartbeat if Marcus was lying. "You're lying. This thing looks good enough to be real."

"The artist was very good. He created it from the same photograph used in that antiquities magazine. You'll note that his stressing work to show age is very good. . . . I've got some work to catch up on in my office. I'm afraid I got a little behind when I tracked you over at your hotel. You drive that little red convertible well, by the way. You'll find everything you need in your bedroom—next to mine."

"You don't possibly think that I'm staying here—"

"Yes, I do. Or you'll never get to see the real brooch that you've been hunting for over a year." He picked up her climbing gear, wound the lines, and, carrying them, walked toward her. "I can call Hatchet and ask him to escort you outside the building. He won't be happy that you've breached his security, and it might hurt his feelings. He's sensitive that way. Or you can stay. But if you do, I'll want your backpack and that nifty leather belt with the handy buckle. We can talk in the morning."

A hard businessman, Marcus's expression revealed nothing, only that she wouldn't get a second chance at the brooch.

If she stayed the night, she might actually hold the brooch. She'd hunted so long, and she wasn't missing this chance. Tempest slid out of her backpack and handed it to him. "Satisfied?"

Marcus unzipped the backpack and smiled at the maid's uniform. He also noted the lightweight basic black dress and pumps that would blend in anywhere. The lady was a chameleon, and he'd caught her. "No. The belt. If I'm not mistaken, that's a knife sheath at your back."

Tempest smiled sweetly up at him as she removed her belt and handed it to him. "I had plans for that."

For the first time, Marcus's smile lit his eyes. "I'll bet. Let me know if you need anything. Good night."

Marcus leaned down to her, and his finger slid down her cheek. Then he turned and walked away from her toward what appeared to be his office.

Tempest leaned down to study the brooch. It appeared to be authentic, but she needed a closer look. She didn't hesitate; she reached for a sleek contemporary statue, held it for a moment, then smashed it into the glass case.

At the sound of a crash, Marcus paused in midstep, then he continued walking. He inhaled sharply; he held his breath and forced himself not to turn.

If he did, he wasn't certain what he would do.

Tempest had actually scaled the side of the building, risking her life to get to the brooch. He hadn't thought she'd go to such lengths. Any ordinary woman would have tried to get past security, and Marcus had deliberately made that easy for her. But oh, no, not his one-night stand, a woman who had definitely gotten to him.

The sight of Tempest moving slowly upward, seeking toeholds in the bricks, hauling herself up and over the high wall of the patio, had shaken him badly—he'd almost reached the line to help haul her up and into his arms. From there, he wasn't certain what he would have done either.

He'd wanted—no, he'd needed her to come after him. The thought that she could have hit the brick patio below or that she could have fallen twelve stories to the street had brought cold sweat to his forehead.

The counterpoint to his fear for Tempest was also his anger at her for endangering her life. He wanted her to pay for raising those emotions in him—and for leaving him immediately after that single night. Marcus had dreamed about her, awakening with his body hard, hating her for that hunger, and now she was here—within reach—and she was going to pay.

Inside his office, Marcus slid aside a wall panel, tapped in the security key to a hidden vault, and placed Tempest's climbing gear and backpack inside. His thumb tested the heavy buckle's prong—it was very sharp.

He studied the knife, then watched Tempest enter his office. "Obviously, you've decided to take a shortcut—effective, by the way—to get to the replica. The original brooch isn't in this vault—sorry. Would you like to look before I set the time lock? Oh, sorry, I don't believe even you—as an experienced burglar— could open this one, without alarms going off at the security company."

"It was a very nice replica, perfectly aged and stressed. The creator drank heavily, though. Too bad. He probably spent the commission the minute it was in his hands. Where did you say the genuine article was?"

"Quite safe, buried deep inside a bank's security vault. And the artist does drink. But then, you'd know everything, wouldn't you? That old hands-on, feeling thing?"

"I suppose you're going to make this difficult—" Tempest frowned; Marcus had somehow gotten her background, but he couldn't possibly understand. "What do you mean, 'hands-on, feeling'?"

He closed the vault and used his back as a shield to prevent Tempest from seeing the code. He slid the wall panel closed and turned to her.

"Yes, I am going to make this very difficult. I deserve that, don't you think? You were a little rude."

"Translated: Since you're the man, the protocol of a one-night stand is that you leave first?"

"Something like that."

As if she weren't interested, Tempest prowled slowly around the room, noting the barren bookshelves, the laptop on the desk, the opened briefcase—and the security cameras lining one wall. Tempest reminded Marcus of a cat, just waiting to spring. But now wouldn't be the time for her to do that, he decided, not while he was so tightly wound himself. She was the one woman he couldn't forget, and for that, he couldn't forgive her.

She paused in front of the monitor that viewed the patio beneath the penthouse. "Very nice, Marcus. I wonder what your neighbors would think if they knew you were spying on them."

"It's motion-sensitive technology, focused only on that one vulnerable spot. I'll disconnect it now—since I have what I want."

Marcus studied the tiny knife, the four-inch curved blade was obviously handcrafted, the grip embellished with a Celtic design. Aware that Tempest had sat in his desk chair, had propped her feet upon his desk and was watching him closely, Marcus tested the tip on his finger. "You use this often?"

Tempest picked up a stiletto-shaped silver letter opener, engraved with Greystone Investments, and appeared to study it. "When I have to. Why do you have the original brooch? Or say you do," she added softly.

Marcus moved close to Tempest and leaned back against the desk. With one swift movement, he swept her feet from his desk. "Simple. I usually get what I want."

Those eyes flashed gold as Tempest abruptly stood. But bracketed by the wall at her back, the L-shaped desk arrangement, and the leg that Marcus had just braced against the wall, she was trapped—momentarily.

"How did you know I wanted the brooch?"

"You were wearing one like your mother's the night we . . . met. I know a private collector—Viking artifacts, his specialty—I'd seen his private collection, not for public viewing. He has friends with the same interest, and he asked around. One of them knew that an antiquities hunter was looking for something like it. He didn't want it to go to a museum, and the price was right. I guess the hunter would be you— you've had a busy nine months since we last saw each other. I thought about coming to your adobe studio, but then, you were hunting the brooch. You were rarely home and constantly on the move. And I wasn't sure what I would do if I ever got you in my hands again."

Marcus noted her grip on the letter opener. Her gloves now were supple black leather, but he remembered the silk ones she'd worn that night, the way they'd glided over his back. Tempest continued staring at him for just a heartbeat, and then she tossed the opener onto the desk.

Marcus moved the leg blocking her passage. Head high, Tempest walked by him and out into the living room. He followed and settled in to watch her prowl around the penthouse. She paused to look at the ultra-modern gym and ignored him as she appeared to study a Monet, but every line of her curved, compact body was tensed and ready to spring. Then, she pivoted to walk slowly toward him, sliding her glove along the back of a leather sofa as she passed. She continued walking past him, catlike, a female predator waiting her chance to take what she wanted—freedom, and the brooch.

Tempest circled the penthouse slowly. She paused at the master suite, arched an eyebrow as she looked at Marcus, and then walked into the guest room.

Marcus came to lean his shoulder against the doorway and watched Tempest prowl around the room and into the bathroom. She came out to open the door of the walk-in closet. "No women's clothing," she stated. "I expected a whole rack of different sizes and women's things in the bathroom."

"Those were high expectations." Marcus wouldn't give her the satisfaction of knowing that since that one night, she was the only woman he'd wanted. He picked up a phone, punched in Hatchet's number, and said, "My guest has arrived."

Marcus could almost hear Hatchet's brain tick, discounting any possible gaps in his security. He didn't ask questions, but tomorrow after Marcus placed the sack with the maid's uniform and a climbing rope on his desk, the Sebastian would be scoured thoroughly. Hatchet would link the unusual appearance of a maid's cart to the rest. He'd probably be grateful to Tempest for revealing the security weakness. Marcus smiled briefly as he cut the connection; Hatchet was like that, appreciative of anything to make his defenses better.

Tempest walked toward Marcus, her hands on her hips. "Okay, Marcus, you cold, calculating bastard. I'm tired of this. Let's have it. What do you really want?

You've gone to too much trouble, just for a little pay-back."

"You. You have something I want," he stated simply, as he pushed away from the doorway. "And I have something you want, so watch yourself when it comes to calling names. I'm very sensitive about that particular one."

Three

_____

"JUST WHAT DO I HAVE THAT YOU WANT?" TEMPEST ASKED carefully as she followed him.

"Open the other file, under the top one, Tempest." His arms folded over his chest, Marcus leaned back against the credenza to watch her.

Taking a deep, steadying breath, Tempest slowly moved toward the sunken conversation area. Marcus held too much information already. If that file folder held the two years she wanted to forget . . . Tempest tried to appear casual as she lifted the folder and flipped it open.

The header on the top paper was Blair Institute for Parapsychology. Her gloved finger traced the top paragraph: "Tempest Bartel, age ten, the middle triplet, talent for psychometry. Not an easy study. Rebellious, uncooperative, a vicious, headstrong, angry, and unruly child. But highly intelligent. Subject has destroyed an entire laboratory by deliberately lighting a fire in a trash basket and holding it up to the alarm sensors. The lab was flooded, the child contained."

The notation went on, and Tempest momentarily relived her childhood terror: With water streaming down upon her and angry, she was more vulnerable, and she'd thought one of the scientists had been her father. "Daddy?"

From that one word, the parapsychologists had quickly linked the triplets' boating accident when they were three to Tempest's guilt that she might have caused the accident, and to a seemingly deeper bond with Daniel Bartel. The scientists deduced that she was vulnerable in water, her psychic gift open and receptive. To test her responses, they had been preparing her for complete submersion in a water tank when her mother had descended upon them.

Tempest quickly flipped through the rest of the papers. Her test results, a few notations that she was the daughter of a psychic, and a list of her responses in relation to her sisters followed. Claire's and Leona's results were not in the folder; Tempest was grateful for that. Her tested responses to her mother were normal, but the ones to her father were unusually fierce and defensive: "I know he's dead, and he's not coming back, and no, I can't talk to him. Stop asking questions about how I felt when he died! I already told you that I broke my arm, and he was driving home too fast."

Marcus's silence seemed to throb around her, and, still caught in the trauma, Tempest reacted furiously. "So their lab got scorched a little. They shouldn't have left me alone with two pieces of flint, asking me which was the oldest," she said, before dropping the file.

Marcus's smile seemed amused, his hard veneer softening for just that heartbeat. "You're right, they shouldn't have."

Tempest dropped the file onto the table. "How did you get that information, Marcus? I thought my mother's attorneys collected it all and legally sealed it."

This time he shrugged again, but without the smile. The soft light caught the reddish lights of his dark hair, the planes of his face, that blunt nose, his sharp cheekbones. The rest of his face was in shadows, the light gleaming on his broad shoulders, catching the power in his crossed arms. "I think we've both had enough for tonight, Tempest. I'm turning in."

"Don't you dare walk away from this, Marcus," Tempest warned as she stepped onto the leather couch, up to the back, and vaulted to the floor on the other side. She covered the distance to Marcus in a heartbeat. "I want to know what you're up to—right now. And you'd better not have involved my family."

A muscle moved in his jaw and his lips thinned. He moved too quickly for her to escape, his hand shooting out to capture her jaw. "It will be up to you to keep them out of it. Apparently, according to what I've read, you're all somehow connected by something other than birth. Since I'm still uncertain how I feel about psychics . . . clairvoyants, extrasensory perception, sixth senses, whatever, I'd advise caution, Tempest. I really would."

"Threats? Here's one for you: You've been stalking me. I could turn you in."

"You won't. You've just broken into my place— picked the lock. And I was just researching you. I'm not the first to be interested in psychics. After all, Ms. Storm, you are one of the famous Aisling-Bartel triplets." He kissed her again, just as brief and hard as the first time; his whisper ran deep and harsh against her lips. "At first, I could have killed you, then I thought I'd have a nice little chat with you about your lack of manners. But then, I saw your mother with that pin—"

Tempest put both hands on his bare chest and pushed free. "Brooch, Marcus, not a pin. It's a brooch."

"Why do you want it so badly that you've run all over the country in the past year and a half to find it?"

If he knew that the brooch was somehow linked to

whatever was happening to her family now, he'd have an advantage—a man like Marcus would use it. "Now that would be telling, wouldn't it?"

"I'll find out, you know, sooner or later. I'm very good at details. We'll talk in the morning."

"We'll talk tonight, and then I'm getting out of here."

He leaned down, his forehead against hers. "You do, and you'll never get that brooch. I'll have it melted down."

Marcus straightened, his stare down at her arrogant and cold. "Now, good night. Unless you want to join me. I feel a little . . . unfinished . . . when it comes to you. No? Well, now that we've had our little chat, I'll see you in the morning, when we've both had a chance to cool down."

As he forced himself to walk away from Tempest, Marcus expected her to attack him, her expression was fierce enough—those dark gold eyes had bored furiously into his.

He'd dreamed about her scent, about her hunger, her passion, and she was just as he remembered—passionate, fiery, but a lot less friendly. When those dark green eyes changed to gold, when she was angry and passionate, reckless maybe, then, he'd have the advantage.

Marcus smiled coldly to himself; that slight tremor of Tempest's body had told him that she remembered their one-night intimacy, her burning like fire beneath him, over him, consuming—and then walking out before he woke up.

He'd known from the moment he'd seen Tempest that she was unusual, and a prize. Graceful, polished, she looked amazing in that tight black dress, those hot pink elbow-length gloves, those black high heels. The bored escort of a woman who was only using him for her "arm candy," Marcus had left with Tempest. The heat and sensuality had stirred around them from that first moment.

She'd been standing by *Predator*, a bird of prey in flight, one long, hot pink silk glove stroking its bronze wing as if to tame the wild beast. Captured in a pool of light that caught the flame in her hair, she'd looked over her champagne glass to him. He'd known instantly that she would be interesting.

Marcus had walked to her, caught her scent—unique, exotic, sensual—above the others in the room. As he had stood near her, she was even more unique, with slanted mysterious green eyes, that pale skin, and soft, glistening mouth. There was a unique edge to her, a sparkle that said he wouldn't be bored—and he wasn't; in fact, he'd been fascinated by each sensuous feminine movement, each sultry look. A short conversation, the purchase of *Predator*, and they were off to a very late dinner in his hotel room.

And he hadn't seen her since that night.

Marcus took his time in the shower, pacing himself deliberately, until he emerged naked from the bathroom. He found Tempest sitting on the edge of his bed. She looked away immediately to *Predator*, gleaming beneath a lighted alcove. "I see the resemblance now— you and *Predator*."

He wasn't going to make it easy. Marcus took his time drawing on black silk pajama bottoms. He usually slept nude, but the concession seemed fitting with Tempest—although he wasn't quite sure how he'd come to that conclusion. That night in Santa Fe, she'd had no problem watching him move, almost as if she were studying a piece of her art and enjoying it; as for her own body, she hadn't been shy in exposing herself. But then, she hadn't planned to stay for breakfast, had she? Or anything else? And that irritated. "This is going to be a long night, isn't it?"

In a restless movement, Tempest was on her feet, facing him. "What are you after, Marcus? Other than a little revenge to satisfy a silly male ego?"

Marcus ripped back the coverlet from his king-size bed and lay on top of the sheets, placed his hands behind his head, and watched her. It wouldn't do to give Tempest too much information too soon. And he had her for tonight. If what he'd read about the nature of psychics was true—and if there was such a breed, Tempest would have more than the usual curiosity, and she was definitely impulsive. Marcus already knew that she would take what she wanted and walk away without looking back—except if she wanted something more. And Tempest wanted that brooch.

He switched off the light. "Good night, Tempest. By the way, I thought you might like an undisturbed sleep, so I took the liberty of turning off the telephones and blocking cell phone reception, too. I'll see you in the morning."

"If you're alive," she murmured quietly as she turned and walked out of his room.

He listened to the sounds as she moved through the penthouse, testing the locks, opening the refrigerator, sliding a drawer open and closed, the big-screen television purposefully tuned too loud.

Marcus held his breath as she came to stand in his bedroom doorway. He remembered that curve of her hips, the way he'd gripped them, how fluid and soft and strong she'd captured him. And now he had her.

Before moving away, Tempest whispered one word, "Bastard."

Every muscle in Marcus reacted, tightly coiled in anger. It was a word his father had often called him.

"I'll want to see the real one, the real brooch," Tempest said early the next morning as she walked into his private gym.

"Sleep well? I imagine you were pretty tired after your surveillance of this place—and that climb last night." The image of Tempest scaling the Sebastian's brick wall still haunted him. She was unpredictable, an element that caused him to be mildly uneasy. In contrast, he'd meticulously structured his life, the aftereffect of a chaotic childhood.

Marcus stopped running, turned off the treadmill, and tossed a towel around his shoulders. Early this morning, he'd found Tempest asleep on the dark leather couch, snuggled in a dark green woven throw, still dressed in her black clothing. She was still wearing her gloves, the file folder papers scattered and crumpled around her. If he didn't know what Tempest could do, like scaling the outside of a building twelve stories up, she would have looked sweet.

He hadn't expected the wave of tenderness and sense of guilt as he'd stared down at her. She'd seemed so vulnerable, so feminine, that he'd wanted to protect her—but then, that would have been protecting her from himself.

He'd approached snaring Tempest in the same methodical way he researched a takeover. But after he'd read the Blair Institute reports and the newspaper clippings of how the ten-year-old triplets had been scooped from their home and tossed into a nightmare of testing, he'd been shaken. No child should have to go through that. With an aunt as emotionally cold as his father, a woman who wanted money for his keep and provided little in return, Marcus's experience hadn't been pleasant either.

And no child should have to go through his own early childhood—a verbally abusive father and a mother terrified for her son and herself.

Tempest's cool tones broke into his thoughts. "I see you cleaned up the broken glass. You appear very talented, Marcus."

"Thank you. I always like things neat, like in saying good-byes, when leaving in the morning."

Tempest ignored the pointed reference to their one night together and took her time walking around the various pieces of exercise equipment, the morning light from the windows shifting around her curved, athletic body. She held her coffee cup and an apple, and sat on a weight lifter's bench, one leg raised upon it. She'd removed her jacket, and the fitted black top clung to her curves, her arms pale and toned as she placed her cup aside. Marcus noted that thick-cuff silver bracelet; it had looked exotic and exciting over her long gloves, an unusual choice for a unique woman.

Tempest studied him as he straddled the bench and sat facing her. Her witch's eyes considered him in a sidelong, speculative stare. "You must want me badly, or what I can do. Or, what you think I can do. Which is it?"

Marcus took the coffee cup from her and sipped the hot brew. "You're going to have to change. That outfit won't work for where we're going. They might mistake you for a burglar, and that would be correct."

" 'Where we're going,' to see the brooch, to see if it is the original," she stated coolly as she took the cup back from him, as if she'd never give him any part of herself. "That's the only place I'm going with you, Marcus."

"We'll see about that," he answered as he stood and extended a hand down to her. "I'm proposing a little bargain, very special and very private. When you're satisfied that the brooch is what you want, it's yours—if you help me get what I want. I don't care why you want the brooch, or what you want to do with it. It's just yours. I want you to stay with me, live with me, until you get that something for me. Agreed?"

"Or you'll melt it down? That's the alternative, isn't it? You'd destroy a piece of antiquity, of value, just for revenge?"

"Absolutely. Consider it a promise."

She glanced at his well-manicured hand, big and hard with calluses. She remembered exactly how it had felt cruising her body, and she understood its potential danger to arouse. Life with Marcus would be like living in a tinderbox, his playing methodical, cool, and determined to her rebellious, impulsive nature.

Tempest had been controlled by a man just once, and she hadn't liked it. She'd betrayed everything she was and what her family was for him. A second time held little appeal. "What was that about living with you?"

Marcus smiled coolly and nodded. "I'm afraid I don't exactly trust you. But then, I have good reason not to, wouldn't you say? After all, you are a woman who runs off without a polite good-bye, then adds burglary into the mix. Do you think I'd trust a woman who can travel at will anywhere, anytime, a chameleon when she wants? No, I want to know your every move, and that means sticking very close to you."

Tempest smiled sweetly and stood. She removed her gloved hand from his and patted his cheek. "Before I make any bargain with you, I want to see the brooch. You're really going to pay for this, you know."

"I always pay—and well. It keeps things so neat."

"At my showing, they said you were rich and cold, ruthless when you wanted something. And those were your business associates. I didn't seem to meet any of your friends."

"They were right."

"And you want me to do something for you."

"A very special something. Let me cook breakfast first. I never do business on an empty stomach."

Tempest followed Marcus into the kitchen area,

watched him expertly prepare bacon, scrambled eggs, and toast. He poured orange juice into two glasses and set two places at the dining-room table. Tempest sat at the bar for a moment, then she took a banana and walked to sit at the table; she crossed her legs, her feet propped upon another chair. "I can't believe you're this domesticated, Marcus. You do this for all your—guests?"

"I learned how to take care of myself at a very early age, Tempest. There were times when the staff wasn't allowed in the house—and my mother wasn't . . . feeling well."

Marcus had chosen his words very carefully. Tempest remembered her research on Marcus. At fourteen, the Greystone heir was orphaned; his parents had died in a car wreck near their Michigan home, one of many homes. Now thirty-five and a seasoned, hard business-man, he headed Greystone Investments' diverse enter-prises.

And he wanted Tempest to do "something" for him.

A powerful man, with every resource at his finger-tips, and he wanted her.

Another man had wanted her to do "a little some-thing" for him—and she'd almost lost her soul for two years.

Dressed in her sleeveless, basic black dress and pumps, Tempest decided not to wear her more noticeable wide-cuff bracelet or her belt; she chose only the silver replica of the brooch. A little light sunscreen, mascara, and lip gloss completed her simple, but go-anywhere look. She allowed Marcus's hand at her waist as they walked into the bank's private viewing room. The clerk carried in the tiny box and glanced at Tempest's black leather gloves. His frown was puzzled, but he nodded and discreetly closed the door behind him.

Marcus, in a lightweight gray business suit, stood back and nodded to the box. He looked as hard and impenetrable as the bank's huge vault door and the gate covering it; he looked as cold as the exterior marble blocks, polished and smooth. But when she'd appeared, freshly showered and in the dress, those gray eyes had definitely heated, before he turned away. Her body had responded immediately to Marcus's heated look, and unprepared for her sensual reaction, Tempest had been shaken.

Marcus spoke abruptly, his deep voice echoing in the bank's viewing room. "You wanted to see it. Open the box. Hold it."

Eager to see the brooch—and see if it was truly the original, Tempest barely controlled herself. She wanted to rip open the lid, dive into the box, and see the brooch. She wanted to tear off her gloves and feel its history, to understand why it was so important to her family, why both her mother and her oldest sister dreamed about this brooch. But Marcus was noting her every expression, stacking up his advantages, and she couldn't appear to be too anxious.

"'Hold it.' You're saying that you actually believe in psychic ability, then? In my ability to hold something and know its history? In psychometry?"

"I'd be a fool not to after researching your mother and your family. Let's just say that since I haven't actually seen anything to convince me, it's a lot to believe. According to experts, the ability can—or cannot—be transferred to descendants. It follows, naturally, especially after reading the reports from Blair, that you and your sisters share her ability. Yes, I think psychic ability is within the realm of possibility. But like anything, there are always a lot of fakes. I've read your mother's books and checked her background. She's definitely tuned in to something to last this long, against naysayers and challengers."

"So that naturally makes me a full-fledged psychic." Tempest placed her gloved hand over the box, her senses shivering with the impulse to open it. "You could just be putting me through some hoops for pay-back, your precious ego."

"I could. And that brooch has something to do with your family. Leona was wearing it in an advertisement for her vintage clothing shop. Is she hunting it, like you? Why?"

"We fancy it," she lied lightly. "What is it you want me to do, Marcus?"

"You've gone to a lot of trouble for a mere fancy. We'll talk after you decide if the brooch is genuine."

Marcus was hunting for insights not contained in his resources; he was circling her, wanting something from her. At twenty, she'd danced to another man's tune, doing one little favor for him, then another and another, until she was tightly caught in her own destructive web. Marcus's expression was shielded, giving her nothing. "You'd play great poker."

"You wouldn't. You're very expressive—in all ways. You're volatile, impulsive, and reckless to a fault when you want something, like scaling the Sebastian. You're very easy to read."

"Maybe you're the psychic then."

Focused on the brooch, Tempest listened to her own terrified, racing heartbeat. Marcus's indrawn breath echoed in the sterile private room. "Just open the damn thing, Tempest. Let's see if we're in the game or not."

One flip of the lid revealed the small box inside. Aware that Marcus watched her closely, Tempest removed the box and placed it on the table. If the artifact wasn't genuine, she was in no danger. If it was real, she had to have it.

She cautiously opened the box and stared down at the brooch, resting on a dark cloth base. Still wearing her gloves, she carefully picked up the large brooch, much larger than the replicas she had created for her family. It wasn't as heavy as she'd expected, concave on the back, probably to allow some kind of storage, which was typical of the period. Bronze would have been more commonly used, but this piece was silver, with some kind of an alloy, and dark with age. The brooch gleamed within her leather gloves, the impression of the wolf's head still sharp beneath her stroking thumb. As the photographs had depicted, the angular impressions circling the wolf's head were marred and worn smooth; it would be impossible to connect the Viking characters for a correct translation. An ornate, intricately woven design circled the piece, the places that might have held gold or amber empty now.

Tempest sat carefully, her heart racing. If the brooch was genuine, she might have the answer as to its link to her family. The legend handed down from mother to daughter of her family was that Aisling, a Celtic seer and ancestor of Greer, and therefore the triplets, had been taken captive by a Viking raider chieftain—she had become his bride. Tempest's gloved thumb traced the marred Viking characters. How was this brooch connected to her family? Why did her mother and sister dream of it and the Viking wearing it?

Tempest carefully replaced the brooch in the box. She both feared and wanted to know what secrets it held, who owned it, what had happened to it.

Suddenly, her gloves were off, tossed carelessly aside and her hands held the brooch. She willed it to lead her—Heat warmed her hand, images flipping through her mind, the channel from her hands open and receptive. She closed her eyes and spoke softly, "You didn't touch it with your bare hands, Marcus. I'd know. The private collector was before you. He never got over his wife committing suicide. He wanted to join her. The archaeologist who discovered it at a Viking dig hid it away, selling it on a private market. He'd already sold artifacts from Egyptian tombs, an older man desperate to keep a younger wife in style."

"That's enough. If you want more, you're going to have to keep our bargain. Then it's yours."

Tempest glanced at Marcus, who stood, both hands braced on the table as he stared down at her. "It is the original, then. What's wrong with you?"

She couldn't breathe, the residual images flying around her, harsh words clashing with flashing swords, metal clanking, death groans all around her. She heard a woman's sharp cry—was it her voice or another's from centuries ago?

Then suddenly, the brooch was ripped from her hands and Marcus held her shoulders, shaking her gently. "Tempest, dammit, come out of it."

He looked as fierce as the warriors. But he was wearing—a contemporary suit and tie. . . . Tempest blinked and shook her head; she struggled to replace this man's image with that of the looting, raiding warriors.

Marcus tugged her up and into his arms. "Okay . . . okay. Take it easy. You're shaking and cold—don't you faint on me now, Tempest."

"Sorry, Marcus—I think I'm going to—"

"You fainted, Tempest," Marcus stated harshly as he placed the cold damp cloth on her forehead. Lying on his guest bed, she seemed so small and fragile, all that animation, power, and passion gone.

She'd terrified him, suddenly going limp and pale in his arms. He'd managed to make excuses and a fast exit from the bank, almost carrying Tempest in his arms. He'd explained her limp body and dazed expression with: "Heat. She's not used to these temperatures. I'm taking her home right now."

Marcus stood, looking down at her on the bed, and rubbed his hand across the back of his neck, where tension—and his conscience—had tightened into a knot. In her too-pale face, her eyes were dark and haunted as if she'd walked into a nightmare, and it still clung to her.

"Do you always react that way?" Marcus asked unevenly.

"You were right. I'm afraid I haven't eaten well in the past few days, and the heat did get to me."

She shook her head, her dark red hair vibrant against the white silk pillowcase. The damp cloth slid aside, and Marcus bent to replace it. Tempest caught his wrist and stared up at him. "You said that if I did something for you, I could have the brooch. I'll do it. What do you want from me?"

"It's the real one, then." Marcus didn't trust himself now; he'd been hit by a guilt he didn't expect, and more—fear for Tempest and the fierce need to protect her. "We'll talk about it later. When you're feeling better."

"You're going to try to back out now, aren't you? Well, you can't. We have a bargain."

Tempest shoved his hand away, and, as Marcus stood, she sat up and wrapped her arms around her bent legs. She placed her head on her knees and rocked her body. With the plain black dress setting off her fair skin and shining red hair, she looked delicate and sweet and young.

He'd been raised in a hell that still circled him. If Tempest came with him, lived with him, he could tear her apart.

Unfamiliar with the need to hold and comfort another person, Marcus rubbed the tension knot at the back of his neck. "This might not be a good idea now, Tempest—"

That brought her head up, her stare fierce. In one fluid movement, she was on her feet, standing on the bed. She reached out to grab his shirt, jerking it in her fist as she leaned down to him. "Oh, no. You're not backing out. I want that brooch, and I'm getting it. I wouldn't trust you not to melt it down—just so I couldn't have it. Tell me what you want so badly that you researched me—and my family—and you laid out that whole entrapment. Tell me what you want, because I won't stop until I know what it is—brooch or not."

Her eyes were that angry, glittering gold—and Marcus didn't trust himself. Back about ten heartbeats, he was feeling like that bastard his father had called him. Now he was angry at Tempest for causing him to feel like scum. He reached to circle her bottom; he lifted and carried her out into the living room. Marcus released her, and she tumbled down onto the couch in a flurry of arms and legs. Her skirt hiked up to reveal a curved thigh and hip, with just a tiny band of red silk—and Marcus's body started heating.

She'd gotten to him, torn him inside out worrying about her, and right now he wanted to dive into that compact, curved body and taste—

Tempest sat up and glared at him, her cheeks flushed. Marcus forced himself to back away from what looked like open combat. He turned and headed for a drink he badly needed to cool down; his hand shook as he poured it. "You recover fast."

The silence behind him almost palpitated with her anger; the back of his neck tingled with warning.

"When do we start?" Tempest asked quietly as she came to stand beside him. "Finding what you have to have?"

Marcus closed his eyes and started to bring the bourbon to his lips—but her hand stopped him. Her tone was soft, as if she really cared. "What is it, Marcus? You're afraid, aren't you? You're actually afraid of the answers you need—you have to have."

Marcus reacted instantly, turning to her, not shielding the savage emotions within him. There was only one person who had really cared, and now she was gone, murdered. "I am never afraid," he said between his teeth.

"You're afraid that I just might be able to give you what you want. No, that's not right. It's what you need, what's buried inside you so deep that it's a cold stone in your heart. It's holding you captive, Marcus, and you can't let go."

Her voice was softer now, her expression compassionate. She was picking up pieces from his attitude, his tone, his expression—psychics did that, didn't they?

He didn't want pity, let alone Tempest's. But she'd dug right into his darkness, torn off his shields, and exposed his private hell.

Marcus picked up the drink and tossed it down. He stared into the mirror and caught his harsh face, a man who lived like a machine, all those dark memories trapped inside him: a beast for a father, a victim for a mother, a picture-perfect wealthy family with ugly secrets—and then it had all been ripped away. "Whatever you think you know—you don't."

Tempest barely came up to his shoulder, and yet she had more impact than a bulldozer. She was dangerous to him, in too many ways. Churning with shifting emotions now, Marcus relied on what he knew best, what he'd learned to protect himself—retaliation. He wanted to step into her darkness, just as she had his, tit for tat. "Tell me about those two missing years I couldn't find. Where were you? What were you doing?"

"That's my business. You need something, and I'm going to get it for you. My guess is that you want answers."

He'd never told anyone what he was about to tell Tempest. "It's a cold-case murder. That's why I'm ready to try—alternative methods."

"You mean psychics. Okay . . . so where did it happen? We'll need to start there."

Four

"TEMPEST SHOULDN'T HAVE AGREED," GREER AISLING SAID as she stood at her office window, overlooking the Northwest's Pacific Ocean. "But she never could pass up a challenge, and now she's with Marcus Greystone—headed toward Lake Michigan. If there's one place any of my daughters shouldn't be, it is near a major lake."

The distant haze seemed to blend sky and ocean. Like white dots on a blue-gray canvas, seagulls hovered in the distance, making use of the wind, while beneath the swells, the whales were swimming, sounding to their young. On the brown sand, sandpipers were running amid the clumps of seaweed. Higher on the shoreline, the tufts of grass bent in the wind that constantly misshaped the trees.

Greer rubbed her brooch, one that her daughter had created—a replica of the real one that Tempest had held in her hands. The genuine Viking brooch was much larger, the angular characters surrounding the wolf's head too marred to read.

Claire, the empath, the youngest and most vulnerable of the triplets, had been attacked while in her Montana home. Before Claire and Tempest could reach the man, he'd destroyed his workplace and computer, and committed suicide. But Tempest had caught the residue of rage he left behind. She'd picked up that same rage while touching items in Claire's home and clothing, and had matched that same rage to the man's computer. Something—someone—had gotten control of the usually placid man, driving him to hurt Claire.

What or who was circling her family? And why?

Greer tapped the file she had developed on Marcus Greystone, owner of Greystone Investments.

"Going to help Marcus with a little problem," Tempest had said lightly on her call from the airport as she waited for the private jet to be readied. "Yes, I know that Lake Michigan could be a psychic portal. But I'm not the psychic that you, Leona, and Claire are. I don't feel things—unless my hands are on them, but I know that the brooch I held this morning was the original. I wasn't strong enough to protect myself or to 'see' everything, but I went deep enough to know it's real. I'm getting it, just after this little favor for Marcus."

From researching Marcus, Greer understood that "little favor" immediately—the Greystones' deaths had been in the suspected hit-and-run cold-case files for twenty-one years, and now Marcus was hunting.

That was why he'd donated a huge sum to the Blair Institute for Parapsychology last October—just after Greer had talked with Tempest about her very successful Santa Fe showing. She hadn't explained, but the vibrations and energy coming from her were heightened; they were purely sexual, frustrated, and terrified.

Marcus Greystone had evidently connected Tempest to her psychic family; he'd left a research trail all over their public history, including the accidental death of Daniel Bartel. He'd researched Tempest, and he'd gotten her.

Now a hardened man, Marcus had successfully rebuilt his father's struggling company by focusing on marina equipment, pleasure and fishing boats, and water sporting gear. Married and divorced with no children, Marcus had been the one Tempest had met at her showing in Santa Fe. Greer had sensed Tempest's unsteady emotions from the first. She'd been careful to ask about the buyer for *Predator*, because the image of the statue had flown into her mind the moment that Tempest had picked up the telephone.

The likeness of a hawk suited the man, who from his early twenties had stepped into the position of Greystone's lead man, his finances and his family gone. A driven man, willing to suffer hardships, Marcus had put himself through college while rebuilding Greystone Investments.

Now, with enough wealth and power in his fist, Marcus wanted to solve his parents' cold-case murders, and he had interested Tempest by securing the brooch she had pledged to find.

And now a contemporary predator had Tempest in his talons.

"It happened there. My father was driving my mother's car."

As they passed an aged brick building used as a tourist center in western Michigan, Marcus's fists tightened on the BMW's steering wheel. In the first week of July, a few tourists were walking on the roadside path, an elderly couple holding hands.

In a black T-shirt and jeans, he looked little like the sleek, perfectly tailored businessman she'd met in Santa Fe and again in Albuquerque. Now, he looked even more honed and dangerous. Marcus looked as if he could handle himself in a back-alley brawl, the muscles and cords of his arms flexing as he drove, his big gold wristwatch flashing in the sunset.

Tempest studied the building's huge WELCOME TO

PORT SALEM sign. She thought of another Salem, one that had condemned those with extra senses. "That's a bit ironic, don't you think?"

"I thought so. Since we met in October, I've come to think of you that way, a green-eyed witch. You left me feeling a little bit used, Tempest."

"Isn't that supposed to be my line?"

"Always right there, your defenses up, right?" In profile, the filtered sunlight from the shaded windshield gleamed on Marcus's cheekbone, and shadows lay in the lines around his lips, that set jaw. He wore designer sunglasses, concealing any emotion in his eyes, but his lips thinned, a tense cord in his throat working before he continued, "No doubt you know this from your research, after our—encounter. My parents' car was rounding that curve and smashed into that brick wall. I was fourteen."

Marcus's knuckles showed white as he gripped the steering wheel, his tone uneven as he continued. "Kenny, our handyman, took me to identify the bodies—what was left of them. I was staying with him that night. I often did. But that night, my mother had asked him to come get me. My parents had been arguing. I can't remember a time when they weren't at odds. My father liked to terrify her—my mother, Winona—and she took it. Dear old Dad was no sweetheart. Jason used to drive like that with me, to scare me. Maybe he tried it once too many times and didn't make the curve. But then, that wouldn't explain the deep dent in the driver's side and the scrapes along the side."

Marcus's hands flexed on the steering wheel. "It was a deliberate hit-and-run, according to the investigator's report. The tulip farmer's pickup truck was reported stolen the morning after they died, and it was found abandoned by a motel. The paint on it matched my mother's car. My parents were hit just as they came out of that curve, and the first impact killed my father. But the scrapes along the side, and the skid marks on the pavement indicated that someone revved up that pickup, burning rubber as my parents' car was forced into that wall, killing my mother. Someone wanted one or the other dead, or maybe both. At one o'clock in the morning, no witnesses were around, or at least any who would speak up. The night janitor was inside, heard the impact, and called the police."

Tempest shifted slightly in the comfortable leather seat. A return to Port Salem had evidently reopened Marcus's emotional scars. She was fortunate to have a few years of a loving father and warm memories, a mother who did nothing to disparage them. And she had been unfortunate enough to believe that almost every man was as honorable and selfless. And then, she'd met Brice. . . .

The insight into Jason Greystone wasn't pretty, and Tempest realized how deeply Marcus had been hurt at an early age. He preferred to distance himself from his father by calling him "Jason," the dislike and bitterness easily detected.

"Where were they going?"

"I have no idea."

"Then, how are you going to explain me . . . why I'm here? It's a cold case, Marcus, and if you say that I'm here to research—investigate—people might not be so willing to share information."

"I told the ones closest to me that you were very special to me, and they can take that however they want. I said you'd be asking questions about my life, my family, and I'd appreciate their cooperation. If deeper explanations are necessary, I'll handle them. I want you to know everything. Everything," he repeated grimly. "I want that murderer found, and if you can help, I want you to have whatever you need."

"They'll think we're involved, and I am considering you for a potential—something. I am not going to play into that gig."

"Then don't. But we are involved, aren't we? You want that brooch, and I want answers." Marcus shifted abruptly, and the car sped by the tourist center for Lake Michigan. He glanced at a curvy woman, bicycling toward town, her shorts high enough to reveal the curve of her bottom. He continued watching her as he spoke to Tempest. "I imagine you're tired. The flight into my private airport here was rough."

Tempest inhaled sharply, surprised at the tiny jealous sizzle; she pushed it down. She told herself that Marcus's sexual interests didn't affect her at all. "You're an expert pilot. And I'm not tired at all."

At ease with any travel, Tempest leaned back in the leather seat. Clearly, Marcus's emotions were churning beneath that cold exterior shell. His lean body had been tense on the flight, his expression grim. He was tightly coiled and too quiet.

He glanced at her backpack at her feet, then at her black shell and black slacks, her comfortable loafers. "You travel light, only a backpack and that overnight bag we collected from your hotel."

Tempest wasn't interested in chitchat. "What makes you think that someone wanted them dead?"

He inhaled as if bracing himself to look back at the past. "I have the photographs and the documentation. That hit-and-run was done on purpose, but what the police didn't know was that my father had been getting threats from people he owed—or whose toes he'd stepped on. Taking on the mistress of an underworld character can make life chancy and nasty. I checked out all those leads and found nothing. You're welcome to all the information I have, the contacts back then, the files and photographs, but they're not pretty."

"No, thanks. I don't work that way."

Marcus nodded. "Apparently your mother does. She sometimes works with the police, using their photographs and files."

"That's her setup, her professional preparation." Tempest sighed impatiently. Earlier, Marcus had said he'd read Greer Aisling's books; that was a large investment of time, and he was using what he had learned.

She took in the passing scenery. Port Salem was a typical Lake Michigan town, nestled on the shoreline and filled with tourists. Sunset touched the harbor that fingered in from the lake. The waterway separated the main part of town from elite houses on the other side, which faced the lake. "You dug all that up, did you? She works differently—so do my sisters. I'm the oddball, and can only feel with my hands. Debts and threats are one thing, but if someone is dead, he can't very well pay off. Now why do you think someone wanted him dead?"

"His enemies, business and private. He ran some small dealers out of business, wrecked a few lives along the way. On the other hand, Jason might have wanted to kill them both . . . maybe he hired someone to do the job—because she knew too much. I wouldn't have put anything past him. Greystone Investments was going under. He'd had to sell off the other houses, and I imagine his women weren't exactly happy when he stopped buying several-thousand-dollar trinkets."

Tempest knew about threats; she'd been receiving them on and off for the last few years. Lately, the tone had changed, and eventually, she would have to deal with the man who had almost ruined her life.

She stared straight ahead at the blue line on the horizon. Lake Michigan was exactly where she shouldn't be, near big water, a potential psychic portal; she could be very vulnerable.

Inside the luxurious BMW's interior, Tempest's body chilled as she remembered how Claire had spoken of the fog along the Missouri River—*I felt the river wanted me. I thought I heard a voice call to me, but I couldn't be sure. It was only a whisper, and there were people all over the campground. But I was definitely drawn to the river. I had to protect myself by focusing, enclosing myself in an imaginary wall. And then, I think the fog I felt lurking around our camper followed me back to my home. At one point, I felt as if it wanted Neil, curling around him. . . .*

Neil and Claire were married now, and bonded with him, she felt so strong—or was she still in danger? What force could take over a quiet, good man, driving him to attack Claire?

Whatever had gripped Claire's attacker and activated him into savagery, it had come through that computer—which he'd effectively destroyed. Tempest remembered the savage energies racing up from her unprotected hands.

As Marcus's car seemed to float over the highway toward Lake Michigan, the water's blue line became larger and glistened, the sunlight hitting the waves—a child's kite flew high in the early-July wind, and seagulls hovered in the sky. If the water had been used as a psychic portal to reach Claire, would Tempest also be susceptible? She could be cruising toward her destiny . . . or her death. The town's name, Port Salem, wasn't exactly thrilling. Centuries ago, her ancestors had been burned at the stake in a town called Salem.

The road curved suddenly, and they were driving along the harbor, packed with fishing boats, cruisers, and small craft. Docks, their slips filled with all kinds of watercraft, lined the harbor. A huge metal-sided building stood at the widest part of the harbor, a platform dock in front of it, a large dock with filled slips nearby, and a parking lot to one side. Several cars and various boats on trailers were parked in another area. Near the top of the five-story building was a sprawling Greystone Marina sign. It offered heated dry storage for boats.

Tempest hadn't been near any large body of water for years, and the sight fascinated her. She'd visited her mother on the Pacific coast, but then the Aisling-Bartel home had always been a safe haven for the triplets. Memories of her father came skipping back, of how much he loved sailing. . . .

"The building is for boat storage and repair. I spent a lot of time at that marina, a kid looking for something to do to fill the hours. Kenny—Kenny Morrison—still works there," Marcus was saying. Then he glanced at her. "What's wrong? You just shivered."

Tempest couldn't look away from the small sailboat coming in from the lake. It was just like her parents'.

She'd caused that boating accident by playing too close to the edge when the wave hit. Distracted for just that one heartbeat, her father hadn't handled the sailboat well. When the sailboat had started to capsize, the triplets had been tossed overboard. They panicked, calling out for their parents to save them—and her father had swum to save her.

Despite the huge waves hitting them, he'd smiled at her as if they were playing a game, and she'd known that she was safe. "Hi, Tempest Best. Let's just do this, shall we? You and Daddy? You're safe now, with me. Mommy has Claire and Leona there by the boat, and we're going to see them. Here we go—hold on tight, honey. . . ."

Since then, she'd been terrified of water, and at an early age, she'd learned to conceal her fear. "From what you say, it doesn't sound like you had a perfect childhood, Marcus."

"Always right there, aren't you? Defensive, closing

off anything you feel might give away a part of yourself—to me, at least. Maybe it's better that way." Marcus's fingers flexed on the leather-covered steering wheel. "I'm like my father, in some ways. It wasn't a perfect childhood. Jason liked to hurt and humiliate. I don't know why my mother stayed with him."

Bitterness and love wrapped together in his reflective tone. But Tempest knew why a woman, who thought she loved a man, would stay with him.

For two years she thought she loved a man as cold as Marcus, then she hurriedly pushed that humiliation away. "Freak" wasn't a label she liked to remember.

As they drove along the harbor toward the expensive homes, she stared at Port Salem's houses on the other side, seemingly built almost on top of one another, a stacked colorful clutter of peaked roofs, the small town's church spire rising above the others. "Where's the tulip truck that hit them? And their car?"

"Probably recycled into lawn furniture now. At fourteen, I didn't have much say about anything. I didn't know at the time that there were people like you who might pick up psychic residue years later. When you held that replica, then the original brooch and reacted, I knew for certain. There's no way you could tap into that information so quickly, on the spot. Here's the driveway to the house." He turned into a paved lane between two brick columns; the lane wound up a flower-lined slope to a massive contemporary redwood home, surrounded by decking.

Marcus parked the car, got out, and reached for his laptop in the backseat. Outside the car, Tempest hitched up her backpack and noted the floor-to-ceiling windows; weather-bent trees surrounded the house and massive lawns and gardens. "Nice shack."

"My mother liked the flowers. She was always working in the flower beds. She always smelled liked that, like flowers." Marcus stood beside her, his hand resting on her waist. Everything in Tempest stilled; it was almost as if he were acting to protect her. Why? Because his ghosts, the darkness of his life rested inside?

He seemed to shake loose of his memories, and asked, "What did you say?"

Tempest moved away from that big possessive hand. "I said, 'Isn't your girlfriend—the one at the Santa Fe showing—going to be a little disturbed by me traveling with you? She could get the wrong idea.'"

Marcus nodded down to her. His wraparound glasses lit by sunset, shielded his eyes, but his lips curved slightly. "You mean, just because I took off with you for the evening and made my excuses to her, that Gabrielle would think we—that you and I, sweetheart—were having an affair?"

"I wouldn't want to break up a real romance." Tempest noted the older, stout woman dressed in a uniform and apron standing on the back deck. The dying sunlight lit her short, gray hair and glinted on her glasses.

"My housekeeper, Opal. She's expecting us. She lives here, but for this visit, I've rented her a condo in town. And I dealt with Gabrielle the morning you skipped out. She was happy with a diamond choker."

"Like I said, I wouldn't want to break up true love."

As they walked toward the massive double doors of the house, Tempest asked, "Is that your usual parting gift for your—ladies?"

"Like father, like son," he stated coldly.

"And you hate that part of yourself—the part that is like him," she remarked softly.

"You're not here as a psychiatrist, but I'm reminded of him every day. If Jason hadn't been so self-indulgent, Greystone Investments wouldn't have almost gone under. He was talented at crafting business plans. I'm using some of them today. But he was a little too reckless when investing, and he made mistakes in his personal life that ruined business."

Marcus waved to the housekeeper but directed Tempest around the house to the stairway leading up to the sprawling front deck. As they stood on the deck overlooking the lake, Tempest took in the comfortable furniture and large hot tub. Marcus removed his sunglasses and inhaled slowly. Tempest understood; he was home among familiar scents, enjoying them, the same as she would when arriving at her mother's coastal home.

He looked out at the lake, the fishing boats bobbing on the swells, a tall ship making the most of the wind, the sails billowing as a speedboat powered by its side. "My mother loved this place the most. I spent most of my time here. It was the first thing I secured."

Marcus looked down at her. "I don't like to let things escape me—unless I'm ready to let them go."

Tempest caught his meaning and wasn't backing off. She smiled sweetly up at him. "Likewise."

"The question is: Are you testing yourself to see if you're as good at the psychic business as your mother? Or are you testing something else? Like me?"

"Now, that's egotism."

"Maybe. But I already know that you're tricky and a runner. I also know you're impulsive, reckless, and driven—and that you're afraid of something."

Tempest fought her irritation. "That's a lot of knowing."

Marcus turned suddenly to Opal, who had opened the sliding front door. "Hello, Opal. You look well. This is Tempest Storm. She'll be staying here for a while."

Behind her glass lenses, Opal's fierce blue eyes took in Tempest's black outfit, her silver cuff bracelet, the big Celtic-style band on her wristwatch, and the replica brooch. She frowned slightly at the black gloves but recovered her professional mask quickly. "Very nice to meet you."

"Likewise."

Marcus's open hand rested on Tempest's back as they entered his home. Inside, she quickly drew away. That glint in his eyes said he recognized the hunger they'd shared, still simmering between them. "Make yourself at home."

Opal's stiff posture and her compressed lips indicated her displeasure. "You'll find the kitchen stocked as you requested. I've left numbers for delivery services, if you need anything. Pointe Maid Service has cleaned thoroughly. Francesca came over personally to supervise. I checked everything. It's all in order, Mr. Greystone."

"Thank you. Would you show Tempest around, please? I need to check some figures and make calls on a new merger. I'll bring our luggage in later."

Opal nodded, and Tempest followed her through the ultramodern house. Done in bamboo flooring and covered by dark maroon and gold area rugs, the rooms were spacious, with cream and dull golds to contrast the darker teak furniture. The larger furniture suited Marcus's tall body. Airy paintings depicted the lake and boats, bringing the scenery outside into the house. The open-room arrangement contained a large bar, suitable for social entertaining.

As she followed Opal, Tempest noted the absence of any family pictures.

"Mr. Greystone has renovated most of the house to suit him. His corporate offices are in Chicago, but he comes here every chance he gets. It's his favorite place," Opal stated with obvious pride that she was charged with the care of his home. "I usually stay here. I have my own room. But this time, I am to take a little vacation while he is here."

The housekeeper's sharp tone underlined her territorial rights. Tempest wondered if "this time" indicated visits with other women. Marcus had been an experienced lover; there was no reason why Tempest should think she'd had an exclusive experience with him.

Opal was brisk and coolly efficient in her tour. "The kitchen—Mr. Greystone can call Francesca's number for daily cleanup if you wish. . . . Here's the formal dining room."

"Opal, I understand that you've been with the Greystone family for a long time. Do you always call him 'Mr. Greystone'?"

"Always . . . as I did his father. And there was Mrs. Greystone, of course. And the second Mrs. Greystone, Marcus's ex-wife. I'm afraid she didn't like this place very much. Tried to do it up with French provincial—imagine that. He would have none of it, not my Mr. Greystone."

As they passed the spacious office, Marcus stood at the large windows viewing the lake; he was apparently deep in a conference call, and Opal continued her tour: "We have four guest rooms. Each bedroom has its own bathroom, all well stocked."

She nodded to a door. "The master bedroom . . . it was the Greystones', Mr. Greystone's parents. It's just the way it was when Mr. and Mrs. Greystone had their accident. Here we are at your room."

Opal's lips tightened with apparent disapproval. "Mr. Greystone wanted you next to his room."

Tempest glanced at the contemporary decor of beiges and dark sienna, the area rugs woven in a design to match the artistic hanging over the bed. The bed, dresser, and highboy were all rubbed walnut, a feminine guest basket sat on the vanity. "Thank you, Opal. I'm certain that everything is in order."

The housekeeper smiled slightly and nodded. "I do my best."

"I was wondering what you could tell me about the Greystones' accident. You were here then, weren't you?"

Opal's smile froze and died. "I have nothing to say about that bad business. I need to check on something in the kitchen."

When Opal hurried toward the kitchen to the rear of the house, Tempest tossed her backpack to the bed and wandered out to the view of the lake from the living-room windows.

Was the lake really dangerous to her? Could it be used as a portal to harm her? What energy could pass over it to her? Or was her fascination with it because she knew of Claire's experience, an empath who could sense energy easily?

Or was the triplets' vulnerability near water simply because at a young age, the massive wave hitting their sailboat and capsizing it had tossed them into the ocean? Fear could enliven psychic ability, and from that moment on, they had been more sensitive when near the ocean. Without their mother nearby, they could never play at the edge, never run in the sand.

Tempest inhaled abruptly as she remembered her father and mother struggling to recover the triplets. They'd been wearing life preservers, little protection against the ocean's swells and icy temperature.

Was it true that the water could be used as a portal? If her father was out there now, could she reach him? She had to know . . . she had to know. . . . Tempest wrapped her arms around herself, her fingers digging in as the nightmare seemed to pass before her.

The horizon was dark gray now, water and sky blending, the fog rolling into shore. Claire had been frightened by the fog; she'd felt that it wanted her. How close had she been? Just feet from the river's edge? Not as sensitive to nature as Claire, how near would Tempest need to be to the lake to feel any energy from her father?

She had to know. . . . Tempest looked at the pathway leading down to the lake and started moving toward it. She had to know if she would have the same reaction as Claire. Maybe Claire was the only one of the triplets who was affected—empaths were definitely connected to nature. But Tempest's ability lay in her connection with her family and in her hands alone.

Maybe after all these years of purposefully staying away from large bodies of water, she was finally immune—now was the time to discover just how vulnerable she was.

Tempest picked her way down the stone pathway, the tall grass brushing at her thighs, the tide lapping at the brown sand just in front of her. She crossed the riprap, the large gray chunks of stone that prevented erosion of the sandy bank leading up to Marcus's home.

She removed her shoes and let her toes sink into the cool damp sand; she listened to the sounds of the waves breaking farther out on the lake. The tide sucked the sand beneath her feet, the froth almost a caress. With her senses tingling, she wondered if some faint energy stirred in the water.

Was it the dark evil energy of her sister's attacker? Or was it their father, waiting to give her final closure.

"Come to me, whoever you are," Tempest beckoned softly as she stood braced against the wind and the tide. "If you want contact, you have to let me know you're there."

The fogbank rose above the dark waves, and the cold, damp wind pushed her body.

"Tempest?" the voice seemed to hiss quietly around her, the sound almost drowned by the wind, the swish of the grass near her.

"I'm here. Who are you? What do you want?" Her skin prickling, she stood very still as that fogbank came nearer, rising and curling above her.

Then it slid around her, almost like a lover, but with moist, airy tentacles that soaked her clothing, causing her to shiver. "Tempest?"

She couldn't breathe, the fog so thick it seemed to be crushing her.

She glanced up at the man beside her, recognized Marcus, and still held by the fog, she took her first deep breath.

Marcus peered down at her. "Tempest?"

"Did you . . . did you just call me?"

"Yes, didn't you hear me? Or were you just ignoring me?"

He frowned, his dark brows and lashes catching the mist in tiny glistening jewels. Instinctively, her finger moved to trace his brow, to wipe away the remainder of whatever had just almost crushed her. Marcus jerked back as if he'd been burned, and then Tempest understood: "You're afraid of so many things, Marcus. You're afraid of me, aren't you?"

In the swirling mist, his smile was coldly savage. "You're full of it, Tempest . . . on some ego trip. No offense, but I have no reason to be afraid of you. Your sisters just called, one after another, and then your mother. I got the feeling they were worried about you. Leona said, 'I should have known. She always was a daredevil. Have her call me back—please.' The 'please' must have been an afterthought. She sounds like she's used to giving orders. Is your family out of this—what we're doing, or not?"

"They're never out of it, Marcus. We're triplets, remember? And if you believe your research, we're connected in another way."

Tempest looked at the fog surrounding them. She had to know what was calling her, wanting her. Tempest eased away from Marcus and so far back into the fog that his features were blurred, and his body seemed to dissolve into the gray mist.

"Tempest?" a voice hissed softly above the wind.

She scanned the waves, crashing in the distance, and for an instant, she was a terrified three-year-old, thrashing in the water, fighting it. A man seemed to be swimming toward her.

"Daddy? Are you out there?" She looked down to see the waves lapping at her ankles, the foam churning like lace, and she felt the sand sucking beneath her feet, drawing her closer.

A wall suddenly hit her from the back, a band looped around her waist, and tore her back from the water.

"What the hell do you think you're doing?" Marcus demanded harshly as he hauled her back.

In that instant, Tempest realized that she'd been drawn into the water. Something wanted her, just as it had wanted Claire. And it wasn't their father. Or was it?

"Let's get out of here. You're freezing." Marcus's arm circled her waist, and he guided her toward the embankment.

Still wrapped in the fear that the fog and water had wanted to draw her into them, Tempest didn't trust anything and struggled free. "Watch it," she said tightly. "No touching."

Marcus's hard look down at her said that, at one time, he'd touched plenty, and she'd loved it. "Okay. Have it your way," he said as he turned and moved up the embankment toward his home.

"Opal has prepared dinner. I'll put it on the table," Marcus said.

In the kitchen, Tempest's back was to Marcus as she turned to look out at the harbor's lights; the fog had begun collecting on the spacious windows and forming tiny snaking trails down the glass. The running lights of a small boat appeared in the distance, and in one gloved hand, Tempest held the glass of wine Marcus had served her. She held out her other hand, studying it as if fascinated. "I wonder if—" she mused quietly.

Marcus glanced at Tempest as he placed a roast chicken on the kitchen's table with the baked potatoes and salad. "Wonder what? Dinner's ready."

Locked in the sensations she'd just experienced near the lake, Tempest set her wineglass aside and slowly removed her glove. She held out her hand and moved her slender pale fingers, studying them.

Marcus inhaled unsteadily. If there was one thing he'd dreamed of, had wanted on his body, it was that nimble, feminine hand.

"What's going on, Tempest?" he asked quietly, as she slid her glove on again.

Instead of answering, she reached for the telephone. "Hi, Leona."

She glanced at Marcus and collected the cordless telephone. "Excuse me. I'll take this in my bedroom."

Marcus frowned. He'd turned off the telephones' ring tones, letting the answering machine quietly filter the calls.

The telephone hadn't actually rung. That had happened before in Albuquerque just before they'd left his suite—that time Claire had called. Clearly, Tempest could sense exactly which member of her family was calling her—before the telephone rang!

Shaken that Tempest's family was connected by their senses and not electronics, Marcus sat down and looked out at the fog. Something had happened out there, and Tempest had asked, "Daddy? Are you out there?"

Was she also connecting with her father, who had died when she was four?

Marcus decided to wait for her and walked into his office. In a few minutes, he watched Tempest walk from the guest room and into the kitchen; she'd apparently taken the call and showered, her hair dark and damp, lying close to her head. Marcus's body tensed at the scent of her and the simple black knit lounging gown. It clung to every curve, revealing her bare feet—he remembered those agile feet stroking his calves in the luxurious aftermath of sex, the sounds she'd made.

The wolf's-head brooch gleamed at her shoulder. She hadn't been wearing that down at the shoreline; wearing it after the incident in the fog could signify that she knew she needed the good-luck piece. Why? What did it signify to them? Why was that brooch so important to the Aisling-Bartels?

He followed her into the kitchen, and said, "I guess your family is worried about you. And that phone did not ring, Tempest."

She smiled blandly and looked at dinner, waiting on the table. "I'm famished. This looks really good."

"Let's eat then."

Later, in his office, Marcus ran a few sales comparison graphs for a teleconference he would hold the next morning. But he watched Tempest prowl around his office. Her gloved hand drifted lightly over the desk and leather chairs, and then she stood in front of a grouping of pictures. All of them were of Marcus as a boy, with his mother.

Tempest turned to him and leaned back against the credenza, her wineglass in her hand. Those green eyes studied him as he turned off his laptop. "Winona had red hair."

Marcus caught the inference immediately and lifted his glass in a toast to her. "Like father, like son."

Her glass clinked softly as she placed it on the desk.

"Don't say that. I need to be in that room—your parents'."

"Tell me what happened out there. I heard you call, 'Daddy.' Did something happen that flipped you back in time to when he rescued you?"

Had her father called to her from beyond? Was she the one Aisling-Bartel woman who could be a medium for the dead? Logic battled with what he'd already read about Greer Aisling's successful work with the police when traditional means had failed. And he'd seen Tempest's reaction to both the replica and the genuine artifact. Perhaps it was possible—If so, was it possible that his mother might want to connect to him?

Locked in a mental debate that the impossible psychic connection might actually be possible, Marcus barely heard Tempest's voice. "Tell me why you've kept that room as a shrine."

"Opal wasn't only an employee, she was my mother's good friend. When she wanted to keep the room as it was back then, I saw no reason to object. There was a time when I was forbidden to go in there, but it really doesn't matter now. Keep ignoring my question, and I'll have to research more, Tempest. I want to know why you called to your father," he warned quietly as he stood and walked to her.

She ignored his question; she returned to the reason the bedroom was kept just as it was. "It's like a private collection that no one else sees."

Marcus ran his fingertip around that soft jaw, just a touch to watch those green eyes light, to know that her body had tensed, just a little private torment—for himself. "Just like the collector who owned the brooch before me."

She smiled blandly. "You're not going to own me, Marcus."

"I wouldn't want to. But that statement leads me to believe that some man 'owned' you before—and you didn't like it," he said as he walked from the office.

Marcus opened the door to his parents' bedroom and let Tempest pass by him, his body sensitized to the nearness and scent of hers. She'd terrified him earlier, and his reaction now was irritation with himself, followed by the normal male sexual one to reclaim her.

She slanted a look up at him. "It's a room with a bed. Don't get any big ideas."

"Wouldn't think of it. But since you brought it up, I wonder if it isn't on your mind," he returned mildly.

"I pass. Been there, done that."

Marcus lifted his wineglass in a toast. "At least you're not denying it, sweetheart."

"We both know I'm not sweet." Tempest smiled slightly as she passed, an acknowledgment of their night in Santa Fe. Inside the large room with a balcony overlooking the lake, she studied the cool, neutral decor offset by the dark woods of an elegant traditional king-size bed outfitted with matching bedside tables, a highboy, bureau, dresser, and a woman's vanity. She picked up the framed picture beside the bed, that of Marcus—the boy, grinning beside his mother, the lake filling the background.

Marcus remembered how he'd come here to be with his mother—when Jason was away. The room seemed still to carry her fragrance, the feminine softness that he remembered.

As Tempest moved, the black knit gown clung to her curves, the thigh-high slit now and then revealing that enticing, pale, long leg. The light from the balcony's window caught the fire in her hair, the smooth curve of her cheek and throat, and lingered on the compact curves Marcus had remembered too well. He'd never forget her walking toward him after that Santa Fe showing, the slight sway of her hips, the way she'd lifted them to him later, hungrily—maybe she was truly a witch, after all. Maybe she'd cast a spell he intended to exorcise.

Tempest suddenly removed her gloves and tossed them to the bed, and Marcus's insides tightened almost painfully with the need to have those slender hands on his body.

She wiggled her bare fingers like a surgeon preparing for a delicate operation. Then she smoothed the replica brooch at her shoulder, her apparent good-luck piece. "Who's been in this room?"

He leaned against the doorframe and remembered his mother crying and his father yelling, verbally demeaning her. Large for his age at twelve and experienced at surviving, he'd faced Mr. Jason Greystone with a threat he'd intended to keep, "Leave her alone, or I'll kill you!"

Jason had been on the boy in one stride, gripping him by the throat. With a cry, his mother had thrown herself between them, a tigress protecting her son. "You know what I can do, Jason," she'd said in a soft deadly tone. "And I'll do it. Leave him alone. Not him, Jason. Not this one. Not my son."

A movement in the room startled Marcus and brought him back to the present. He looked at Tempest, who seemed to be choosing the right place to start. What was it that Winona Greystone could do? What threat could she have held over her then-powerful husband?

Not him, Jason. Not him. Had there been someone else that Jason had hurt? That question had plagued him forever.

Marcus shook free of the ugly past, but knew he was

enough like his father to make good his threats. "Not that many would have come in this room. I suppose it was some sort of a makeup gift to my mother. Dear old Dad had this property set aside from the rest of his property and investments. With the help of friends, and an anonymous benefactor—probably a friend, too, who didn't want to get involved, maybe contaminated by Jason's financial problems—this place survived almost as it was."

Memories crowded around Marcus as he answered, "Opal maintained what she could. I owe her for that. Once, when necessary, she borrowed against her life savings to keep this place going at a minimal level while I was rebuilding the company. I've repaid her with interest and bonuses and whatever she needs now. Kenny, who runs the marina now, has probably been in this room through the years. I imagine if there was an electrical problem, or whatever, he would have been in here. He still does some handyman work around the house. Francesca Pointe owns a cleaning service, but she oversees this house herself. She would have been in here."

Tempest's bare hands fluttered around the dresser, his mother's vanity, and then both hands gripped a brush his mother had used. Suddenly her body began quivering, her face paled, and her forehead began to dampen.

It was the same reaction she'd had at the vault. Alarmed, Marcus moved quickly toward her and caught her shoulders, turning her. "That's enough."

She held her hands away, but her eyes shimmered with tears. "It must have been horrible for you. She loved you very much. She stayed with him because of you."

"It wasn't sweet. I begged her to leave him, but she wouldn't. Let's get the hell out of here."

But even as he urged Tempest from the room, the echoes of the past followed him. *You know what I can do, Jason,* his mother had said. *And I'll do it. Leave him alone. Not him, Jason. Not this one. Not my son.*

Not this one.

Who else was there?

Five

AS THEY LEFT HIS PARENTS' ROOM, MARCUS'S EXPRESSION was grim and guarded; he took Tempest's hand and drew her to his side. The gesture was possessive and protective, and Tempest quickly moved away.

Shaken by the energy remaining on the brush's single red hair, her own emotions battering her, she was too vulnerable now, careful to keep her hands free of contact. "My gloves," she whispered unevenly as she held her hands away. "I need my gloves."

Tempest had expected sarcasm but instead received a curt, "I'll get them. Stay put."

Marcus collected the gloves and returned to watch her slide them on and flex her fingers within the supple leather. Tempest's hands were shaking so badly she could barely manage. "That bad, huh?" he asked softly, his hand resting upon her shoulder.

"You're right. It wasn't sweet . . . and don't touch me." She sensed that Marcus wanted to hold her, but she didn't trust herself. Not exactly in control of herself yet, she was apt to grip anything for an anchor, and that wouldn't work with Marcus. In her open, responsive state, without her shields tightly around her quite yet, Tempest just might want that hard powerful body and lose herself in the pulsing heat of sex deep within her, with the only man who just might hold her high and waiting in an orgasm—just to prove his point, that she was susceptible to him.

Sensual tension heated the inches between them, as those gray eyes darkened. "But I've already touched you—intimately, haven't I? And you liked it."

"You were okay . . . average. But I'm not planning a repeat performance."

Marcus's finger trailed down her cheek and tapped her lips lightly. "Aren't you?"

She backed against the wall as his head lowered. Marcus's intent expression reminded her of a predator ready to pounce. He placed his hands flat on the wall beside her head, trapping her and increasing her wariness. Tempest tensed as his cheek brushed hers, his skin rough against her own. His teeth caught her earlobe, and then he whispered huskily, "How long do you think you can hold out?"

Her body was already softening and heating, her legs weakening. She eased her head away and Marcus's lips moved to her throat. "I've got you, Tempest. I'm in your blood and you're in mine. We'll finish this game, and you know it as well as I do."

At that challenge, she turned to him, licked her lips, and managed a sultry, confident smile. "You'll lose if we play games. I'm fast, and I'm good. Where is Opal, by the way?"

Marcus didn't move. "I'll have to slow you down a bit, won't I? So you won't run as easily next time. Opal is in the laundry room downstairs. She always starts my laundry the first thing. I'll finish it later."

He pushed away from the wall as Opal's footsteps sounded, coming up the stairs. Tempest breathed deeply, aware that every cell in her body wanted to devour Marcus's, to feel him deep inside her, to be wrapped so closely that he couldn't escape until she was ready.

Marcus's eyes pinned her, taking in her body from head to toe as if he remembered how she looked without clothing. Aware that she couldn't hide her blush, Tempest refused to look away as she spoke to the other woman. "Hi, Opal. Thank you for preparing dinner."

Opal's blue eyes narrowed behind her tinted lenses, and her brief smile seemed forced. Clearly, Tempest had invaded a territory that the housekeeper considered hers.

Marcus turned to the other woman. "I need to catch up on how a merger is going. Would you please help Tempest get settled? I put her bag in her room."

Opal nodded. "Yes, sir. I'll just put your things away, Miss."

Inside the guest bedroom, Tempest watched the older woman grip the overnight bag's handle and prepare to open it. Just that one touch should be enough. . . . Then she said, "There's no need for that, Opal. I rarely use anything but what I can carry in my backpack anyway. Could you please tell me about Marcus's mother and father?"

The housekeeper seemed uneasy, clasping her hands in front of her. "He told me you'd be interested in his life and his parents. They argued. Marcus's father was not an easy man. Mrs. Greystone was a lovely thing— sweet, kind. The hit-and-run driver was never found. Why are you really here?" she asked abruptly.

Tempest decided not to lie. "To do a job that Marcus wants. I'm sorry if you feel I'm intruding. How long have you been with the Greystones?"

"I came just after Mr. Marcus was born. They hired other help, but Mr. Jason was difficult. I was the only one they needed, and the others left." Opal straightened with pride; her mouth tightened into a hard line. Then her words seemed to burst from her: "Why do you want to know about his parents?"

Tempest decided to go with her instinct to take Opal by surprise, to get that first important impression. "Because I'm going to find that hit-and-run driver, Opal. Marcus wants me to. And I'd appreciate anything you could tell me about that time."

Opal paled; her gnarled hands clutching each other. "You're a detective? He's already done that years ago, as soon as he got on his feet and got back—"

"I'm very specialized, Opal. And I'm very good. May I call you to answer any questions?"

Opal nodded, and clearly upset, hurried out of the room.

Tempest moved toward the handle of the luggage, stripped off her glove and gripped it as Opal had done. She took the first impression from the layers of others, opening herself to absorb the housekeeper's energies. If she could connect them with the others in the Greystone's bedroom, she could start identifying a potential killer.

Opal's energy belied her controlled appearance. Tempest closed her eyes as she absorbed the housekeeper's poor, struggling childhood, a faithless husband, multiple stillborn babies, and fiery jealousy. Tempest pushed deeper into the jealousy, seeking a motive to harm the Greystones. Anger and frustration burned her hand—hatred of Jason, and . . . and love of Winona. Opal had worshipped Winona and had planned to murder Jason, to parent Marcus with Winona. Fear moved icily through Tempest's grasp and up her arm. Opal was deeply afraid now—of what Tempest might discover.

Tempest forced her fingers to uncurl from the luggage grip. In love with Winona, hating her abusive husband, Opal just might have wanted to kill Jason that day—and had mistakenly forced Winona to her death, too.

Tempest looked at her naked palm. She needed more—

In his office, Marcus glanced at Tempest as she passed, moving quickly toward the kitchen. If she was on the run, he intended to catch her. He finished noting a few changes to the outboard motor in the package deal with a fully outfitted johnboat, and jotted a note to his marketing department.

He found Tempest in the kitchen, bent low into the refrigerator and apparently scanning the contents. The view was worth hurrying for, her curved bottom wiggled as she poked through the crisper drawer. Marcus couldn't resist coming up behind her and placing his hands on the sides of her hips, bending over her back to view what she was retrieving.

Held against Marcus's body, his face next to hers, Tempest stayed very still. "You know what you're doing," she stated unevenly.

Oh, he knew. But Marcus couldn't think about anything but the cucumber in her hand. Her gloves wrapped around it, just the way her gloved hand had held him.

Already hard, his body close to hers, only a few layers of fabric held him from that feminine heat. He nudged a little closer and pulled her back against him, as they straightened.

She held very still as his hand flattened low on her stomach and the other near her breast. "If I'd wanted you, I'd have already had you," she whispered unevenly.

Marcus forced himself to remove one hand from her body and close the refrigerator door. "Don't be too sure about that."

He managed to step back and cross his arms over his chest. That posture did little to ease the tension riding low in his body, but it did save a little pride.

"Make yourself comfortable. Let me know if you need anything. I'll be in my office."

At three o'clock in the morning, Tempest stood on the front deck overlooking the lake. The hanging ferns swayed in the wind; the mist had beaded on the fronds and caught the dim light within Marcus's home.

She had to go back to the water—to open her hands and feel if her father was trying to contact her. Or had she really sensed an evil dark enough to hurt Claire?

Earlier, as Tempest had stood with her feet in the foam sliding upon the sand, she'd seen flashes of a man, struggling against the powerful ocean swells, swimming toward her. She'd felt so small, the life vest enclosing her, the water so cold, and she'd been a terrified child again. Claire and Leona had been bobbing on the waves, just as terrified and screaming for their parents, the sailboat overturned in the distance.

Fear of the water had heightened the sisters' sensations, making them more vulnerable in later years despite expert tutoring from their mother: *Stop. Think. Focus. . . . Build that wall, protect yourself. . . .*

But Tempest had had an easier time than Leona and Claire—because she could wear gloves as protection.

She tightened her gloved hands on the redwood railing and thought of Marcus's mother. Winona Greystone's gentle nature would have had no protection against a demeaning husband . . . or a woman like Opal, who knew how to use her misfortunes to wring sympathy from a tender heart.

Tempest had rolled the single gleaming red hair between her naked fingertips. With her bare hands, she'd selected it carefully from Winona Greystone's hairbrush.

The brush had been held by others, but once Tempest linked that single red hair to that individual's touch, she'd known she could trace it back to that one person—Winona. Tempest had skimmed over the different energies and decided to do a more in-depth probe later when Marcus wasn't watching—she knew that she had revealed too much.

Holding an object and discerning what had happened to it, the people who had held it, wasn't an ability she'd wanted—but her DNA, tracing back to that Celtic seer ancestor, couldn't be refused. Tempest could have let her ability remain dormant, undeveloped, but she had developed her skills to a slight level to suit another purpose, another man. Only when her mother had dreamed so specifically of the brooch had Tempest really started using her hands for what they'd been intended.

The fiery red hair had turned slowly almost as if alive, and Tempest remembered the sensations without her gloves. Winona had loved her son desperately, enough to sacrifice her body and soul for him.

Because she knew what Jason Greystone could do. But Tempest had caught something else on that brush: Layers of Winona's energy blended with a man's, a true bond of love. From how Marcus had spoken of his father and his parents' relationship, that bond wasn't likely to be deep and loving as the swirling, complete energy of the man and woman on the brush. This other man was her lover, her true heart, and together, their love had created a child. The man had also used the brush—in this same room. Winona had treasured the brush, because it was from him. She had loved the stolen moments with him, her lover— not Jason. *Winona had taken a lover; the bond was true, and together they'd had a child. Was it possible that Jason Greystone was not Marcus's biological father?*

Stunned by that thought, Tempest leaned out into the fierce wind that pasted her night clothing, a worn T-shirt and loose shorts, against her body. The railing creaked ominously, and she stepped back, testing it gently. It gave slightly, apparently not that sturdy, and she stood back.

The lake beckoned to her, slowly, inevitably, as if it had waited for her. Was it her father's spirit? Or was it more, the evil that had caused her sister to be attacked, the evil that might be tied to the brooch?

At any rate, her senses told her she was being summoned, and she had to know why. Tempest glanced back at the rest of the house; Marcus seemed to have retired for the night, and what she had planned was a very private affair.

Ignoring the wind's chill and the damp mist, Tempest picked her way down the path toward the lake. Cloud cover prevented an easy moonlit stroll, but then, Tempest wasn't feeling cautious. She slipped on a rock, went down to slide on her bottom, and skinned her knee slightly.

On her feet the next instant, Tempest hurried across the margin of sand and tall grass down to the shoreline. "Dad?" she asked cautiously.

Intent upon every sound, picking through the hiss of the wind, Tempest leaned into the wind. But nothing came except the crashing of the waves and the foam slipping sensually along her feet. Then, "Tempest . . . I've been waiting for you. Come to me."

Tempest tore off her gloves and tucked them into her waistband. She reached into the mist and stood riveted to the darkness it held. The evil she had sensed earlier wasn't there. She felt only the warm droplets on her skin. Growing up, she'd been a tomboy, ready for any challenge; she had been just that heartbeat closer to her father—could that bond reach across death?

Was she the one descendant of that ancient seer to communicate with the dead?

Tempest held very still, pouring all of her energy

into sensing the mist, filtering through it to find some small particle of her father. "Who are you? What do you want?"

"I want some sleep," Marcus stated quietly beside her ear as he slipped a blanket around her shoulders. "What's going on?"

She held very still, stunned that he could come so quietly. She wished him to disappear and leave her alone with the energy drawing her to the water.

Marcus turned her face to his; he gripped the edges of the blanket in his other fist and used it to tug her to him. The wind whipped at his hair, the mist gleamed on his shoulders, and there was nothing sweet about his expression. "Your family just called—again. They wanted me to check on you—again. You weren't in your room. They have an eerie way of doing that, at just the right time. They sounded upset. Any reason why?"

Still wrapped in the sense that the mist held a presence—and just maybe the father she'd missed her entire life—Tempest shook free of his hands. "Get away from me."

But it was too late, her hand had slid down to Marcus's, and her naked fingers had laced with his. The link jolted Tempest. Suddenly she felt everything, all at once, sensations riveting her. While the wind whipped at her face, she stood helpless as images of a lonely boy circled her. He'd found shelter with a man connected to him somehow. Another man, Jason, yelled at him, challenged him beyond his years, demeaned him. Marcus wanted to free his mother, and couldn't. A fiery pain riveted her—anger, frustration, fear, a boy on the edge, held by one person, one bond— his mother's love.

Tempest almost wept at his pain and loneliness—his mother died, a cold paternal aunt had become his guardian.

So many layers slipped through her fingers, down to the essence beneath that hard exterior. Then one trembling winding thread felt the same as Winona's lover, the man who had used the brush. That thread twisted suddenly, became angular, raw, and savage, but it was still the same man, and his essence ran through Marcus.

The fierce drive in Marcus to rebuild Greystone Investments hit Tempest; she saw him working too hard and long for a college student, driving himself.

Because Marcus had dedicated his life to getting the resources for revenge, to uncover his parents' killer.

The wind caught his hair, mist beading on those harsh features, that dark stubble on his jaw. "What's going on, Tempest?" he asked quietly.

"You—just you. I know everything, Marcus, and I'm so sorry."

His head jerked back. "Did I ask for sympathy? I made it okay."

The ache inside his heart curled slowly up her arm and lodged in her heart. The fast pace of his quickened hers. "No, you didn't. I'm sorry that your aunt couldn't find love, or some warmth for you."

He seemed stunned at the mention of his aunt and fired back angrily. "I don't know how you got that, but you're wrong."

"That's not true, but I don't blame you for denying it," Tempest murmured softly, her senses filled with the need to erase the harm done to Marcus. She stood on tiptoe to comfort him with a kiss, but he turned, and her lips brushed his. They brushed again, tasting him as a man this time, with hunger and heat.

She flew back to another time, when her senses had been tangled with Marcus's, their lovemaking so fierce it had marked her—and she had thought she could escape.

"Tempest?" he asked cautiously as she moved closer, lifting her arms to circle his shoulders.

She stroked his hair, damp with the mist, and moved into the heat of his body. "You're so afraid, Marcus. Don't be."

He frowned and shook his head. "Of you?"

"Of me. Of tenderness and caring for someone. Your mother didn't leave you because she wanted to. It wasn't her choice. She didn't desert you. She would never do that. And you're not like him."

"Her murderer didn't give her a choice—I know that."

There was more Tempest wanted to say—that the man who wasn't his father of record but with whom Marcus had shared precious comfortable and enjoyable hours, was linked to him by blood.

As the moonlight slipped through the clouds and mist, Marcus's face was hard above her. "You know so much, do you?" he demanded.

His lips were just as fierce and hot as she remembered, demanding everything; he gathered her closer and lifted her back to dry sand. Her fingers sank into Marcus's bare skin, that hard rib cage, those powerful shoulders, and the impact of his aroused body against hers tossed her back to that night in Santa Fe.

This time, without her gloves, that link had been sparked, and for a heartbeat, she'd become one with Marcus, an intimate, riveting lock, her heartbeat in sync with his.

She shook free, shaken by how easily he'd handled her and that connection shimmering now within her, aching for more. She knew her passions—taking challenges was as much a part of her instinctive nature as breathing. And Marcus was a living, breathing, exciting challenge. He was too smooth, too controlled, too cool, and every bit of her rebellious nature needed to tear away his facade, to meet him on some primitive plane without restraint.

She'd wanted the battle between male and female, anticipated it. She'd felt that way the first time she'd met Marcus, and the need had grown. It could consume her just as before—the need to please a man, to do his bidding.

"Accidents waiting to happen," Tempest murmured to herself, and hurried to draw on her gloves. The saying went well in her situation with Marcus.

He rammed his hand through his hair and shook his head. He turned abruptly to look at the lake, his hands on his hips. "Look . . . I'm sorry. I was out of line. It's been a long day and night. And you bring something out in me that—"

"I know. You don't like feeling whatever you do for me. It seems like everyone in your life has walked out on you—and then I did the night after we made love. You feel protective of me, and there's something else— other than the usual sexual one. You feel tenderness. And you don't like it," she added uneasily. "Your pride and your scars won't let you admit any of that. You can't admit that you just want to be with me. You don't know how."

Marcus turned to her, his angry expression reflecting his frustration. "You're damned irritating. What is it with you? Why did you come down here in the middle of the night? What were you doing with your gloves off and your hands stretched out to the fog like that? And why did your family call at almost the same time?"

Tempest scanned the lake. The mist was cold on her skin, the waves breaking a little farther out on the water. But whatever she'd sensed out there had gone. Had it been her father wanting to contact her? Had she just missed her one chance to find closure with him? "They're worried about me."

"And they're afraid for you to go near the lake? I read the reports about the sailboat accident affecting all of you, making you terrified of water, and how you in particular didn't want to face your father's death . . . that you felt guilty about distracting him when that wave hit. You were a kid, Tempest. Kids play. But I can see why you'd be terrified of water. If that's true, why did you come down here?"

"It's a long story, and I'm tired." Drained and unwilling to talk about what she couldn't explain, Tempest turned and started to walk up the sand dunes toward his house.

"You're just coming back when I'm not around," he stated flatly.

"It's a private affair, and you're not invited."

"That's my girl . . . scrappy, defensive, and—"

That one statement stopped Tempest. She should have walked on, away from that single challenge—but she couldn't. She turned and walked back to him. Her finger prodded his chest. "I'm not your girl, buddy."

Marcus's smile was a little boyish, a little wicked. He reached out to trace her ear, his fingertip sliding down across her cheek, and then over her lips. He tapped them softly. "You want me, sweetheart. Admit it."

Of course she did. She wanted to sink so deep into lovemaking with him that she'd forget everything, but her pride wouldn't let her admit it. Armed with that admission, Marcus would be too dangerous. "Damn you."

"The truth hurts, doesn't it?" Marcus's hands cradled her face, and he bent to kiss her gently. The seductive brush of his lips crossed her cheek and returned to her lips. "Yes, damn me, but it doesn't change this, does it?"

The tension shifted between them, stilled and warmed into sensual need. Tempest knew that her emotions were riding high and that Marcus was the perfect settling-down remedy, just as he'd been that night in Santa Fe.

"No, I guess not," she admitted truthfully, her pulse already kicking up, her body hungry. "But not here."

In the house, Marcus stood in the shadows for a moment, considering her, and then he walked into his bedroom.

Tempest inhaled and held her breath and frustration for a moment. He was deliberately giving her the choice to follow—or not. She'd have to come to Marcus, to his bed. She could go to her own—and be unsatisfied and restless for what was left of the night—or she could take what she wanted.

Her need to take what she wanted, to take challenges, had most likely come from her Viking ancestor. Or she could be riding on some other energy, that connection with the lake. But more likely, it was because her uneasy feminine senses told her that she simply needed to be held by Marcus for a few hours, until daybreak, when the night had passed.

She centered on something else she'd discovered when she'd touched Marcus: As irritating and macho as he seemed, she could trust him; his essential energy was honorable, and he would protect her with his life.

With a shrug, Tempest stripped off her damp T-shirt and shorts and walked into his bedroom. Marcus was lying beneath the sheets, his arms behind his head. "Let's just do this, and get some sleep," she managed unevenly as she slid in beside him.

Marcus turned on his side, his arm drawing her to him, then his hand stroked the curve of her hip. His hand came up to capture her wrist and bring it to his lips. He tugged the edge of her glove with his teeth. "First, tell me something. I need to know what I'm dealing with."

"That sounds fair." Tempest settled against his hard body. She nuzzled his throat and his chest, enjoying the textures and scent of his hair and skin against her face.

His essence was darker, more masculine than she remembered, but there was something else now, aside from the soap and aftershave. It spoke of the sea and the wind, of leaping into new challenges, and of strength.

She rubbed her face against the side of his throat, prowling for more. Just there, his pulse was heavy and deep, waiting, and soon she would have him, all of him, claiming him. She would possess him.

Marcus's big hand smoothed her bare shoulder, his deep voice slow and thoughtful. "You're wearing your gloves. You did that night. Did you wear them with him—whoever hurt you?"

She wanted her naked fingers to cruise over that hard warm body, to enjoy the powerful shape of neck and shoulder, the mound of muscle in his upper arms, those hard pecs, and lower to that sculpted six-pack stomach and lower yet. But she couldn't risk any more with Marcus tonight; her gloves would have to do. Tempest eased her knee over his thighs, rubbing the rough texture, her body already soft and aching for the hardness against her. She bit his ear lightly. "Do we have to talk now?"

His fingers tightened just that bit. "Did you ever touch him with your bare hands?"

Somehow, she'd never trusted Brice enough. Some dark instinct told her to protect herself, and for once, she'd listened. "No, I didn't. Does it really matter—now?"

His smile curved against her throat. "Yes, it does. I feel like a virgin."

This time, she smiled. "You're a long way from that, buddy."

"But you aren't. I'd know." Marcus moved over her, settled intimately against her, and brushed his thumbs against her temples. "Okay?" he asked softly.

"I'm here, aren't I?" she returned as she wrapped her arms around him.

"Take off the gloves."

"No."

He leaned down to kiss her, his tongue playing along her lips. When she arched instinctively to capture him, Marcus smiled sensually, his tongue matching the elusive rhythm of his hips. "I could make you."

"Try," she invited.

"I'm going for a walk."

Freshly showered, Tempest glanced at Marcus, who was holding his morning cup of coffee and standing at the windows overlooking the lake. He was wearing only his boxer shorts, and Tempest inhaled as she noted the barely visible, long, dark scratch marks on his tanned back. In her passion, as he'd held her on that edge, she'd held him tight, her fingers sinking into those hard, sleek muscles, locking him to her. He'd possessed her, giving her no quarter, and she'd returned the favor, and something had clicked the moment she'd flown out of herself, something she just might have given to him—or taken from him. She resented the feminine intuition that said she would only crave more.

Unshaven now, his jaw dark as his mood seemed to be, Marcus was locked in his own thoughts.

Damn him anyway. He'd brought her breakfast in bed, the worst crime he could have committed. Exhausted by the previous hours, Tempest hadn't a chance to reclaim herself, before she awoke to his lovemaking. And damn him again—his exquisite tenderness was worse than the first offense.

"Don't get all worked up over spending the night in my bed, Tempest." Marcus's tone seemed distant and offhand, as if the night hadn't mattered. It had, and had left her senses shaken.

In an attempt to be unaffected, she snatched an apple from the bowl of fruit, tossed it in the air, and tucked it in her bag. "Just don't get any ideas, Mr. Greystone. You deliberately played that scene. You've probably played the same one too many times to count. Think of it as just a moment in time."

"I don't take advantage of women in a trauma. Remember that it was your choice to come to me. You made that choice." His look at her was slow, dark, and brooding, and Tempest's senses started heating. "I've got a few e-mails to get off this morning, and Francesca is coming over. If you wait, I'll show you around Port Salem."

"No, thanks. I'll just take my little broom and fly off to see it for myself." She tried to sound flip, but Tempest had to escape the house, and Marcus. She needed to reclaim whatever Marcus had taken in that storm where nothing else mattered.

Now she understood more than she wanted about his boyhood and his struggle to rebuild his father's company. She understood why Marcus had created that cold shell, why he kept others at an emotional distance, and she ached for him.

"You married her to get ahead," Tempest stated impulsively, and wished she'd kept that piece of information to herself. "Your wife, I mean."

Marcus carefully placed his cup aside. His movements were slow and determined as if he were mentally preparing an intense conversation. He walked to Tempest and stood studying her. "You got that, did you? When your gloves were off, and you reached inside me. I thought you could only feel things—not people."

"I've had to learn a few things, to protect myself. People aren't my usual, but I've done enough to survive."

"Evidently. Last night, on the beach, you weren't protected, were you? You want to tell me about it? And what you sensed in my parents' room? And what you're holding back from me?"

The man who Marcus thought was his biological father— wasn't. Deep in the layers of Marcus's essence, Tempest had caught the same energy as the man Winona had loved and one other tidbit: Marcus's father wasn't Jason Greystone. "I'm here to earn that brooch, remember?"

Then Tempest couldn't resist asking, "Um. . . . Last night, did you feel anything? On the beach, I mean?"

Marcus stared out at the shadowy beach. "Oh, yes, I felt something, like little curious feathers running all over me. I guess that would be you, right? I'm not sure I like the invasion."

He rubbed the back of his neck as if rubbing away something else. "You mentioned my marriage. Grace, my ex-wife, was okay. We each got what we wanted. She got a hungry executive, the power-couple image she needed to satisfy her family, and I got shares in her father's company. When she wanted someone else, I wanted her to be happy. She's the only woman who's been with me in Port Salem. She didn't like the quiet and lack of her kind of upscale social life. It's very casual here. There is no way she or her family would be connected to my parents' deaths. I'd know."

Tempest tensed as he reached to caress her earlobe; the touch riveting and taking away her breath. "You're afraid of getting caught, Tempest. You're ready to run right now. It must have been really bad."

"It was."

"As bad as the Blair Institute for Parapsychology? That couldn't have been pleasant."

She looked down at the wolf's-head brooch Marcus was tracing with his fingertip. "What do you know about me—that you're not telling?" he asked softly. "I've seen you react enough and caught the connection between you and your family. You hadn't called them, but yet they knew you were outside and by the lake. Just how did they know that?"

"They knew I was coming to the lake. Of course, they knew."

"But not beside it at that very moment. You were fascinated by it, and you took off your gloves to feel it, didn't you? Feel for what? What do you think is out there? And just for your personal information—that's the second time I've sensed that you were burning off excess energy, whatever is going on with you—like that high you were on at the night of the showing—by making love with me."

"Boy, you're just loaded with questions and information this morning, aren't you?"

"Yes, and you don't like being cornered. I respect that. Neither do I. But if there's anything I should know about you, or what's happening, I'd like to know—and I want to know what you're hiding."

Jason isn't—wasn't—Marcus's biological father.

"You just tensed and looked away, a sure sign that you're hiding something. You're expressive, very easy to read, even when you're not zapped by something you've touched." Marcus tapped the brooch on her shoulder. "You're wearing this, and it's almost like a good-luck charm. Why do you—and your family—need good luck?"

Marcus was too close to finding answers she'd prefer remained secret. Tempest moved away from his touch. "I'm here to do a job, Marcus. That's all. But I need movement, to stretch my legs, and I'm leaving here now."

Wrong phrase. She'd used her legs plenty last night,

and now Marcus's expression mocked her. The memory of how she'd met his fierce claiming with her own shot through her. Horrified that she'd just blushed, Tempest said, "See you later."

She hurried out the door, aware that Marcus was watching her. She lifted her face to the mist and tried to feel if anything waited for her. Was her father out there? Or was it something else?

Across the harbor, Port Salem was already filled with milling tourists, gaily dressed with cameras strapped to their necks. On the beach, brilliantly colored kites caught the wind and flew high against the clear blue sky. Just on the horizon, where the sky blended into the darker swells, a tall ship passed, its majestic sails filled with the wind. Fishing boats bobbed on the waves; a dinghy motored toward a large yacht.

Was it still out there, waiting for her? Had her father wanted to make contact and she'd missed closure forever?

Keeping her distance from the water, Tempest made her way down to the waterfront. Sunlight danced over the waves now and the wake of a passing fishing boat splashed against the bank's concrete wall. Seagulls were already aloft, and elderly men sat on the bank, bait buckets at their sides, fishing lines gleaming. Across the harbor's waterway, a mother pushed a stroller on the park's walkway, another child racing ahead of her. A woman sat at a picnic table; she held an easel with one hand to brace it against the wind and dipped her brush into the paints on the table. Boys on bicycles raced by, and a family seemed eager to get to the sandy beach, the father carrying a picnic cooler.

Tempest stared at the harbor's water splashing against the concrete barrier lining it. Claire had probably been this close, just feet away, when she'd sensed the river calling her. Tempest waited—but she caught only the sounds carried by the wind—waves hitting the barrier, the rev of boat motors, children's happy yells. "Who are you? Where are you? Come out," she whispered.

That trickle of her senses told her that Leona was calling. Tempest pulled her cell phone from its holder, and Leona didn't waste time: "You just had to do it, didn't you?"

"Did what?" Tempest asked quietly, because as an older sister by three minutes, Leona could admonish like their mother. Make love with Marcus? Sensed more than she ever had about another person? Had Leona been able to use the lake's waters as a psychic portal?

"You know what. I can hear the sounds of major waves. You just had to test yourself against the water, didn't you? Well? Don't you remember what happened to Claire when she got too close to the river? The water wanted her, and you did it, didn't you?" Leona demanded.

"It only made sense to see if—"

"To you, maybe. You've always been impulsive, a rebel, just out there looking for challenges to test yourself. Okay, well, what did you feel—anything?"

"I felt—I felt as if it might be Dad, maybe. I felt he was trying to contact me."

"'He'? You think it's a man?"

"The energy felt like a man," Tempest stated carefully. "It felt warm, like him, the way he used to hold us, Leona."

"We were four when he died. That's a long time to remember, Tempest." Leona's silence trembled across the line. "Tempest, be careful. None of us has ever been mediums for the dead, not even Mom. Her sensations, the images, whatever, stop at the point of death, they don't go past it. She can feel what happened in the room, the emotions of the dead person while they were still alive, and parts of the murderer's life, where he lived—but nothing after that. Tempest, you could be projecting something, growing it in your mind, something very dangerous, and it could obsess you. You're too impulsive, too ready to take challenges."

With the sense that she was being watched, Tempest scanned the crowd of tourists and found one woman standing and staring at her. Opal stood, tightly gripping her handbag; she didn't return Tempest's wave, but turned and walked briskly away. "Leona, stop. You're sounding like—"

"Don't you dare. Don't you dare say I sound like Mom."

"Tell me you don't have dreams like her. You dreamed the same dream, about the Viking. You saw the same wolf's-head brooch. And we've always known that you were potentially the strongest of us— if you developed."

"Well, I'm not trying to develop. I hate it. I'd give anything to be like other people, but oh, no, we have to be psychics." Leona paused then and returned to warning Tempest. "Port Salem. Just the word 'Salem' should scare you. Centuries ago, people like us were dipped into ponds until dead, or burned at the stake."

"I know our history, but—" Tempest began.

"You're not like Claire and me, Tempest Best. If ever there was a female swashbuckler, it would be you. Sometimes you lead with your heart, Tempest. That's not always wise, but to be truthful, I sometimes envy you. You'd better be wearing your brooch like ours. I don't like what you're doing one bit, flirting with danger—but you always were that way—bullheaded. And you never let yourself grieve for Dad like the rest of us. You held him too tight, Tempest Best. It's time to let him go. . . Customer just walked in the door. Have to go."

Tempest stared at the cell phone, the line dead.

" 'Tempest Best,' " she repeated with a smile. The triplets still used their affectionate names for each other, Tempest Best, Claire Bear, and Leona Fiona.

Leona had always been defensive when compared to their mother, Greer Aisling, the world-famous psychic. Leona resented the flashes of the future that could unexpectedly leap at her, and she'd never gotten over her vision of her husband being crushed to death in an avalanche.

The morning was bright now, and Tempest traced a small sailboat, using its engine to motor out of the harbor. It looked so much like her father's.

Was Daniel Bartel out there last night? She had to know. The car accident had ended his life too soon. Maybe he needed to say good-bye.

Men yelled, machines creaked, and Tempest turned to Greystone Marina. A small, sleek speedboat had been pulled from the harbor and was being hoisted onto a machine. Men stood on the dock, watching the process, and Tempest walked across the large parking lot to them.

One man was clearly the young owner of the flashy speedboat on the hoist. He was all neat and clean, wearing a designer name T-shirt and shorts with cargo pockets. Clearly the speedboat was his pet, his expression anxious, his body tense.

A man speaking into a small walkie-talkie device directed the crane operator. "Leroy, a little to the left—no, back a little. Okay, start lowering it."

The other was an older, stooped, gray-haired man with shaggy hair beneath his ball cap and a full beard that reached his chest; he wore a stuffed, worn tool belt and stood, cradling his right hand with his left. He suddenly turned to her, his expression fierce. "Lady, get back. That boat could slip at any time, and you could get hurt. If you've got business, go wait in the office. It's inside the building."

"Okay," Tempest agreed slowly, a little nettled by the man's sharp order. Then she shrugged, and decided that if Marcus had spent time here as a child, it might be a good place to check for anyone who might want to harm Jason or Winona Greystone.

Inside the Greystone Marina, Tempest noted the enclosed office space. She looked up at the various small boats, cruisers and sailboats, stored in layers above her. A glance at the building's huge open entrance revealed that the men were busy securing the speedboat to some sort of device—the same that supported the other boats above her. A forklift stood nearby, the motor running.

The large, airy structure was long, four rows of boats stored all the way to the end, and Tempest wandered the full length. To the rear of the marina's building was a large, sleek, beautiful cruiser. A large scroll labeled it the WINONA. Winona. Marcus's mother. . . The sign in front of the cruiser read, PRIVATE. PROPERTY OF THE OWNER.

The *Winona* gleamed in the shadows, safely away from the rest of the heavy equipment and people. Marcus didn't want her touched, and that meant she held special memories for him . . . and possibly secrets that Tempest could discover.

She had get on that boat. But first, she scanned the building to find it empty, and then looked outside to the men standing in front of the open entrance. Marcus stood talking with them. Then he turned and started walking toward her. With the bright morning sunlight behind him, his silhouette appeared in the sunlit rectangle of the entrance.

Suddenly a hissing sound from above her caused Tempest to look up—just as a heavy cable and an anchor were falling toward her.

Marcus's body hit hers hard, taking away her breath;

his arm wrapped around her tightly as he half carried her to safety.

The heavy metal cable and anchor hit the concrete floor with an impact that jarred the building. Tools tumbled from the wall supporting them, and the boats rattled slightly in their bays. Something fell from the *Winona* and shattered on the concrete floor; the cruiser's windows shimmered slightly in the shadows.

Tempest locked her arms around Marcus and held tight, as she stared at the heavy anchor and chain pooled over it. She could have been killed. . . .

"Are you okay?" Marcus asked quickly as he held her upper arms and studied her.

She'd just escaped death, unable to move as the weighty cable and anchor plummeted toward her. "Of course, I'm okay," she managed as she shook free of Marcus.

But her knees started to give way, and Marcus tugged her back against him, holding her tight. Tempest leaned against him, her body shaking. "Maybe I'm not okay," she admitted unevenly.

Marcus cursed harshly, cupped the back of her head, and pressed it to his chest, then ordered, "Don't you move. Stay put."

"Kenny!" Marcus yelled, his heart pounding fiercely beneath Tempest's cheek.

She closed her eyes, dealing with the conflict waging inside her. She put aside the fear's aftereffects, and dealt with how she felt, tucked closely, safely against Marcus. Some part of Tempest's pride scoffed at how she'd reached for him, how she was clinging to him now. The other part, her body and her instincts, recognized that, for once, she was glad to have someone else protect her. And that someone was Marcus, a dangerous man, a man her instincts and her body trusted. She felt stronger, more feminine, softer against him. At the moment, it had nothing to do with sensuality, and everything to do with something else, something terrifying.

The man with the full beard hurried inside with the others. He glanced at the heavy cable and anchor lying on the concrete and glanced up to the small cruiser trembling in its storage bay. "That's the *Born Free*, Marcus. I just checked her. She was secure."

His hand rested on Marcus's back, but Tempest noted his other hand, held against his midsection—his right hand—was withered, resembling a claw. "Are you okay, Marcus?"

"I'm fine, but she isn't. Meet Tempest Storm. She's my guest." Marcus glanced at Tempest, who had cautiously eased away from his arms. "You're shivering. Let's get out of here. Kenny, let me know what you find, okay?"

"On it," Kenny stated briefly as he went to a metal stairway and started moving up the stairs to the cruiser's storage bay.

Tempest remained locked in place, staring at the cruiser to the rear of the marina. "The *Winona*. Your mother's name."

Marcus hustled Tempest outside into the sunshine. "Just one of those little favors Jason granted my mother from time to time—a gift to give the appearance that he really cared for her. They were arguing on that cruiser the day they were killed."

"How do you know? Were you with them?"

Marcus urged her toward a sleek black Corvette with its top down in the parking lot. He started to open the door for her, but, locked in the near escape from death, Tempest reacted by habit—she slipped over the door and into the passenger seat.

"That's the quick way, I guess," Marcus stated. He eased into the driver's seat, and the powerful engine quickly leaped into life. "I could tell my mother was upset by the way she came back that evening. She'd been crying and trying to hide it from me. God, I hated Jason then. She called Kenny to come pick me up, and he did."

"Kenny would know a lot about that night, wouldn't he? I'd like to talk with him, and I'd like to get on the *Winona*, Marcus."

He shifted abruptly, driving onto the highway running parallel to the harbor's waterway. "Not now. There's a drawbridge over there. It lets the tall ships and sailboats go up the harbor. See it?"

"Uh-huh." Tempest considered what she knew: Kenny had been around when the hit-and-run had taken place. Kenny was the handyman at the Greystone house and probably privy to intimate family matters. "Tell me about Kenny."

"Right now, he's not happy that you're asking questions about my parents. Opal called to warn him about you. He knew both my parents, and he wants them left in peace, and he's afraid of what it will do to me, raking up the past. I told him that was just what I wanted you to do, get any leads on my parents' deaths. I didn't tell him how you might do it. He wasn't happy, and he's leery of you. I said I'd back anything you did because I want that hit-and-run driver."

She noted that they were driving away from the harbor and the lake. "I thought you were tied up with the maid service—Francesca, wasn't it?"

"She wanted to meet you, to see if you had any special preferences, flowers that sort of thing. She's my unofficial hostess and has helped with different parties, just as she helped my mother. I came down here to see if you wanted to ride back to the house with me. I said I'd call her when we were back at the house."

Tempest looked around at the tree-lined road; they were moving eastward, away from Lake Michigan.

"We're not going back to the house. Where are we going?"

"Wine tasting. I own a small winery and cafe near here. After what just happened, I think you could use a little time-out, don't you?"

Tempest looked out at the big wooden shoe sign in front of a greenhouse; the Dutch clog represented the early settlers of the area. "Frankly—no. I want that brooch, and I want any debt to you finished. Pull over at the tourism center. I want to see that brick wall up close and personal."

"After what just happened—I don't think so. I know what happened the other times you took off those gloves. You could have been killed, and right now, you look too pale. I didn't bring you here to die."

Tempest settled into her seat and began eating her apple. "I'm just fine. But evidently you're not. Maybe I wouldn't be either if I knew that a business I owned could cause a death because it lacked safety measures. . . . Fine. Have it your way. Wine tasting, and then the brick wall. A glass of wine or two could take the edge off of what happened. Or not."

"Idiot," Marcus muttered as he shifted again. "And every safety measure possible has been taken at the marina. I have complete confidence in how Kenny runs the place."

He glanced at Tempest, who was lifting up from her seat and stepping over it into the back. He quickly shifted down again, slowing the car, and then looked back at her. "What the hell are you doing?"

She needed distance between them. Something had happened when she'd touched Marcus, and later when they'd made love—something that had bonded her to his energy and now, after a frightening accident, she could almost feel his heartbeat. She'd never been that intimately close with any other man's energy, except her father's.

Tempest propped herself up on the back of the convertible and braced herself against the wind. Marcus was driving slowly now, maneuvering the car through traffic and glancing fiercely back at her. "You like that, don't you? Living on the edge, taking risks? What is it with you?"

She didn't answer as she remembered how safe she'd felt tucked against Marcus.

She had to find the hit-and-run driver and get that brooch, because she had to escape Marcus, a man too dangerous to her—for what he caused her to feel.

Six

##

"DADDY? ARE YOU OUT THERE?" TEMPEST HAD CALLED
softly to the mist as she'd stood in the moonlight, the
mist swirling around her.

Marcus decided he didn't trust her now. She was on
a very personal hunt, apart from his need to know
who had forced his parents' car into that wall.

"Dad?" she'd called another time, as if beckoning
her father.

At four o'clock in the afternoon, the lake breeze
swept gently through the open windows of Marcus's
home. The visit to the winery had been brief, and Tempest had eaten little and drunk less. She had seemed
locked in her own world. Even after an escape from
death, she couldn't look away from the beach.

Kenny had called, clearly upset. "Trouble, Marcus.
Looks like someone has been up here, playing around.
I just checked the *Born Free* last week, and she looked
okay. That anchor was secure, but there were tool
marks on the metal where it had come loose. One of
the customers saw some guy running down that back
flight of stairs after it happened. No one goes up there
but me, but the padlock on the door was broken. I can
put in a camera and an alarm sensor up here if you
want."

"Do that. And install the closed-circuit at your place and mine."

"Do you want the police in on this?"

"I think we can handle it. I don't feel we need to involve them any more than we have to. Every once in a while someone from the past turns up with big ideas about blackmail or payback. I'd rather not spread any more of that around Port Salem than necessary." Marcus remembered how years ago the dark side of crime had come calling, wanting his father's debts paid—with interest. If any of them had surfaced and had any information about the death of his parents, Marcus wanted a very personal conversation with them.

"But you want that girl stirring up the past, nosing around."

Marcus understood Kenny's reluctance to step back into the pain of his parents' death. "She's very special. If something has been missed by the investigation and everything I've done so far, she just might find it. I'd appreciate your helping her with everything you know."

"We've been over all that. You and I talked over everything. All those years ago, the investigations tore you up. I don't see how this girl can do anything that professionals couldn't do. What do you know about her anyway?"

"I know I want her doing just what she's doing. I trust her."

"I don't."

After the call, Marcus swirled the wine in his glass as he watched Tempest prowl around his home. He didn't blame Kenny for not wanting to open the past; it had been a nightmare. But if there was any slim chance that Tempest's psychic ability could lead to the driver, dead or alive, who killed his parents, Marcus would back her all the way.

He turned his attention to the restless woman who had walked away from the window overlooking the lake several times and always returned to it. Tempest's fascination was easily read in the tense lock of her body, the way she leaned toward the lake. "Want to talk about it? What's got you on edge?" Marcus asked as he walked to her.

Her quick "No" only caused Marcus to push for more. "You're upset because of the anchor almost killing you. That's reasonable."

"Sure." Her answer was too quick, cutting off further conversation. Then she added furiously, "And your remedy served your own purpose, didn't it? You deliberately wanted me to have enough to drink— dulled enough to answer questions that I do not want to answer. Isn't that rather clichéd?"

Marcus set his glass aside and leaned back against the teak credenza. Last night, they'd made love, hurried and hot, and then slower, deeper, dreamlike. This morning, Tempest seemed even more distant, deliberately avoiding any contact with him, and that irritated. *She* irritated. "Okay, exactly where did I go wrong? At breakfast—when I set that tray down by you, you looked at it as if it would bite you. Ever since then, you've been on edge. You held on to me at the marina. You reached out to me, and you didn't like it—he must have burned you bad."

His second probe into her life caught her. Tempest whipped around to stare at him, her lips parted. A slow blush started working up her cheeks before she recovered. "Could we just pass up a rehash of last night? You already know everything about me and my family. I knew what I was getting into by coming here."

Marcus briefly gave her credit for the recovery; she must have had a lot of practice concealing her life. "But I didn't. You called 'Dad' and 'Daddy? Are you out there?' last night—and you can't stop looking at the lake."

"So what if I do? It's beautiful and I was raised beside the Pacific Ocean. Maybe I was a little home-sick. And just maybe I was talking to my father, people do that, you know, talk to loved ones who are gone. I came here to do a job and you're standing in my way. I get the feeling that you're guarding me. I don't need or expect that. When we came back from the winery, you didn't stop at that wall where your parents died. Okay, I get that. It's not somewhere you like to be. But later, you didn't want me to go back alone. Do you want to know what happened there or not?"

"You know I do. I've never stopped hunting for that killer. I never will. I still have nightmares about that faceless SOB and what I'll do when I find him."

"You'll do the right thing."

"You can't be sure of that."

"But I can." Tempest folded her arms and faced the lake; she seemed fascinated by it again.

Unwilling to be locked out of her thoughts, Marcus moved closer to her. He nudged her with his shoulder, and she still didn't look at him. "This morning, I fixed that breakfast tray because I thought you might be getting sick. You dreamed last night—it was a lot of threshing around. You called out 'Dad,' like a terrified child."

The intimacy in which he'd given comfort was unlike their sexual needs; desperate to help, he'd responded to comfort her, and his own tender emotions for Tempest had shaken Marcus as well.

She pivoted around so quickly that her gloved hand brushed a glass tower of seashells and beach pebbles, toppling it. For a moment after it crashed, Tempest stood pale and transfixed, as if locked in another time.

"Don't worry about it, Tempest," Marcus stated carefully. He didn't have to be a psychic to know that

something in her had just clicked, as if she were remembering other seashells and pebbles. He crouched
to collect the shards of broken glass and reached to
place them in an earthenware bowl. He collected the
rest and stood. "I picked these up on the beach with
my mother. I guess you've done the same."

Tempest hadn't moved, staring at the shells and
pebbles that Marcus was holding in his hand. "Yes, I
did, with both my parents. Then just with my
mother."

"What happened in those two missing years, Tempest? The ones where you disappeared without a
trace?" Marcus asked as he carefully aligned the shells
and pebbles on the gleaming dark teak credenza. He
caught just a flash of pain in her expression before she
turned away to stare out at the lake again.

"Stop pushing me, Marcus," she whispered unevenly.

"How do you think I got where I am? I'm enough
like my father to push when I want something badly
enough, and you're on the run. Why? From what? And
what does that—" He tapped the brooch at her shoulder. "Why do you want that badly enough to come
here—with me, a man who scares the hell out of
you?"

"You didn't really think I'd come, did you?"

"I had my doubts." Marcus frowned when he
recognized Tempest's expression. It was one his
mother often had, that of confusion, of wanting to
speak, to share something deep inside her, and
suppressing it. "Tell me about those two years,
Tempest. You were never married, and yet you
changed your name from Bartel to Storm. Was there
another name between those, something you're
hiding? Maybe I can help."

Tempest's green eyes widened for just that heartbeat, and Marcus knew he'd touched a secret that she'd

kept close and dark. "Okay, the next question is, are you running because of him? Is someone after you?"

Those eyes flashed to gold, and Marcus knew that he had her on the edge, just where he wanted her. "Blackmail," he supplied softly, pushing her just that bit more.

"I'm going out for some fresh air," Tempest stated suddenly as she turned and opened the sliding door to the front decking. Marcus understood: He was hunting, and he had gotten too close to those hidden two years of her past. She closed the door and the conversation, then stood with her arms folded as she stared at that lake again. Suddenly, she was moving over the railing.

It was just like Tempest not to use the obvious, safer pathway. Marcus jerked open the sliding door; he hurried out to see Tempest making her way around to the rear of the house, her hair fiery against the blue sky, her black-clad silhouette slight against the large gray rocks serving to hold back bank erosion. "Tempest!"

As she balanced on one large rock and prepared to leap to another, the rock shifted. She stood outlined against the sparkling harbor waters, her legs braced for balance, her arms held out from her sides. A fall could break a bone, or if she hit her head—Marcus cursed and found himself moving over the same railing. He knew in that moment that he would follow her anywhere, *because she was his*.

The railing creaked ominously, then cracked, and Marcus found himself falling. He managed to catch one board and cling to it. It was only a slight drop to the foliage below, and Marcus landed on his feet. Shaken, he glanced up at the heavy board railing, falling toward him. A leap away, and Marcus was safe, the railing crashing down amid the rocks and brush. "Two accidents in one day is a little much," he muttered as he carefully followed Tempest's path.

Quick and athletic, she made it to the powerful Corvette, swung over the side, and bent out of sight for a minute. In the next heartbeat, the engine fired and the convertible was racing down the driveway, away from the house.

Tempest glanced at the tall man beside her, his body tense. "Yes, I hot-wired your toy," she admitted as she studied the brick wall in front of her.

"You could have been killed," Marcus stated softly. He bent to pick a gorgeous red rose from the tourist center's flower bed and carefully removed the thorns before handing it to her. His eyes were dark and fierce, a pulse beat heavily in his throat, and the lines deepened beside his lips. "Enjoy yourself?"

Then he smiled tightly, and added a curt, "Sweetheart?"

"Uh-huh. Yes, I did." Her light, flip answer was a shield for the emotions running through her. Tempest shivered slightly; as she had driven from the house, one glance in her rearview mirror had told her that Marcus handled the BMW with ease, but he wasn't happy.

She was flying high with excitement. She'd loved the chase; he'd risen to the challenge so well, perfect in fact. She lifted the rose to her face and caught the scent. Tempest looked over the petals to Marcus—and enjoyed the contrast of stormy eyes with those strange golden brown flecks in the center, that tense hard muscle in his cheek with the delicate petals. "Do you like chasing after women?"

"I never do. But one headstrong woman seems to be the exception. You can drive well, by the way, but don't do it again," he stated tightly. "I get the picture. I pushed, you didn't like it. That still leaves us with a few questions, doesn't it?"

"Not really." Using an excuse to move away from

Marcus, Tempest held the rose and backed away from the wall, studying it for impact damages. He could upset her too easily, and he knew and understood too much. Worse—Marcus could touch something deep inside her, too scarred to be freed. "Maybe you do deserve a few answers. Where did they hit?"

"The bricks had to be replaced. They're gone. I'm afraid you wasted a lot of effort getting here."

She turned to him, this time her anger had sparked. "You could have told me that earlier."

Marcus nodded, his body tense and hipshot, and the sunlight glinted off the reddish sparks in his neatly trimmed dark hair. "I could have. Now shall we just go somewhere and have a nice quiet chat?"

There, still holding the fragrant rose he'd just given her, with the late sunshine warming her back, and the lake in the distance, it seemed the right time to tell him. She brushed the soft petals across her face again. "You asked who had hurt me. Maybe it was someone like you, someone who wanted more than I want to give. He wanted to—control . . . contain me. I didn't like it."

"No, you wouldn't. You were with him for those two years?"

Tempest ran the fingertip of her black leather glove over the fragrant red rose. The gift was sweet and had touched her, dammit. Brice Whitcomb's roses had been delivered by a florist—while he had entertained someone else. "I scared him."

"I can understand that," Marcus stated grimly. "Let's get out of here."

When he took her arm, Tempest jerked away. She'd been led into cocktail parties and private soirees just like that—to glean any tidbits from which Brice might ferret out information he could use. Then Marcus's hand slid down her arm and linked his fingers with hers. "Ready to go now?"

Tempest considered the feminine sensations racing through her: Did they date back to Aisling, the Celtic seer, the captured bride of the Viking chieftain?

In Leona's and Greer's dreams, the warrior had fought for her, but he'd probably had much more of a battle getting his way with the seer. Tempest had always known that her restless, rebellious nature leaned toward that strain of Viking blood. It was her nature to test herself, and Marcus seemed to be a perfect opportunity.

Marcus tipped up her chin and studied her. "What's going on?"

She smiled and stepped close, looking up at that hard rigid face, those gray eyes with the strange bronze flecks filled with her image. His shoulders blocked out everything else, and he'd be a worthy opponent—intelligent, a physical man, determined, strong, and just unpredictable enough to be exciting. Maybe that was what she'd first sensed about him at her showing—that he was the perfect, delicious opponent. "Lots."

"Nothing like a thorough explanation," Marcus muttered, as they walked toward their cars. As they stood between the Corvette and the BMW, Tempest couldn't resist smoothing that little windblown stand of hair at his temple. Every line of his face was masculine, beautiful, a contrast of planes and shadows, of suntanned skin and coarse black brows and lashes. The curve of his lips was just perfect, not too soft, but with enough width to be very tempting. The hard shape was deceiving, because she also knew how seductive his lips and tongue could be, how skilled. "You've likely had every woman you've wanted, haven't you? It was probably all so easy."

Marcus leaned back against the BMW, folded his arms, and studied her. "Tell me that you didn't have a few guys chasing after you—and you enjoyed every minute."

"But you keep up better, Marcus," she murmured sweetly. She tossed the rose into the convertible passenger seat and prepared to slide over and down into the driver's seat.

"That's something, I guess." Marcus reached to quickly lift her up into his arms. He held her aloft. "I'd rather you rode with me. I'll have someone pick up the 'Vette later."

Perfect, Tempest thought as he grimly stuffed her into the passenger seat of the BMW. Though the gesture was a bit primitive, Marcus meant well; he simply wanted her safe and under his care. In his own way, he was quite gallant, and that played to her feminine side. She might as well enjoy the benefits while she could.

"I want my rose," she called, as Marcus started to circle to the driver's side.

He stopped, shook his head, and returned for the rose in the Corvette. This time, he thrust it at her. "Here."

"Thank you," she murmured, and fluttered her eyelashes at him.

"You could have been killed!"

Tempest stared at the railing crumbled on the rocks below. "You could have been killed, Marcus. That railing was loose. I should have told you earlier."

"He's in the kitchen, cooking your dinner, lady," Kenny stated beside her, as he and a younger man carried in boards for the new railing. They stacked the lumber in the living room, and Kenny glanced at the other man. "Okay, Cody, that's enough to start in the morning. See you here at eight. And don't stay up too late at that computer. You're going to have a hard day tomorrow."

"Yes, sir. I will, sir." Cody Smith, the younger workman, glanced warily at Tempest and nodded. "Ma'am."

"Cody." Tempest noted the youth's sly glance down

her body. In fact, he was taking in everything in the house. As a woman who had sometimes hunted in unusual areas where she wasn't supposed to be, Tempest recognized that intent expression.

So did Kenny. "He's just a kid, lady. He can't help looking. In the wrong crowd maybe, at one time, but a good kid just the same. And that railing wasn't loose the other day. I just checked it before you came. I keep up things around here. We haven't had any accidents for a long time—until you turned up."

"A long time—there were accidents like today at the marina and here at the house?"

Kenny rubbed his disfigured hand as if it hurt. "Some. Every once in a while something happens that shouldn't have. We'll work on the railing tomorrow, and then clean up down the bank after that. Could be some stray nails and such around, so be careful."

If Tempest had had her sister Claire's empathic gift, she could have touched that clawlike hand and eased the pain. Instead, she touched it with her glove. "Does it hurt?"

"Stupid question." As if burned, Kenny quickly drew away. His scowl came too late; Tempest had already caught a flash of fear. Why would Kenny be afraid of her? Was his unfriendly attitude because he was hiding something? Something that might concern the Greystones' deaths?

"I'm new around here. Give me a chance. I'm sorry I've upset you. I think we've just gotten off on the wrong foot." Tempest studied Kenny's face more closely and noted something very familiar around those light eyes. She held her breath as she realized they matched the color of Marcus's, with the same strange bronze flecks. That full gray beard could also conceal a familiar jawline—Marcus's. And Winona had had a lover—the father of Marcus. Was it possible that Kenny—? "You were here when Winona Greystone was alive, weren't you?"

Kenny inhaled abruptly and looked out at the lake as if visualizing a face. "I was."

"What color were her eyes?"

"As blue as the sky on a clear summer day—" Kenny's soft tone changed into a harsh one as he asked, "Why the hell did you ask that question?"

Her question had been deliberate, to test his reaction to Winona. She was definitely a tender memory. Kenny was in charge of repairs at the marina and at the house. Maybe Jason had been the intended victim, not Winona. Just maybe Kenny had hurt his hand when he'd forced the Greystones' car into that wall. "I just wondered. How did you hurt your hand?"

He straightened defensively, and the eyes staring down at her from the shadow of his ball cap held the same arrogance as Marcus's. "Boy, you're nosey, for someone who wears gloves all the time and could be hiding your own scars."

"I'm a sculptor. Sometimes I work with flame. It's only logical that I'd have scars. Have you tried physical therapy? I know a great—"

Kenny inhaled abruptly, then released his breath with his anger. "I'm a workman, lady, and accidents happen. You should have stopped asking personal questions while you were ahead. Since you've stepped in where you're not wanted, I guess it's fair to come out and tell you what I think of you. You're trouble, if I ever saw it. I heard about Marcus chasing you and how the Corvette had been hot-wired. Since you were driving it, I guess you would know about that. Not exactly the kind of skills I'd expect in a woman Marcus brought here, and there's something going on between you two. You've got the restless look of someone who doesn't stay around long. Marcus should have some-one to make him a home."

"I agree. But Marcus needs answers, and I'm going to help him. You spent a lot of time with Marcus when he was a child. You've probably developed quite the attachment, right?" *Like a father for a son?*

"I've been around for most of his life. I worked for his father." Kenny's harsh reply bit into the air between them. "Now, if that's all the questions you've got in your bag, I'd better get back to work."

He turned suddenly and walked toward the kitchen, leaving Tempest alone with more questions. She stud-ied his walk, a rolling seaman's stride. Though his clothing was loose and shabby, and his shoulders slumped, his body build was definitely familiar—just like Marcus's. She turned to stare out at the lake and made a note to visit the marina and touch Kenny's tools with her bare hands. If there was that paternal link to Marcus, she'd find it. When questioned about the color of Winona's eyes, his voice was as soft and distant as if remembering a lover—and perhaps she had been.

Tempest listened to the indistinct, rumbling blend of Marcus's and Kenny's deep voices. Kenny had been wearing gloves when he'd handled the boards, and probably as he worked around the house. She'd have to have his naked touch to compare him to Marcus.

She looked at the closed door of the Greystones' bedroom. What other secrets did that room hold?

She hurried into the room and surveyed it. Fran-cesca Pointe's maid service usually cleaned the house, and apparently she took a special interest in it. That seemed to be a very personal thing to do, almost pro-prietorial. Tempest carefully stripped off one glove, held it in her other hand, and walked toward the im-mense bookcase-style bed.

She placed her open palm on the massive walnut headboard and felt a jolt of fear, the essence the same as on Winona Greystone's brush. Tempest jerked her hand away, but it was too late—she caught more than she wanted of Jason's abuse. Winona wouldn't leave him, yet she loved another man, who just could be Kenny.

Tempest looked at the vanity where she'd found the brush with its single, gleaming red hair. The various feminine cosmetics were gone, but to dust the gleaming walnut surface, that tiny feminine lamp would have to be lifted. She slowly closed her bare hand around it and moved carefully over the crystal stem until she found Winona's energy again, on the tiny metal flowers. If Francesca had dusted in here, she was using gloves or cloths, something Tempest's gifted hands couldn't penetrate—she needed the naked touch.

She replaced the lamp and ran her bare fingers over the picture frames on the wall. She found nothing but a woman thinking about what to serve her family for dinner that night and how to pay her bills. On the bedside table, Tempest found more of the same daily problems, the hardworking carpenter's struggle with a wood supplier. There had to be something more in the house, something that would lead to that hit-and-run driver. Tempest drew on her glove, stepped outside the room, and closed the door. The men weren't talking now, and she called, "Marcus?"

When he didn't answer, Tempest found him in the kitchen, bending into the refrigerator. She put her hands on her waist. "You shouldn't have gone over that railing. You could have been killed, Marcus."

"Mm. It held you, didn't it? I had no reason to think that it wouldn't hold me."

"But you must weigh—"

"A few more pounds than your 125. I'm hungry. It's

almost six, and I've got a conference call later. I need to prepare for it—dull stuff, presentation of a new speedboat, sponsoring a hydroplane race up in Washington state and Idaho, a recall notice on an inboard motor. I'm afraid you'll have to occupy yourself. Maybe feel around a little bit?"

"Not in the mood. Maybe I'll just call it an early night. I need to catch up on some e-mail, polish my toenails, that sort of stuff."

When the usual odd tingle ran up her nape, Tempest automatically reached for the telephone. "Hi, Claire."

Marcus's eyes narrowed for a moment, then he shook his head and began building a Greek salad. Tempest selected an olive and popped it in her mouth. She moved carefully away from him—any touch now and Claire, a very sensitive empath, would know everything, including that Tempest had made love to Marcus last night. "What's up?"

Claire's quiet, serene tone floated over the telephone line, enclosing Tempest in a gentle cloak of love and patience. "I'm worried," she said softly. "We're so vulnerable to large bodies of water, and something is going on with you. Does it have to do with Dad? Or something else? Are you wearing your brooch?"

"Yes." Tempest turned from Marcus and walked to the window overlooking the harbor. In the setting sun, the water seemed serene, and people were walking in the park. Everything looked perfectly normal. "Please don't worry, Claire."

"I always worry about you, Tempest. You're very different this morning. Softer, more feminine. We already know you're involved, Tempest Best. And this isn't a game. Marcus Greystone is a very—oh! That's him, isn't it?" Claire asked as Marcus's body brushed Tempest's.

Marcus frowned when Tempest moved away. He

watched her while he crumbled feta cheese into the salad and followed it with a sprinkle of parmesan. The pasta was already buttered and topped with fresh chives and parsley. He opened the foil wrapper of the salmon he'd just taken from the back-porch grill, and it looked delicious.

As she spoke to Claire, Tempest lifted the rose she'd placed in water and lifted it to her nose. Over the fragrance and the petals, she studied his backside as he bent low into the refrigerator. Marcus Greystone was a man with a really nice butt, a man who wore his jeans well. It really was sweet of Marcus to give that rose to her. He could cook, and he was rock solid in an emergency, like when the anchor fell. It was really nice to be tucked up close against him, feeling fragile and feminine, despite her fear.

"Tempest? Don't challenge this thing. Don't try to fight it. We're vulnerable near water and—my God, you were almost killed weren't you? And Marcus pulled you to safety? Neil?" Claire called to her husband. "Tempest was almost killed!"

Tempest should have known that Claire would snag the terror she'd felt as the anchor and heavy chain had fallen toward her. "I wasn't hurt. It was an accident."

"You're going back to that boat, aren't you?" Claire's tone was alarmed, and that little tingle at the back of Tempest's nape started to prickle.

Tempest looked at Marcus, who was leaning back against the counter, watching her and sipping a glass of wine. She was careful not to correct Claire that the "boat" was a fifty-five-foot luxury cabin cruiser. "Maybe."

"I think Neil and I need to come and—"

"Don't you dare."

"Okay, then it's Mom or Leona. Take your pick. Or it's both."

"Boy, Claire Bear, you've gotten pushy since you've married Neil. You know that Leona resents Mom." Tempest glanced at Marcus, who was too still. "Big ears are listening. I'm fine. I'll talk to you later."

"You're invited anytime, Claire," Marcus stated loudly.

"No, you're not," Tempest corrected. Amid her family, Marcus would be on the trail of her past and every secret she'd ever had. "I'm on a job, you know that. There's no reason to make this a family affair. I have to go. Bye, Claire. Love you. Truly, I do."

"Real nice," Marcus said as he handed her a glass of wine and swept his hand toward the dinner he'd placed on the table. "What are you afraid of, that they'll tell your naughty little secrets?"

Tempest ignored his taunt and slid into the chair he held out for her. She realized she was still holding the glass with the rose, and Marcus had noticed, too. She quickly placed it on the table, fearing the attachment to him. "Thank you. Could we just move on?"

Marcus sat and studied her before filling their plates. "Sure. If that's what you want."

"I want. But first, tell me about Kenny. What happened to his hand?"

Marcus neatly swirled the pasta onto a fork and held it out to her lips. "He never said. I never asked."

"Because you trust him?" The fork remained poised in front of her lips, and Marcus's expression said she wasn't getting answers until she accepted the food. She did. "Mm. Good. You didn't answer my question."

After a silent moment in which his expression didn't change, Tempest inhaled and slowly returned the favor, holding the fork up to Marcus. He took the offering and studied her. "I've known Kenny since I was a boy. He's been better to me than my own father. Yes, I trust him, implicitly. I can't remember a time when his hand wasn't like that."

Better to me than my own father. But with those matching eyes, Kenny could be Marcus's father.

To avoid Marcus questioning her further, Tempest dived into her food. Eager to be away from him, she ate quickly. "Thanks. That was great. Excuse me. I have things to do."

When she started to stand, Marcus suddenly reached out and caught her wrist, tugging her down to straddle his lap. His arms held her in place. "Going somewhere so soon? Before we finish our conversation about our little race this afternoon?"

His hand had slipped under her tank top, smoothing her back. Tempest sucked in her breath as his other hand caressed her bottom. She wished her fingers hadn't dug into his shoulders. She wished her hips hadn't reacted instantly to the heat and the pressure below her, already pushing down on him—only a few layers of fabric separated them, her body already moistening. "My, my. . . ." she murmured. "What have we here?"

His lips moved against her throat. "You scared me today, Tempest. I didn't like it."

"Time to pay? I owe you some relief, something like that?" Perfect, she decided, instant satisfaction only a heartbeat away, and then she'd be finished.

He smiled and settled her more closely against him, and what Tempest had to have. She framed his face and took a long, deep sensuous kiss. His skin was so hot, or was it hers? That big hand caressing her back slowed, and in another moment her bra released. His fingers smoothed her side, his thumbs just at the edge of her breasts, and she held her breath, waiting for his caress.

Instead, Marcus leaned back from her kiss. "Time to do the dishes."

She had to have more of him. He tasted of excitement and heat and— "Later," he said firmly as he eased back, separating their bodies.

It was then that Tempest recognized his dark, grimly satisfied expression. Marcus had deliberately set out to arouse her, and then leave her untended. His brand of revenge had left her trembling and unsatisfied and furious. "Playing games, Marcus?"

"You like games. I thought I'd give you one," he stated as he eased her to stand on unsteady legs.

He stood, but he held her upper arms. "Want to tell me why someone is asking about you in Albuquerque? A man?"

"What do you mean?"

"Just that. Yesterday, someone was asking a lot of questions about your work at the gallery there. One of my friends was browsing. He knows that I bought *Predator* and called to tell me about the guy. Very slick, they said, but definitely not the kind who might appreciate art. A tall, blond guy . . . an aging playboy sort, with a definite eye for the ladies?"

Tempest stepped back from Marcus. The description fit Brice Whitcomb perfectly. She'd been just twenty and ready to explore the world when she'd met him. An experienced thirty-five-year-old then, Brice had charmed her into selling her soul. In their two years together, she'd learned about the dark side of life. By the time she was twenty-two, she was free of him, but world-weary and emotionally scarred.

With Marcus hunting every detail of her life, she lied, "I have no idea who he might be. I'm not that famous, but a few people do appreciate my work, and you found me, didn't you?"

"That I did." Marcus's fingertip circled her jaw as he smiled. His expression seemed tender, but then maybe that was what Tempest wanted it to be.

"Why am I really here?"

That fingertip tapped her lips lightly. His answer was soft and dangerous. "Because I want you and because I want to find that hit-and-run driver. Because you want that brooch, and you do not want to be indebted to me. Have I got that down right? Or is there something else?"

Seven

TEMPEST TOOK OFF HER BELT, HELD THE BIG CELTIC-STYLE buckle, and gripped the prong in her fingers. In the shadows, standing on a Greystone Marina landing four flights above Port Salem's harbor, she turned to scan the night once again. At ten o'clock, the harbor was well lit, with a loud party going on the small yacht opposite the marina. Lights inside the cabin silhouetted people on the deck and those dancing to the music of a reggae band. The multicolored lights strung along the deck reflected upon the dark waves below.

Marcus had just started his extensive overseas calls and conferences, and she'd supposedly settled in for that leisurely night. Her bedroom window had offered an easy escape, and she had quickly raced toward the marina. With any luck, she'd be back before Marcus took a break.

The harbor's waves splashed upon its concrete retaining walls. The small platform dock in front of the marina and the boats moored in their slips on the nearby large dock creaked softly as they rode the waves.

A low layer of fog had just covered the water; it

dimmed the reflection of the party's colored lights, but the view was still breathtaking.

Across the harbor, a vivid array of neon signs traced Port Salem's curving main street, headlights flashing now and then. On the hill beyond the main street, lights of the houses twinkled almost like a Christmas array. In the distance, streetlights lined the park walkway leading to Lake Michigan. Everything looked perfect for a night in early July.

Tempest held very still, trying to absorb whatever presence she'd felt that night on the beach. "Are you out there, Dad?" Tempest questioned softly.

As if in response, the fog seemed to churn over the dark waves.

A round of laughter from the party startled Tempest, and she realized that she'd once again become fascinated with the water. She scanned the harbor below, and it seemed normal. She turned toward Marcus's home, where she'd first felt that presence on the beach. The jutting contemporary structure stood out against the night, the windows of his office softly lit. She had little time before he'd miss her, and she wanted to be alone when she searched the cruiser. If Kenny were Marcus's biological father, she'd soon know, and she just might feel something else on that cruiser— someone who wanted to kill.

She bent to pick the lock of the metal door high on Greystone Marina. She only had a brief time to get on the *Winona* and look around. When the Greystones had their last argument, perhaps someone else was on board, too—someone angry enough to kill either Jason or Winona Greystone, or perhaps both.

The door's lock clicked open, but a gentle test proved that something else held it from the other side; she would have to try another entry.

On her way to the metal ladder attached to the building and leading to the roof, Tempest carefully stepped over the fragments of the outdoor lightbulb. Breaking the bulb had been necessary; if anyone were passing by, the light would have revealed her too easily.

She tugged up her gloves, grabbed the ladder's metal rungs with both hands, and tested it briefly. It held securely. Tempest braced one foot on the landing's railing, then hauled her body upward. She had just gotten both feet on the lowest rung and was starting upward when she felt a chill, the mist damp upon her face.

"Tempest?"

She held very still, and realized that even with her leather gloves on, the metal rungs of the ladder were wet and slippery with the fog that now enclosed her. One glance downward told Tempest that the fog had thickened, blocking everything else from her view. She couldn't see above her. The mist seemed so thick that it pressed close against her, almost too thick to breathe.

Panicked, Tempest tried to breathe evenly and failed.

"Tempest?"

When she glanced down again, a man stood on the sidewalk below, his image softened by the layers of fog surrounding him. He could have been looking at the party across the water—or he could have been looking up at her. Had Brice Whitcomb finally found her? After all these years of threats, which had increased lately, had he finally come for revenge?

Tempest closed her eyes and remembered his last threat: "I'll kill you before I let another man have you. You're mine, you little freak. You owe me."

Her heart racing with fear, Tempest quickly forced herself upward, racing toward the safety of the roof. Just as she gripped the edge of the roof, her rubber-soled shoes slipped on the damp rung. Pushing her muscles to the limit, Tempest hiked her body upward and grabbed on to the roof's railing with both hands. Breathing hard, aware that one slip could take her falling five stories to the ground, she hung, feet dangling out into the mist.

She thought she felt the cool stroke of a hand along her cheek, a man's raspy whisper, "Tempest? Careful."

"Yeah, right. Who are you?"

Had Claire felt this same fear when she'd been by the river and sensed it wanted her?

Then out of the fog a man's hands reached toward her; they gripped her wrists. She couldn't let him have her, she had to hold on to the railing. Panicked, Tempest worked her legs, trying to find some footing.

If Brice had already tracked her here, now was his chance for revenge. "Brice, don't you dare let go. I know you want payback, Whitcomb, but—"

"Let go, dammit. Can't you see I'm trying to help you?" Marcus's voice was rough and frustrated, his grip tightening. "I've got you, Tempest. Now let the hell go."

The fog seemed to evaporate suddenly, and Tempest saw Marcus scowling above her. She'd never been so glad to see anyone. At the same time, he'd caught her prowling again. "Oh, hi. What are you doing here?" she asked lightly.

"What does it look like I'm doing? Let go, so I can haul you up here."

Tempest obeyed, and Marcus pulled her upward and over the edge of the roof's railing. He caught her tight and held her, his heart racing beneath her cheek.

"If you say, 'Idiot,' I won't be happy, and you have no idea what a problem I can be when I'm not happy," she managed shakily, as Marcus held her at arms length.

"Okay. But I'm thinking it. And I knew from the first

minute I met you that you were a class-A problem. Now let's get down from here."

Marcus led the way to a lighted doorway and gently pushed her. "In."

She moved lightly, quickly down the metal stairway, and paused as she looked down at the fifty-five-footer on the ground floor. "It's unusual to keep a boat that big in dry storage, isn't it?"

"The weather here is rough in the winter. There's no reason for her to be out in it. I keep intending to check her out myself, but never have." In no mood to discuss the *Winona* further, Marcus's hand closed around her forearm. "Keep on going."

"I'll just be back, and you know it. I want to see that cabin cruiser up close. How did the calls go—the overseas ones, the conference calls, all the sales projects, yada yada?"

He sighed deeply. "They stopped the minute Kenny called. When I flipped on the closed channel used for security, guess who I found on that landing—four stories above ground?"

"Oh. I have no idea. But thanks anyway."

On the ground floor, Marcus glanced at the *Winona* at the rear of the building. His sigh was tired and frustrated. "You want to get inside her? Fine. I'll turn on the lights. Do your thing, and then we're going home."

She didn't question his use of "home." Right now, still shaken by the terror of falling, of that fog wrapping around her, it sounded very welcoming. Marcus had called to her, or else she'd imagined someone—but then, she was linked to him, wasn't she? She'd actually touched Marcus without her gloves, locked on to some energy that had lodged inside her, the odd sense that he was just what she needed to complete herself.

But, then, she'd been wrong before.

As they stood on the ground floor and walked toward the cruiser, Marcus asked, "Brice? As in Brice Whitcomb? Payback for what?"

Tempest stepped up on the ladder, leading to another attached to the *Winona.* "Okay, I used to know him. We didn't part on good terms."

"Tell me more. An ex-lover?" Marcus's deep voice cut at her, his eyes glinting in the shadows.

"Sure. Aren't they all?"

Her flip remark was automatic, defensive, and smoothly denied by Marcus's narrowed stare. "I guess I'd know your track record, Tempest Best. Your list of lovers is pretty short."

Tempest shivered as she realized how much care he'd taken with her that first time in Santa Fe—until her body accepted him more readily. She didn't bother to deny his statement, but climbed on board, and asked brightly, "Coming with me?"

"I'll wait. Do what you have to do."

After circling the deck, Tempest made her way down into the luxury cruiser, sometimes called a "motor yacht." She found the switch for the lights and flicked them on. The spacious salon area was fitted with gleaming wooden cabinets and flooring, several conversation areas, and a liquor bar. A large television dominated one area, couches arranged for viewing in front of it. Red leather benches lined the area, which included a view of a well-outfitted galley, with a washer and dryer at the far end, and at the opposite end of the salon was a view of the cockpit. A luxury chair sat in front of the controls.

Tempest made her way around the cruiser, checking the two staterooms with televisions and the well-stocked, very upscale "heads."

She let herself feel what might have happened that last day in the Greystones' lives. The liquor rack was empty, but had probably been filled years ago—

according to the file she'd seen, Jason Greystone liked to drink in his later years, and he had been drinking that night.

Smelling of cleaning agents and lemon wax, the air seemed thick, almost pressing against her. Tempest held very still, wading through the energies she hoped to catch. She wasn't like Claire, who could pick up sensations when near a live person; she wasn't like Greer, who could stand in a room and sort through the residue of energies remaining there. Tempest's heart suddenly began to race, and fear clogged her throat. The hair on her nape lifted as though another person had just touched her.

She inhaled and held her breath, her body tense. It was as if there was a presence waiting for her, wanting her to know something. For a moment, Tempest panicked, just as she had while dangling five stories above ground. She placed her hands flat on a granite countertop, focused internally to calm herself, and waited for her panic to subside.

But she was alone, the windows of the salon catching the light, reflecting it back at her. Tempest remembered that instant in time when the anchor had hit the concrete floor, jarring the building. Well secured, the cruiser had evidently been jarred by the vibrations. Something had crashed to the floor, and the windows had shimmered, catching the light, for just that heartbeat. Was it possible that some energy wanted to draw attention to itself?

Tempest noted that the red leather benches could be used for storage and could be made into a full-sized bed. Then Tempest caught a metallic gleam on the floor, near one of the benches. Walking to it, she saw that a thin gold chain had slipped out from the storage beneath the bench and gleamed on the varnished planks. She tried to gently pull the chain free, but it was stuck. "Is this what you wanted me to find, Winona?" Tempest whispered to the eerie silence. "Is this what you let slip from your keeping, just for me, when that anchor hit?"

Tempest raised the bench lid and sorted through plastic-wrapped blankets and linens until she found what she wanted; the chain was attached to a small heart-shaped locket. "Is this it, Winona? A necklace you loved?"

She carefully eased the necklace free, then straightened to study the locket in her open palm. Ornate, decorative filigree covered on one side, the other smooth side held the initials, W.R. She opened the locket to find it empty. The chain had been broken, and Tempest held her breath as she held the necklace in her fist and removed one glove.

She slowly gripped the necklace in her naked hand. Instantly, waves of anger, feminine and masculine, fueled by jealousy and defiance, hit Tempest. The energy was of a woman pushed past the point of caution as she revealed a secret she'd held for years. Her necklace had been a gift from her lover.

A man's angry shouts seemed to echo, ricocheting against the gleaming cabinets; Tempest's body jerked as she felt the sharp pain at her throat, the necklace being torn away.

Emotions racked the salon and Tempest closed her eyes, absorbing everything. And then she knew: That day, the final argument was about Winona's lover and possibly the father of Marcus, and her unborn child. But this time was different, because Winona Greystone wasn't backing down. That evening, she'd set the scene in the cruiser, away from any danger to her child. Winona planned to face down her husband, to take her child, and to leave. She knew enough about Jason's corrupt dealings to use as leverage, and she had proof that Jason was sterile and could not have sired his heir. Her lover and a new life had been waiting for her and their son.

"Tempest?" Marcus called from outside the cabin. "One minute, no more."

"W.R. not W.G. He'd given it to her . . . the man she loved," Tempest whispered, her body cold. "And if Jason couldn't have her, then no other man could—she was blackmailing him. His so-called macho image would be ruined if the public knew he was sterile, and she had the living proof. Jason had to let her go—or he had to kill her."

Marcus's next call was louder, distracting Tempest, and she shuddered, quickly pulling on her glove. She struggled to pull herself free from the storm of emotions still rocking her.

When she left the cabin and slowly made her way around the deck to climb down the ladder, Tempest was uncertain just what she should tell Marcus. He took one look at her and lifted her face to the light. "You found something. What?"

She held out the necklace, and he took it almost reverently, his voice uneven. "This was my mother's. She was wearing it that day—she always wore it. The chain is broken."

"The initials on the back—did her maiden name begin with R?"

He nodded slowly. "Roberts. Winona Roberts was her name. I guess she didn't want to add the G."

"She was going to make her stand—for you and herself, to start a new life. She wanted to talk with Jason away from where there might be any repercussions to you—so he couldn't hurt you. You have no idea where they were they going when they hit that wall?"

"I never knew. I knew they had argued. They came back at sunset, and that's when she called Kenny to come get me. My God, they'd been arguing, and I knew they would, after I left. He probably tore this from her, didn't he? She was wearing a bandage on her throat. She told me not to worry about anything, that things were going to be better and that she would be fine. . . . I never should have left—"

Tempest read the stark pain in Marcus's expression; he was reliving that day all over again, his finger tracing that slender golden chain resting in his palm. She needed to get him away from the cruiser, and touched his arm. "Let's get out of here, okay?"

Suddenly, Marcus turned to her, his face harsh in the marina's stark overhead lighting. "What else did you get? Why had she chosen that one day—after all the other days before it? Why *that* day?"

Because Winona had just learned that she was pregnant again, determined to pull herself and her children to safety. She knew her time and her strength would be limited later on.

Still rocked by the violence echoing from years ago and uncertain of how to begin—because Jason was not Marcus's father, and he had no idea—Tempest whispered, "Very simply, she wanted a better life. For you both."

"He wasn't a man to let go easily." Marcus studied her, his expression concerned. "That must have cost you. You look like hell."

"Thanks. Marcus, she . . . she was pregnant again."

"That's what the report said. Let's get out of here. Did you touch anything else?" He scanned the dark windows of the cruiser, and added, "Kenny is touchy about how he finds this place in the morning. He already knows you've been prowling around. I'd better double-check."

Tempest watched Marcus enter the cruiser, then she hurried to the rack where Kenny kept his tools. The tool belt he had worn was hanging nearby, and she had to touch it—to know his touch, to know more about the man who could be Marcus's real father . . . and the father of Winona's new baby.

Tempest eased off one glove and carefully reached for a battered wrench. . . . Intelligence, education, and class mixed with rage and jealousy and frustration and hatred—and love. For Winona? Or did he hate her for not leaving Jason and keeping Marcus's true paternity secret?

Tempest closed her eyes, opening herself for more, needing more.

On the wrench, remnants of Kenny's energy ran parallel to Marcus's, a familial link. But then it changed, swerved into an elusive direction, running like a scarlet ribbon through the dark layers of frustrations. Tempest fastened on to a glimmering tiny bit just beyond her reach, and stretched her senses toward it. She closed her psychic fingers around it and held tight, shocked by the waves of bitterness and pain and frustration. She forced her sensations back away from that hard brittle nugget of hatred, and breathed quietly. Did Kenny love Winona? Or had something happened between them? Did he hate her, enough to kill both Greystones with a hit-and-run? But then, Jason wasn't letting Winona go, not alive and holding the secret of his only heir as blackmail.

She needed more time, but one glance told her that Marcus had finished checking the *Winona*. He was walking toward the building's side door, where the light switches were located. In a second, he'd be turning to call to her.

Kenny's hatred for Jason burned Tempest's bare hand, and she carefully replaced the wrench and drew on her glove, before turning.

Her mind raced on. So far, three people could have been involved with that hit-and-run. First of all, Jason could have plotted to murder his wife—and the plot could have misfired, killing him. Opal wouldn't have liked Winona's pregnancy, because she wanted Winona all for herself. She could have tolerated Marcus because she'd had to. But Opal wouldn't have wanted a child from Winona's true love, a reminder of how willingly she had moved in his arms, loving him. Then there was Kenny, who had hated Jason for having the woman he wanted and his son. Or maybe Winona had changed her mind at the last minute.

The question remained that after the Greystones' furious argument in which Jason tore away her necklace, and she'd faced him down, where were the Greystones going that fatal midnight hour?

Tempest was holding a bag of secrets, and Marcus intended to get all of them.

At midnight, he tossed the broken chain and locket in his palm, studying it, remembering how his mother always wore it— the bandage and thin cut at her throat when he had identified her body. Jason had probably torn that chain from her throat. Why? Because he was angry? Because he didn't want another child?

Marcus glanced at the guest bedroom door; Tempest had closed it after their arrival back at his house. The moment they'd stepped outside the marina building, she'd tensed and stared at the harbor's waters as if fascinated. He'd turned to lock the side door and reset the alarms. When he'd turned back again, Tempest had been walking toward the marina's platform dock.

She had been wrapped in the heavy fog by the time he reached her. She seemed fascinated by the water, crouching to place her hand in the waves, her position precarious if one hard wave hit the dock. Tempest had been unaware that he was near, until he put his arm around her. "I could be the one, Marcus," she had whispered unsteadily as she gripped that brooch at her shoulder. "No one in our family has ever been a medium, but I could be—do you think I could be? Do you think my father wants to contact me?"

The fog had settled damply into his clothes, the entire night pulled out of some nightmare from the moment Kenny had called that a burglar was trying to get into the marina.

Marcus would never forget seeing Tempest dangle from that railing, her face pale and terrified in the mist. If anything had happened to her . . .

Marcus tossed the locket again, and watched the chain pool back into his palm. If he hadn't let Tempest into the *Winona*, she would have just come back again; he'd read about the curiosity of psychics and now he believed it. Tempest hadn't changed from one Blair parapsychology assessment: "Very expressive, impulsive, emotional, headstrong, almost driven by curiosity."

He remembered how shaken Tempest had been when she had emerged from the *Winona*; she looked as if she'd been tossed into a nightmare—and probably had, if she'd caught the echoes of his parents' argument. His mother's necklace had been there all those years and Tempest—a hunter—was the only one to find it.

Kenny had checked the *Winona* immediately after that anchor fell, and a few things had been slightly jarred from their places. The impact must have been just enough to free the necklace.

It glittered in his palm, taunting him. Where were his parents going when they hit that wall? It didn't make sense, not after an argument—they usually kept their distance from one another, rather his mother tried to keep her distance all the time. But she was pregnant again. . .Marcus didn't want to think how that child had come to be conceived, because she couldn't bear to have Jason touch her.

Marcus studied that closed bedroom door. Beneath it, a strip of light, periodically disturbed, indicated that Tempest was pacing her room. She was talking quietly, and Marcus waited until she was finished. Then he swung open the door and leaned a shoulder against the frame. "We need to talk."

Tempest shoved her cell phone into her backpack and sat on the bed, staring at the floor. Then she was on her feet, facing him, her body rigid, her fists at her side. "About what?"

"Brice Whitcomb."

Her head went back as if he'd dropped a miniature bomb at her feet. Marcus noted the flashing gold of her eyes, the way her body tensed, but he wasn't backing up. "If you're in danger, I need to know."

"No thanks."

"Want to tell me about it? About Brice Whitcomb, and why you think he might be stalking you?"

Tempest shrugged and bent to untie her shoelaces. She stood and opened that big ornate buckle, tossing the belt to the bed. "I was twenty, he was thirty-five. It was a bad two years—it took me a while to realize just how bad. He wasn't happy when I left."

"You walked, and he didn't like it? Because?"

She leveled a stare at Marcus. "No, he didn't. He was using me."

"To do what?"

She stripped off her sweater and shimmied out of those form-hugging black pants. "I'm taking a shower."

Marcus's body had already started reacting to her nude body. Athletic and feminine, she was all pale curves. "No underwear?"

"Not all the time. I've never liked it. Too hampering. Worn only for necessity or when I'm feeling girlie and want to dress up." She stretched her arms high, and then lifted one leg to the bed, bending over it to touch her toes. She repeated the exercise with her other. She was deliberately distracting Marcus, and he was reacting just as she wanted. And that irritated.

Marcus took two strides and tugged her against him. "You like to test the boundaries, don't you? Well, test this."

She was all open and hot, ready for him, diving into his kiss. Her legs wrapped around Marcus's hips as he lifted her, her arms locked around him, her gloved hands in his hair. "Take them off."

"No."

Marcus eased down onto the bed, aware that Tempest's hand was already seeking him, stroking him. Her lips were parted, those green eyes dark with passion, her hips lifting to him, an age-old invitation. In another minute, he'd be locked inside her, the heat building into the storm she wanted to divert him.

Marcus removed her hand and held her wrist, staying it. Tempest frowned, looked up at him, and the flush in her cheeks deepened. "What do you want?"

"A promise. No climbing buildings, running off in the middle of the night, and no walking along the water unless I'm with you. Tell me about that—the water, why you're drawn to it. You were raised by the Pacific Ocean, is that it? And the lake reminds you of home? Am I supposed to believe that? Or do you want to tell me the truth?"

"Didn't that sweet little Blair parapsychology report on us tell you anything?"

"The only link I saw was the sailboat accident when you were three. When that wave hit, you and your sisters were tossed into the ocean . . . retrieved by your parents. Your father died when you were four, and at ten—when you were all tested—all three of you demonstrated some sort of a link back to that time in the water. You seemed to be the one closest to your father. I can understand why you would be terrified of the lake, but that isn't it. Terror doesn't draw a person to anything, it makes them want to stay away. You want to reach your father, don't you? To reach him somehow by using the water as a medium?"

When she trembled and shook her head, denying an answer, Marcus allowed Tempest to push him away. "You want me. I want you," she whispered unevenly. "Can't we just leave it at that?"

Aware that he'd pushed enough for the moment, Marcus smiled and drew her into his arms. "We could. But I'm fragile—"

Tempest's feminine snort mocked him. "Like a bull-dozer."

Marcus smoothed that sleek taut curve of her bottom. "You've got one man chasing you. But I'm the one who has you, and you like it."

"You mean, you own me? Been there, done that." She started tugging his shirt up, and Marcus allowed her to remove it. He allowed her to unsnap his jeans and slide the zipper down, her gloves brushing against his skin, wrapping around him. He watched her eyes close as Tempest went into herself, coming down upon him—and then while every cell in his body wanted to forget everything but making love to her, Marcus ordered quietly, "Tell me about Brice. Why you think he owned you."

Tempest stilled, that vein pulsing along her throat, and then she lifted slowly away; she moved away to sit on the edge of the bed, her back to him. Suddenly, she was in motion, striding toward the bathroom. "I'm taking that shower now. Alone."

Marcus fought the impulse to go after her, to prove that she was his. The need to possess her held him, a contradiction to any feeling he'd had for other women.

He stood, stared at the closed bathroom door, and tugged up his zipper. He put his hands on his hips and frowned at that closed door. Okay, so the possessive-male instinct was a little antiquated, but Tempest could nudge his primitive emotions. He glanced at the rose she'd placed beside her bed and thought of those green eyes studying him over it—eyes as green as the sea, witch's eyes, meant to enchant and to beckon, holding secrets that he had to have . . . dangerous secrets, or Tempest wouldn't be guarding them so closely.

Was he obsessed? Maybe.

More importantly, would she come to him tonight?

Marcus shook his head and stepped outside her bedroom, closing the door behind him. "Lady's choice," he murmured as he walked into his office and sat in front of his computer. "Now for Brice Whitcomb and those two years Tempest is hiding."

Marcus ran a search for the name and came up with articles about notable European events and high-society parties. Marcus noted one event in France; it was at an exclusive resort, and Marcus just happened to know the very efficient Le Paix manager. A quiet call to Phillipe, a promise to go deep-sea diving off the coast of Greece, and Marcus quickly had a complete guest list for those events occurring in the two hidden years of Tempest's life. Each event had included Whitcomb. Phillipe's e-mail also included a note that ten years ago, Whitcomb had a companion, a mysterious woman wearing a veil. Phillipe had networked with other managers and had obtained Whitcomb's name at their events. A woman called "Dominique," who was supposed to have a scarred face was his companion, though she preferred to stay out of the limelight Whitcomb apparently loved.

According to Phillipe, Whitcomb hadn't been around in the past few years and more than one resort said that he'd skipped without paying his bill. Their collectors had found that Whitcomb had no known means of support, and with rumors of blackmail and extortion, he had been declared persona non grata.

In those two years, with Tempest's gifted hands and circulating among the wealthy set, Whitcomb wouldn't have needed to work. He could have used her in so many ways, including helping him in high-stakes poker games. "She probably made him a fortune. No wonder he wants Tempest back."

Moments later, Marcus sat back, steepled his hands, and stared at his computer. He'd found Tempest's missing two years, ones she wanted to hide. He'd already found that she'd emerged Tempest Storm, after those two years.

A shadow passed his office doorway, and Marcus quickly turned off his computer. He cursed softly. Tempest hadn't had enough for the day—she was on the move again.

But this time, he found her at the window overlooking the lake. In the room's soft lighting, she appeared as a small silhouette outlined by the deck's lights. She seemed so lonely, wrapped in her thoughts.

Fog churned outside, the deck's ferns heavy with it, and Tempest's gloved hand reached to flatten against the window.

"Everything okay, Tempest?" he asked, easing closer to her. An athletic woman, Tempest could move quickly. If she decided to go over that railing again, Marcus wanted to be ready to stop her.

Her arms wrapped around her body, the movement lifting her white T-shirt high enough to reveal her panties below and that one sweetly curved buttock, those two long legs. Marcus breathed deeply, and desire lodged low and hard and slightly painful in his body. The problem with dealing with this one particular woman was his fascination with her. Whitcomb had had her for two full years, and Marcus reluctantly admitted to his dark, simmering jealousy of her former lover. "Tell me about Brice."

"It's a long story."

After his research on Whitcomb, Marcus understood a little of Tempest's distrust of men. A woman with her talent could bring a fortune to a con man. "I've got the time. But we've both had enough for today. I'd rather not chase you over that railing again."

She turned suddenly. "Could you just hold me?"

"What's going on?" he asked, as Tempest held very still against him.

"I'm testing something." Her face warmed his neck, her breath stroking his skin. "You smell like the ocean. Salty, clean . . . fresh."

"Okay, so much for expensive aftershave and soap," he agreed uneasily. "And?"

Tempest snuggled closer, wrapping her arms around him. "I hate it, you know, this sixth-sense gift, this curse."

"Want to tell me about it? Why you're so fascinated by the lake?"

Tempest sighed wearily and moved sensuously against him. "I thought you'd read up on psychics. A lake could be a portal—for psychics. Like communicating or broadcasting without electronics, only more because it involves sensations and emotions. There's something out there, and it's calling me. Its energy wants to link with me. I feel its need for me, so it already has something of my energy."

Marcus stilled and held his breath. His fingers stopped sliding under the elastic of her panties; he felt as if he'd been caught in a car's backseat by his girlfriend's parents. "You think it might be your father?"

"Maybe. The energy feels like a man. I don't know. I never wanted to be clairvoyant or 'intuitive,' to see things that weren't real. None of us did, we only wanted to be like other people. With inherited ability we couldn't erase or destroy, we didn't want to open ourselves to it. We didn't want to get stronger, and we pushed it away, my sisters and I. But we can change, and our gifts—if that's what you can call this curse—can change. We can become like hybrids, our abilities swerving all over the place, depending on how strong and how much we practice. Until now, I haven't practiced that much—I just used what I had, my sisters didn't. I'm not that strong, and I knew it for certain when I held that brooch. That's why it has to go to my mother."

She looked up at Marcus. "You're all tense. What's wrong?"

"If that lake could be a portal, a potential connection with other psychics, then your mother and sisters could link with you? Know what you're doing?"

"We haven't really tried it as adults. Mom tested us when we were younger, enough to know that without her protection, large natural bodies of water could be dangerous to us." Tempest smoothed his hair and stood on tiptoe to kiss him. "Afraid?"

Uneasy now, Marcus removed his fingers from her panties and placed his hand firmly and properly on her waist. "If someone is strong and using the lake as a portal, then it could be your mother, couldn't it? Claire lives in dry rural Montana and Leona lives in an area of ponds and—and the Kentucky River. That leaves your mother, and you said she's strong."

"When I was growing up, she cleansed everything in the house, imprinting her energy over everything that I might hold with my bare hands. Yes, she's very strong, and practiced."

He eased away from Tempest. "Does . . . does she know that you and I—?"

"Probably. She can sense everything over the telephone lines. But we're a distance away from the lake, and that would be where she might be able to reach my energy without a telephone—because I'm weaker. Scary, huh?" Tempest grinned impishly and moved against him again. She looped her arms around his neck and wiggled her body against his. Marcus swallowed uneasily; she was soft in all the right places. He pressed his fingers a little deeper into her waist, keeping them firmly anchored.

"So . . . when we're . . . together . . . your mother and your sisters aren't in the bedroom, right?" An uneasy sensation caused Marcus to feel as if he actually were that hot-pants high-school kid after her mother's sweet little girl.

"Oh, you look so guilty. That's so cute." Tempest suddenly grinned, leaped upward, and circled his hips with her legs. She kissed him slowly, fully, playfully until his hands were back cupping her bottom— beneath the panties. "We are a package deal, Marcus. Born three minutes apart and as psychics, I'd say we're pretty connected. But no, I'm not about to stun them with whatever we do—together."

Marcus smiled against her lips and realized that Tempest could do that—relax and make him feel light and carefree. She simply fascinated him, a woman with a myriad of facets, and he wanted to explore each one. "And you like to push the limits, don't you? Just for the rush?"

"I don't know. I haven't had one yet tonight. We're all alone, big boy. Do your thing."

"Like what?" he murmured against her lips, his fingers already stroking that damp, hot cleft.

Her fingers wrapped in his hair, tugging his lips closer as she dived into the kiss, nipping at his lips. "You know what."

Greer awoke to the grunt of battling men, to the metallic crash of swords, to a dark, bitter curse in a language time had forgotten or corrupted.

She tried to breathe, forcing each breath, listening to it move in and out of her trembling body. In her vision, she could see them moving in the smoke, rough-hewn warriors, wearing leather and fur and coarse woven goods. Their shields gleamed, their blades and hatchets at work.

The screams were horrible, women and children trying to run into the woods.

A massive hand clenched Greer's throat, holding her still when she would run, terrified by the Viking invasion. A giant towered over her, his gray eyes cold and ruthless, his blond hair catching the wind. He held her in his grip as he stared down at her body, those cold eyes darkening. "They say you are a seer. What do you see now, woman?"

She recognized the heavy brooch at his shoulder, the wolf's head circled by the Vikings' angular symbols. In her dreams, she had seen it before, and knew then that her fate had been sealed.

She could not tell this warrior that she'd seen him as her love, the loving father of her children, the thoughtful, considerate man who would come to seek her counsel. "Take me and not the rest. I am worth more than anything else you will ever possess."

He laughed at that, a great roaring laughter that beat at her ears. "I have slaves. I have women. You will be no different from the rest."

"I will be your wife or nothing at all," Greer heard herself say firmly.

The Viking leaned down to peer at her. He smelled of the sea and wind and freedom, and she knew she had to conquer him—perhaps in a soft and tender way a woman did best. Already his hand was gentler at her throat, his thumb stroking her flesh.

"We shall see," he murmured, before hoisting her over his shoulder.

Greer dug her fingers into her sheets as the warriors

passed through her vision, and as suddenly as she had been lifted to the chieftain's shoulder, she was torn away and dumped upon the ground.

A heavy foot pressed against her chest, taking away her breath and pinning her still. When she looked up, it was into the face of evil.

Terrified and fully awake now, Greer pushed free of the bed and the shards of the nightmare. As she walked unsteadily out to view the Pacific Ocean, she placed her hand against her chest, willing the fear and the memory of his foot away from her. She focused on the ocean waves, then on slowing her racing pulse.

Whatever had circled Claire was still out there— Greer could feel it closing in on her and her daughters.

It was getting stronger.

Greer knew her daughter well—Tempest would not stop until she possessed the genuine brooch. Childhood guilt and pride demanded that she bring it to her mother, and set on her course, nothing would stop her.

Greer held the replica wolf's-head brooch in her hand and traced the designs with her finger. Centuries ago, Aisling had tossed the runes to give the appearance of a seer, when actually she was probably a first-rate psychic and needed nothing but her extra senses.

On the other hand, Tempest had only her sense of touch. The unreasonable guilt she felt over her father's death could make her more vulnerable now—close to Lake Michigan. A false calling could take Tempest to her death.

Greer shook her head. This was Tempest's journey, and Greer would not interfere.

She looked out at the heavy mist, saw it bead the windows and catch the light. Was it possible that Tempest could be the first of the Aisling line to connect with the dead? Was Daniel really out there and waiting? "Oh, Daniel. . . ."

Then she looked to the waves and pulsed her thoughts out into the night, over the land, to Lake Michigan. "Be careful, Tempest. You want this so badly that you can be led into danger by false signs."

Then Greer looked to the sky and whispered, "Keep your daughter safe, Viking."

Eight

"I COULDN'T CATCH MY BREATH IN THAT NIGHTMARE. I FELT
I was being crushed, the weight so great, I couldn't
escape—there was no way out, just that darkness
squeezing in on me." Leona's uneasy tone slid through
the cell phone to Tempest.

Tempest sipped her morning tea and watched Kenny
Morrison and Cody Smith working to clear away the
broken railing from the rocks below Marcus's house.
He was in his office, finishing the conference calls he'd
begun last night, and Tempest spoke quietly, "I felt the
same when I was—"

Leona's tone changed instantly, sharp with concern.
"What? When you were what?"

Dangling from the marina's railing, almost five stories up? Tempest shivered as she remembered the cold
damp clench of the fog around her, the slippery ladder.
Someone had been out there watching her. Who was
it? Was it Kenny, fearful of what she might discover?

"I'm just fine, Leona."

"No, you're not. Just like always, into things that
challenge you, testing the boundaries. Tempest, you
are *not* the reason that our sailboat tipped that day—
you are not the reason for Dad's accident. Okay, he was
hurrying home that day because you'd broken your

arm, and you shouldn't have been climbing that wall. But then, you were always climbing. All this stuff happens to other families, too. . . . Okay, I caught that 'I've heard all this before' sigh. You're bound and determined to—"

"Uh-huh. I want that brooch free and clear. I want to earn it."

"Sure. And you want to help Marcus. Admit it?"

Leona's proven ability to read Tempest easily irritated. "Maybe."

This time, Leona sighed deeply as if deciding that pinning Tempest down was a lost cause. Paper rustled in the background as if she were working at her desk. "Anyway, Claire just sent a small shipment of handbags perfect for my shop. You should see them. I love the way she makes them, no two ever alike. The last bunch just flew out the window. I guess marriage is taking up her production time. Speaking of that window—I need to redo the display. My new vintage-style clothing will suit any track the horsie crowd attends."

Leona's pause had been a fraction too long, as if she'd changed her mind about what to say. Tempest's senses quivered, the way they did when her sisters were disturbed. "You're holding, Leona Fiona. What's up?"

"Maybe I'm just worried, and maybe that disturbs the rest of you. Maybe the attack on Claire set us all off. But there's something stalking us, Tempest Best. I feel it. I'm in Lexington, miles away from the Kentucky River, which is the nearest large body of water. It's not even that large when compared to the Missouri River where Claire was camping when she first sensed the fog. But last night—I dreamed I was climbing a ladder to a tall building, the fog wrapped around me, and I could just barely hang on—OhmiGosh, that was you, wasn't it?"

"Well . . . ah. . . ."

"I went to bed early. We're in the same time zone, and since I dream things in advance—" Leona's sigh sounded again. "I knew it. You went back to the boat, didn't you? Why?"

Tempest tensed, aware that the harbor's water could have been a psychic portal to her sister, linking them without serious effort. If they could be linked by genetic DNA passed down from Aisling and by birth, the water acting as a universal medium, then who else could be out there, seeking them? Their father? Or something else, some predator, just as powerful?

Tempest carefully picked through what she wanted to tell her sister and came up with, "Marcus could be in danger. I was just checking out a few things."

Leona pounced on that admission. "On the other hand, maybe I don't want to know. It might scare me too much. And there was a guy in the shop today. He picked up a handbag and seemed interested in everything in the shop. Men don't usually browse that much. I'm trying not to 'open' any more than necessary, but he was unusual."

Tempest knew how Leona had fought her clairvoyance for years; after her husband's accident, she'd formed a tight, protective shield around herself. But when worried about Claire, she had allowed her sixth sense to be more receptive. A psychic could pick up fragments from the way a person looked, their jewelry, how they moved, enough to be intrigued and unfortunately for those with extra senses, curiosity was always there. But if Leona had purposely allowed her psychic fingers to feel around that man, she must have been quite disturbed.

"Unusual?" Tempest thought of Brice's threats to her, then quickly realized that her sister could pick up residue from that humiliating time in her life. To block her sister, Tempest forced away everything but images of her work, the flow and design of a new project: intricate Celtic designs circling runes that could be detached from the necklace easily, if the wearer wanted to lay them for a reading.

Leona sighed heavily. "Okay, I know what you're doing—blocking me. But I am worried, Tempest. I don't like to agree with Mom, but she's definitely uneasy, too."

"You were saying this guy was unusual?"

"Very. I knew it the moment he walked into my shop. I felt as if everything were shaking around me, those little feathers on Claire's handbags almost stood up. I've never wanted anything to do with our family's psychic abilities, but at the time, I almost wished I could read auras."

"What did he look like?"

"Attractive . . . a blond with sun streaks, very Nordic-looking, crisp waving hair, blue eyes—very shielded, cold eyes. He may have been wearing contacts, I don't know, and I can usually tell. There was something strange about his eyes. An outdoors sort of guy, by the way his skin looked, athletic. He touched one bag, ran his hands over it. His fingertip traced the red beads—it was the bag Claire was working on when she was attacked, 'Date Night.' It was almost as if there was a connection, and he understood—maybe he was seeing what was happening—or maybe I was just imagining that weird little smile."

Leona paused as if bracing herself, and then continued. "I dreamed about him all night, and no, not pleasant dreams, either. I dreamed I was in a car, riding with him, and suddenly everything stopped—stopped, as in dead stop. I woke up in a cold sweat. Then, this morning, I thought I saw him passing the window again, and I thought I heard—"

"What, Leona?"

"Nothing. I don't know. I don't like this, Tempest. I'm worried."

Tempest mentally visualized the X design of the *geofu* rune. The *geofu* implied complete harmony and matters of the heart. But on the inner level, the rune may issue a perilous "as you sow, so shall you reap" warning. Tempest had certainly sowed danger when she'd been with Brice.

"You're blocking me, Tempest Best," Leona said mildly. "Any reason? What are you hiding?"

Only that the man's description might fit Brice, a man whose threats had recently become more bold. Once she finished her task to claim the brooch, Tempest knew she would have to reckon with Brice. In her time with him, she'd learned a few things, like very effective blackmail.

"I don't know what you're talking about." Tempest held her breath. Leona had just sent a powerful energy probe, her psychic fingers lightly kneading Tempest's sensations. Leona had definitely become much stronger in the past few months. To block her sister, Tempest quickly visualized a tiny lobster-claw clasp that would fasten the rune to the bracelet's link. Leona might not know it, but her ability was stronger now than it had ever been, despite her efforts to push it away.

Still blocking her sister, Tempest placed her teacup aside and picked up a tablet and pen and began sketching a square, to be framed by silver. The rune designs would have to be cut deep and darkened, laying in the stain, and then wiping it from the indentations. "How old was this guy? What did he say?" she asked.

"That's the odd part. He wanted something suitable for the horse races here, something that a lady could use with a dressy hat and gloves. I sensed that he was older, despite his appearance. He seemed very worldly, very classy, I suppose, but his eyes seemed almost flat, as if nothing was inside. I keep remembering those eyes. He was definitely seeking something, and it wasn't a handbag for the races. He left without buying anything."

"Send me the handbag he touched. If this guy is trouble, I'll feel it." Tempest realized that Cody was staring up at her from the rubble of the broken railing. Uneasy with the boldness of his expression, she moved slightly back into the room's shadows. Could he have been standing out in the fog last night, watching her, calling to her? Why?

"Okay. Are you wearing your brooch?" Claire asked suddenly.

"Sure. I may be a little on the impulsive side—" Tempest waited for Leona's burst of laughter to stop, then added, "Okay, I admit to being impulsive—but I usually have a reason. I know when to be cautious."

When Tempest hung up, she quickly sketched the detachable silver runes idea and tucked it in her jeans. Then she started thinking about Brice; he wanted to either have her or kill her. Until ten years ago, he'd been careful of his treatment although their relationship had already been strained by his gambling debts. Then Tempest had overheard a very special conversation with a woman he'd apparently been supporting— with Tempest's draining work. Tempest had confronted Brice with the true picture of what she actually was to him. He'd described "Dominique" to the woman in bed with him as "my private little freak, the little gold mine."

Tempest inhaled sharply as she remembered that one stinging slap from Brice's open hand—and the satisfaction of tossing him on the floor before she walked—or rather climbed out the window of that locked room.

It wasn't a moment she wanted to share with her family. They hadn't asked why she'd resurfaced, throwing herself into her clay, blowtorch, and metal, into a life she could control. "The little freak," she repeated darkly, still angry because of how Brice had used her.

As an artist with public and private showings, she'd expected him to turn up at any minute, and she'd been prepared. Brice could have easily traced her family; in the two years they were together, he'd probably picked up bits. But Tempest had been careful because some instinct had told her not to trust him completely.

With the ability to foretell the future, like the triplets' seer ancestor, Leona might have just picked up on Brice's need for revenge. Could Brice have already found her? Was he the man standing near the harbor's fog? Was that low laughter his, or from the party yacht? Or had Kenny come to watch her fall? And then there was Cody, who seemed more than a little interested in her.

The hairs on Tempest's nape lifted, and she turned suddenly to Marcus, who was in the shadows, studying her. "Problem?" he asked casually.

"Of course not," she lied. She was pretty close to falling in love with another exciting, challenging man—Marcus. She'd just realized how her senses could pick up his proximity, almost like a pulse running separate and different, yet with her own.

"I don't believe you. But I can understand." He walked past her and into his office.

Tempest couldn't let him get away with that and followed. His office held his scent—morning aftershave, soap, man, and his coffee. She realized that she had become addicted to that unique blend of scents—and just probably Marcus, the way he moved, like a sleek predator, waiting for a chance to strike. That little sensitive tingle low in her body tightened into a warm knot as she remembered his lips moving down her body, that lick of his tongue. "What do you mean, you 'can understand'?"

Marcus leveled a look at her and took a sip of his coffee as he tapped a note on his computer keyboard, then straightened and studied her. "You look good in the morning—not at all like the experienced burglar you actually are. You could have fallen and been killed last night."

"So I've done a few things. So what? Hasn't everyone?" Uneasy with Marcus's narrow look, Tempest knew what she looked like—like a woman who had been thoroughly pleasured, who felt tingly, rosy, and soft. Near him, that fluttery, feminine sensation was unnerving.

She needed payback—to turn the tables on Marcus, who had used sex to make her pay for trespassing on his well-guarded emotions. She studied the pictures on the wall, aware that it would take very little to walk to Marcus and slide into his arms, to capture all that male strength and begin testing him in a return bout.

Last night, their lovemaking had been rawly primitive. Tempest had intended to finish quickly and move to her own room. But Marcus had pinned her, making her wait, withdrawing, licking and nibbling on her breasts until she'd almost come, then he'd retreated, holding her on that pinnacle until she'd cried out for release. Still, he hadn't stopped until her skin seemed on fire and ready to burst. "Don't you ever do anything like that again, Tempest," he'd ordered roughly, just before she ignited.

She knew then that fear had driven him, that he considered her to be his, and that terrified her. Exhausted and sated, she'd only been able to curl against him.

In the morning, Marcus had slid from her arms quickly. His look down at her had been dark and brooding. "I mean it. Don't try anything like that again."

Apparently, his mood hadn't lightened since they'd awakened. Tempest had badly needed those two hours to paste herself back together from that last ultimate shattering, when she'd pooled into a warm, smiling, satiated despicable puddle.

She'd spent the last two nights in his bed—just where Marcus wanted her . . . just where she wanted to be. Tempest frowned slightly. Marcus was dangerously addictive. She met his cold stare and felt the stirring of heat, the need to take Marcus right there on his desk, to prove that she could walk away, unaffected.

On the other hand, maybe she should make him wait. Just maybe she should dress to kill, set him up, and pay him back.

Marcus placed his finger beneath her chin and lifted it. "Your eyes just turned to that dark gold shade, and that means you're angry. About last night? You had it coming, you little witch. You're not alone in hiding something you're ashamed of. I've done a few things I wasn't proud of, either, because I wanted to rebuild this company. I've tried to make up what I could. You, on the other hand, feed on risk and challenges and take them because you can. Everyone has things they don't want exposed. But I'd like to know what else you found on the *Winona* last night—other than the obvious."

"Your mother's energies seemed to be all over the place. I wasn't there long enough to find much of your father." Tempest omitted details about Winona's energies—the fear, the struggle, and her rigid, defiant anger. Jason's energy had crackled with rage, a bully at work, but this time, Winona hadn't backed down. "I'll kill you first!" Jason had shouted.

Had he done just that? After that horrible argument,

somehow arranged to kill Winona and gotten caught in his own trap?

Marcus stood with his back to her, apparently overlooking the harbor. "The cruiser was basically my mother's. She took it out—sometimes with me, sometimes Kenny helped. She loved the water, Jason didn't, and that was her escape. But the day they died, they went out on the lake together. I've always wondered why."

And Kenny? Was Kenny like Brice, a man who would kill a woman before letting her go? As a handyman, with free rein in everything that was the Greystones', Kenny was in a murderer's perfect place to strike. She needed to know more about him. "I suppose Kenny is upset over last night. Were you standing near the water last night, watching me on that ladder?"

"No, I didn't have time. I knew where you were, and I came in through the side door from the parking lot. Do you think someone was watching?"

Tempest shook her head. "I don't know. Someone was down on the sidewalk beside the harbor, but I couldn't tell if they were looking at me or at the party across the harbor. Did someone see me there and call you?"

"Uh-huh."

A chill rippled through her as she remembered that eerie whisper, *Tempest?*

"I didn't see anyone, but you're right about Kenny. He is not happy. He doesn't trust you, no matter what I say. I should have warned you that he was sensitive about his hand and that he doesn't like questions about himself. After that stunt last night, he has reason to think that you're trouble. But I already knew that."

Marcus turned to her, his expression intent. "And the *Born Free*'s anchor didn't come down by itself. Kenny said someone had been up there, tampering with it. Now, want to tell me about it—Dominique?" Marcus asked quietly as he tugged her into his arms.

Dominique, the name she'd used when living with Brice. Tempest struggled, but Marcus held her firmly. "You're not going anywhere. If you're in danger, and accidents are happening around you, I want to know about you and Whitcomb. I have some idea about how Whitcomb used you. A man answering his description tried to find you at your hotel in Albuquerque."

"How would he know I was there?"

"Apparently he went to a gallery showing your work. They thought Whitcomb was a potential buyer, and since you were supposed to be in town, maybe you'd want to meet with him. You'd left a phone number of the hotel for a contact number—they gave it to him, and your cell number. That's pretty poor business practice."

"I know. I'll speak to them about it." Tempest shivered, chilled by the past that she'd hidden for years. When Marcus released her, she stepped back, found the credenza behind her hips, and leaned against it. She gripped it with both hands as she stared out at the harbor and Port Salem beyond it. Denying her past wouldn't work; Marcus was too good. He'd have all the facts in his fist before releasing them to her. She felt so tired, so worn and ashamed.

"He's been threatening me. When I first left him, I thought he'd get over his possessiveness. I didn't hear from him for five years, and then he contacted me through the Santa Fe gallery where you and I met— just a light, easy letter asking for forgiveness. I didn't reply, and then a few more letters, and then the tone changed to vicious threats and blackmail. Somehow he always got my phone numbers and my e-mail address—I changed them often. Brice is very intelligent, and it is a mistake to underestimate him."

She folded her arms over her chest; she didn't want

to remember her time with Brice. "I made a bad mistake."

"And you became 'Dominique,' the mysterious veiled woman with him at high-class European events. From Whitcomb's records, the photographs of him with some notable, but discreet crime lords, you probably circulated in the shadows, right?"

Tempest inhaled slowly and nodded. She watched a fishing boat, loaded with men, motoring out of the harbor toward the lake. "Those pictures were taken later, when Brice really got in over his head. When we were together, I had long hair, brown contact lenses, and I'd darkened my eyebrows and lashes. Supposedly the veil hid a badly scarred face. Some people actually felt sorry for Brice—because he was handsome then and charming, and he seemed to be stuck with me. I insisted on a disguise. At least I had enough sense to know then that my family would be shamed if they knew what I was doing."

She rubbed her gloves together, and the buttery-soft leather created a hissing sound. It echoed in the taut silence as she continued. "One touch of a hand, and I knew the person's weakness, what dirty secrets they wanted to hide the most, what they desired over everything else. And Brice used whatever tidbits his 'little freak' picked up. He made a lot of money off me."

"I see," Marcus stated grimly. "If you're susceptible to oceans, how did you cross them?"

"I took something to sleep, to relax. As for the rest, I could go a short time without being affected, and I always kept a distance away. We must be relatively close to be as affected as I have been here, down by the lake." She stretched out her gloved hands and looked at them, her shame refreshed. "I made my choices. It's no one else's problem."

"An aging crook on hard times might play rough, Tempest."

She thought of Brice's first and last slap, when she'd tossed him to the floor. "True."

"Everyone has something they'd rather forget. I've seen your reaction when you touched that brooch with your bare hands and when you came from the cruiser. Playing Whitcomb's game must have cost you."

"After a 'feel,' it would take me days to recover from their energies, from the evil and lust and whatever else they were going through. And it was never enough for him."

Tempest shook her head. "I never should have gotten involved. The first time, I thought I was helping him repay someone who had cheated his family, his dying mother, who was losing the family plantation. But then, that would be difficult to do when his mother had died years before, wouldn't it? I found that out later, and then the women, of course. It was quite the little learning experience. I betrayed myself and my family for him. I sold out everything that I was, that they are."

Marcus looked out at the harbor, his expression hard. "Does your family know?"

Tears burned her eyes, and she wrapped her arms tightly around her body again. "Not the details. When I came back from Europe I was twenty-three and a real wreck. I'd taken a year to paste myself together before facing them. They've never asked questions, but they couldn't have missed it—either visually or in their senses. I had to be very careful of Claire—she absorbs energies too easily and can make them her own. She's stronger now—with Neil."

"Neil Olafson," Marcus repeated as if making a mental note to himself. He turned suddenly to her. "Tell me about the brooch. Why you want it? To buy off Whitcomb?"

"Definitely not." The thought of Brice possessing the brooch caused her to shiver.

"Why then?" he pushed.

Tempest met his stare. Wrapped in her own ugly past, she'd forgotten for a moment that Marcus was a predator at heart, suiting her hawk statue. "I think I'm going for a walk now. I need to pick up a few things."

"You just do that."

"Going shopping? 'Need to pick up a few things'? Like hell. You're hunting, Tempest." From his new deck, Marcus watched Tempest walk along the sandy beach, then stop. Set against the expanse of Lake Michigan, she seemed small, fragile, and alone.

He didn't trust the way Tempest had looked when she left. Those green eyes had flashed at him over her shoulder, but then, he'd been busy studying her hips, covered in loose cargo shorts. Her black T-shirt was tucked into those shorts, and that belt with the Celtic buckle circled her waist. That wasn't a little change purse attached to the back of the belt, it was her knife. She was definitely on the hunt, and Marcus hoped Whitcomb wasn't in the area.

Unable to wait longer, Marcus dialed Tempest's cell number.

The wind and waves crashing against the shoreline almost drowned the sound of her "Storm here."

Marcus narrowed his eyes at the figure on the beach, curved, long legs, the sunlight catching the fire in her short hair. She must have been preoccupied, her tone crisp.

"Did it ring, your cell phone?"

For a few heartbeats, he heard only the waves and the wind. Then Tempest's uneven, curt answer, "No."

"So, you sensed me calling you? Is that what happens with your sisters?"

Her silence said that he'd caught her off guard and that his probe had been affirmative. "Hey. Greystone. I'm busy here. You can call your watchdogs off."

Marcus tensed and noted the slender man a distance away from Tempest. He hunched against the wind, his hood up, and was unrecognizable in the distance. "I never sent anyone after you. I prefer to handle you myself. I trust you to get back here by noon. If you don't, I'm coming after you. Do you know who that is?"

"The kid who helped Kenny. . . . Hi, Cody."

She might trust Marcus with her body, but not to protect her. If Whitcomb was on her trail, Marcus would protect her—if she let him. "Anything I can do to help?"

"I told you, I needed a few things."

"Back by noon, Tempest. Okay?"

"I've never liked being on a leash, Greystone. I'll turn up when I get ready. I've got a few things to do, and I thought you were tied up with some big new promotion campaign."

"You'd better be here."

"Or?" she asked lightly, that challenge in her tone.

Marcus disconnected the call and watched her talk with Cody. Then he called Kenny's number.

"Cody is hanging around the beach. I thought he was supposed to be working at the marina." Marcus pushed away an edge of jealousy. He'd noted Cody's interest in Tempest earlier, but what male wouldn't be interested in an exciting redhead with a body like Tempest's—agile, strong, and feminine, soft in all the right places.

A bright flash drew Marcus's attention to a battered gray van parked across the channel. A youth leaned against it. He appeared to have his binoculars trained on Cody and Tempest as they walked along the shoreline.

"Cody put in overtime last night cleaning up a gas spill from one of the inboards. I said he could have the morning off." Kenny's voice sharpened. "He's not with a gang, is he?"

"Alone. But someone in a gray van is pretty interested in him and Tempest."

"That would be Sean. Cody brought him over to my house to play games. He's a little rough around the edges, but he hasn't had many breaks. He's quite a gamer, though. It was good to have the two kids in the house, yelling up a storm and having fun. He's probably waiting to pick up Cody."

Uneasy about the boys' attention, Marcus decided to have a talk with both of them later. He ended the call and looked at the white beach pebbles and shells that he'd placed in the earthenware bowl. Tempest had gathered the same with her father, and she missed him, feeling for him in the mist. Marcus shook his head. If she was any indication of the rest of the family, he would have his hands full—because there was more than sex between them, a lot more, and he was seeing it to the end.

As Marcus walked back to his office, he noted that his bed was neatly made, as if Tempest wanted no reminder how she had melted in his arms. "It's not that easy, sweetheart."

At his desk, Marcus used his computer to hunt for a Montana address, then dialed Neil Olafson, Tempest's brother-in-law. A woman like Tempest could make things move real fast, and Marcus might need help from someone with experience. "Hi, Neil. This is Marcus Greystone."

A few hours away from the intense situation with Marcus was just what Tempest needed. She had to get away from Marcus quickly—before she lost everything that she'd fought to reclaim. He'd researched "Dominique," and he wasn't stopping. Neither was Tempest; she had definite plans to check out anyone around at the time of the Greystones' deaths.

Tempest eased into the tiny backyard of Kenny Morrison's home. The small white house was located in Port Salem's older residential district, across the harbor from the Greystone house. On a clear day, Kenny would have a perfect view of Marcus's home. The shady street and quiet neighborhood indicated that in the morning, residents were probably either out enjoying the clean air and sunshine or at work in the tourist trade. Tempest noted multiple high-tech antennae and satellite dishes on Kenny's roof, the cables running from the street poles; Kenny was definitely well equipped for electronic communications.

She eased around the well-used, freestanding barbecue grill, glanced at the sheets hanging on the line, and noted the privacy afforded by the bushes.

Then she noted the man standing and watching her from the small garden. His injured right hand was cradling tomatoes against his body. "Hello, Kenny."

He walked to the back porch, and with his good hand placed the two large tomatoes on the grill. Kenny quickly rolled down the shirtsleeve that exposed his scarred and emaciated forearm. He stuck out his claw-like hand to her. "This is what you came to see, isn't it? Why are you snooping around my place?"

"No one answered my knock at the front door. So I thought maybe you might be back here," Tempest managed lightly and gave him her best smile.

Kenny wasn't buying her excuse. "No, lady. You thought I'd be at the marina. We had a little burglar problem last night, and I had to check out the marina first thing this morning. I replaced a lightbulb on an outside stairway, and I came home just minutes ago. Now what do you want?"

"Those are great tomatoes," she said, going for a compliment to soothe Kenny. "Did you go down to the marina last night? Did you see the burglar?"

Was he the man standing beside the harbor? Did he whisper, *Tempest*?

"No need to. Marcus took care of it." Beneath the shadow of his ball cap, those gray eyes with that rim of bronze flecks around the iris pinned her. "You're trouble," he stated bluntly. "Things happen around you, and you ask too many questions."

That challenge caused Tempest to angle her head up at him. "And you're afraid I might learn something you don't want known; otherwise, you wouldn't be so defensive. We can talk here, or we can do it later in front of Marcus."

A slight breeze riffled through the shade trees and the rosebushes and a warning tingle shot up Tempest's nape. The shadows moved around them, darkening then lightening Kenny's face, just as love could turn to hatred. If Kenny had anything to do with the Greystones' deaths, Tempest intended to know.

Eyes like Marcus's narrowed, and Kenny seemed to loom over her. But Tempest wasn't backing off. "I'm here, doing a job for Marcus."

"Yeah, and I know what kind of a job. He's rich, and you're in his blood. He'll pay, in the end. You've fed him some cock-and-bull story about finding that hit-and-run driver. You didn't see what he went through. I did. Now you got him all revved up again, wanting to go over the whole mess again. You already stirred up trouble between us, because he wants you to have free rein to nose into people's business."

Kenny clearly wanted to argue, but Tempest noted that flash of fear in his expression. She knew that he was terrified of her questions. But nothing could change the color of his eyes or Marcus's, father and son. "You were here when the Greystones died, weren't you?"

Kenny rolled his shoulders and settled his chin into his full beard, his stare shadowed and wary. "Why?"

"I'm trying to find the driver of that hit-and-run. He—or she—is a murderer, Kenny, and has to pay."

Kenny no longer seemed defensive; he seemed startled and upset. "You think I did it? That's why you're asking me questions?"

"I just need answers. If you're afraid to answer my questions, I'll ask Marcus to ask them. He will. He's determined, but I doubt that he knows you have several degrees—engineering right?"

He inhaled sharply. "How do you know that?"

"I just do. Now tell me what happened to your hand." If Kenny as Marcus's biological father was blackmailing Winona, she might have threatened to expose him. If murdering Jason was the motive to get Winona to go with him, Kenny just might fit the bill.

Kenny's good hand immediately covered his scarred one, the movement protective. "So you're going to hightail it back to Marcus and play your little games and get me fired, is that it? If I don't give you what you want?"

"I'm good at getting what I want." Tempest ignored Kenny's knowing snicker. "And I want to know what happened to your hand."

"That's for me to know," he stated roughly, and then stepped inside his house, firmly closing the door. But there had been that glimpse of fear again, an insight into why he wanted to avoid her questions; Kenny feared she was getting too close.

Tempest stared at the two red tomatoes on the charcoal grill. "I'll find out, you know."

She studied the tools braced against the shed and started toward them. She had almost removed one glove when a familiar chill lifted the hairs on her nape. She slowly turned to the shadows beneath that old oak tree and found Marcus's tall body.

Tempest pulled on her glove, walked to him, and tilted her head up to look at Marcus. If he wanted to leave his good friend out of her research, that wasn't possible. "I have a job to do, and I'm doing it. Kenny was here at the time of your parents' accident."

Was it possible that Marcus's biological father would have wanted to kill Winona and her unborn child? Why?

Marcus's grim expression was a younger version of Kenny's anger just moments earlier. "Figures you'd want to talk with him. But you could have asked me to come along instead of your little 'shopping' story. He's a little sensitive to you now, and already suspicious. Sneaking around in his backyard doesn't help. I don't want any miscommunication between you now. He knows I'm backing you, but sometimes, Tempest, you can come at people wrong. Kenny and I went over every detail for years, and he knows how badly I want that killer. But you might put a different spin on something we've missed and open up a lead. Did he tell you anything that might help?"

Tempest decided not to tell Marcus that Kenny's unfriendly reaction to her was probably out of fear. He definitely wanted the past to remain untouched. "I think he can help. How did you know I was here?"

"Next time, I want to be with you. I saw Cody downtown, and he told me you had asked where Kenny lived. He said you'd headed this way. From what I know of Kenny, Jason hired him to take over the marina when I was two or so. He's been here ever since. I trust him. When I was a kid, I stayed over here more than at home. I grew my own tomatoes right in that garden over there. He could have lived in my house, or I would have given him a nice place and enough to live on. He didn't need to work such long hours at the marina, but maybe it keeps him going. . . . Let's go."

"You're uncomfortable digging into his past, Marcus. But I can't leave him out of this."

Marcus's expression was grim. "I don't expect you to. He's worried about me, that's all. He wants to protect me from going through everything again. I'll talk to him. What did you and Cody talk about, other than where Kenny lives?"

"Kenny. Cody said that he and his friend—"

"Sean."

"Uh-huh. Sean and Cody sometimes go to Kenny's for gaming. Cody has a little sister, and he's worried about her, that something might happen to her. He didn't say why, only that he had to help her. He's obviously upset and nervous and needed a friendly talk. Meanwhile, I discouraged his crush on me. He's a good kid, but scared."

Marcus glanced at a side street. "There's that van again, that kid Sean. It's driving too slow and looks like it's circling the block. Did Cody say anything about Sean?"

"Just that he's changed in the last two days. I think Cody might be scared of him."

Marcus's jaw tightened. "Or someone. I'll want to talk with Sean and see if either kid knows Whitcomb."

"That's a long shot, Marcus."

"Long shots sometimes pay off."

Nine

"I'LL STILL HAVE TO TALK WITH KENNY. AND WITH YOU around, I might not get the reaction I need," Tempest said, as Marcus took her hand.

"You're not pushing him now. Wait until both of you cool down." Moving swiftly away from Kenny's house, Marcus pulled her into the back alley and past the backyards of several houses.

"But—" When Marcus slashed a grim, set look at her, Tempest opted for a later, better moment. She wasn't exactly in a good mood herself. If she'd pressed the point, she might have revealed her suspicion that Kenny was actually Marcus's father.

Marcus didn't stop pulling her away from Kenny's house until they reached a vacant house two blocks away. He walked across the backyard to the BMW waiting in the driveway. Marcus pushed her into the passenger seat and lowered his face to speak to her. His tone was quiet, but fierce. "Okay, you obviously didn't go shopping. What's next on your hit list?"

"Okay then, take me to Opal or to Francesca. They were both around at the time." In love with Winona, Opal definitely had reason to kill Jason. Or rebuffed by Winona, she might have wanted to kill them both. Francesca might know some tidbit that could lead to answers.

Marcus inhaled abruptly, impatiently, and then closed her door. As he crossed in front of the car, he leveled a dark "stay put and don't try anything" look at Tempest.

He reversed the car onto the street. As he drove, Marcus glanced at Tempest, the shadows from the trees above the street periodically darkening his face, emphasizing the silver of his eyes. "They were both questioned at the time of the accident . . . everyone was. Opal almost had a breakdown. Be careful with her, too. Like Kenny, she's suspicious of you already."

"I think it's strange that she wanted your parents' room kept as it was."

Marcus shrugged. "It didn't matter to me. I thought if it helped her get through her grief, then fine."

Tempest leveled a look at him. "It matters to me. You want answers, don't you?"

He might not like the answers she got—one in particular, about Kenny. Marcus handled the car easily through Port Salem's narrow, winding residential streets down to Main Street. "She's an old woman, Tempest. Be careful how you ask questions, but ask them anyway."

"She's tougher than you think, and she might know something—someone connected to their deaths. I need to talk with her, watch her reactions—without you. I hunt better without you around, and that includes talking to Kenny," Tempest stated firmly, as Marcus pulled into a parking spot on Main Street. "And you probably have other business, don't you?"

He watched that gray van drive slowly by, two silhouettes in the cab. The youths seemed to be appearing a little too frequently for Marcus's comfort. "You wanted to talk to Francesca. We're parked in front of her office. I'm walking to the marina . . . it's just across the drawbridge. You can reach me on my cell or the marina's number when you're finished. Do it."

Inside Francesca's office, Marcus was warm, friendly, and charming—unlike the man who had taken Tempest's hand and practically dragged her away from Kenny's. He returned the tall blonde's hug with obvious affection. "Francesca, this is my friend, Tempest Storm. She's staying at the house, and we're not going to need maid service until I call you, okay?"

Francesca's very blue eyes seemed to brighten, pinning Tempest, going over her black shirt and cargo-style shorts, the big silver cuff bracelet and large multipurpose watch, both with Celtic symbols. Francesca took in Tempest's well-worn running shoes and quickly concealed her distaste. "Hello, Tempest. Please sit down. What an unusual name. That silver brooch is unusual—but very attractive. Is that a dog's head?"

"Why, I believe it is, Francesca," Tempest returned with a smile she didn't feel. As she sat across the desk from the older woman, Tempest studied Francesca. Tall, classy, artfully made up to conceal her midforties to fiftyish age, the blond woman had had some reparative nip and tuck.

Meanwhile, Francesca's cerulean blue eyes—aided by tinted contact lenses—studied Tempest.

"Tempest created that brooch. She's a sculptor and designs jewelry," Marcus stated. "Francesca, I'm needing a little favor. I'm having a party, and I was wondering if you—"

When Tempest turned to him, stunned by his abrupt plans, his smile was brief and bland. "Oh, did I forget to tell you, Tempest? A little business, a little poker. You'd be bored, and the other men aren't bringing their ladies. Francesca helped my mother with parties, and she's continued to help me."

Francesca evidently wanted to draw the conversation back to the potential money she could make. "I'd love to take care of the party, Marcus. At the house, or on the lake?"

"The lake . . . fewer interruptions that way."

"The *Titan* then, a perfect yacht for a party. Just tell me the date, and I'll have my people out there cleaning. Is the *Titan* here?"

"I'm not using the *Titan* this time. It's time the *Winona* had some lake duty. She'll be anchored offshore, just in front of the house."

Francesca blinked suddenly, seemingly stunned. "The *Winona*? But she hasn't been used . . . she's been in dry storage for years."

"That's why I think she needs to be used. I want something a little different. Something suitable for an all-night, high-stakes poker game. Kenny's kept her cleaned, but your people might go over her. If you could stock the refrigerator and the bar, supply the heads and the rooms, freshen the sheets and towels, provide gift baskets, that sort of thing, I'd appreciate it. I want my guests to be comfortable."

Tempest stared at him. Poker? High stakes? Marcus had wanted to know more about Brice, and he was a high-stakes poker player.

Francesca quickly jotted down notes. "How many?"

Marcus's gray eyes flickered at Tempest. "I'm not sure. I just sent out the invitations . . . four at the minimum, six at the maximum, including me. It's more business than a game, Francesca."

"Of course. You've always had a good head for business."

Tempest didn't trust Marcus's guarded expression. He'd done something she wouldn't like—something that involved her, and he was hiding it. If it concerned Brice, who was apparently hunting her, she wanted to know. Tempest didn't wait—she simply jerked off her glove and took his hand.

The bond was stronger than she had expected. But then she'd given him that integral part of herself; at the same time she'd taken something of his energy into her, hadn't she? She'd touched him before, but was still unprepared for the masculine jolt, the layers of his past. Then anger, revenge, disgust for another man ran up her arm like a ribbon, the energy burning her, the savage emotion possessive and territorial. She closed her eyes and saw Brice. A high-stakes poker game with Brice! "You didn't."

"I did. Francesca, the game will take place in a couple of days, three at the most, depending on when the other gentlemen accept my invitation. Do you think you can have the *Winona* ready that quickly?" As he spoke, his eyes never left Tempest, his fingers laced with hers. A sexual force pulsed from Marcus, caught her midsection, and sank lower. She could feel him in her, pushing, throbbing, the heat riveting her until she barely caught her breath.

Skin against skin, bodies wrapped in lovemaking, breathing hard, caressing. Marcus smiled slightly, his eyes shielded but hot. She could feel his lips tugging at her breasts, his hands going over her, touching her just there— Tempest suddenly realized that Francesca was watching the play between them, and fought the blush rushing up her cheeks.

He wanted to imprint his lovemaking over any other man's because she was his. His fierce need for possession terrified her . . . she had to pull free. Tempest closed her eyes and tugged her hand free, breaking the bond. Her hands shook as she drew on her glove; Marcus knew exactly what he was doing. He was reminding her that they were lovers, that he had undeniable status and therefore rights in her life and her protection.

Francesca frowned, evidently understanding the play between Marcus and Tempest. The older woman stared at Tempest's gloved hands, clenched tightly on the arms of her chair.

"I thought you had something you wanted to do, Marcus," Tempest managed huskily.

"Yes, go ahead if you want, Marcus. I'll take care of the *Winona* and make certain your guests are comfortable. I am really surprised you're using the *Winona*."

"It's time to put her back in the water. I'll leave you two ladies alone. Francesca, I would appreciate your spending time with Tempest and giving her whatever information she needs."

Francesca tensed slightly. "Information?"

"Places to shop, beauty shops, girl stuff," Tempest said easily, concealing her real reason to talk with Francesca. She also wanted to place distance between Marcus's fierce sexuality and her own reactions to him. His sensual energy still pulsed in her, and she was very close to reaching a climax—right in front of the other woman. "Go ahead, Marcus. I'll catch up with you later. I'd like to talk about that poker party."

"Oh, I know you'd like to know every detail. But stay here until I come back, will you?" Marcus squeezed her hand with enough pressure to let her know he wasn't exactly asking. He didn't trust her not to stay away from Kenny now, or to visit Opal.

Marcus glanced at the street beyond the office's window. "There's that van. Francesca, do you know anything about a boy named Sean and Cody Smith?"

Francesca smiled and shook her head. "Cody works for Kenny, you could ask him. I don't know a Sean."

Tempest watched Marcus stride away, a sleek, powerful predator on the move, his long legs quickly crossing the drawbridge over the narrowest part of the harbor. She glanced at Francesca and noted the other woman watching Marcus as well.

Now, facing Francesca Pointe in her sleek blue suit—a little overdressed for the casual inhabitants of Port Salem—Tempest understood that look: Francesca was definitely attracted to Marcus.

Tempest had wondered why Francesca, the owner of a maid service business, would take particular and personal interest in cleaning the sprawling Greystone home. And now she knew.

"I see you wear gloves," Francesca said. "That's odd in July, especially with such casual wear, and they're leather, too. I hope your hands are all right, dear."

"I have a little hand problem."

Francesca's sympathetic tone did not match those bright, watchful eyes. "There is a lovely shop in town— La Femme. It has gloves. Perhaps you'd like to shop there for other gloves."

She smiled and spoke as if sharing a confidence. "You will get better service though, if you dress differently. It's a little upscale. Tell me, how long have you known Marcus?"

"Not quite a year. We met last October. I was doing a showing of my work—I'm a sculptor, as Marcus said. He purchased a piece of mine."

"Ah." In that one syllable Francesca inferred that Tempest was after a wealthy lover. "Will you be attending, after the game? And do you have any suggestions for food or sleeping arrangements? The *Winona* has two bedrooms as I remember and two bathrooms."

Sleeping arrangements. Francesca was already well aware that Marcus and Tempest were lovers. She'd just witnessed an intimate lovers' scene in which Marcus had concentrated on making love to Tempest. From that call on the beach, he'd noted that she was highly receptive to him, and he was right on target in assuming that she'd pick up any sexual energy he projected.

Fine. Just great. There she sat in an office chair, her thong slightly damp in the aftermath of Marcus's sexual probe. He would have to pay for that, and if he had really invited Brice Whitcomb to his poker party.

The offshore poker game would certainly draw

Brice, if invited. Marcus was stepping into her life and taking over, but then boys will be boys—and given another name, this poker game served the purpose of an old-fashioned duel. Over her. A little helpless female. Just great.

Tempest smiled sweetly. "I haven't been invited, before or after the poker party, and Marcus can answer any of your questions, I'm sure. I was wondering. . . Marcus doesn't talk much about his parents. I was wondering what you could tell me."

Francesca hesitated only a heartbeat, but it was enough for Tempest to note a quick frown, a tightening of those artificially full lips. "I think it would be best if Marcus answered your questions, don't you?"

She'd deflected quite nicely, but Tempest wasn't giving up. Intuition told her that Francesca was hiding something, and Tempest was going to dig it out. Without touching, she didn't have Claire's empathic gift, but she could read body posture and expression. Tempest sensed that this initial encounter might be the most important, that Francesca would be well prepared for another round.

What was that Marcus had said? Like father, like son? Attracted to one, attracted to the other?

Tempest decided to push that tidbit, and added, "I am seeking specific information about Jason Greystone."

"She's after something," Kenny said as he entered and closed the door to Greystone Marina building's interior office. He placed a sack filled with garden vegetables on a side table, stuffed some cut roses into a jar, and sat facing Marcus. "You're going to have to watch out for that girl. She's after something," he repeated darkly. "And she's trouble, just like I said. And those roses are for Fred's wife. He puts in long hours here, and she deals with a whole houseful of kids."

"Don't worry. I get the point. The roses won't go to Tempest. You told me what you thought of her when you brought the boards to fix the railing." Marcus looked up from the marina's computer; he'd just tele-connected with his own laptop in the house. He'd been going over plans for pontoon boats and his notes about Greystone's new line of bass boats that would be man-ufactured in the Midwest. He signed off and glanced at his wristwatch. It had already been a good half hour since he'd left Tempest at Francesca's. How much longer before she called?

He drew a deep breath, aware that his intended sexual probe, focused on making love to Tempest—had a backlash. For just those few heartbeats, he'd felt the shape of her breasts, the pliant warm flesh beneath his hands. He'd felt the slick warmth of her body en-closing his—and he'd hardened instantly. Fully aroused, hungry for Tempest, his walk to the door and across the drawbridge to the marina hadn't been pleas-ant. Concentrating on business was necessary to force his mind and body away from making love with Tem-pest.

Marcus studied the hot pink roses. She'd actually blushed. Think of that—as if she were embarrassed and sweet and—

"You look like a damn lovesick fool," Kenny noted curtly. "She came to my place, hunting around the backyard. I ran her off. There's no reason for her to come see me. None at all."

Kenny hadn't known that Marcus had observed the exchange. Tempest wasn't the only curious one now. Kenny's dislike of Tempest had been apparent from the start, and for no apparent reason. Kenny was uneasy now and restless, his expression guarded and tense. He'd always been very private about his back-ground, and Marcus suspected that the damaged hand was connected to Kenny's reticence somehow. Kenny might not purposefully withhold information, some lead, but he wasn't going to be very open with Tempest now. Marcus decided to give Kenny some time before asking him questions about that hand. "She's just naturally curious, and she's a little impetuous. But I want her working on this. I'll talk to her. I'd like you two to get along."

Marcus glanced across the channel to the slow-moving van. Kenny wasn't the only uneasy one; Sean's van had appeared too often for comfort. With Whitcomb hunting Tempest, anything out of the ordinary around her was suspicious. It probably wasn't anything, but still, Sean better have good reason to be hanging around so much.

"I know you want that killer, but I don't see how that girl is going to turn up anything but a whole lot of trouble. Jason made a lot of enemies when he took up with that woman. Her boyfriend didn't like it much, and he was connected to some criminal types. You have to be careful, Marcus. You know that," Kenny stated quietly. "Every once in a while some filth from back then surfaces, and you deal with it."

"It's a nasty little inheritance. But Tempest doesn't have anything to do with my father's enemies." Marcus was watching Francesca hurry down the sidewalk opposite the marina and disappear in the direction of her home. She was moving quickly, her head bent. Then she glanced around and behind her, as if fearing someone followed her.

Tempest wasn't with her. Marcus quickly dialed Tempest's cell phone, and she didn't answer. There was one other person she'd wanted to see—Opal—and Tempest had said that she couldn't work well with him around. Okay, so maybe he was a little protective of his friends, but Tempest needed protection, too. That anchor almost fell on her, and that near accident four stories up would make an ordinary woman just a little cautious about being out on her own—especially since Whitcomb wanted her either back, or dead.

As he hurried out of the office, Marcus said, "Kenny, I have to go. Get the *Winona* down and ready, okay? Maybe it's time she saw a little lake duty. I'll need her for a little party in two–three days."

Kenny frowned and said, "That's quick, isn't it? Any reason why?"

"To settle an old debt."

On his way back to his BMW in front of Francesca's office, Marcus dialed Opal at her condominium. Tempest had two down and one to go on her list, and that was Opal. His casual call pleased her, but she hadn't seen Tempest. Marcus noted the distaste in Opal's tone; she didn't like Tempest either. Her appraisal of Tempest agreed with Kenny's—Tempest was definitely hunting. "If she turns up, have her call me, will you?"

His next call was to Francesca's mobile phone; she wasn't answering, unusual for her given the good relationship they'd had over the years.

Apparently in just two days, Tempest had managed to upset the people who were most like his family.

Marcus reached Pointe Maid Service's locked office and looked around. Tempest was nowhere in sight.

"Hi, Cody." As she left La Femme with her purchases tucked into her backpack, she met the youth. As before on the beach, he seemed uneasy, but he swung in beside her. He kept looking around, his eyes avoiding hers. "Is something wrong, Cody?"

"Nah, I'm just worried about my little sister, that's all."

"Do you want to tell me about it? Maybe I can help."

He shook his head and stuck his hands in his pockets as they walked along. He looked at the busy street, the tourists standing in front of the shop windows.

"She's just getting a little wild, that's all, running with the wrong crowd. The folks can't do anything with her, and I'm sure nothing to look up to. Look, you haven't been here long. If you want to go somewhere, I could show you around and walk you there."

"That would be nice. Do you know Opal, the house-keeper at the Greystone house?"

"Yeah. That old lady lives over at the condos by the lake. Everybody is talking about why she had to move out of the house when you moved in. News travels fast here. It's this way."

She should have heard the gray van coming up behind them. The parking garage of Opal's condominium was quiet, dark, and lonely, with only a few cars in it.

When the tires squealed on the concrete behind them, the vehicle coming in too fast, Tempest pushed Cody to safety. To avoid getting hit, she rolled over the hood of a parked car and came down on her knees. When she rose to her feet, Sean was already upon her, holding her. Despite her struggle, a cloth covered her face, the smell pungent before she slid into unconsciousness.

Tempest surfaced slowly, and felt as though her brain were full of cotton. Metallic sounds and hard rap music beat heavily all around her, pounding, increasing her headache. She was lying on the floor of the van, her arms tied behind her, her legs tied at the ankles. The van's doors were closed, and the space was filled with dirty clothing and blankets. Her backpack lay beside her, the contents evidently rummaged. Her small sketching notebook lay open. Her billfold had been emptied of bills and credit cards. She heard male voices outside the van and wasted no time in working her small knife out of the sheath and cutting the cord around her wrists and feet. She prayed that Cody was safe.

As an extra precaution, she drew her cell phone from its holder on her belt and dialed Marcus. "I can't talk now," he murmured curtly before ending the connection.

Great. Marcus was busy.

The throbbing music stopped, and she heard Marcus's voice. "Hello, boys. Nice place you have here. Of course, the Evans family might not approve of you moving in while they're away."

Tempest tensed, her body chilled. If Marcus hadn't brought help, he'd be outnumbered; she'd counted at least two different voices, and one of them was yelling, "Shoot him, Cody! Give me the gun!"

Cody? He was in on this?

At the mention of the boy's name, Tempest's anger ignited. She tried the van's double doors, and then pushed them open. One door hit a man and he yelped, sprawling to the floor as she leaped from the van. She quickly went into action, taking down Sean. His gun went skittering across the garage floor. The man on the floor was on his feet, making for the closed door; she had just raised her fist for a blow when she recognized him. "Cody!"

He cowered away from her. "Don't hit me. You weren't supposed to see me. You wouldn't have known anything about me. You weren't hurt, see? You're okay," he tried lamely.

Marcus was holding the handgun now; he placed it on a work counter. "Okay, is she? After being manhandled and pushed into that van? Oh, I'm sure she's just fine."

The two young men cowered back against one wall and froze as a police siren sounded, coming nearer.

"About time. I called before I crashed this party," Marcus said as he flicked a button on the wall and the garage door opened. Instantly, Sean bolted toward freedom.

Unfortunately for him, he had to pass Tempest, who stuck out her foot. He tumbled and fell, sprawled on the concrete. Then he jackknifed to his feet and went for her. The momentum threw Tempest back against the van and for just a heartbeat, while he pinned her wrists, she saw his eyes, filled with rage. There was something else in Sean's expression, like satisfaction, as if he finally had her, and she deserved to die. In that second, that blink of time, Tempest recognized the same burning rage that had been on the objects her sister's attacker had touched.

She had to move fast; her knee jerked up into his crotch.

For an instant, Sean seemed unharmed. Her glove had slid down so that his fingers touched her naked palm, and she caught his energy. A wave of darkness and evil, deep and contaminating everything it touched, burned through her; it prickled with the need for revenge past this moment, for something she'd done. Stunned by the fiery need to hurt her, to make her pay, Tempest couldn't take her eyes away from the youth's. They were locked in silence with only the sound of her racing heartbeat in her ears.

"Tempest," he whispered so softly, his lips barely moving.

She shivered, recognizing the voice as the one from the fog, his energy the same as the fog she'd held in her bare hands. It felt like the rage of Claire's attacker. "Who are you?"

Suddenly, he was jerked away, and Marcus's fist sent him against the wall. The youth slid down slowly to the floor, still pinning her with those flat, black eyes. They were cold now, as if something had retreated in him, slithering back where it couldn't be found.

"Later," he whispered, as if promising revenge at another time.

She couldn't look away, still trapped by the moment when something between them connected and terrified her.

"Stay put," Marcus advised the youths quietly as several police cars pulled up on the street.

The officers quickly secured the young men. One officer walked to Marcus and Tempest; he apparently knew Marcus. "It looks like everything is under control here. The Evanses aren't going to like these kids using their home, and they're facing a list of charges. Good thing you saw that van and those two boys pushing her into it. You handled it just right, Marcus. Miss, do you need to see a doctor?"

"No. I just want to go home." She allowed herself to lean against Marcus, who held her tightly against him. Tempest realized she was clutching his side as if he were necessary to her, and that she had just stated her "home" was Marcus's.

"She's staying with me, Mac. Meet Tempest Storm. Tempest, this is Mac Henderson, our police chief." Marcus continued supplying information as the other man jotted down details. "Glad you arrived when you did. Thanks."

"Heard about you, Miss Storm. You'll both need to make statements. It looks like these boys have moved up from petty theft. You'll have to testify. Marcus, follow us to the station."

"Will do." Marcus went to Tempest, who was still leaning back against the van. "You're safe now, Tempest."

"Am I?" She couldn't move, frozen in those few heartbeats when Sean's eyes had locked with hers, had connected in a way she didn't understand. She rubbed her hand where the skin seemed to have been branded—marked by his rage. Cody thought that they were just taking credit cards and money, and that she wouldn't be harmed. But Sean's expression said he had had other plans. She didn't want to think of what he might have done to her if she hadn't been found. But it wouldn't have been pleasant.

Cody was standing on the sidewalk, ready to be loaded into the back of the police car. He glanced at her, then hung his head. "Wait a minute," Tempest called as she walked toward him.

"I'm sorry. Sean said you wouldn't get hurt . . . he promised," he said as tears ran down his cheeks. "He said if I didn't help him get your money and credit cards, Sissy was going to pay real hard. I didn't know what to do. He was okay, and then he just changed. He got real mean, and I was afraid for Sissy."

"Who changed, Cody?" Marcus's hand was on her shoulder now.

Cody's eyes shifted to the other police car; Sean stared back at them from the rear window. The tinted glass did not hide his hatred, which seemed locked on Tempest.

As the police car drove away, she shuddered, because she knew that whatever her life experiences had been, she'd never been so close to such living evil.

Ten

———

"YOU HAVEN'T STOPPED STARING AT THE LAKE SINCE WE got home from making our statements at the police station. Is anything else bothering you, other than what happened today?"

Tempest couldn't stop shivering throughout the tea and toast Marcus had quickly prepared for her when they'd returned home. Now, at seven-thirty, the fog was rolling in from the lake; she could almost feel it beckoning her.

She'd been terrified for her sisters, and angry and deeply ashamed, and she'd grieved—but she'd never experienced pure terror since she was three and that sailboat had overturned.

That afternoon, she had been terrified . . . because of what she'd seen in Sean's eyes and how his rage had burned her palm. Whatever was inside the young tough named Sean O'Donnel was stronger than he was. It had simply enveloped him—owned him. She shivered as she remembered his voice, like the one she'd heard in the fog, *Later.* . . .

According to the police, her kidnapping was a new twist for Sean. He'd grown up in foster homes, never quite fitting in; he was a loner, and shy. A heavy computer "gamer" and electronically linked to others, he'd never been a leader, or instigated any crime worse than minor theft, and that had been because of hunger and necessity. Until today, Sean's only crimes were breaking into homes to raid a refrigerator, steal a few groceries, warm clothing, and, once, a sleeping bag. He'd been staying in a run-down shack just inside the city limits. According to Cody, two days ago Sean had suddenly become cruel, dominating, and had threatened the life of Cody's little sister. He had changed from a friend into a driven bully.

Or something had changed him.

Behind her, Marcus was evidently frustrated. "All right, Tempest. What gives? What's going on with you? I saw how you reacted to that kid."

The telephone rang, and Marcus's voice sounded impatient. "Greystone."

Tempest felt his tension seep into her. When she turned, Marcus looked at her, and said, "Okay. Yes, I thought it was something like that. Thanks for the call, Mac. Good-bye."

When Marcus stood and stared at her, prickles rose up Tempest's nape. Sensitive to his uneasiness, she asked, "What is it?"

"Two things: Cody said that Sean had been in the marina. Cody admitted that he had deliberately left the marina's door on the top story unlatched, and Sean used it to get in. He was up there when that anchor let loose and almost killed you. Figures . . . someone was seen going down those back stairs just after it happened."

That anchor could have killed her. Sean had probably tampered with it. It wasn't an accident—Sean had meant to kill her!

Tempest's fingers bit into her upper arms. She had an eerie sense that she knew what Marcus's next words would be. If Sean followed the same path as Claire's attacker, who committed suicide—Marcus's next words hit her like mallets. "Sean hanged himself in his cell. He's dead, and all hell has broken loose down at the station. A full investigation is getting set up, a state forensics team about to descend on them. Mac says the media are already swarming the place. He's had to call in extra men and ask for overtime."

Tempest's blood ran cold, and the image of Sean's face, his fury and need for revenge flashed in her mind. *Later. . . .*

Her sister's attacker had committed suicide, too! He'd been reached through his computer by evil and rage so great that it had burned Tempest's hands. Sean's touch had burned her like a brand. He wanted to destroy her; he wanted revenge. For what? What?

She rubbed her hand, trying to wipe away his touch. Whatever had been in Sean had reached into her, linked to her energy somehow. "I've got to get out of here. Right now," she whispered as terror spread over her. She looked outside to the bank of fog, now almost at the windows. Her panic rose and spilled into words. "It wants me. I know it does. At first, I thought it might be my father, calling to me—but it isn't. It's ugly, and it's evil, and it wants me. It's locked on to me, and it knows me. It knows how I breathe, how my heart sounds. No—don't answer that, please!"

Marcus had started toward her, then he stopped as the telephone rang. Tempest shook her head that she didn't want to talk to her sister, Leona. He picked up the telephone. "Greystone."

Marcus wanted to hold Tempest in his arms, to protect her. She was all nerves, obviously terrified, and he was in no mood for Leona's abrupt, "What the hell is going on?"

"She's okay." Marcus noted the sound of tires on pavement; Leona was in a car somewhere, and emotional drivers were more likely to have accidents. "Take it easy."

"Don't you lie to me. This is my sister, and I know when she's okay. She's not."

"Okay, she's not." Marcus quickly filled Leona in on what had happened to her sister, then watched Tempest enter her bedroom.

"I knew it," Leona said quietly. "Get her away from that lake and do it now."

When Tempest quickly emerged, carrying her backpack and leather jacket, Marcus watched her hurry toward the rear of the house, which led to the driveway. "I think she's leaving now. Bye."

Marcus found Tempest on the back deck, clutching her backpack in her arms as if it could protect her. She was staring at the fog curling around her ankles. "Tempest?"

She looked terrified, unable to move, as if she were standing amid a nest of snakes. Her cell phone was ringing as it had each time she'd been in danger, and Tempest hadn't anticipated the call this time. Marcus didn't hesitate; he looped an arm around Tempest's waist and carried her back inside. When he tried to stand her on her feet, her knees gave way, and he caught her. Still locked in whatever had happened outside, her green eyes seemed to glow within her pale face. She stared at him blankly and shivered as if freezing. On the second call, Marcus took the cell phone from her waist, flicked it open, and said, "She's okay. She's with me. She'll call you later, Leona."

"Marcus, this is Claire," the woman's soft but alarmed voice stated. "Let me talk to her."

He handed the phone to Tempest, and she gripped it like a lifeline. "I know, Claire. It's here. I felt it. . . . Yes, I'm okay." Tempest glanced at Marcus and her expression softened, her skin began to color again. "Yes, I know what he is. No, he doesn't know. I'll think about it. I just had a bad scare, but I'm okay. . . . No, they didn't hurt me. . . . I can't change what I am,

Claire Bear. I love you truly, I do, but I have to finish this. I have to. . . . I just got scared, that's all—and you felt it? I'm so sorry, I didn't mean to upset you. . . . I'm okay."

After Tempest ended the call, she moved away from Marcus, walking slowly to the window to stare at the fog outside. He followed, noting the unusual way the droplets formed on the windows, snaking down the glass, the patterns curving toward Tempest. In her customary black sweater and pants, she looked very small and vulnerable when framed by the ceiling-to-floor windows. The porch lights were on and reflected in the mist, causing it to sparkle against a gray background.

Marcus came up behind Tempest and wrapped his arms around her, nuzzling her face. Her skin was warm now, when it had been so cold during their time at the police station. When Sean had whispered to her, her eyes had widened in fear, and her skin had paled as if the blood had drained from it. Until then, she'd seemed in control, vibrant, furious, and ready for revenge. Her emotions had been clearly written on her face. But after that moment when she'd been trapped against the van, Tempest had been too quiet, her face like a mask.

She'd changed in that moment when Sean whispered something to her. With Marcus's arms around her, she seemed to relax slightly and leaned back against him. Her gloved hand pressed his against her body, the other gripping her wolf's-head brooch.

"What happened when that kid, Sean, held you against the van? You didn't react immediately. It was as if you were looking inside him, trying to find something. What was going on? What did he say to you?"

"He said, 'Later.' You wouldn't understand."

"Make me. He's dead now. He can't hurt you."

"If he sabotaged that anchor and tried to kill me,

then it's also possible that he was standing out in the fog last night, isn't it? When I was on the marina's ladder? His voice sounded the same."

"That's possible. But there's no way he would know in advance that you'd be on that ladder. Maybe he was just passing by and saw you up there. Maybe he called out to you. We'll never know now." Marcus glanced at the dark figure moving across the front deck. It stopped in the center of the windows; only a black shape outlined by the porch light, it could have been peering either into the house or toward the lake. He placed Tempest aside and hurried to the door—if it was one of Sean's friends, he was in for a surprise.

Marcus was on the cloaked figure in two steps, tearing off the hood. The bones beneath his hand were fragile, the woman's upturned face pale, a match to Tempest's. A strand of vibrant red hair cut across her cheek. "Get me in the house," she ordered unevenly.

"Leona!" Tempest had already moved past Marcus, quickly drawing her sister into the house. Marcus followed and secured the sliding door. The two women held each other; Leona's long, dark green cloak swirled around them as they stared, transfixed by the fog churning outside the window, their hands joined as if facing an enemy.

Marcus closed the reflective blinds and turned to the two women. The sisters matched perfectly, the same striking shade of dark red hair with fiery highlights, though Leona's was longer, shoulder-length, and smoothly turned; she wore bangs that accentuated her green eyes. Their skin was the same pale shade, almost translucent now with the fear hovering around them, their cheekbones bore the same Celtic slant, and their chins were a little to the edgy side. In contrast, Tempest's jaw was a little fuller, and she was shorter by about four inches, more compact and curved than her triplet.

Leona quickly removed her cloak as if it chilled her; she tossed it to a chair and rubbed her arms. Beneath the long, loose green sweater, with a low-slung chain belt and flowing green slacks, her body was leaner than her sister's. Marcus noted Leona's stylish, long, beaded necklace and the silver brooch that matched Tempest's.

"I knew you'd come," Tempest stated quietly.

"Leona, I presume? Want me to take that?" Marcus indicated Leona's overnight bag and another smaller parcel that had been tucked beneath her cloak.

Leona lifted the bags to him, but her eyes never left him. She seemed to see inside him, right down to the bone, what he was beneath layers of civilization to the essence of what he was, his honor, his strengths and weaknesses. "Yes, you'll do," she said quietly.

A chill ran up his nape, and Marcus rolled his shoulders to ease the tension. If all the Aislings were like this one, he'd have to be on his best behavior with them around. "Sisters, huh? You could have fooled me."

Her lips curved at the obvious tease, and her head tilted, shifting that sleek gleaming hair across her smooth cheek. Graceful, cultured, Leona silently exuded class and sensuality. A contrast to Tempest's expressive face and impulsive nature, Leona would be thoughtful and poised even in the worst of situations, always in control, her expression amused now. "And a sense of humor, too."

The two women stood, arms loosely looped around each other's waist, and faced him as if considering what role he played in their lives. Marcus briefly wished he could see the triplets and their mother all together, alike and so different. "I'm glad you came, Leona," he said quietly, meaning it. "Tempest needs you. I don't understand what's going on. Maybe you can help. I hope you're staying here. I'd like that."

"That's why I'm here—for my sister. She's afraid of you, you know."

"Leona Fiona, I am not," Tempest declared vehemently and moved slightly away.

"Sure you are. If he's going to protect you better, he needs to know why. Would you mind terribly showing me the kitchen? I'd love a cup of tea."

"I'll put your things in a guest room, then I'll set the kettle on." Marcus moved quickly away. He sensed that Leona had come to check him out. He also sensed that if she wasn't pleased, there would be hell to pay. From the sound of the women's fierce arguing going on behind him, hell might have started without him.

"I said I was finishing this. I need to. You know that," Tempest stated adamantly.

"You've always been too impulsive." Leona's voice was soft, but no less fierce. Marcus sensed that this sister-older-by-three-minutes wasn't a woman to test lightly.

The argument continued while Marcus placed the overnight bag and parcel in the bedroom next to Tempest's, which was next to his. As much as he wanted Leona to spend the night, he knew it would be a lonely night without Tempest snuggled next to him. After today, all he wanted to do was to hold her tight against him and know that she was safe—either that, or paddle that cute fanny because she'd attempted to see Opal without him. He should have known Opal was on Tempest's agenda the moment she could get free.

If he hadn't known what a stubborn woman Tempest was, he might not have driven to Opal's condominium. He might not have noted the van ahead of him, or saw the youths putting an unconscious Tempest into the back of the van.

Aware that any fast moves on Marcus's part could have resulted in harm to Tempest, he had used the element of surprise.

The women's argument moved past the guest-room doorway and seemed to be headed toward the kitchen. "What do you mean, you have to 'finish' this? Don't you realize it could finish you?" Leona was saying.

"You always were bossy."

"Because you are too impulsive. You always were."

Marcus sighed and followed the women. It was going to be a very long night. His conversation with Tempest—okay, it would probably be an argument— would have to wait. He leaned against the doorway of the kitchen and watched the two women move almost in sync, as if they'd made tea together many, many times.

They rummaged over the basket of teas that Opal had provided, discussing the proper one for the night. Marcus hadn't been aware that tea flavors were selected on the basis of mood and time. Apparently, green tea with a touch of orange seemed just right. "Cups are up there in the cupboard. He doesn't have a teapot. I've looked. Just toss the bags into the pan after the water boils. We can have our tea while we fix dinner," Tempest stated briskly.

For some odd reason, Marcus felt suddenly deficient, incapable of providing the simplest thing for his woman; it was an uneasy feeling.

"I can order in," he suggested as he watched Tempest bend into the open refrigerator, studying the contents. His senses locked on to the wiggle of her bottom. He remembered the way it felt, soft and cupped in his palms as Tempest rode him, and hoped his tone was conversational. It came out a little deep and husky. "Did you fly or drive all the way, Leona?"

"I packed myself into the car the moment after I talked to Tempest this morning. You're just lucky our mother didn't come. She can be a real witch."

"Nice thing to say about our mother, Leona," Tempest reprimanded as she whipped something in a bowl. She tossed fresh blueberries in flour and added them to the mixture. Then she ran her hand over a griddle heating on the stove as if expertly testing the temperature. "Dishes are over in that cupboard, Leona . . . silverware in the drawer. Butter in the French butter keeper on the table and there's quite the selection of syrups in that cabinet. Marcus, would you like bacon and eggs with your pancakes?"

"Ah—" But Tempest had already started the bacon sizzling. "Yes. That would be great. I didn't know you could cook. Why have I been doing it?"

"You seemed so domesticated that I didn't want to interfere."

"'Domesticated' sounds like a tamed animal." Marcus settled in to brood about how Tempest saw him—a man without a teapot. Strange, how something so insignificant nagged him, but then time with Tempest was never the usual. Just how did she see him, anyway? Suddenly, her appraisal of him seemed very important. Did she think he was the cold bastard that others had called him?

Marcus rolled his head, trying to dislodge the tension in his neck and shoulders. Their lovemaking was definitely fantastic, but Tempest had him on edge, and he wanted her to see him as—well, someone she wanted to settle down with.

He inhaled abruptly. Today's nightmare proved one thing was for certain—she couldn't go running off into every dangerous situation when she wanted. She'd have to adjust to a few rules.

He considered that compact body, the curves over those athletic muscles and decided to make himself more appealing.

Leona had set the table, then leaned back against the counter to sip her tea. "This is heavenly. We've got some lovely teapots in the shop, Marcus. I'll send one."

"None of those china, overdecorated things . . . something sturdy with big handles. Marcus has big hands, but he can handle very delicate things when he has to," Tempest said as she flipped a pancake, then another.

Marcus allowed himself a small tidy smirk; he had taken very good care of Tempest and her "very delicate things." It was nice to be appreciated for good work and patience, when Tempest would have rushed right on through to the mind-blasting finish line. On the other hand, he really appreciated the wait and building the hunger, too.

"No teapots like little houses or cabbages? No little flowers with vine handles?" Leona teased.

Tempest scooped the pancakes onto a platter. "Give me a break."

"You need one—a break, I mean," Leona answered grimly. "I brought the handbag you wanted to hold, the one that eerie guy touched that day in my shop."

Though the July evening was only mildly cool, Marcus lit a small fire in the living-room fireplace. Leona had appeared chilled clear through; the warmth and sound of the fire seemed to take the edge off their awareness of the fog outside. Settled in his chair, Marcus studied the two women, who seemed to be of one thought at times, murmuring quietly, the firelight catching sparks in their hair. Leona was sleek, stylish, and poised, her eyes shadowed as she took in her sister and Marcus. Watchful and protective, she considered Marcus over the rim of her wineglass. "I had to see you in the flesh," she said.

He lifted his glass and tried a light probe into Leona's psychic gift. "You've seen me before, then? In your dreams?"

"Maybe." Her tone gave him nothing and yet everything. He wondered what she'd seen, this sister who could see into the future. What had her psychic feelers gotten from the times they'd talked? Marcus had the uneasy sensation that he was being checked out; he hoped he passed muster. He felt very delicate, his very first adult experience with that emotion.

Tempest sat beside her sister and held a box on her lap. She carefully removed the lid and eased a lady's handbag out of the white tissue paper. The firelight caught on the red and black beads. At first, Marcus thought it might be a gift; Leona's hand rested on Tempest's shoulder. "Be careful, Tempest Best."

"Just a quick touch, and I'll know," she said as she slowly drew off her glove.

Marcus was instantly alarmed; he had seen how Tempest had reacted when touching the ancient brooch and in his parents' room. "Know what?"

"If they're the same," she whispered as she quickly gripped the bag.

Fire burned her fingers, snaking up her arm, darkness and evil churned in the flames, the same need for revenge that she'd felt when Claire had been attacked, the same fierce rage she'd sensed in Sean.

Leona reacted quickly; she tore the handbag from Tempest's hands, stuffed it back into the box, and placed it aside. "That's enough."

"Damn right it is," Marcus stated and moved to sit at Tempest's side. He carefully slid her naked hand inside the glove and held her hand tightly in both of his. "Whatever is going on has to stop. She's too tired now and too vulnerable. It's costing her."

"It could cost all of us, and she knows it." Leona's voice seemed to hover eerily in the room, and momentarily their combined fear skittered over the bamboo wood flooring and danced in the firelight that lit the women's faces.

"It's the same. . . ." Tempest whispered unevenly.

"Do you think it's Brice?" Leona asked.

Tempest shook her head, her tone drifted, as if she were remembering. "I don't know. I never really opened to him . . . I never touched him with my bare hands. And maybe then, thinking that I was doing something heroic and wonderful by helping him, I wouldn't have believed what I'd felt. I wasn't as strong as I am now. I could only catch the top layers when I held an object. He was quick enough and smart enough to ferret out more information and use it to his advantage. Maybe not touching him with my hands was the only thing I did do with him that was smart. At that point of my development, trying to push away my ability on a personal level, but trying to help him, I probably couldn't have withstood how evil he really was. He's a scam artist . . . smart enough to seduce a weaker mind by using a computer. He definitely manipulated me into—"

"Working as Brice Whitcomb's masked companion, Dominique," Leona added as if just remembering something she'd forgotten, something she'd intentionally pushed into a drawer.

"Companion? I was his 'freak,'" Tempest stated darkly, the emotional burn still apparent after ten years.

"I know about Dominique," Marcus informed Leona, as she glanced warily at him. "That's why I want Tempest to visit you for a couple of days."

Tempest's frown pinned him. "Marcus is having a high-stakes poker game, hoping that Brice will attend. Some macho-protective contemporary duel that is utterly senseless. I can handle myself with Brice. I have before. And I'm not going anywhere. I just got scared for a minute and wanted to run away and hide, but I won't. I'm seeing this through."

Leona's reprimand was cool and silky. "You always

were like that—taking every challenge tossed at you. Tempest, this could be deadly. Use your head."

But Tempest was clearly puzzled as she stared at Leona. "I never told you his name or mentioned 'Dominique.' Don't tell me—"

Leona suddenly stood and paced the floor, her loose slacks flowing around her long legs. "I'm getting stronger. I opened to help Claire, and now it just keeps growing. I'm a clairvoyant—okay, I admit it. I'm a true-blue precognitive. But our extra senses can morph at any time, and mine is. I've never wanted it. I never wanted to wake up in the middle of the night and know that Joel, my husband, was going to die—not while he was safe in my arms. I think that must be why I dream of being crushed—because Joel . . ."

As if unable to say more, Leona shook her head.

"It isn't our mother's fault. She couldn't help it, any more than her mother could, or we can—"

"Our grandmother killed herself because of it . . . because of what we are. She simply went mad because she couldn't deal with it anymore. It wouldn't go away, and it kept getting stronger—"

When Leona turned furiously on Tempest, Marcus wondered how many people actually had seen inside Leona's smoothly concealed emotions, her cool tones, and her poise. She glanced at Marcus, who felt as if he was a spectator watching gladiators spar. Leona shut down instantly, the cool poise returned, as if caution had come too late.

Tempest turned to Marcus. "You wanted to know why I want that brooch, why it means so much to us, why we wear my replicas for good luck? Well, I'll tell you—because it belonged to a Viking chieftain who captured our ancestor, a Celtic seer named Aisling. About a year and a half ago, Leona and Mother started dreaming the same dream—oh, don't even try to deny it, Leona. The Viking was wearing it at his shoulder, wasn't he? In your dreams? I created the replicas from both their descriptions, but I decided to use Celtic designs instead of characters that had been marred beyond recognition. The real thing looks so different."

Marcus frowned, mentally connecting the Celtic seer, Aisling, with the triplets' mother. "As in Greer Aisling, your mother?"

"Right. We were just four when Dad died in that accident. We were five when she had to manage her very unusual children and bring in money. She took Aisling as a professional name to protect us. She started a small business, working from home, and it grew."

"But she failed," Leona stated furiously. " 'Protect us?' They came and took us anyway on some trumped-up child-neglect charge, even though we had caretakers around, didn't they? And dear mother was away working a case when it happened—yes, I know you read about the case, Marcus. Tempest told me you'd researched the Blair Institute of Parapsychology, that you were a benefactor and probably invested somehow. Wonderful how parapsychology interests everyone, isn't it?" she asked bitterly. "Two days of bloody hell, that's what it was, and Claire suffered the most. All because our mother did not protect us enough."

"You've got to give that up, Leona," Tempest said quietly. "She did everything she could. There was no way she could have known that Blair parapsychologists would use false claims of child abuse and neglect to get to us. Marcus won't let that happen again . . . I've seen some of his correspondence with the Institute. He's made it clear that behavior would cause the loss of his backing, and he'd see that others withdrew as well."

"She should have expected something like that.

We've been the objects of every witch doctor wanting to make a name for himself since Greer Aisling started working as a full-time, high-profile psychic."

"Be honest, Leona," Tempest said, and this time, she was the more poised of the two women. "You knew they were coming, didn't you? You saw them in your dream the previous night. I remember how you screamed, so terrified, calling out for Mom and begging them to stop."

Leona seemed to crumble, her hands covering her face. "I was ten years old, dammit. I just thought it was a bad dream. I wanted it to be a dream, not the hell of the reality. At ten, it was a lot for Tempest and me, but far, far worse for Claire. As an empath, she absorbed every emotion from all the psychologists, and the people who wanted to make money by writing about us."

"And it just feels like we're being stalked," Tempest finished unevenly.

Marcus inhaled and leaned back. He smoothed Tempest's rigid back with his hand; she'd just shivered in spite of the room's warmth. "Someone is trying to hurt your family?"

"Some *thing*," Leona corrected. She stood, opened the blinds, and looked out into the night. Then she lifted her wineglass to the window, her tone bitter, as she said, "I'll bet we could contact Mother if we tried. We could put our little brains to the task and just broadcast a psychic connection straight to her, clear across the country to the Pacific Ocean."

"Take it easy, Leona," Tempest whispered, as Marcus drew her back into his arms. She settled against him, her arms tight around him. "I thought it was our father at first. But then, I knew. It's strong enough to seduce and kill. I have to get into Sean's place and see if I can trace that computer link."

"There's no way. Mac said they're all tied up with

Sean's suicide, and as soon as he can get some extra manpower, he's sending men out to investigate the place."

"Well, we'll just have to get in there before they do, won't we?"

Leona shook her head. "No, you don't. It's getting stronger, and you have to leave here, Tempest. If Brice comes here, he might find you. He's been threatening you for years, but now he's stepped up the pace. You could have told the police, but then, they would know that you—"

"Had helped him scam people out of their money?" Tempest finished. "Yes, that's true, but what Brice doesn't know is that I chose his victims well. They were people who had ruined others and deserved payback. I wouldn't have lasted long in prison, even temporarily, without my gloves—I'd feel everything, know everything, and I'd go mad like dear old Grams. I'll leave here when I get what I want, that hit-and-run driver."

"You should tell him," Leona said fiercely. "He has a right to know."

Tempest glanced at Marcus, and then looked down at her tightly clasped gloved hands. "I can't. Not until I'm sure."

Marcus ran his hand through his hair. There was no way he could protect Tempest without enough details. Brice Whitcomb was one thing—a living man, a vulture preying on others. But when psychics started holding secrets . . . "Oh, hell. If you're witches, and I'm in some coven, you might as well tell me now."

"That's disgusting," Leona stated. She crossed her arms and stared at Tempest as the fire crackled, the flames casting shadows on the walls. "Of course we aren't witches. We can't levitate either, or shape-shift. Rule out vampires, too."

"Okay, I guess that about covers everything." Marcus

stood and quickly crossed to a liquor cabinet. He flipped a squat fat glass from one hand to the other and poured in two fingers of bourbon. He downed the drink, appreciated the burn to keep him focused, and considered both women. Both psychics had been unraveled by the fog and the water, and it was more than a childhood accident at the base of their fears. He turned to Leona and Tempest, who now stood facing each other, their faces pale, their hair gleaming in the firelight.

Unless he missed his guess—which everything was at this point in nonreality—they were communicating, rather they were arguing silently. Leona nodded, and Tempest shook her head. He'd heard of twins doing this same thing, understanding without words, but now he was seeing it in action. "Then tell me about the brooch, why it's so important."

Tempest's voice was thin and uneven as she stared at the fire. She stood close, as if she couldn't get enough of the warmth. "It has something to do with the curse."

"What curse?" Marcus asked unevenly.

"We don't know," both women answered at once.

Then Leona said quietly, "We only think there's a curse. It feels like one, dreams like one—the both of us, Mother and I—have dreamed of some shadow filled with violence and speaking something that sounded like a curse."

Tempest glanced at Marcus, who leaned back against the bar, the empty glass in his hand. He tapped it against the gleaming teak finish as though trying to balance sturdy reality with what he'd just heard. "How do you know that whatever is out there is linked to that brooch?"

"Because when I held the brooch, I felt the energy. Not everything, but just the top layers. Something is buried beneath them, and it has to do with that curse.

It would take someone stronger than me to hold that brooch and not—"

Marcus's expression changed, those silvery eyes searching hers. "'And not' what? Die?"

"Maybe. Maybe just lose a few gray cells and turn into a maniac, or vegetable."

"It would take someone strong like Mother," Leona stated bitterly. "The Queen Mother of us all."

"Or you, if you practiced like she did. You're the strongest of us, you always were, and you know it, so lay off. We're in this together, Leona Fiona."

Leona paced in front of the fireplace. "You think I don't know that? Do you think I want it? No, and neither do you. And he's in it—another protector like Claire's Neil."

Marcus stirred uneasily, and Tempest shot him a keep-out-of-this look. She turned on Leona. "You could have told me and saved me a lot of trouble."

Leona crossed her arms and smiled smugly. "But Tempest Best, you always liked trouble and the challenge. I'd say Marcus is a whole lot of both."

Tempest glanced at Marcus. The look held and sizzled, the heat wrapping around her. If Leona wasn't present, Tempest and Marcus would likely be in bed now. The glass in his hand came down with a thud, his eyes the color of smoke, the tension in his body all spelled lovemaking and plenty of it. His look stripped the clothes from her as if he were seeing her naked. Tempest's blood heated, pounding in her ears, her body aching for his, a pulse starting deep down inside her, the hunger building. In another instant, she'd be on him.

"Um. Am I Interrupting something?" Leona purred smoothly.

Marcus's stare never left Tempest, the heat burning her as he spoke. "Let's get back to business. I get the feeling that I'm missing something. Walk me through this, so I can understand."

Tempest was too restless, her body and her nerves stretched tight. Since making love with Marcus right now wasn't an option, she began a tai chi stance.

"Claire's attacker had the same essence as the brooch, what I could feel of it. Sean had that energy, too. It's the same as what's in the fog. It holds rage as if it needs revenge. The question is why?"

"If you think your mother can unlock this thing, I'll send the brooch to her."

"That won't work. It has to be rightfully earned—I think. I'm earning it. I'll get that hit-and-run driver's name for you."

"She has to take it to our mother," Leona supplied quietly. "Tempest has to earn it and deliver it in person. It means everything to her."

"Yes, it does," Tempest agreed. "I betrayed everything about my family. I sold out and I lost myself. I may not be able to get back those two years, but just maybe I can do something that will make me feel as if I can repay that debt."

The brackets around the compressed line of Marcus's lips deepened. "You can't very well repay anything if you're dead, can you? Did you ever think of what Sean had planned for you? Cody may have thought that theft was the motive, but if what you say is true and the way Sean looked at you, he had other plans. And he couldn't leave a witness."

"I get the picture." Tempest tried not to shiver as she remembered the flat, hollow darkness of Sean's eyes, the evil she'd felt inside him, and his *Later.* . . . As if *Later.* . . . meant they'd meet again—but maybe this time that evil would have transferred to someone else.

Marcus walked to her and cupped her nape in his hand. He tugged her to him, his arm wrapping tightly around her. "Okay, maybe we'd better get this out of the way. You were too shaken up earlier to get into it, but I thought we had everything settled before you took off for Opal's. You were supposed to wait for me, and you didn't. The first thing I know is you're not with Francesca, you're off someplace, and I can't find you. It made perfect sense that you were doing just what you wanted and not what I'd asked."

"Told is more like it. I thought I'd shop and call you later. I intended to, and then I decided that Francesca would probably head for you. So I decided to make good use of my time by chatting with Opal. She may know something important."

"Know what for instance?"

Tempest managed to catch her thoughts before they passed her lips, no small task when Marcus was glaring at her, pushing her. There was no way he could know that Opal had wanted to be Winona's lover. "Opal was close to your mother," she managed.

"Of course she was. She helped her—and me—in every way she could. But that doesn't change the fact that you do just what you want. Just today, you've seen how dangerous that can be. I told you I'd be back. . . . if I hadn't seen Francesca running down the street— probably away from you—I might not have gotten to that van in time. What did you say to Francesca anyway? She's a longtime friend, and she looked pretty rattled, and you just might be the reason."

"I just asked her a few questions. Maybe she was upset about something else—some maid quitting or something."

"The point here is that you can't exactly be trusted, so I'm calling your mother in to babysit."

Tempest's fists gripped the back of his shirt. "You do and—"

"And you'll be safe."

"I have to do this for myself, Marcus, to pay for selling out. It's my penance, my right, and I'm claiming it. Don't you get it?"

Leona collected the handbag's box, labeled with the name of her shop, Timeless Vintage. "Mother won't come unless Tempest asks her. I've already asked. Children, this has all been interesting, but I'm tired and have a long drive back tomorrow."

Marcus stared down at Tempest. "And you're taking Tempest for a few days."

"Not a chance. Leona, are you game to go down to the beach tonight—with me? We'd be stronger together."

"I thought you'd never ask."

Leona and Tempest held hands as they walked down the path to the beach; Marcus followed a short distance behind them.

"Another protector," Leona murmured, as the wind lifted her hair, webbing it across her cheek. "You've bonded."

"Temporarily. It's pretty irritating. He's irritating. But it's true, dammit."

"First Claire with Neil and now you—and you know that, too. You're linked to him. I knew it the moment after that night in Santa Fe, after your showing. I knew Marcus would come after you. It's stronger now, and he's in your blood. You can't turn that off easily, Tempest. Marcus challenges you, and that's one thing you can't resist. You're running scared, Tempest Best. You're afraid he'll leave you like Dad, or somehow betray you like Brice."

"I've already gone through hell with one man. I don't know if I'm up to trying again with another. And why do you think he'll still want me when I hand him the news that Kenny is probably his father . . . and just maybe the murderer of Jason and Winona? Kenny's jealousy and anger are too strong . . . I felt them."

"That would be difficult," Leona murmured as she watched the waves swell and crest, breaking into foam that slid upon the sand. "Timeless, isn't it? And with a sense of peace. I've missed it."

"Marcus worshipped his mother. To discover that she'd taken a lover, and that he wasn't his father's biological son, would upset anyone." Tempest lifted her face to the wind. "What do you feel, Leona?"

Silent for a moment, Leona whispered, "Whatever energy was in the fog has slipped away, but I feel something else. . . . I feel—"

"Mother," Tempest finished. "She's out there, thinking about us, fighting to keep us safe, putting everything she has into wrapping that safety around us. We're stronger together, but she's added heft to the mix. Whatever this thing is, it's strong enough to hide from her."

"Except when we're alone and at our weakest. It's killed, Tempest. It caused the man who attacked Claire to commit suicide and now that boy, Sean. It's very strong and very evil, and it's waiting for us. You're playing with danger by staying here."

"I disagree. Of the three of us, I'm probably the safest. I'm not a precognitive—my dreams run to nightmares of how I used my gift, of partially developing it for a man who used and deceived me. I'm not an empath like Claire, who is far too vulnerable to people and to nature."

"She has Neil now, and she's stronger."

"You're the strongest, and you know it."

"But I'm not asking for trouble. I don't live by lakes or the ocean. Kentucky has a few large ponds, and—"

"And it felt you tonight. It knows your energy. It's like a bloodhound, and it will remember you. Don't forget that for a minute."

Marcus stood close behind the women, then his hand rested on Tempest's shoulder. "We should go back now. You've had a long day."

Leona hid her smile. Marcus spoke as a man who needed to hold his lover close and safe in the night.

Throughout their impromptu meal, he'd drawn Tempest to his lap as if he'd needed the comfort of her body after the traumatic day. She'd snuggled to him with a sigh as if she had just come home forever. She'd fed him slowly, carefully at the last, as if it were a new, intense experience, and the intimacy between them, the looks they shared, were promises, whether Tempest fully realized it or not.

The stroke of her hand over Marcus's hair, as if she loved touching him, that brief flick of her tongue to taste the syrup on his lips, was age-old proof that Tempest was playing the feminine role to her lover, the man bound to her and she to him.

The experience of seeing Tempest's intimacy with Marcus in reality, and not just in fragmented dreams, was reassuring to Leona.

Later, lying in her own bed, Leona smiled again as she heard Tempest's bedroom door open, then Marcus's door close. Her little sister had gone to her lover, the man who would hold her safe—if he could.

Eleven

AFTER TEMPEST QUIETLY ENTERED MARCUS'S DARKENED
bedroom, she closed the door behind her. She found
him lying on the bed; his hands were behind his head,
his chest bare, and a sheet covered him from the waist
down. She noted the contour of that sheet; Marcus was
definitely aroused.

"About time," he stated roughly, as she crossed the
room to him.

Because she was uneasy about his reception and the
scolding she was certain to receive, Tempest decided
to trim some of his anger and frustration by seducing
him quickly. The sexy negligee she was wearing could
jump-start their lovemaking. She lifted her foot to the
bed, giving him a good look at her legs, and then
slipped one strap down her shoulder, shimmying a
little to emphasize her breasts. Marcus didn't move or
show any reaction. She slid the other strap down, until
all that held up the lacy shortie was her breasts, then
she deliberately let one peek through.

Marcus studied her black short lacy nightgown,
then gripped it in his fist, drawing her down to him.
"What's this about?"

She'd had time to shop at La Femme and pick up the
sexy nightie, and then she'd met Cody outside the

shop. Now she knew that he'd been waiting for her. "I thought you might—"

One tug brought her tumbling down on Marcus. "You thought what?" he asked grimly. "That this little number would make up for your doing exactly what I told you not to do?"

"Something like that."

Marcus rolled her beneath him and held her wrists beside her head. "If I hadn't come when I did, you could have had a very . . . bad . . . time."

"I know. Thank you. I'm sorry you were worried." Tempest tried to appear contrite. She knew that Marcus had to go through the admonishment, and then she'd make it up to him. It was a necessary man-woman ritual before life and lovemaking moved on, and she really wanted him close tonight. Sean's *Later*. . . . threat still frightened her; the youth had committed suicide, but whatever was in him at the time could have moved on to someone else. If something—someone—had gotten to him through his computer games and had directed that evil toward her, there were others out there, just as susceptible.

She lifted her head to kiss him, but Marcus drew away. "Take off your gloves."

"Not tonight. I'm not in any kind of control . . . rather, I'm not strong enough to control myself, and I feel all this energy sizzling inside me. I could send out enough psychic heat to fry both our brains." Her statement was true enough; her extrasensory ability was changing and getting stronger, because she was pushing, and because Marcus's inner strength of character and his energies were blending with hers. Controlling her impulses had always been difficult for her and, aroused, she could hurt him. On the other hand, she wasn't certain how their bond worked. It might be a two-way reception if he could sense what she knew and felt. If Marcus sensed that she suspected Kenny might have been the hit-and-run driver, forcing his parents' car into that wall, he might—she had no idea what Marcus might do.

Francesca could also be a candidate. While Francesca had suddenly needed to go to the bathroom—probably to calm herself—Tempest had slipped off her glove and placed her hand on the businesswoman's date book. Hatred, greed, frustration had slithered up Tempest's arm; she'd passed through layers of narcissism, fear of aging, loneliness, bitterness, and jealousy to find one startling nugget—Francesca wanted Marcus to notice her as a woman, to take her as a lover. An older woman fearing age, she wanted his youth and vitality for her own—and she resented Tempest enough to hurt her.

Above her, Marcus scanned Tempest's face. "You were just somewhere else. What's going on? What are you holding?"

"You?" she teased. "I'm not anywhere else. I'm right here—um, under you, I believe."

Marcus scowled down at her. "Cute. Now get this straight, sweetheart. You're leaving with your sister in the morning—"

"Am I?" She wiggled a little beneath him, stroked her legs against his, and smiled up at him. Pillow talk with Marcus was perfect after the traumatic day. Tempest settled in for the relief and pleasure of being with him. "You're so cute when you're playing big boss man."

"I'll show you 'cute.'" Marcus stared down at their bodies, her breasts pale and exposed now, rubbing against his chest, her nipples peaking with the slight abrasion. Stretching her arms high, he bent down to catch her nipple in his mouth, rolling it on his tongue, then moving to the other.

When Tempest let out a whimper, her hips lifting to his, Marcus quickly skimmed her nightgown away.

His hand ran down her body, gripping her hip, his fingers pressing in possessively, then crossed to her lower belly. She waited, arching restlessly, for him to touch her intimately, stroking her gently, teasing her as his lips demanded everything, sensitizing her until she almost cried out, and then Marcus was sliding deep, slowly at first, and then faster.

His lips covered Tempest's just as she cried out, arching up to hold that riveting fiery sensation, her eyes closed as she went deep inside, aware only of his heartbeat, his pulse pounding with hers. "Stay put," he ordered roughly against her throat as his breath stroked her skin. "You're not going anywhere."

"As if I could." His lovemaking had been dominating and fierce, staking his claim, and it was just what she wanted—to test herself against him, to feel everything, wide open, that searing need with nothing held back. She hadn't expected the intimacy, the love play, or the deep chuckle at her throat, followed by a gentle nip.

"Stop smiling, you little unpredictable beast," Marcus murmured with a lazy smile in his voice; his weight was heavy, but perfect, upon her.

Tempest circled her emotions; she'd run a lifetime, fearing entanglements, just keeping the minimum of affection, fearing too much intimacy—and now here it was, with Marcus, and she wanted it to last forever. She ran her fingers through his hair, enjoying the crisp short length, the flutter of his eyelashes against her throat, the way his breath swept over her skin—as if she were so much a part of him, wrapped tightly, hearts slowing. She rubbed her breasts against his chest, felt the leap of his biceps against her softness; her thighs slid along his harder ones, her insoles caressing those bulky calves. Being a part of Marcus's life wouldn't be so bad; with him, she'd have an exciting challenge every day.

He nuzzled her throat and ended up tugging her earlobe with his teeth. "I'm supposed to be making my point."

"Oh, you did." Tempest smoothed his back, her thin, supple gloves allowing her to feel the power rippling beneath his skin. She felt drowsy and warm and safe, not a bad place to be at all, rather like a safe harbor where nothing could touch her, and the past was in another galaxy.

Marcus caressed her breast, shifting a little to ease his weight from her, but he still held Tempest close, his hand cupping her chin to lift it for his kiss. "I want you to leave with Leona. I don't trust Whitcomb. It's a nightmare at the police station now, state investigators coming in, interviews of the guards, paperwork, and the media gnawing at each word. After we made our statements, the newspaper reporters outside the station took your pictures. Whitcomb could recognize you and I don't want anything to happen to you."

"Is Brice anywhere around now? He is coming to that game, isn't he?"

Marcus tensed, and whispered, "Always right there, hunting, aren't you?"

She caressed his back with her gloves. "I could get it out of you now, you know. I've relaxed a little. I might not fry you quite as much."

He chuckled again, a low, rich sound Tempest loved. "I don't think you could do much more damage right now, but it might almost be worth it."

"Are you going to tell me?"

"Not a chance. Want to tell me about him—and you?"

In Marcus's arms, Tempest rubbed her toes against his, enjoying the physical afterglow, the warmth of their bodies, the small cocoon of the bedding around them. Her stint as Dominique seemed like such a long time ago, as if she were another woman. "I scared him.

That last time, I'd seen him for what he was—a scam artist and a thief and a user—and I just may have lost my temper. He ended up lying on the floor, staring at me as if he didn't know me. Those first years, after I left him, I think Brice was glad to get rid of me."

Marcus caressed her back and murmured, "I wouldn't be so sure that's true now. 'Bitch, next time I see you, you'll be crying to take me back. Either that, or you'll be dead,' sounds pretty serious to me. You cost him, Tempest. Whitcomb used the information you gave him to get in with the right people, to scam some of them. When you left, he no longer had that insider information. He's hard-up for money now."

Tempest leaned back in Marcus's arms; her fingers tightened on his chest hair. Marcus's quote was exactly the one she'd received when retrieving her cell phone messages. "I never told you exactly what he said."

"Okay, just maybe I accidentally listened to your cell message when you were in the shower earlier. I didn't delete it, because I want you to know how dangerous he sounds."

"'Accidentally?'"

"You said he had your cell number. It makes sense that he'd call. The point is, I intend to deal with him."

Marcus sat up, his body tense as he appeared to be listening. "Stay here," he whispered as he slid open the bedroom window and eased through the opening.

She was on her feet in a heartbeat. "Marcus, what is it?" she whispered.

"Someone is prowling around the back deck. If I go through the house, they'll see me." Then he slid into the night.

Tempest quickly rummaged for her nightie, slid it on, and followed. There was no balcony or patio outside Marcus's bedroom, but she managed to grip the handrail on the decking a few feet away, just outside Opal's former kitchen-side room. Marcus moved stealthily ahead of her, his nude body a blur in the night. At the end of the decking, he eased around the corner, and Tempest hurried to catch up.

When she turned the corner leading to the back deck, she saw Marcus standing with his legs braced, his hands on his hips peering out into the night. Tempest came to stand behind him, her hand on his shoulder. "What was it?"

"Probably just a stray dog, rummaging for food. Opal sometimes feeds strays." Marcus turned and searched the back door; he tested it and shook his head. "It's still locked."

Tempest heard Leona calling for her and noted her shadow inside the house as she moved to turn on the lights. Marcus was still bent to the door, studying it for marks. "Ah, Marcus, honey?"

"Yeah? I don't see anything." He looked around the steps and found a shred of cloth clinging to the hand railing. "I don't remember seeing this before, do you?"

"No, but I am seeing Leona coming this way, and you aren't wearing anything."

He stared at her blankly, then down at his body as if just realizing he was nude. "Oh, dammit."

Marcus looked so cute with his stunned look that Tempest couldn't resist laughing.

After scowling at her, Marcus moved quickly around the decking and disappeared. Tempest waited just a heartbeat, and then knocked on the door's window. Leona immediately let her in. "What's going on?"

"I thought I'd forgotten something out here. Nice night, isn't it?"

As usual, Leona didn't waste time. "Get in here. You shouldn't be out here by yourself."

Tempest hid her smile as she moved into the house and turned to lock the door. "Oh, you're right. I really shouldn't be."

Leona leaned close to whisper, "Don't bother going

back to your guest room. I know you're sleeping with him, and he's probably wanting to see more of that negligee. You'd better get back before he misses you."

"He is cuddly. I was just tucking him in."

"Sure. He's a little bit large for 'cuddly.' See you in the morning." Leona's soft laughter floated after Tempest as her older sister returned to her room.

Tempest couldn't stop giggling as she entered Marcus's room. He was sitting on the edge of the bed, studying the scrap of red cloth. He looked shaken. "I haven't done any window-sneaking since I was a hot-pants kid. Come to think of it, I didn't do it then, either."

"Oh, poor baby." Tempest came to sit on his lap. She wrapped her arm around his shoulders and stroked his hair. "Can I make it better?"

Marcus eased her around to straddle him. He eased her nightie away and positioned her close and tight against him. He was hard and hot and definitely needing to be "made" better. "You can try."

Much later, Tempest lay tangled with Marcus, his arm and leg over hers as if keeping her close to him even as he slept heavily. She turned her head to find the scrap of red cloth on the nightstand, and she had to hold it, to know who was out there in the night.

Marcus sighed as she carefully reached above his back to slowly remove her glove. Tempest reached her naked hand to the scrap and fisted it. Hatred, envy, and frustration blended into one burning energy and snaked up her arm, and she knew that Francesca was the night visitor. Why?

Above Marcus's back, Tempest eased the scrap inside her empty glove and began inserting her hand, when she stopped. Just once, while he slept close and safe, she wanted to hold him with her naked hands—when he wouldn't pick up her energy. She needed to know what ran between them, the strength of their connection.

Tempest carefully eased her other glove free and

placed them both on the bedside table. She had only gotten his basic energies from her hands, but she had bonded with Marcus, become a part of him somehow, and psychic ability could morph in all directions. It could also boomerang and hurt those with lesser ability. In no way, did Tempest want to "fry" Marcus, or even come close to hurting him. Slowly, gently, Tempest placed her open hands on his back, gathered him close to her, and closed her eyes.

Her gentle probes searched beneath the painful, lonely, frustrating layers, more than she already knew, more than he perhaps knew. She let her energy flow through him, easing, cleansing, focusing on sweeping the darkness away to give him peace.

Tempest held her breath as he shifted slightly and sighed. She held very still and probed again and found layers of peace and harmony. Somehow, when she'd held Marcus, her energy rebounded on herself, taking her psychic ability into another dimension. Marcus had the ability to change her into something she'd never been, the bond between them growing stronger with each heartbeat.

He would demand everything, just as she would. In the end, they just might hate each other.

Marcus held her closer, his hand caressing her lightly, but Tempest shivered. She knew that Marcus wouldn't let her go easily, even when he learned of his biological father.

After carefully replacing her gloves, she gathered Marcus closer.

"Later. . . ." Sean had said. Were there others with that same dark, evil essence wanting to hurt her—or worse—all the Aislings? Why did he and the man who'd hurt Claire need revenge? For what?

On the Pacific Northwest shoreline, just outside her home, Greer stood by the doorway, marked by winding, interwoven Celtic symbols. She traced them with her hand as she closed her eyes and let her senses pulse over the water, skipping slowly, swirling, seeking. The ripple began, opening larger, until she found that psychic portal in Lake Michigan, and then she pulsed through it. The safety check to feel her children was the second of the night; the first had found her two daughters by the lake, the protector looming behind them—Marcus Greystone wasn't letting anything happen to either one of them while they were under his care.

That wouldn't be easy with Tempest's impulsive nature and addiction to challenges.

"A handbag. It was more than that. Leona wanted to see that Tempest was safe. If only Tempest wouldn't feel that she needed to do penance for her mistake . . . she was so young and vulnerable."

Greer smoothed the replica brooch and sighed. Like Aisling centuries ago, Tempest had met her match, and Marcus didn't know his bloodline wasn't of the Greystones. A woman who held a secret like that from her love might pay a heavy, heartbreaking price.

Tempest awoke slowly to the rumble of Marcus's voice and Leona's smoother, feminine one. As she entered the kitchen, wearing one of Marcus's dress shirts over her nightie, they turned to stare at her. They were standing close and leaning back against the counter, sipping from mugs, the discussion apparently serious.

Heat tangled between Tempest and Marcus, the reminder of the night sizzling between them. Too aware of her sister's appraisal, Tempest smiled brightly and tried not to think about the warmth moving up her cheeks.

In a T-shirt, worn jeans, and bare feet, his hair

slightly mussed and his jaw dark with stubble, Marcus looked even more delectable. "Come here, sleepyhead," he murmured in a husky tone that tingled every sensitive nerve in her body and went to all the parts Marcus had loved so well.

Leona was smiling softly as if she understood Tempest's hesitation, as if she knew something Tempest didn't. Another tingle shot up Tempest's nape, warning this time. "What's going on?"

"We were just getting ready to have a bite before I sail off on my broom," Leona said smoothly. But the warm, secretive smile said she was withholding something Tempest had yet to discover.

Marcus hadn't moved; his eyes never left Tempest as he placed his mug on the counter. "Come here," he ordered, more softly this time.

Tempest studied him and weighed what crossing those few feet of kitchen flooring could mean. Nothing, or everything, that he could get her to obey him? Was this a power play for Leona's benefit, to demonstrate that Tempest would behave upon his orders and stay safe?

Marcus shook his head and grinned at her. "Scared? You're thinking too hard."

"It's very early." Tempest studied the circles beneath Leona's eyes. Had she dreamed last night? What had she seen? "You didn't sleep well, did you? You weren't worrying about me, were you? I can take care of myself, and none of you should worry about me."

It seemed only natural to walk to Marcus and kiss him. She settled into his arms with a sense of homecoming.

As if seeing something yet to pass, Leona took in the way they stood and smiled. "We always worry about you. You're impulsive, Tempest Best. As a child, you were always into everything that even slightly challenged you. You've always been restless, eager for the next turn in your life."

A shadow crossed Leona's expression as she added, "I'm worried for both of you."

Tempest understood immediately. Leona had dreamed of her husband last night, and seeing Tempest and Marcus together had churned all those loving memories into one heartbreaking ache. "You couldn't have stopped that avalanche."

Leona's face paled, her eyes reflected the grief and guilt that she rarely let anyone else see. "I could have warned Joel. I could have kept my husband at home somehow. . . . I need to go. I have a full day's drive ahead of me. Are you coming or not?"

"No. I must do this, Leona. Everything that I am says I was born to do this, that I must bring the brooch to the one person who can unravel its secrets. That I must earn it rightfully. I have to." Tempest moved to hug Leona, and the sisters clung to each other.

"Stay safe, Tempest Best," Leona whispered unevenly. "I love you, truly I do."

"Likewise."

At the car, the sisters held each other tightly, prolonging the moment when they would separate. Leona leaned close to whisper to Tempest, "You touched him last night, didn't you? Easing him? He's much lighter this morning."

"I didn't know that I could. I'm glad."

"You're opening more to find the brooch and pushing yourself. Be so careful, Tempest. I couldn't bear it if anything happened to you or Claire."

"I'll be safe. Drive carefully."

Marcus came to stand beside Tempest, his arm around her, as they watched Leona drive away.

Tempest missed Leona instantly, their bonds drawn even tighter as adults. There was nothing she could do but turn to Marcus and hold him close. "She'll be okay," he soothed as he rocked her.

"She's upset. She's usually so calm and in control. She's afraid for me, terribly afraid. They all are." Tempest brushed her damp lashes against Marcus's T-shirt. "Thanks for playing host. I know we can't be easy to understand."

"Well, Neil says—"

Tempest looked up at Marcus. "Neil? Claire's husband? You've been talking to him? Why?"

Marcus seemed wary, looking off to a sailboat motoring slowly out of the harbor toward the lake. "I needed a little tutoring on how to handle you."

Tempest stepped back. "I don't believe you. You actually called my sister's husband for a tutorial?"

"Now, don't get upset, honey. I usually research pretty thoroughly—ah. . . ." He peered down at her. "You're mad, aren't you?"

Tempest's hands were on her hips now, her temper rising. "You betcha. You research acquisitions thoroughly—not me."

Marcus grinned and reached out to waggle her head. "Come on, babe. Be reasonable. I've got you, don't I?"

"I should have locked you outside that window and turned on all the lights. I should have staked you out there, nude, for everyone to see. So what did your new buddy, Neil, say?"

"When I told him that you were with me, he laughed, and said, 'Good luck, buddy. Try to keep up.' Sounds like a good guy, easygoing. He told me that if things got really rough, and I was at my wits' end, just to call your mother."

"Don't . . . you . . . dare."

Marcus's grin was boyish and devastating as he patted her bottom. "You'll have to keep me busy then, won't you?"

In another heartbeat, he put her over his shoulder and hurried back to the bedroom.

When Tempest stopped laughing, she looked up

into Marcus's tender smile, and her heart stopped, flipped, and settled warmly. She smoothed his jaw, his hair, and knew she loved him.

"Figures," Marcus stated as he glanced in his bathroom mirror. Tempest stood, leaning her shoulder against the doorway. She still wore that slumberous afterglow following their morning shower; it looked good on her. He noted the black leather gloves and remembered the rubber ones in the shower—they really didn't feel wrong on his body, when they were soaping in the right places.

He swished his razor in the sink and angled his jaw for another swipe. That big belt buckle secured Tempest's outfit; her olive tank showed off those clean, feminine muscles, and her khaki shorts had the usual pockets. Her running shoes looked as if they'd had better days.

Marcus recognized the look; Tempest was going hunting, geared to move fast. In addition, she also wore that good-luck replica brooch, her wide-cuff bracelet, and the large, multipurpose wristwatch, all embellished with Celtic designs. Someday, Marcus promised himself, when Tempest wasn't keeping him so busy, he'd research Celts and the Vikings and would try to understand her better; Leona had said that Tempest's instincts had always leaned more toward their Viking ancestor. From what Marcus knew of that ancient culture and of Tempest, Leona was probably correct. "So where are we going?"

She lifted an eyebrow and walked toward his vanity. She turned suddenly, and hiked herself up to sit on the counter as she watched him. "You missed a place."

Marcus studied Tempest, a wave of pleasure enfolding him. She wore his touch, and she was his—on the flip side, being a part of her life wasn't that bad either.

Afterglow suited that pale skin—he frowned at the slight red patches at her throat. Lovemaking in the shower had been sensuous, and once he had carried her to the bed, Tempest had ignited, demanding, challenging him. His girl moved fast, and as yet unprepared for her unpredictability, Marcus's control had slid right off that bed.

He reached over to caress briefly her smooth thigh and leaned down to kiss her. The intimacy he'd never allowed himself with another woman felt good, as if Tempest and he had done this forever. In fact, everything seemed brighter and lighter this morning; he felt almost carefree. "Honey, why are you all dressed up for hunting?"

"You won't like it." Tempest studied the towel wrapped around his hips, and Marcus's senses quickened—or something did beneath that towel.

"I'm sure I won't. After you do what you think you have to do to earn that brooch—and that is bull, by the way—I have big plans. And where did you say we were going again?"

Tempest's gloved hand roamed over his shoulder and his biceps. The appraising, hungry look didn't hurt, that sexual heat simmering around her. "I thought you had a little boys' party to arrange—which is also 'bull,' by the way."

If she had a little sexual hunger left over after that marathon in his bed, Marcus didn't want it wasted. He let the towel at his hips slip just that fraction. Tempest's stare locked on to just what he had available.

Then she grinned and lifted to kiss him, adding a little bit of tongue and that little nip before stating, "It won't work. I'm not going back to bed with you."

Resigned that Tempest wasn't taking his bait, Marcus sighed and continued shaving. She was still studying him as if trying to make up her mind about something when he finished. He studied her reflection in the mirror. "Want to talk about it? Whatever's on your mind?"

"I'm just trying to decide what to do about something."

"It's probably something I won't like, or you'd be talking." Marcus lifted her into his arms and walked into his bedroom; he tossed her on the bed and started dressing. With Tempest on the move, he wanted to be prepared. He didn't want to be caught in the nude again, as he had been last night. "Okay. Give. What's up?"

"I need your help. Just one little phone call to Kenny." As she watched him, Tempest lay on his rumpled bed, her hands folded behind her head, those long legs crossed. "You look—nice—in that shirt and jeans and those loafers. Sort of upscale tough. You've got a sort of animal appeal, I suppose. That's what attracted me to you at the showing. The way you move—sleek, powerful, like some arrogant lord and master. My little heart just fluttered."

Tempest's playful mood shielded something she wanted to hide, and Marcus wasn't buying. His good morning feel-good slid away into a questionable trust issue. Tempest was hiding something, and it must be good. "Flattery will get you—laid. Give me one good reason I should call Kenny. He's busy with the *Winona*, and he's pretty upset about Cody."

Because Marcus knew that Kenny had been trying to help the youth, he'd already intended a phone call and an offer of help. If Kenny hadn't been around to help guide Marcus, he could have ended up just like Cody, looking at a hard life in or out of prison.

"Kenny might be able to give us directions to Sean's. He and Cody and Sean played games together."

"Why not just ask Cody?"

"Because he's in jail and probably watched pretty closely. Because you said that Mac was pretty overwhelmed at the moment by Sean's suicide investigation and doesn't have the manpower to get out there right now. Because I want to get in there before anything gets touched. Because asking Kenny may be the quickest way to get to Sean's place, before Mac's people can get out there to investigate."

Marcus glanced at the bedside table; he needed thinking room—Kenny was already wary of Tempest and Marcus didn't blame him. If they were caught at Sean's place, it would be difficult to explain Tempest's psychic ability and their reason for being there, especially when Mac had said the place was going to be investigated. "I thought I put that scrap of red material down there."

He didn't trust Tempest's wide-eyed expression. "I have no idea."

"You're not going to let this go, are you?" he asked finally as he sat down on the bed.

"I think—but I have to know for certain if what is happening to my family, the stalking feeling we all have, has anything to do with Sean's computer. Sean self-destructed, committed suicide like the man who attacked my sister earlier this year. I have to know if there is a connection, and there's only one way to do that."

Marcus shook his head, then he reached for the telephone. He searched again for that red scrap as he spoke to Kenny. After yesterday, Kenny's distrust of Tempest had grown. Kenny had wondered if she'd encouraged the two youths, flirting with them. "She's not the kind to do that, Kenny. I believe everything she tells me," Marcus had stated flatly. "For your sake, I'm going to try to help Cody and get a good attorney working for him. But I'm not listening to any more about Tempest in that regard."

When he finished the call, Marcus circled his thoughts about Kenny's dislike of Tempest; a longtime friend and father figure, Kenny seemed to fear her seeking answers from the past. He was too defensive and wary each time her name came up. His actions were unlike anything Marcus had ever known about him. Why? Was Tempest too close to something Kenny didn't want known? Something to do with that damaged hand?

Marcus turned to Tempest. "All set. Sean's place is a rental shack at the edge of town. The police are set to investigate it early this afternoon. The things down at the station are pretty hot right now, and they're tied up until then."

"I'd better move fast then." Tempest came to her feet in one lithe move, but Marcus captured her wrist and stood more slowly.

"Correction: We'd better move fast."

She stared at him, and then quickly moved to the other side of the bed. "Help me make this bed. Hurry."

"Huh? Why?" Of all the problems brewing and despite Tempest's hurry to get to Sean's, she wanted to make the bed?

"I always make my bed."

"Why?" At the moment, Tempest's little quirk really interested Marcus more than anything else.

Tempest tilted her head and frowned at him. "Okay, I'm just not too sure Opal or Kenny or Francesca or whoever can get into this house won't come in while we're gone. The bed is all messed up. One person wouldn't have done that. They'll know."

"That we're sleeping together? I imagine they do."

"Well, they don't need proof, do they?"

Marcus tried to wade through the intricacies of Tempest's mind and came up with, "So you're ashamed of sleeping with me."

"I'd prefer not to broadcast it," she said in a prim tone.

"Honey—" God, she was sweet and cute, Marcus

decided. Who would have guessed that she was an old-fashioned girl at heart?

"Stop grinning, you big idiot, and get to work." Tempest began picking up the pillows that had ended up on the floor and smoothing them, tossing them to a side chair. "Well, don't just stand there. Help me. This thing is massive."

"Hey, I'm a big guy. I need space." Marcus began to help. He found that nifty little nightie and held it up. "I love this thing."

"I got some more—pull up that end. No, the sheet first . . . fold it back."

" 'Some more'? Like what?"

"Oh, you know. Black thigh-highs with a lacy band, a black bra and thong to match—that kind of stuff."

Marcus tried to focus away from the image of Tempest wearing that sexy outfit and crushed the slinky nightie in his hand. He stuffed it under the pillow. "You're not using the guest room," he stated firmly. "And no arguing about it."

Her hand in his, Tempest followed Marcus to the small wooded area, the run-down shack nestled within it. Junk of every nature—furniture, tires, rusted auto frames—circled the wooden building. Every pile of that junk seemed to have small wildlife peering at them.

She noted a crow atop the leafless limb of a dead tree and a tiny frisson ran up her nape. Its feathers gleamed blue-black in the early-morning sunlight. The crow seemed to be watching and waiting—for what?

Marcus stopped so suddenly that she almost ran into his back. He turned to her. "What did you say?"

Her own whisper echoed in her mind, "Bad omen." But to Marcus, she said, "I said, 'This is disgusting.' "

He scanned her expression. "Okay, little Miss Witch. I

know the word 'omen.' You've been uneasy since we got in the car to come out here. Want to tell me about it?"

She shivered and glanced up at the leafless limb, bobbing slightly with the weight of two more crows. "Spooky place."

Marcus nodded grimly. "It was probably all he could afford. Kenny said the kid had tried to go straight, but like Cody, he was having a hard time of it—battling a juvenile record. Come on, we don't have much time before Port Salem's finest come to investigate."

She wondered about Kenny's apparent attachment to the youths. Was it all fatherly-do-gooder? Or was he connected to them in another way, a way that involved getting rid of her?

Kenny was hiding something big, and he had been around the time of the hit-and-run. No one— including Francesca and the clerks at the La Femme, or Cody—knew much about him, but Tempest knew that he wasn't as he appeared. She glanced at Marcus, who was scanning the electrical and phone lines running into the shack. The line of his jaw could match Kenny's, beneath his beard. Their eyes were definitely a match, and the hard contour of that brow and forehead, those cheekbones. Winona's lover and the father of her son just could be the potential father of her unborn baby—and Kenny was definitely a part of Marcus's life. He could have wanted control of the company through Marcus, but then his prodigy had taken to business like Jason.

As a handyman, Kenny would have the know-how and opportunity to cause the railing to come free. Put all that together, and Kenny definitely figured in as a potential murderer.

"It's hard to believe that Sean could get good Internet service out here." Marcus used his foot to push aside a pile of beer bottles near the front door; he tried the knob and found it locked. But Tempest had already taken off her belt and with a shrug, he moved aside. "We could get in a whole lot of trouble if the investigators show up now."

She felt the prong nudge the lock and eased it around until the mechanism clicked open. "Let's just get this done."

"Stand back."

Tempest stared up at Marcus, who was about to push open the door. He'd used his shoulder to nudge her aside. "Huh?"

"Get out of the way, short stuff. Stay behind me."

"But—" Tempest looked up at Marcus's set expression and decided that this was not the time to argue. "Okay."

The smell stale of beer and cigarettes hit her like a wall, the shack's interior dark and cold, despite the warmth of the July day. The single room held a grubby stove area at one end, stacked with dirty pots; a bed with a sagging, exposed mattress, and a ratty recliner occupied another side. Tempest spotted the computer screen against one wall and made for it, aware that Marcus's hand warmed and weighted her shoulder, somehow linking her to his strength. Tempest turned on the machine and waited for it to come to life. She slowly removed one glove.

"I don't like this. You fainted after holding that brooch, and I saw your reaction to the handbag. Be careful, honey," Marcus warned quietly.

"Something changed Sean in the space of two days. If it's in there, I'll find it."

The screen's cursor blinked, waiting as she slowly lowered her bare hand to the keyboard. That first touch caused her to stiffen, the burning ribbons of hate winding up her arm. "That would have been what Sean felt—it feels the same as the handbag Leona brought in last night. Something wants revenge."

"Take it easy."

She found the gamer controls, wrapped her hand around the stick, and focused. "It came through a game."

Marcus checked the electronic games lying beside the computer. "These are all from the local discount store. Kenny buys ones like these. He spends a lot of time playing games, too."

Tempest swallowed the fear in her throat; the evil pulsing beneath her hand was almost alive, like a snake wanting to sink venomous fangs into her flesh. "It was something else, something designed to program Sean."

Marcus took her wrist and lifted her hand away from the game controls. "That's enough. Put on your glove."

"Something is wrong. . . . I didn't get—"

"You're shaking, and you're pale. We're leaving. Come on, we don't want to be here when the police come."

Inside the car, Tempest sat hunched into the passenger side, her arms around herself. Despite the warmth of the July sunshine passing through the windows, she couldn't get rid of that dark energy. "The energy is getting stronger somehow. It's feeding off them—the people it uses—and getting stronger. I got less than I did when I held that handbag. I think he—it—is learning how to block me."

Could it be that after all these years, her sensitivity was diminishing? That she was losing the sixth sense she'd never wanted? Why now?

Marcus reached to take her hand and draw it to his thigh. He laced his fingers with hers. "You think a game set Sean up to yesterday?"

"Yes."

"Uh-oh. Look."

Tempest followed Marcus's nod toward the cabin.

Flames were crawling up the ragged window curtain. A sudden explosion caused the windows to shatter, and the flames burst into the air. "We'd better get out of here. It won't do to be seen around here—not the day after your kidnapping and Sean killing himself. Did you see anything that might act as a detonator?"

"The computer. You turned it off, but it didn't want to die easily."

Marcus reversed quickly and headed back toward Port Salem. "That seemed strange. But I thought it was off."

"It appeared that way, didn't it?"

On the highway, Tempest looked back to the wooded area of the cabin. Smoke billowed against the blue sky. "Like I said, 'a bad omen.' "

The whine of a volunteer fireman's siren cut through the air, and Tempest hugged herself tightly.

Marcus took her hand. "What you said about feeding off the weak . . . people can do that, you know. Get others to bend to their will. Usually they pick a weaker person because then they're in control, they're stronger. Cults are established every day by someone with a gimmick to sell and with enough charisma to suck people in. If there's anything left of that shack, the investigators may find a link to someone, something."

"They won't find anything."

"How do you know?"

She removed her glove and stared at her hand. It looked like the same, but was it? Was she as strong as before? Or was the dark energy stronger than her? "I just do. Everything would have been on that computer. Worms are unseen and unknown, twisting through the guts of a computer until they do their job. This one recognizes touch from the keyboard and gaming control and starts activating the game from the last point. It challenges with points—I would have been worth one hundred. . . two hundred dead. If Sean failed to kill me, he lost, and he had to 'erase.' Meanwhile, he had a deadline to check in—when he missed it, the machine fried itself."

Marcus glanced at her, his wraparound sunglasses reflecting her image. "Sean was to erase the game?"

Tempest drew on her own sunglasses; she needed the silver protection to shield the fear crawling through her.

"No, the worm would do that and fry the computer. He was to kill himself."

Twelve

"NICE OUTFIT." SEATED IN THE FRONT DECK'S LAWN CHAIR,
Marcus looked up from his laptop; he took in Tempest's modest gray short-sleeve sweater, slacks, and black loafers. He also noted the absence of the silver brooch, her bracelet, and large wristwatch.

Shaken by what she'd felt on Sean's keyboard and gaming stick, Tempest had dressed carefully. Marcus had arranged the midafternoon meeting with Opal; he'd agreed that she might remember some small detail that would help Tempest. After an argument, he'd agreed that she could talk with Opal alone.

"I thought I'd make Opal feel more comfortable with me. Or at least try," Tempest said. "She might know something that didn't click back then—some detail that I can research."

"She probably remembers some unsavory types. When Jason's business started to slip, he took in the wrong kind of investors—under pressure. I researched all of them I could find, including the mistress he took from an underworld type, which was a real bad mistake. But none of his buddies thought the woman was worth killing for, and they had already bled Greystone Investments dry."

"Still—it's the little things that might lead to something bigger."

"I'd really like to sit in on this session. I might pick up something I'd missed before, some lead she doesn't even think is significant. I could help, maybe stir some memory she'd forgotten."

"I know you want to help, but you're so tense that you could interfere with my read of her. I have to concentrate on every small nuance. How's the little boys' party coming along?" Tempest stood at the new railing, testing it as she looked out at the brilliant July day, the tourists already on the beach, and kites sailing high in the sky. So much had happened in the four days since she'd arrived.

"It's all set." Standing behind her now, Marcus braced his hands on the railing and nuzzled her throat. "While you were in the shower, Kenny came by. He's upset about Sean's death and Cody's upcoming trial."

Tempest's sense of danger quickened. Kenny wouldn't want his secrets discovered, and he could have set the youth into action. She turned slightly to meet Marcus's brief kiss, and ask, "Really? What else did he say?"

"He wanted to thank me for getting the best attorney possible for Cody." Whatever Marcus wasn't saying trembled on the breeze between them, but his expression had closed. She didn't believe his, "That's all we talked about."

Tempest leaned back against him; in another situation—one in which he might learn through her, that his life had been a lie—she might have admitted to him that she was already in love with him. Instead, she took the precious moment now, the closeness of Marcus, the warmth between them, and wrapped it tight inside her.

Sunlight seemed to kiss the waves, sea foam sliding like lace upon the brown sand. Across the harbor, Port Salem seemed to be all colorful houses stacked one on top of another, the single church spire pristine white against the brilliant blue sky. Everything seemed too peaceful, unlike the churning darkness in the fog and unlike Francesca's jealous energy on that tiny scrap of red cloth Tempest had hidden.

"You're not going to keep out of the poker party tomorrow, are you, Tempest?"

"So it's tomorrow, and he's coming. I'm not into payback or the mine-is-bigger-than-yours game. I just want to actually feel Brice's hand to see if his touch is connected with everything else—to see if he was the person who came into Leona's shop and touched that handbag."

Marcus's lips moved against her ear, his breath warm against her skin. "Strange that you never touched him."

"I can feel you smirking, you know." Marcus's statement was so quiet and pleased that she wondered if he'd felt her probe last night, her naked hands on his back. "You're comparing how I am with you, and how I was with him. I was too inexperienced, and I trusted him."

"Trust is hard to regrow." He nodded, watching her with those smoky gray eyes. "I wondered. From what I gathered, the woman at his side was always in the background and very quiet. That doesn't sound like you."

"I wasn't . . . 'me.' I was Dominique, someone running his errands and his scams for him, sucking off energy from the things others had touched," she admitted, not bothering to conceal her bitterness.

"And Whitcomb's energy was never left on anything?"

"I told him that it would dilute whatever he wanted. He was always very careful not to touch with his bare hands."

"He touched you," Marcus stated harshly as if he hated the thought of another man's hands on her. This time his arms closed tightly around her, his hands open and possessive.

"I was flattered, a man as sophisticated as he was and moving around with the high-society crowd. It was a different world, a new adventure, and I wanted it all. I knew I'd made a mistake and that it was over even before I heard him call me his 'little freak.'"

Marcus's breath hissed across her cheek, and then he released her. "He shouldn't have said that. Just focus on why you are here and forget about him. I have no doubt about your ability to get that driver, dead or alive. What you're doing is very important to me."

As if he had suddenly lost interest, and the discussion was closed, Marcus bent to tap in a few notes on the laptop. His expression was hard and determined, then he closed the laptop and placed it aside. The wind riffled his hair slightly, and the scent of his soap and aftershave carried to Tempest as he looked up at her. He spoke slowly as if mulling his thoughts as they left his lips. "I've begun to think that maybe, just because Kenny and Opal and Francesca have been around most of my life, that I may have missed something. Or maybe they wanted to protect me and omitted it purposefully. If so, I've made a mistake by not pushing them to remember more. There might come a time when they won't remember anything at all, and some detail that could help might be lost."

When Tempest nodded, he continued, "Opal gets touchy sometimes when we talk about my family. Maybe I haven't asked the right questions. She can be difficult when cornered. That's her nature, because she doesn't like to be challenged, and she considers you a challenge to her domain and me. Do what you have to do. If you need me to smooth things down a bit to keep the conversation going, I'll be around, and I'll take the heat."

The close friendship between Opal and Winona nagged at Tempest. Winona had been described as kind, but no woman would have been kind in a situation of unwanted attention. "Marcus, exactly why did your mother hire Opal? Was there some obligation, some tie?"

Marcus looked out at the lake. "Opal was down on her luck at first, and my mother wanted to help. Then they were friends. I think my mother admired Opal for her strength and independence, the way she'd just pick up and decide she was going to travel, to visit cities and landmarks. She'd come through hard times, and maybe my mother saw a little of herself in Opal. I know she felt sorry for her."

Tempest recollected the running survey she'd made of Opal's room near the kitchen. Other people, probably the maids, had been there, one who had multiple lovers and worried about balancing her schedule; another was a single mother, struggling with online college programs and worrying about how her children would get a better education.

But the single most potent energy had to be Opal's, startling in her desire for another woman—Winona, worshipping her as much as she hated Jason Greystone. The prospect of another baby could have caused Opal to respond, to plan Jason's murder. Jason would stand in the way of an abortion, and a second child would tie Winona even closer to Jason. There would be no escape, no happy ending with Winona. The plan to murder Jason could have gone wrong and killed Winona. Or perhaps Jason was not intended to die. Perhaps Opal had believed Winona had betrayed her by conceiving with her lover and in her fury had wanted only Winona dead.

Naturally Opal would be uneasy when questioned about Winona and Jason. Especially if she killed them.

"Tell me about what you remember of Opal as she was back then."

Marcus studied the seagulls gathered on a fishing boat left on the shoreline while a man and a woman, obviously involved with each other, lay on a blanket. "She was always there. Quiet and in the background—for the most part. Very efficient. Mom trusted her implicitly, even when they argued. Opal was always with Mom when she was needed, always with me. She didn't like Jason, that was apparent."

"And when Winona and Jason argued?"

Marcus shrugged and collected his laptop, tucking it against his side as if it were his armor, his weapon and a part of him. "I don't know. I suppose I was too young and unhappy already, so my memories might be confused. They were probably protecting me as much as they could. I do know that Opal wanted my mother to leave Jason."

Winona couldn't leave Jason because she was protecting her son—until the day that she defied her husband. "And how did Jason feel about Opal?"

Marcus checked his watch. "With you asking questions, this thing could move really fast. Opal should be here at any minute. Jason didn't like anyone who protected us. He threatened to fire her, but he never did. I think that may have been the last straw for my mother. I think he liked treating Opal like a lowly servant. He needed to bring others down to elevate his own miserable personality."

Or just maybe Jason understood how Opal felt about Winona, and in his perverted mind, he was enjoying the older woman's unrequited love for his wife.

Either that, or Opal might have had her own little blackmail going, holding some tidbit over Jason that he feared might destroy his social position . . . such as he was sterile despite his very public heir, a son who couldn't be his biological child.

Marcus watched the couple on the beach, obviously wrapped up in each other, but he seemed to be wading through memories. "Opal always hated the times my mother went out in the cruiser by herself. I suppose she was worried, but that cruiser was my mother's only relief. She could handle it beautifully. I don't know how she learned. I asked her once, and she said she'd learned from my father. I don't know how she could have. Jason was good in business but pitiful on water. Instinct clicks in then, and experience, and his were in business."

And Kenny would have had both. What had Opal known of that relationship? Had she known who fathered Winona's baby? Had she known that when Winona went out by herself, it might have been to meet her lover?

Tempest looked at the dark blue sedan moving up the shadows of the driveway, but her mind prowled through the last few days with Marcus. She was changing. Was it because she had temporarily bonded with Marcus, and she was becoming stronger? Or was she becoming stronger because she was reaching for more, opening her senses to more, real and unreal, what she could see and what she could feel?

In another few minutes, she might know more about Opal than perhaps the woman understood about herself.

"You're wearing his mother's locket," Opal stated harshly. Seated on the living-room couch, she held her handbag tightly on her lap; she placed her teacup in its saucer on the teak coffee table. Her glasses flashed as she tensed and leaned forward. "Did Mr. Greystone give it to you?"

Her tone implied another question: *Or did you steal it?* Tempest ran her gloved thumb over the smooth engraving on the back, the initials W.R. "This is all I have left of her. She always wore it. I want you to have it," Marcus had said.

"What? No diamond tennis bracelet?" Tempest had asked, teasing him. His simple gift had meant more to Tempest than expensive jewelry; she'd been so touched that she'd almost cried. Instead, she'd made light of the moment.

He'd lifted her face with his fingertip and brushed his lips across hers. "Diamonds are for the other girls, green eyes. Let me know if you need help with Opal, okay?"

Still stunned that he would give her something so precious, Tempest had murmured demurely, "As you wish."

Marcus had chuckled and kissed her briefly. "Behaving isn't something you do well, sweetheart. I should know."

Upon Opal's arrival later, Marcus had chatted a bit, then tactfully removed himself to his office, leaving Tempest to forage for answers. "I found the necklace on the *Winona*, and Marcus wanted me to have it."

Opal's lips tightened. "He let you on that boat? It was his mother's . . . it's been in storage, and Kenny said that—"

"Kenny said what?" Tempest asked when Opal stopped abruptly.

The older woman regrouped quickly, a sign that she'd had practice. "Kenny said that—that you'd been at the marina and that Mr. Greystone saved you from falling. Why were you up on that back ladder anyway? And at night?"

"Marcus was working, and I thought I'd look around without disturbing him. I couldn't get the combination right on the ground floor, and I thought I'd try the other way to get in." Tempest remembered that figure in the fog, and it could have been a woman. "Were you at the marina that night?"

Opal sniffed. "Of course not. Funny way of looking around, climbing up a back way at night—and what for anyway? And if you don't watch yourself, you'll be kidnapped like you were yesterday. Oh, yes, word gets around Port Salem, it does for a fact. You're here to get him and everything he has, and he's already told me to help you find that driver. Told me, the woman who practically raised him. You've turned him against me. He wants me to 'cooperate' with you. Mr. Greystone doesn't think that you're trouble, but I do."

"Am I? For who?" Tempest asked quietly, because without Marcus nearby, Opal wasn't afraid to speak her mind. Apparently she was just getting warmed up.

"Twitching around here in those tight pants and that red hair, cut like a boy's . . . always wearing those gloves, black leather, not the kind a lady would wear even if she wanted to dress up. You're not his type—he likes women with class, like his mother. Anyone can see you're just after his money."

"I have a little hand problem, and that's why I wear gloves. Leather is just more practical. And I know you loved his mother."

"Of course I did. Winona was sweet and kind."

Tempest rose from the couch where she had been sitting next to Opal. She sat in the chair opposite the other woman; she needed every nuance of Opal's expressions. Tempest settled into the calm she needed before launching her very precise question: "Tell me about Winona, Opal. The woman you loved and wanted."

"As if I'd give you any insight into family matters, even if Mr. Greystone wants me to." Opal sniffed again and looked out of the window to the harbor. "I'm only here because he asked me. This was my house once. I'll be back when you're gone, taking over as I've always done."

Suddenly, she turned back to Tempest, her blue eyes widened. "What do you mean, 'loved and wanted'? Of course I loved Winona, she was my friend, and I wanted only the best for her. Jason wasn't good enough for her."

"Was any man? Any other man?"

Opal sat back as if she'd taken a blow, her lips parted as if she'd just issued a silent cry. Then her fury began to build. "I don't know what you're talking about."

Tempest slowly removed her glove and ran her fingertip around the teacup handle that Opal had just used. She shivered with the dark, hateful, jealous energies snaking up her arm and quickly replaced her glove. She had to stay focused on this interview, to get more from Opal than her energy; she needed a visual reaction. She'd caught something else on that teacup, a scene Opal had recently witnessed, and Tempest used it. "You saw them put that cloth over my face, and you saw them push me into the van. Anyone else seeing that would have called the police. I checked, and no one had called in—except Marcus."

"Why—why would you think something like that?"

Because Opal's energy was filled with jealousy, anger, and disgust. She had wished for something bad to happen to Tempest, and she'd been pleased. "I saw you watching, just before they pushed me into the van," Tempest lied.

If Opal questioned just where Tempest had seen her at the time, she could lose the moment. She was running on pure intuition now, picking up sparks from the other woman and massaging them into a probe that could get information. "You wouldn't want me to tell Marcus that, would you? That you saw me being drugged and manhandled, and you didn't call the police?"

"You saw no such thing."

"Try me. Let's call Marcus in here right now and

settle just who he believes. He knows you were home at the time, because he'd just called you. He wanted to know if I was there." Tempest inhaled and regretted the challenge the moment she'd issued it. Marcus clearly loved Opal, and he still held a margin of disbelief in psychic powers.

When Opal tensed, Tempest knew she had the advantage. She wasn't certain how Marcus would have reacted, when put to the test. Impulsive threats didn't always pay off.

But sometimes they did, and this was one of those times. Tempest decided to push her advantage, giving Opal no time to consider the location of her condo in reference to the covered garage. "All I want are the answers to a few questions, and Marcus will never know that you want me out of his life."

Opal's distaste, fear, and need to escape warred with Tempest's threat. "Ask," she said finally, resentment in her expression and tone.

"Okay. I understand that Jason rarely went on the cruiser, except for an occasional party. Do you know why Jason and Winona were out on that yacht together that evening—without guests? Do you know why she was upset when they came back? And finally, do you know where they were going the night that they were killed?"

Clearly alarmed, Opal's hand went over her chest. Had Tempest pushed too hard? Could her questions cause the older woman to have a heart attack?

Tempest reached and held Opal's hand as she spoke quietly, soothingly. "I know you loved her, and you were frustrated that she stayed with Jason—Marcus told me that much. But he doesn't know how you loved her—"

"As a friend, just as a good friend."

Tempest decided to let Opal hide behind that response. "You wanted to kill Jason, didn't you?"

This time, Opal's fury burst into the air between them, her expression savage. "Of course I did. He was perverse, hurting her in all sorts of ways."

"What did they argue about? Maybe it will shed some light on what happened that night."

Opal's anger slid back, carefully concealed, but still simmering in her blue eyes. Obviously, she still loved Winona, wrapped in what-might-have-been. But she had to protect herself, too, and chose her words carefully. "Jason wanted to get rid of me. She loved me—as a friend. She needed me. Her son needed me, too. He was just a boy."

Tempest leaned back and tried to ease the other woman, giving her time to recover, before the next questions. The path to answers was open now, and she eased Opal into it. "I understand. Jason was a bully."

"Yes, a bully. I would have protected her, if she'd just listened. She wouldn't leave him. We argued about that—Winona and me."

"The night they died, did you argue about the coming baby?"

Opal's gnarled hands dug into her black handbag, her answer a hiss in the sunlit room. "Yes."

"She got pregnant again, and you didn't like it."

"He'd have her then, bound up too tight to get away from that bastard."

"Jason would have held that over you, wouldn't he? That he had Winona, and you couldn't have her? Or did she really want you?"

"Of course she wanted me. We were like sisters."

Or would Opal have preferred like lovers? Tempest smoothed the locket again, and Opal's eyes traced the movement. "Opal, tell me about this locket. Marcus said Winona always wore it. Do you know when she got it? Was it something from her parents? The W.R. engraved on the back stood for Winona Roberts?"

Quickly shielding her expression, the older woman

looked down at her purse, clutched in her hands. "Roberts was her maiden name—maybe so. Maybe someone sent it to her later. Her parents had been dead for a long time when she started wearing that. Maybe she started wearing it after her son was born, maybe just before. She wore through a few chains with it. You take good care of it, and leave it when you go," she ordered abruptly as she glared at Tempest.

"I'll be very careful with it." Something had happened about the time of Marcus's birth that had caused Winona to wear the necklace. What was it? Did it have something to do with Marcus's biological father?

Tempest thought of how Jason had called Marcus a bastard. "Do you know the actual meaning of the word, 'bastard,' Opal?"

When the other woman paled and glanced toward Marcus's office, Tempest understood: Opal knew that Jason hadn't sired Marcus—and probably not the coming baby, either. Which led to Tempest's next question: "You might know this—since you were Winona's confidante—did she ever talk about another man?"

Anger leaped into Opal's expression, too much for her adamant denial. Opal knew that Winona had taken a lover, the father of Marcus and perhaps the new baby, but she didn't want to admit it to herself, denying Winona's preference to another to the end. "Of course not. She was a good woman. Why are you asking all of these questions?"

"Marcus is after that hit-and-run driver, and so am I. We're not going to stop until we discover who it was, neither one of us."

"After all these years? Mr. Greystone has that hellfire and damnation look again. It's because of you— you've got him all stirred up. He's got Kenny getting the *Winona* out of storage, fixing her up for some poker party. You're here, messing in business that you have no right to be in, tearing up people's lives all over again. You've got no right, none at all, even if he says you do."

"Don't I? " Tempest met the other woman's eyes. Opal was obviously dangerous, and she saw Tempest as a challenger for Marcus. Her energy was that of frustration, anger, unrequited love, and jealousy. Any of those elements could have caused her to ram that tulip truck into the Greystones. "Love dies hard, doesn't it?"

Marcus leaned back in the restaurant's chair and considered Tempest.

From the moment they'd joined the dinner crowd at the Homeport Restaurant, she'd drawn attention. As they'd followed the waiter to their table, her hair had caught the subtle light in a fiery halo, the line of her body athletic and feminine. Marcus had kept his hand at her waist. A little old-fashioned and proprietorial perhaps, he decided, mocking himself.

In the table's candlelight, her features seemed more pale than ever, her eyebrows more arched, her eyes more slanted and her lips definitely glossy and soft. In a silky black camisole and short-skirt number, with dainty pearl studs in her lobes, she looked quite civilized and definitely tempting.

Marcus considered her civilized look, a silky veneer for what he knew lay beneath, an impulsive, restless, rebellious woman who brought him warmth and excitement. Wrapped up now in solving the hit-and-run, Tempest might not see herself as he did, perhaps as a wife, perhaps as a mother.

His mother's locket gleamed against Tempest's soft skin, a little reassurance that she wore his possession.

Marcus had another reason for giving her the locket, that of protecting her. Tempest had already proven that she was too impulsive, reckless, and not easily contained; she set her own terms on where she would go and when. With Whitcomb in the area and because of Sean's fixation on her, or any other threats to her, Marcus wanted to know where she was at all times. The small transmitter inside the locket would track her, if and when she decided to go anywhere without him. Keeping tabs on Tempest wouldn't be easy, and after yesterday's terror, the transmitter was a little insurance that he could find her—within its range—and protect her.

Kenny hadn't asked why Marcus had asked him to deliver the transmitter and handheld tracking device. "I don't even need to ask who this is for. After yesterday and after her climb up the marina's back way—I can guess," he had stated. "She's pure trouble, but I guess you can't help it. You always were one to work at what you wanted bad enough, but this says you don't trust her either."

"It's just her nature to move fast," Marcus had said. "Yesterday is proof that she needs protection. This is just a little insurance."

Marcus not only wanted that killer, he wanted Tempest "bad enough" and for a long, long time. If he needed to resort to tracking her to keep her safe, he would. When Tempest turned to study the tiny dance floor, Marcus locked on to the line of her throat down to the rise of her breasts above that lace and tensed. If there was one place he wanted his lips and hands, it was on this woman. As if sensing the chemistry heating between them, Tempest turned to him. "Why are we here?"

"I thought you might like a night off, and we could relieve a little tension with a good dinner. And I've never danced with you. The band is good here."

She ran the tip of her black silk glove, embroidered with hot pink roses, around the rim of her wineglass. "It feels like a date. A reservation for two, dinner and dancing, us all dressed up."

"A little out of the usual order of things, but I like to think I have some gallantry left in me."

"Ye old cart-before-the-horse sort of thing?"

Marcus took her hand in his and lifted it to his lips. He turned Tempest's hand over and nudged that glove slightly aside to kiss her inner wrist. "What can I say? I'm a romantic at heart."

Tempest leaned close to brush her lips with his. "Tell me another one. I'm headed for Kenny, and you want in on the action. You're starting to wonder if you've missed something. Tell me about him."

He cupped the back of her head and held her close to his face. She resisted slightly, her eyes flashing just that bit, picking up the candlelight. "You've been through hell, answered all the questions, filled out all the forms, and we both deserve a little relaxation. I've wanted answers since I was fourteen, but don't you think that we could take a breather, enjoy tonight and start again tomorrow?"

She didn't answer but leaned back and considered Marcus. "As I understand it, Kenny basically ran the day-to-day things at the marina. Jason managed, or later mismanaged, the business, thanks to his involvement with the wrong woman."

Marcus sighed, sipped his wine, and shook his head. "Neil told me I'd have to get used to the curiosity, you more than the rest. Don't you ever relax? Yes, that's pretty much how it went. Jason used a few people on his way up, but Kenny made the reality of the marina work."

"The man behind the scenes. The man with practical knowledge of the products—a smart man."

Marcus inhaled uneasily. Tempest was hunting, and she'd locked on to his dearest friend. She may have put Kenny into the pot with Sean's gaming addiction and had guessed that he may have influenced the youth. "Don't go there. Kenny wouldn't have put those kids up to anything. He's worked with Cody, too, and Cody acted because Sean had threatened him and his little sister."

Tempest looked at Marcus over her wineglass. "We're drawing quite a few stares. Why is that?"

"I suppose it could be because when you dress up— or when you don't, there's something to stare at. Or, it could be because other than my ex-wife, I haven't brought a woman to Port Salem."

Tempest placed her glass very carefully on its coaster. "They think we're—committed. They're hoping this is when you pull out a ring, and I'll ooh and ah."

She leveled a dark look at him. "Don't you dare."

Marcus remembered his conversation with Leona on the morning she left; he intended to marry Tempest. Leona had laughed softly, chiding him. "She's a runner, and fast. You'll have to keep up."

"That's what Neil said," Marcus had agreed. "You can tell your family that I'll take good care of her."

Leona's expression said that she agreed, but her impish smile indicated he had a lot of surprises in store.

He focused on the woman seated close to him, who had already experienced one bad relationship. He intended to make Tempest see the positives of a relationship with him. "I'm feeling committed. It's not a bad feeling. And I like to think that I won't be getting up one morning to find you've taken off."

"Ah. That's why we're here, and you're not placing international calls or working on the great poker game. You want a public display that I'm under your protection. You want to protect me."

"And I want to dance with you. Aren't you curious about what else I've got planned for tonight?" Marcus noted Francesca talking to the maitre d' of the filled restaurant. "She needs a place to sit. Okay if we invite her over?"

Tempest's curiousity was usually primed and ready, but this time she didn't question him. Marcus didn't trust Tempest's too-bright smile and that narrowing of her eyes as she looked at Francesca. "Sure."

"Behave yourself."

Homeport's "little girl's room" proved an excellent chance to get Francesca alone. After dinner, Tempest followed the other woman into the restroom.

At the vanity, each woman stood warily looking at the other's reflection. Tempest freshened her lip gloss. When she replaced it in her bag, she withdrew the red scrap of material. "Did you lose this last night?"

Francesca's reflected image stiffened, her eyes widening. "I don't know what you mean."

"When you visited us—at Marcus's home. I saw you, but I didn't tell Marcus." The lie had worked with Opal, but Francesca was a different matter.

Tempest released her breath when Francesca's expression turned to panic; the lie had worked. "I wanted to talk to him alone."

"Really? That late?" Tempest had gotten the admission, now she needed more.

"Marcus often works late. I've come over late before, and he hasn't minded. Then I saw that the lights were out in his office and the rest of the house, and I changed my mind."

Tempest turned, crossed her arms, and leaned back against the vanity. "What did you want to talk about? Maybe I can help."

"Nothing that would concern you. Nothing, but you're upsetting everyone in town, asking all those questions. You're just a passing fancy, using sex to get what you want. It won't last. Marcus doesn't go for your type at all, and you're stirring up a lot of pain— his pain—the way his parents died," Francesca hissed angrily, the careful professional woman's mask slipping from her well-tended face. "Opal is very upset. She said that you asked horrible questions. How dare you!"

"Marcus wants to know who killed his parents. He's given me permission to ask. I'm just doing what he wanted, and I know he's asked you to help. If there's something you don't want known to Marcus, I might be able to help. But he's actively involved in this, and he might be asking questions himself that you don't want to answer. One of them might be why would Opal would discuss this with you in particular?"

"She called Kenny, too. Kenny is going to talk to Marcus. Marcus has always listened to him. You stood out there on the beach and flirted with that boy, Cody. You probably set up that whole kidnapping and caused that boy's, Sean's, death. Kenny said the boys weren't bad, but you're upsetting everyone. If you continue this with me, I'm going to slap a harassment suit on you."

"Go ahead. Try it. It will just look like you're hiding something and make Marcus suspicious, and you wouldn't want that, would you . . . especially since you want him. Oh, am I upsetting you? Too bad. What do you know about the tulip truck hitting the Greystones?"

Francesca's hand went to her throat, a protective gesture. "Are you accusing me of murder? If you are, I'll sue you for slander."

"I'm only asking questions. Marcus wants answers, and if you want, I can have him ask the same questions."

"He's already questioned me, so many times through the years—if I knew anyone, did I know anyone who might have killed them. There was that awful mess with the gangster and Jason, and now Marcus is asking me questions again—because of you. He's called and talked with me. He wants to go over every minute of all those years ago. He's looking for something that was missed. He's asked me to go over any old photographs of his parents, of other people around then . . . He's paying you, isn't he? I never thought that Marcus would—You're really a prostitute, aren't you?"

Tempest remembered Francesca's expression at the dinner table when Marcus had leaned close to whisper in Tempest's ear. Once catching Francesca's jealous expression, Tempest had turned to kiss him. Francesca's anger had been barely sheathed, but now her claws were visible. Tempest pushed her just that bit, probing for an angle that could cause a reaction. Unless her female instincts and her definitely morphed-and-tangled-with-Marcus sixth sense were wrong, Francesca just might have been Jason's lover—and that could be a motive for murder. "Marcus is quite the man—he wouldn't have to pay any woman. You're overly jealous, don't you think?"

"I've practically raised him. What do you mean?"

"Like father, like son?"

Thirteen

"WHERE ARE WE GOING?"

In the convertible, Tempest snuggled close to Marcus as they passed the Port Salem city limits sign. After dinner and a few slow dances, he was definitely hot and revved and perfect. She couldn't wait to see him all rumpled and sweet in the afterglow of their love-making.

"I thought we'd take a little edge off whatever is going on with you—before getting you back in the vicinity of the lake."

"That would be one way to cool my plans for you, Greystone. I thought I'd top off the night with you, and sleep like a log."

"You didn't that first night with me."

The reminder of the fog curling around her, sucking her warmth, chilled Tempest again. The lake and the fog were still out there, beckoning to her. The night she'd climbed up the marina's back stairway, someone had been out there, standing in the fog, watching her. Opal had denied it. Could it have been Kenny? Or Sean? Who was it?

Tempest eased away from Marcus's arm and looked outside at the passing stand of timber. Life with Marcus was too easy, and yet too challenging—and she was quickly becoming addicted to his other side, the gentle, loving, boyish one. She had never felt so safe or feminine and normal as when she was cuddled close against him. Not a good thing when she didn't exactly know her limits, and she was definitely a work in progress—psychically speaking. She'd heard of psychics frying others, putting them on overload and wrecking their lives—she couldn't do that to Marcus.

"Where are we going?" she asked again.

"A favorite spot of mine." Marcus pulled off the highway, onto a side road, and drove up a rough winding road. He parked the car on a knoll overlooking Port Salem.

"Mm, I like," she murmured as she stretched her arms up high and scanned the city's twinkling lights. The view was just close enough to show the harbor's lights and those of a yacht, anchored a distance from the shoreline.

Marcus settled back in the seat, his hand caressing her back. "I thought you would."

She glanced at the way Marcus sprawled back, his hand on the steering wheel, his arm across the back of her seat. "You used to come here to make out, didn't you?"

"Good times. . . . Lost it in the bed of an old pickup I'd rebuilt. I was fourteen—just before the wreck— and I really loved that old pickup. I took my girl for a ride in it late one night and did the deed. Pretty proud of myself on both accounts back then." His hand caressed her nape, his thumb brushed her cheek. Marcus had that well-satisfied, laid-back look as though he was going to enjoy every minute of a very private dessert.

"You were underage, Marcus. You could have had big trouble from the girl's folks—and your own. But I bet you lost it a few times after that, too."

"Maybe." He looked at her, and Tempest's little tingling sensuality hiked into a full simmer. He eased his seat back. "Come here."

What was a girl going to do? Tempest thought as she kicked off her heels. She hiked up her skirt and eased over the gearshift on her way to him. As she straddled him, Marcus's hands slid up her thighs to test her thong, her garter belt, and then down to the lacy black tops of her thigh-highs. He tugged on her garter straps. "Are you going to let me see the rest of it?"

For an answer, Tempest eased her camisole away. Marcus's hands tightened instantly, his eyes just silvery slits in the shadows as he traced her lacy black bra with his hands, running his fingers just slightly beneath the cups.

Tempest unbuttoned his shirt and lifted to undo his belt buckle. She eased his zipper down and cradled him in her hand. He was ready and—she looked at him. "I've never done this before."

His hand caressed her back. "That's what I'd guessed. I thought I'd give you a new experience to remember."

She moved her hands to his shoulders. "Just how would you know that?"

He lifted his hips, nudging her rhythmically. "Do we have to spoil the mood? Or are you the kind of girl who works a guy up on the dance floor and then doesn't pay off?"

If he hadn't grinned after that last statement, she might have taken offense. As it was, Marcus looked so cute and boyish and pleased with himself that Tempest couldn't resist playing to the tease. "Steamed you up good, did I?"

"Me and every other male in the place. But I'm the one that's getting the payoff from the cozy feel of it. Is this where you take off your gloves and melt me?"

"No, but I was going to do a little striptease at the house, but by coming here, you've ruined that plan. I'm pretty good at dancing around a pole."

"Damn."

His curse sounded so frustrated that Tempest smiled; she lifted to ease his shorts down just that bit until she could hold him in both gloved hands. "But let's be practical about this. Maybe the night isn't a total loss. We might salvage a little something."

"Mm. . . ." Marcus was already busy releasing her bra and bringing her down to his hungry kiss. While he was working his way down her throat to her breasts, his fingers eased inside that thong—

"Strings at the side," Tempest whispered, as Marcus's lips played her nipples gently.

He found the bows instantly and drew away the thong. She held her breath as he slowly stroked her intimately, then slowly slid inside. In another minute, Tempest was flying, wrapped so deeply in Marcus that she didn't care about anything else.

Later, lying soft upon him, treasuring the way his heart slowed, his hands gentle upon her, she nuzzled his throat. "You're right, this was a first experience."

"I thought so."

She snuggled closer to him, enjoying the warmth and intimacy. "Was it her first time, too?"

"Hm?"

She smoothed that bit of chest hair, nuzzled it, and appreciated his scent and texture. "Was it her first time, too? I mean I can't imagine a girl's first time like this."

He'd suddenly gone too quiet, and Tempest lifted slightly. "It wasn't her first time?"

Marcus was evidently choosing his words carefully. "No. She was a bit older and wiser."

"How old? Someone married or divorced?"

When he tensed and looked away, she tugged his chest hair gently. "Marcus?"

"Okay, she was experienced. Okay? Are you done asking questions?"

Marcus eased her away and onto the passenger seat, then moved his seat upright. But Tempest wasn't being put off, and he was definitely hiding something. "Who was she?" she asked carefully, alerted by her tingling senses.

When he glanced in the rearview mirror, he said, "Someone is coming—Ouch!"

Tempest had gripped his chest hair, hard this time. He wasn't leaving here without an answer. "Tell me?"

"Okay, it was Francesca."

"Francesca!"

He'd caught the incensed anger in her tone and hurried to explain. "Okay, it happened. It was probably better an experienced woman first than me fumbling with a virgin."

Tempest crossed her arms over her bare breasts. "I don't believe you. You brought me here—right here where you learned from Francesca. You said it was your favorite spot. We just had dinner with her. Marcus!"

"Everyone learns somewhere, sometime. Don't get all worked up." Marcus ran his hand through his hair, and then gripped the steering wheel. He glanced in the rearview mirror. "That truck is headed right for us."

He started the car and began to reverse, but the truck was upon them; the massive bumper hit them from behind. The truck's headlights blinded Tempest as she looked back. Grimly focused, Marcus had already started the car, putting it in reverse, the tires spinning, pitted against the force of the truck. But it was slowly, inevitably pushing them toward the edge of the knoll. Tempest noted a clump of trees below them and beyond them, the brick building. "If we hit that, we'll kill anyone—"

"It's abandoned. Get out," he ordered quietly. "Jump.

Put everything you've got into getting as far away as you can."

"What about you?"

Marcus jerked on the hand brake, setting it. "Right behind you."

The car had already started to slide, and Tempest held her breath as she leaped as far as she could. She hit the ground hard and rolled, coming to her feet instantly. She held up her hand against the blinding headlights of the truck as it quickly reversed, backing into the night.

"Marcus?" Terrified for him, she called into the darkness. After crashing through a small stand of timber, and into the brick building at the bottom of the hill, the car suddenly exploded. "Marcus!"

Without shoes, Tempest carefully picked her way to the edge of the knoll and found Marcus working his way back up. "Marcus? Are you all right?"

"I'm okay." At the top of the knoll, he tugged her to him. It was hard to tell whether she was shaking or if he was, their hearts pounding. Tempest held him with every bit of her strength, her face pressed against his throat. His pulse raced against her skin, and she could feel Marcus's fear before he spoke. "Are you? Are you hurt?"

"I'm fine—but you've got a cut on your head. You're bleeding."

Marcus lifted her face to the moonlight, then ran his hands over her head and throat, and down her arms. He removed his shirt and wrapped her into it, then looked down at the car in flames. "I don't suppose you've got a cell phone tucked into that garter belt, do you?" he asked.

She held up the cell phone that she'd gripped on her way out of the passenger door.

"Good thinking."

After Marcus had called Kenny, asking him to bring

something for Tempest to wear, and then the police, Tempest asked, "Who else would know about this place?"

His answer was succinct. "Just about everyone. Did you get anything on the truck?"

Tempest shivered within his arms. "Big. Maybe diesel. I couldn't see because of the headlights. It was bulky, though, not like a pickup with a bed. It was bigger."

Fifteen minutes later, Kenny arrived; he quickly took in Marcus's disheveled look and his shirt covering Tempest. He tossed a mechanic's coveralls to her. "Looks like a city gravel truck parked down by the highway. I called the police. They're on the way."

While Tempest dressed in the coveralls, Kenny walked to the edge of the knoll with Marcus. "It hit that old grocery store. You'd have died."

He glanced at Tempest, who had come to stand beside Marcus, her hand holding his. Kenny's expression was that of distaste, and he turned away. "Things are stirred up here lately."

"That's enough, Kenny. Leave her alone," Marcus ordered grimly.

The police chief arrived a few minutes later, the red light cycling on top of the patrol car. When questioning Marcus and Tempest, Mac's comments ran the same. "Let's see now. You were just kidnapped yesterday, Ms. Storm, and that kid, Sean, killed himself. Then his shack burned down. Then here you are—"

The police chief's flashlight roamed over Tempest's overlarge dirty coveralls. "Are you a mechanic, by the way? You're wearing coveralls."

"I manage," she answered tightly, and eased away from Marcus's protective arm. "Can we just come in tomorrow and make our statements?"

"It's getting to be a regular appointment. Better put that on your calendar. You, too, Marcus."

After Kenny dropped them off at the house, Marcus quickly turned on her. "What's with you? Every time I come close to you, you move away."

"Let me see that cut on your forehead."

He looked at her warily. "What are you going to do to it?"

"Bend down here. I'm mad at you, but that doesn't mean you have to end up with an infection from an untended cut. What would people think of me if I let that go?"

Marcus bent, but he seemed uneasy. "I don't get it."

Tempest frowned at his injury, then went into the bathroom off the kitchen area. "Where is the antiseptic?"

She found it and returned to order Marcus, "Bend down here."

He obeyed and held still while she cleaned the small wound and applied a bandage. "There."

Marcus stood in the kitchen looking as if he'd lost his mooring and was adrift, his shirt unbuttoned and his slacks dirty and torn. Her thong dangled out of one pocket, and Tempest quickly snatched it. She hurried to the trash and tossed it away.

"I still don't get it—why you're mad. And I wanted to keep that. You could use it again," Marcus stated.

"Well, you can't keep it, and I'm not wearing it again. You and Francesca, that's why I'm mad. Don't you see how wrong it was to take me to the same place as your first time with her?"

"Hell, no, I don't. I went there with other girls."

"And me. Oh, glory be, I'm just one of the herd."

"But you're the only one who drives me crazy. The only one I brought home and wanted to keep, and who I helped make our bed this morning. Do you think I ever cared enough to do that after sleeping with a woman? Was that what your private chat with Francesca in the little girls' room was about? Sorting out territory? Because you started getting really cozy just after you came out, and she was breathing fire."

"I don't know what you are talking about," Tempest lied as she unzipped her coveralls and stepped out of them. She crossed her arms over her bare breasts; she let him stare at what he was going to be missing until he understood that her first experience parking on a moonlight night was coming in second to Francesca's. Maybe she was a little jealous . . . maybe . . . perhaps. But then she knew how much Francesca still wanted him—even if he didn't. "You could at least have taken me somewhere else."

"Dammit, you're in my house, living with me, aren't you? What the hell do you think that means? You sleep in my bed and I—"

Marcus stopped talking when Tempest turned and walked away. He let out a frustrated groan, then followed her through the house and into the bedroom. It was his bedroom; at least he didn't have to go through that argument, because he was too tired and frustrated. He flicked on the light. "Stop right there. I want to see the damage."

Tempest frowned at him and slowly unfastened her garter snaps, quickly rolling down the ruined stockings. With a flourish, she whipped off her garter belt and tossed it to him. "I'm just fine. A few bruises here and there. Now you strip."

Marcus wasn't certain how he felt about a woman ordering him to undress when it wasn't sexual foreplay. He undressed and tossed his clothing aside. Tempest walked to him and studied his body. "Turn around."

"You first."

Despite his frustration and the brewing argument about Francesca, Marcus was shocked at the scratches and bruises on Tempest's back. He ran a gentle hand over her skin and wished that he could have protected her. He smoothed the small scratches on her bottom.

268 I Cait London

The fear that she could have been killed, lying in a morgue right now, terrified him afresh. "You should have told me."

"I landed in the bushes. No big deal. Now turn around."

"I've never gone in for the dominatrix stuff, sweetheart."

But Marcus obeyed, and Tempest carefully examined his body and the long scratch on his arm. She tested it with her gloved fingertip. "It's not deep. I have a sister who could heal that. Make sure you clean it well, and you'll be okay."

When Marcus turned to her again, she carefully picked the small fragments of leaves and rubble from his chest. Tears shimmered in her eyes. "We're both going to be sore in the morning."

Marcus smoothed her waist. Tempest seemed so small and delicate, and he needed to hold her. Still, Tempest was unpredictable, and he didn't want to push his luck at the wrong time. "You're not mad at me anymore?"

Tempest stiffened. "Oh, yes, I am."

In the shower, Marcus stared down at her, the water streaming around them, flattening his hair to his head, emphasizing his rugged features. He glared at her. "Is this going to be an issue? We could have been killed out there, and you're nagging—"

"I never nag."

Tempest stepped out of the shower and began to dry herself. Marcus got out, took away her towel, and continued the job. "I don't get it."

It wasn't until they stood facing each other in the steaming bathroom, and he looked so puzzled and vulnerable, that Tempest's reaction set in. A lifetime of self-protection slipped away and pooled at her feet. "We could have been killed."

He blinked as if trying to find footing on a slippery slope. "Uh-huh."

"You could have been killed!" Tempest wrapped her arms around him and held him tight. "I don't want anything happening to you. Everything is happening now, with me here, close to you."

"And that's the way it's going to stay, honey. You and me. Together," he said, so gently that Tempest could almost forget his Francesca faux pas.

Still careful of her, Marcus eased her into bed. He held her close. "Feeling better, honey?"

Tempest smoothed his chest, his shoulders, his hard ribs and flat stomach; she placed her hand over the beat of his heart; they were both alive, and he hadn't been hurt. She fought the tears burning her eyes. "I wanted tonight to be so special. It was a great outfit, Marcus. I was going to seduce you."

He'd been right about Tempest's territorial need to claim him in front of another woman, and that had shocked her—because it was true. To discover that she didn't really know the depth of her feelings for Marcus, how she wanted to claim him had thrown Tempest off-balance. She'd always been so certain of her emotions—after Brice. She'd always protected herself so well, and now—

Now, she couldn't think about anything but that Marcus was safe in her arms, warm and alive. His kisses along her temple led to her mouth. "You can seduce me another time. Waiting will just make it better, honey."

"I think I'm going to cry. I mean, really cry. I never do that. I feel so weak and in pieces. I thought you'd been killed, and I couldn't stand that. I couldn't bear it if anything happened to you."

"I'm just fine, and so are you." Marcus gathered her closer and kissed her damp lashes. "You'll be okay, honey. We'll get you a new outfit. You looked great, standing up there on the top of the hill, all pale and long-legged, just wearing that black garter belt and those stockings. . . . Sorry they were ruined. I really liked them. And I'll get a stripper pole installed."

She sniffed and nuzzled his shoulder; she'd wake up in the morning and Marcus would be lying there and breathing, alive beside her. It was enough for now. "It is good exercise."

"Something everyone should do," he agreed easily as he rocked her against his body.

Tempest listened to his breathing, the way his heart beat against her cheek, the way his arms were strong around her, and decided that they were both safe and tomorrow could wait.

But Kenny was right; she'd stirred up the past, and someone didn't like it. To protect Marcus, she might have to leave.

"Don't even think about it," he murmured sleepily. "You're not going anywhere."

The order didn't feel like an order. It felt like something she wanted to hear, that she needed to hear.

But Francesca was definitely on her unfriendly list.

"Lucky thing you jumped clear. The girl, too," Kenny stated, as Marcus and he stood in the predawn, staring at the convertible's burned and crumpled wreckage. The abandoned brick building was streaked with smoke where the vehicle had struck. Kenny poured coffee from his thermos and handed an extra cup to Marcus. "How's she doing?"

Marcus shook his head and looked at the police chief making his way down the embankment. When Marcus had left their bed, Tempest had only sighed in her sleep and gathered his pillow against her. He'd almost groaned aloud when he'd stood, his muscles protesting the way he'd landed on the hard ground. "Sleeping. She had a few scratches, and she'll be moving slow today."

Mac looked at the bruise and bandage on Marcus's forehead. "Looks like you are, too."

"I've had better days. 'Morning, Mac," Marcus said to the police chief as his officers circled the wreckage.

Mac Henderson nodded grimly. "Busy night. Add this to that kid, Sean, 'offing' himself, his place burned, and kids partying too hard, and we're up to our ears in investigations with the county and state guys. I hear you referred the news hounds to my office. That was the right thing to do, but I had to call my wife in to answer an extra line. I had to promise her a winter vacation in Florida to get her. It all adds a few years to this old man. How's the girl? Got some more of that coffee, Kenny?"

The police chief took the refill on his travel cup and circled the wreckage, speaking quietly to his men. The flashlight beam ran over the convertible's back bumper and the deep dent and scratches there. He walked back to Marcus. "Someone stole the city's gravel truck last night. I'm going to have to ask a lot of questions that I'd rather not. Your girl is at the top of the list. Those boys grabbing her was bad enough, and now this. We can't have stuff like that happening in my town. Got any idea who might be wanting both of you dead? Or one of you? Or why anyone would want to burn down Sean's place?"

"Not a clue, Mac." Marcus had plenty of ideas, but none that he would give Mac. The police chief was smart and logical, putting pieces together. But Tempest's psychic pieces didn't fit logic, and neither would Marcus's explanations. If Whitcomb was involved somehow, he was running up an even bigger and more painful tab with Marcus, who intended to collect.

The police chief shook his head. "Your girl has already stirred up gossip. She's asking a lot of questions about your folks' accident. You understand that I'm going to have to run a check on her, see if anything unusual turns up, Marcus. If much more happens, I'm going to have the Feds breathing down my neck."

"You do that. But I'll vouch for her. I've asked her to look into my parents' deaths, and that's why she's asking questions."

Mac frowned. "That was, what? Twenty-one years ago? What makes you think she can turn up anything new?"

"It never hurts to put a fresh look on a cold case with someone new, does it, Mac? She's a sculptor, not a detective, but she's extra sharp. Tempest looks at things from a slightly different angle than a trained pro. I wanted her to take a look at the case. Any problems with that?"

"Suppose not. But I have to check her out, just the same."

Marcus thought about those two missing years in Tempest's life. He hoped they were safely tucked away, but Mac might just lift the mask on Dominique's face. If he did, and connected Tempest to Whitcomb and his scams, Marcus would put everything he had into protecting her. "I'll tell her to give you a call."

"Good enough." Mac flashed the light at Kenny's face. "What about you, Kenny? Got any ideas why things are starting to stir up lately?"

Kenny's answer was guarded. "What are you asking, Mac?"

"I just have to ask—you knew those boys pretty well. Cody was working for you, and Cody was a friend of Sean's. Both of them were seen at your place. Cody says you played games, but I'd like to hear it from you. One of my deputies stopped by your place with some questions last night, and you weren't home. I just want to get the right picture about it all. Where were you?"

"You have a problem with me, Mac?" Kenny asked carefully.

"Just asking. That's my job. By the way, no one leaves town until I say so."

Kenny's chin lowered, his beard settled on his coveralls, and his eyes leveled at Mac's. "I went to check on the marina."

"Yeah, that so? My man checked there, too. No one was there."

"He missed me then."

Marcus knew Kenny very well, and his tone said he was hiding something. What was it?

After making their statements at the police station, Marcus and Tempest had dropped by the marina to collect a pleasure boat inventory. As Tempest stood outside the marina's office, looking up at the boat's dry-storage bays, Kenny said, "She's wearing your mother's necklace, Marcus."

"I gave the necklace to her. She found it in the *Winona* after that anchor hit. You said some things had been jarred and out of place. The necklace slipped free somehow."

Kenny's stare narrowed at Tempest. "I never saw it in all the time I cared for the *Winona*. Makes no sense at all that she could just walk in and find it."

"Well, she did." Marcus watched Tempest stroll around inside the marina building. Unpredictable and curious, she'd pushed Francesca last night and wasn't talking about that conversation in the ladies' room. Whatever it was, Francesca had been visibly angry.

Marcus watched Tempest bend over, that shapely backside causing him to remember how soft and pliable, yet strong, it had felt when she'd straddled him in the car and how much he'd liked that sexy outfit.

"You're drooling, boy," Kenny noted quietly. "She's got you under her thumb, hasn't she? Got you all stirred up, doing things you don't usually do, like this poker game and taking the *Winona* out? Since when have you wanted to do either?"

Marcus turned back to Kenny, who was cradling a coffee mug on his stomach, his feet up on the office desk. His affection for the older man who had practically raised him still ran strong, and he hoped that the tension would ease between them. "Maybe I should tell you that I went after Tempest for one reason, and now that's changed. She is unusual, but I'm getting used to that particular little bit of her. The rest is all woman. As for how she feels, she's not exactly happy about being in a relationship."

"And why is that? Most women her age are married with kids, or thinking about it."

"I'll take her any way I can get her. I like her. I like how she makes me feel."

Kenny lifted an eyebrow. "It's more than that, I'd say. She's flashy, cheeky, and a mover. I can't see her staying long with anything. And you've got that settling-down look if I've ever seen one. You should be thinking about that—it gets lonely when you get older."

"I'll take my chances."

Kenny lowered his head and placed the coffee mug on his damaged palm, letting the warmth sink into the scarred tissue and broken bones. It was his habit when deep in thought. "She's mixing in old business, you know. Opal is pretty upset, and I heard Francesca had dinner with you two last night at the Homeport. She called here and wanted to know all about your girl. She's asking too many questions and stirring up problems, Marcus. Sometimes the past is better left alone."

He turned his injured hand, setting the mug on top of it. "You see what happened last night—you're moving as though you're sore. You could have been killed. You caught those boys, but no telling who else is out there wanting payback. Last night was a real big warning that trouble is brewing—"

Interrupted by the ring of Marcus's cell phone, Kenny stopped talking, but he continued to study his hand, running the mug over the crushed bones.

Marcus wondered if Kenny was remembering the past and another warning as he answered. "Hi, Francesca."

Her voice was professionally smooth and cool, lacking the usual warmth and moving directly into setting up a business meeting on the *Winona*, a final checklist. Marcus would have trusted her judgment, but if she wanted a private consultation—about anything, including Tempest—he owed her that, for old times' sake. There was one place where no one would interfere, and that was out on the lake. "I'll set it up and we'll talk, privately."

Her tone brightened, and the call ended; then Marcus turned back to Kenny. "If the *Winona* is ready, I'd like to take Francesca out on a test run this afternoon."

"She's ready. I've kept her in good shape. The motors needed a little priming, that's all. You're usually out on the lake, when you come home, doing a little relaxing. Don't you want to take your girl out on the lake? Cody said she seemed to like it."

"She doesn't like it."

"Can't see you with a girl who doesn't like water as much as you do. Your mother used to take you out. Well, I've said enough."

When Kenny stared off toward the *Winona*, moored in front of the marina, Marcus realized the subject was closed. Kenny was definitely quieter since Tempest had arrived, and something was troubling him. "If there's anything you want to talk about, I'm listening, Kenny."

"Don't forget to take the *Winona*'s key and put it back where it belongs." Kenny stood abruptly; his good left hand cradled his damaged one as he turned and walked out of the office.

Marcus studied Kenny's slumped, shuffling walk into the marina building. Kenny had effectively closed off any further discussion. He was definitely upset about Cody, but something else was disturbing Kenny. And it had to do with Tempest's questions. She'd raised some fear inside Kenny and raised his defenses. Why? What secret was he protecting?

Later that morning, Marcus sat on the edge of the front deck's hot tub and rubbed Tempest's taut neck and shoulders. His private phone call with Mac had chafed; the police chief was seeking a connection between Kenny and the youths, and some reason why Sean would commit suicide. But Mac was right: Kenny's response to where he had been last night didn't ring true.

Based on his trust in Kenny, Marcus had already decided that if the older man needed privacy, he wouldn't question him; he just hoped he wouldn't have to pin Kenny down to protect him. But he intended to ask his own question: Why did Kenny seem to fear Tempest enough to be on the defensive with her?

Marcus looked down at Tempest's nude body in the hot tub, the froth from the jets causing her pale curves to shimmer. She shifted uneasily, as if her body still ached; though she was athletic, the leap from the car would hurt anyone in good shape. "We could have a masseuse come to the house."

She leaned back to stare up at Marcus. Those green eyes closed slowly as he kissed her. "In fact, why don't we order in? A masseuse, a little girl feel-good stuff, and you could get some rest."

Her eyes remained closed as he massaged her temples. "I don't often get a headache, but when I do, it's usually a top-rated one. I just need some rest, and you're right, a massage would be perfect."

Marcus didn't quite trust her answer, or the one to his next question: "You won't try anything while I'm taking the *Winona* out for a test run later today, will you?"

"Would I do that?"

He framed her face with his hands and shook gently until she opened her eyes. "I mean it. Stay out of trouble while I'm gone."

"You're hunting Brice, aren't you? Where is he?"

"In the vicinity."

Those eyes changed into that dark gold shade, and Marcus could have sworn he felt a hot sizzle running up his hands. But then, with Tempest, he was usually simmering.

She'd definitely tensed, the water rippling around her breasts. "Where is he?"

"All that I'm asking is that you stay put and out of the way, just in case he's playing tourist. I wouldn't want a psychic-fry collision on Port Salem's Main Street."

"And I don't like the scenario of the 'womanfolk' waiting at home while the big strong man goes out to fight for her honor, Marcus," Tempest stated darkly as she eased away from his touch. "I'm not worried about Brice. He's smart, and he knows that I can pin him to things he'd rather not have known. He likes to bully, that's all, and it isn't working with me. He'll get bored, and he'll move on. He has before, he will again."

"Keep lying to yourself, and you'll be even more susceptible to someone stalking you." Marcus intended to make certain that Brice never contacted or threatened Tempest again. "One question: You said you hadn't touched-connected-with Brice. But you couldn't sense where he's at, could you? Some little psychic fingers out there hunting for him?"

When she shook her head "no," Marcus bent to kiss her again. "Just let me handle it, okay?"

He didn't trust Tempest's sweet smile or her light, "Okay."

Fourteen

"MARCUS IS TAKING FRANCESCA OUT IN THE *WINONA*, AND I've got to make use of the time. If Brice even feels like a connection to Sean or the attack on my sister, I swear I will fry him," Tempest swore as she watched the *Winona* glide out of the harbor and onto open water. Kenny stood on the marina's dock, watching the cruiser, and that was just where Tempest wanted him—away from his home.

She slid on her cuff bracelet, her wristwatch, and the wolf's head brooch, then tightened her belt in one jerk. So she was a little peeved. What woman wouldn't be? Marcus had taken her to the place where he'd lost his virginity to an "older woman," Francesca. Now they were on that boat—alone. "I hope you're both very happy."

Meanwhile, Marcus's absence served Tempest's purpose. As she left the house, headed toward Kenny's home for a second time, she put her thoughts in order. Kenny just could have been the person driving last night's dangerous truck; it had been obvious that his answer about his whereabouts hadn't satisfied the police chief. The link between Kenny and the youths, the gaming Kenny and they engaged in, could all be tied together in one big psychic knot. Addictions made certain weaker personalities vulnerable, and that's exactly what a stronger one would sense.

Without a family or an heir, Marcus would have bequeathed a substantial amount to Kenny, should anything happen to him. Maybe Kenny just needed that money sooner than later. He was definitely fearful of Tempest's prowling around the past. There were too many unanswered questions and too many links to Kenny.

Tempest was certain that Kenny was Marcus's biological father; she also suspected that he had been the father of Winona's unborn baby. If Winona hadn't wanted to leave her husband, killing them might be the response of a jealous lover—and that would leave Marcus susceptible to Kenny's influence. The Greystone empire had been down at the time, but not gone. Under-the-table deals could have landed Kenny a fat payoff. He wouldn't want those deals discovered, and her questions were making him uneasy.

An unlocked window to the rear of Kenny's home provided an easy entrance. Tempest eased through it and into a neat bedroom. The bed was neatly made, almost military style, tight enough to make a quarter bounce. The dresser had a small tray that a man would use to drop his pocket change and keys into to prevent scratching the surface of the dresser. Tempest eased open a top drawer and found the usual assortment of folded socks and a neatly ironed stack of men's handkerchiefs. The blue monogrammed initials were K.R. K.R. not K.M. . . . Could that R. mirror Winona's R.? Could the locket's initials, W.R. be linked to Kenny's, K.R. and not Roberts, her maiden name? "Okay, now just who are you, Kenny Morrison with the initials of K.R.?"

The furniture was old, well preserved, and dusted. Clothing and shoes in the closet were neatly arranged.

The bedside table's lamp and stack of books—thrillers and romance novels—indicated that Kenny read in bed.

Tempest picked up a small thick album from the bedside table and opened it. Winona's happy face looked up at her, the wind lifting her hair. Then another photograph of Winona with her arms around a younger Kenny, whose face mirrored Marcus's. The Golden Gate Bridge marked the scene as San Francisco. The photographs were all of Winona: Winona in a T-shirt and shorts held on to a sailing mast as she smiled impishly at the camera. The picture of a proud father, Kenny's open hand had lain on Winona's bulging stomach.

Tempest's gloved hand went to the locket that Marcus had given her. The following pictures of Winona revealed that same locket. In every picture, Winona wore the warm sensual look of a woman in love, a vivid contrast to descriptions of her relationship with Jason. Sprawled on the decking, his arms folded behind his head, Kenny's expression was at times boyish and playful and at others, deeply sensual. A woman's lipstick formed a kiss on his photographs. They'd been lovers, and the pictures were very private, treasured mementos, the album well-worn as if handled frequently.

Tempest replaced the album and smoothed the locket again. She felt as if she'd invaded the privacy of a man and woman in love. The locket obviously meant a special endearment to the lovers. From his expression at the marina office earlier, Kenny had noted Tempest's wearing the locket, and he wasn't happy about that.

Tempest moved through the silent shadows to the small, tidy kitchen, a living room with a big-screen television and stacks of gaming CDs and controls. Several games and cartridges were neatly stacked on a shelf. She flipped through the gaming CDs, recognizing the titles she'd seen at Sean's. But she needed more.

She carefully opened a CD case and removed her glove; she had to see if Sean's CDs matched the touch on Kenny's. She had to know if the darkness, the hatred and need for revenge on Sean's games, were the same as on Kenny's.

As she ran her fingertip lightly over the silver grooves of one gaming disk, she found a boy's natural excitement, competition, hope, and nurturing. The next held fear for others and pain so horrible it sank into Tempest's flesh and deeper into her bones. Her hand clenched into the same shape as Kenny's damaged one, and she bit back a scream of pain.

Stunned, Tempest dropped the CD onto the couch and quickly tugged on her glove. The residue of fear and pain she'd felt beneath the excitement of the games trembled through her, lessening gradually. There were other emotions simmering, waiting to spring at her: frustration, depression, revenge, hatred.

She forced herself to breathe steadily, pushing away the negative forces. She replaced the CD and quickly headed for the bathroom. Just as neat as the other rooms, it smelled of cleaning and men's soap. Tempest noted the absence of female scents and slowly opened the medicine cabinet. On the back of the mirror, Winona's photograph looked at her, and next to it was a row of cheap photographs, taken of a happy Winona and Kenny in a machine's small booth.

Tempest studied the shelves' contents: pain medicine in different doses, toothpaste, antibiotic salve, bandage strips. Then she noted a shaving mug with an elaborately scrolled Ragnar across it. The straight razor beside it had also been embellished with Ragnar. Tempest held her breath as she connected K.R. to Kenny Ragnar. The initials on Winona's brooch were W.R. According to Opal, Winona had started wearing the locket around the time of Marcus's birth.

Tempest closed the cabinet door and braced her hands on the sink below. Her mirrored reflection searched her face, her mind tracking dates, stacking them together into one seamless reason for murder.

In her first research of Marcus Greystone, she'd discovered that the time line of Marcus's birth was about three years after the Greystones' well-publicized marriage. Winona Greystone was already married when she began wearing Kenny's locket.

In the heart of a woman, that sentimentality could only signify that Winona considered herself truly married to Kenny.

If Winona had then rejected him and had turned to Jason Greystone for the birth of a new child, that could have given Kenny cause for murder. And if so, he might want to kill again to keep his secret.

Tempest remembered the headlights of that big truck as it steadily shoved Marcus's car toward the edge of that hill. Add that to Kenny's unproven whereabouts last night, his ability to move around the Greystone house, and the weakened railing, and Kenny was definitely at the top of Tempest's "possible suspect" list.

"Dammit." In the *Winona*'s cockpit, Marcus studied the handheld tracking device. Tempest was wearing the locket with the transmitter chip inside, and she was on the move, headed for Port Salem's downtown district. And he wasn't around to protect her.

Fear for her leaped into full gear as Marcus clicked on the cruiser's ignition and revved the *Winona*'s powerful twin diesel motors. If Whitcomb decided to leave his hotel a few miles north of Port Salem and look around the area, he just might spot Tempest. She had dismissed Whitcomb's threats too easily. Marcus didn't. An aging playboy with dwindling resources had plenty of reason to want to either get her back—or kill her for what she knew about him, since his demented mind reasoned she'd ruined him.

"What did you say, honey?" Francesca asked as she came up behind him and placed her hand on his shoulder. When the *Winona*'s twin motors started to lurch into full speed, quickly closing the distance to shoreline, Francesca braced herself against Marcus's body, her arms around him.

"Problem? In some hurry to get back?" she whispered in his ear.

Marcus remembered Tempest's fury when she'd discovered Francesca had been his sexual initiator. He tried gently to shrug Francesca away, but she held firm, whispering in his ear. "You think my arrangements are okay then, Marcus? The food and drinks?"

At the moment, Marcus could have cared less; he feared for Tempest. "If you think the refrigerator and freezer are working properly, the wet bar stocked and the galley in working order, then we're set."

"You can always count on me, Marcus. You know that. I stocked the condiments, and the serving supplies. I checked the coffeemaker, the washer and dryer, just in case someone needs that, and the sheets on both beds are fresh, the bathrooms stocked. I'm glad that you brought me out here to see how everything works when actually on the water. I've never been on board the *Winona* before. She's beautiful."

Dammit. With Tempest on the move, he didn't have time for the discussion he'd planned, that he intended his relationship with Tempest to deepen, and that he wanted everyone in his life to get along. Opal usually came around to changes, but it would take time to convince her that Tempest wasn't going to interfere with their long-standing relationship.

It seemed only reasonable to tell Francesca of his

plans, since she'd been such a big part of his life. After those hot, youthful days, they'd settled into a good comfortable working arrangement which Tempest apparently was not going to understand.

"You might want to sit over there on the bench and hold on. I just forgot that I've got another appointment and need to get back. Checking out the gear and the dinghy took longer than I thought." Marcus was certain that Kenny had done everything properly, but he'd been waiting for the right moment to discuss Tempest with Francesca.

Francesca moved sensually against his back, her breasts rubbing him, and Marcus gripped the controls more tightly. "I mean it, Francesca. Back off."

Her answer was curt and angry, the tone of a woman who had been used and now discarded. "Fine. I heard about last night—how your girlfriend was dressed in mechanic's dirty coveralls when Mac turned up. What were you doing out there?"

Marcus caught the slight inflection of her tone. It indicated that she remembered a boy-virgin years ago and how she'd initiated him in the same place.

He glanced at Francesca as she settled gracefully onto the bench by an open window, her face lifted to the sun. After all these years, Marcus could still see the woman who had fascinated his father but had disdained being near him. Marcus owed Francesca for the comfort she'd given him when he'd needed a softer touch. He owed her for the years she'd helped keep the one place he called "home" waiting for him.

All those years ago, Marcus had started flirting with her for one reason: to upset Jason, who clearly wanted her. But he couldn't have her, because Francesca wasn't interested in a married man and because she was Winona's friend.

Having a woman that Jason lusted after was a definite boyhood coup, especially when his father had found out somehow. At that point, Jason's threats meant nothing, and Marcus's only fear had been for his mother, who seemed to be changing, becoming stronger.

And maybe that was the reason Jason had hired someone to kill her and accidentally found himself the victim of his own plot.

"That girl isn't for you," Francesca stated suddenly against the rushing wind that lifted her hair away from her well-tended face. Her hand rested out of the cruiser's window, her fingers playing in the wind and sunshine.

Marcus anxiously checked the tracking device. Tempest had stopped momentarily, somewhere on Main Street. He relaxed slightly; Main Street was filled with arty shops and cafes. Maybe she'd stepped into an art gallery. It was only reasonable of him to ask an active woman like Tempest to stay put—for her own protection. But she clearly wasn't taking orders.

Apparently, Francesca was also thinking about Tempest. "You need someone to create a home for you, like your mother did for Jason. And that girl is just plain odd, Marcus. She's upsetting everyone, Opal and Kenny and me, people who have considered themselves to be your family for years."

Marcus didn't miss the guilt-nudge; Opal and Kenny had already made their dislike of Tempest known. Francesca had probably experienced Tempest's little psychic feelers, or her unnerving steady stare that had a way of seeing straight to a person's bones. Then he remembered how Francesca had looked as she'd left her office. "What did you two talk about in your office and in Homeport's ladies' room? How did she upset you?"

"You've got to stop her from asking questions. I would think you'd want that gossip to remain dead, not ask some very strange woman to bring it back to life. I got all upset, just remembering how horrible that wreck was."

Marcus slowed the cruiser as they entered the harbor, careful of the wake the powerful fifty-five-footer could cause; other boaters appreciated the courtesy and waved. "I asked her to come for just that reason. She's good at what she does, and I want that hit-and-run driver."

Francesca stared at him. "But I thought you'd given up on that years ago. That day in my office, I knew you were sleeping with her. But surely you can see that there's no way she could get the identity of the driver after all these years. Why open up all that pain now?"

"Maybe I was waiting for just what I needed."

"Which was?"

Marcus did not state that Tempest filled him with warmth and life, and that he knew he needed her. Instead, he answered, "I need Tempest for what she does."

"I don't get it. What does she do? Other than the obvious?"

There were limits to what he was willing to reveal, and Francesca's questions were beginning to nettle.

"She makes me happy," Marcus stated firmly, and decided that was really true.

"It's just sex, nothing more. You'll get over it. She's not your kind, not the kind to really put down roots, anyone can see that," Francesca stated darkly.

"Could be. But it feels right."

Marcus eased the *Winona* along the Greystone platform dock, then looked for Tempest. Every cell in his body locked on to how much he'd wanted to see her, waiting safely for him.

Kenny helped moor the *Winona*, then quickly returned inside the marina building. Francesca had never been a woman Kenny liked being near, yet he'd never expressed his exact sentiments to Marcus.

Marcus helped Francesca out of the *Winona* and did not return her searching, pleading look.

Instead, he hurried to Port Salem's Main Street, hoping to find Tempest, safe and without Whitcomb nearby.

Tempest stepped out of La Femme and into the mid-afternoon sunshine. She slipped on her sunglasses and looked down the street. The grip on her upper arm was too familiar, so was the scent and tingle of sensual energy that spread over her. She didn't turn. "Hi, Marcus."

"Hi, yourself. I thought you were staying at home and taking it easy."

"I thought I'd use the time to promote my sister's handbags. I took in some sales brochures from Timeless Vintage. It could work out. Hey, where are you hauling me off to?"

Marcus used his body to push her down the street, his arm around her waist, his expression grim. "I thought we had an agreement."

"Your agreement, and it was more like orders. Have fun with Francesca?"

Amazing how the male energy bristles, Tempest thought. Or perhaps part of that energy was hers, since they were definitely linked.

"I wanted you out of sight because I don't want Whitcomb hurting you, threatening you, or even looking at you."

As they walked across the drawbridge to the marina, Tempest glanced at the water below. It shimmered, sunlight dancing on the surface. She felt the tug, but last night's upsetting discovery about Marcus's first lover overrode any other sensations. "Now about Francesca. I hope that went well," she said sweetly.

"Give me a break."

"No."

Marcus sighed tiredly as they stopped in front of the marina's building. He placed his hands on her waist, but Tempest's quickly crossed arms prevented him from coming closer. "Okay, Tempest, don't make things easy. I wouldn't know what to do if you did. I need to talk with Kenny, and I have some calls to make. Do you want to wait? Or do you want to walk home by yourself? And yes, I realize you need the exercise, as if last night wasn't enough."

"My butt still hurts," Tempest admitted truthfully, though she had other plans for the minute she got her hands on a computer keyboard again. Her time at the Internet cafe had been too short. "I'm going home—to your house—and I'm getting in that hot tub again."

"I shouldn't be long. But I expect to find said cute butt in that hot tub when I get home. Okay?"

Tempest tilted her head to one side and challenged him. "Are you asking? Or are you ordering?"

He sighed again. "Asking. Please?"

She didn't have much time.

Tempest hurried to boot up her laptop. She needed to find out more about Kenny Ragnar. Her brief stop at the Internet cafe had led to the name, Kenneth Ragnar, owner of a fledgling sailboat company in San Francisco. The article was dated over forty years ago, years prior to Marcus's conception.

San Francisco, as in the Golden Gate Bridge in the photo of Winona.

If Kenny and Kenneth Ragnar were the same man, he was definitely hiding something big.

Her mind on Kenny, Tempest wasn't prepared for the message that popped up on her screen: *Port Salem is a perfect place for a witch to die.*

Greer smoothed the wolf's-head brooch at her shoulder. Fear had trembled in Tempest's hushed call, which had quickly ended when Marcus entered the house.

Tempest's brief, heartbreaking description of Brice Whitcomb's use of her psychic gift infuriated Greer. She walked out to her garden, the lawn where her triplets had played. She lifted her face to the salt-scented air and willed herself to calm.

But the tingling moving up her nape indicated that Leona was calling. Greer braced herself as she retrieved her cell phone from her jacket pocket. Leona rarely called, her tone bitter with continuing resentment that Greer did not fault; she only hoped that one day Leona would understand.

Leona wasted no time. "Tempest is going to get herself killed. All because she wants to deliver the original brooch to you—in person. She's up to her neck there in Port Salem, and already she's had three attempts on her life—well, okay, one was a kidnapping that could have gone wrong for her if Marcus hadn't arrived. You've got to talk to her. You've got to tell her that she isn't to blame for Dad's accident and that whatever restitution she feels she has to make for those two years is just plain dumb."

"It's her honor, Leona. Tempest feels she's betrayed us, what we are."

Leona's silent anger bristled over the lines. "Do you have any idea of how she looked when she held that handbag, the one I brought her? The one that guy touched when he shopped in Timeless? I'll tell you . . . like someone had just rammed a hot poker into her hand. Did you know that someone tried to force Marcus and her over the edge of a hill? Did you know that the boy who led the kidnapping said, 'Later,' as in if he couldn't get her, someone else would? You've got to talk her into getting herself out of there and that mess. She and Marcus can be together anywhere else, *but not by that lake.*"

Greer walked to the edge of her lawn and stared down at the beach where her children had gathered shells and stones, laughing as they danced away from the waves sliding on the sand. She looked out at the cerulean blue sky where the seagulls hovered, to the Pacific Ocean's waves, where their sailboat had overturned years ago. Tempest had blamed herself for dancing on the deck, for leaning too far over the handrail and distracting her father at the helm. Then that wave hit, and the boat capsized.

And Tempest blamed herself for her father's death.

"She needs to do this, to find Marcus's parents' hit-and-run driver. She feels it's her redemption, and I will not take that away from her."

After the call ended, Leona's last accusation echoed in Greer's mind: *She's in danger, and you're not doing anything about it!*

"The hell I'm not."

In her office moments later, Greer carefully pushed away one set of index cards, those containing names and information on the cases she had helped solve, killers with motives to harm her. She placed another set beside them, the names of professional competitors whom she had proven to be either psychic fakes or of lesser ability. Under extreme pressure, she'd reluctantly met their challenges, and they'd sworn to "dethrone" her.

Greer lined up another set of index cards on her desk, those pertaining to her family's connections. She had written one fact on each card; no matter how she lined them up, one fact did not logically connect to another.

Claire, as the youngest and most vulnerable, an empath, had been the first to be attacked. Tempest had discovered the link between the attacker's computer and the dark evil possessing him.

Greer frowned and slid the card with Daniel Bartel's

deadly vehicle accident above Claire's card. She placed the card with the sailboating accident above that.

Then she hurriedly remixed the cards, placing the card with Neil Olafson, Claire's new husband, beside Claire's. Beneath Tempest's card, she placed Brice Whitcomb's, a man Tempest had actually never touched with her naked hands, and then Marcus Greystone's card at the side.

Greer studied Daniel's card, Neil's, and Marcus's, all in a line. While Marcus was unaware of his biological parent, Ragnar was definitely Nordic and possibly dated back to a Viking heritage. Bartel and Olafson were definitely connected to the same heritage. She held her breath as one fact stood out above all the others. The men in the Aisling women's lives had definite connections to the same origins. Daniel and Neil were definitely protector types, and Marcus fell into that category, too.

That left Brice Whitcomb, a part of Tempest's life for two long years. She wasn't frightened of his threats, but now, with Marcus drawing him out, Tempest would protect her love; she would seek Brice out, and she would deliberately feel his energy. The next thought caused Greer to tense: If Whitcomb was connected to the rage Tempest had felt when her sister was attacked, she would react instantly, impulsively, and perhaps brutally.

Greer smoothed the brooch Tempest had created from mere dreams. The Celtic designs weren't the angular characters of the Vikings. What did the original inscription mean? Whatever it was, it held the key to her dreams of Thorgood. And now, reaching into her psychic ability to help her sisters, Leona was dreaming of the Viking, too.

Tempest's Viking blood ran to restless and revenge when aroused. She was definitely on the hunt now, determined to earn that brooch, but also to protect

Marcus and her family. There was no way that Tempest could protect Marcus from the truth of his birth.

Greer studied Brice Whitcomb's index card and heard herself whisper, "Whitcomb just could be the one. If I interfere, Tempest may never reclaim what she's lost. She has that right."

When Marcus entered his house, Kenny's warnings about Tempest still echoed in his mind. "Some man called here, wanting to talk with her. The phone number checks out to El Fandango, the place where your poker buddy is supposed to be staying. Now, why would he want to contact her?"

Good question. As Marcus passed the kitchen on his way to find Tempest in the hot tub, he noted the opened box labeled La Femme and smiled. The replacement outfit from La Femme had obviously arrived, and since the box was empty, he could only hope that Tempest was wearing it.

He found her in his bedroom, one foot on the bed as she rolled up the black hose, attaching the lace at her thigh to the garter snap. The angle presented a view of her breasts cupped within the lacy black bra, her body pale and curved, the black garter belt crossing her hips. She angled her face to look at him, and Marcus settled his shoulder against the doorway to enjoy the view. "Can I help?"

"I'm almost finished, but thank you." Tempest placed her foot on the floor and started walking toward him. Her arms went around his shoulders, her gloves in his hair, toying with it.

Marcus slid his hands down her body and tugged at her thong. "I thought you were going to soak in the hot tub."

She nuzzled his throat. "Now, how could I resist this?"

Marcus brushed his lips against hers and enjoyed the comfort of her curves against his. A homecoming like this was something he hadn't experienced in his lifetime. The unexpected pleasure only heightened the contrast of his life previous to Tempest, which now seemed very dull and mundane, stripped of delight and play. He hadn't known the leap of laughter and joy she could bring to him, or the excitement of every minute. Of necessity, he'd survived, he'd worked and he'd lived, but never with such absolute delight and almost boyish anticipation. Layers of his dark past slid away as Marcus felt himself wrapped up in one big, very happy grin. "The pole will have to wait, but it's coming."

Tempest's lips were at his earlobe, nibbling slightly, her tongue flicking it as her hands ran over his shoulders and down to unbutton his shirt. "Maybe I prefer some other kind of exercise."

Marcus sucked in his breath, cupped her bottom, and drew her close against his hardening body. He could really get used to homecomings like this one. "Like what?"

Tempest nibbled a trail to his bottom lip and sucked it gently. "I'd even take off my gloves for a total effect. You'd like that, wouldn't you?"

"Oh, yes, I truly would. Any special reason for this celebration?"

"Uh-uh," she answered too easily as she began to unbuckle his belt.

With his heart pounding, his instincts telling him to take her quickly and toss away caution, his need to be inside her, feel that tight, moist glove, her body joined with him, Marcus shook his head. "It wouldn't have anything to do with locating Brice Whitcomb, would it? You wouldn't want to 'feel' that while we're . . . exercising, would you?"

Tempest blinked up at him; she was expressive and

totally delicious. Marcus couldn't resist backing her against a wall and holding her wrists. With or without gloves, Tempest's hands did things to him that stopped his mind from clear thought. He asked again, "Brice Whitcomb. You want to know where he's at, and of course, you could get that from feeling me, right? And then what?"

"You're not very romantic, Greystone."

"Not when I know you have ulterior motives. He knows you're here, doesn't he? After all, you've caused quite a stir around here. Even if he's located miles away, he's bound to pick up news and photos of that kidnapping attempt. Has he been e-mailing you?"

"He may have mentioned something about Port Salem as a perfect place for a witch."

The fierce need to protect Tempest burned through Marcus. "Dammit. And you want to take him down, don't you?"

"I want to see if he's connected to whatever is stalking my family, and there's only one way to do that." She glanced at her wrists, where Marcus's grip had pressed the cuff bracelet slightly into her flesh.

Marcus understood immediately and eased his hold. "You want to touch him with your naked hand."

"You've got it. And you're jealous, aren't you? Now, that's odd, when earlier you reeked of Francesca's perfume."

Marcus released her wrists and pushed away from her. "That was over before it began."

When Tempest rubbed her wrist, he instantly lifted it for his inspection. A red line marred her smooth pale flesh, the mark of her bracelet. In his anger, he'd hurt her, and Marcus was instantly alarmed. He bent to kiss the line. "I'm sorry."

"I'm okay. You're not."

He smoothed the Celtic designs on the silver bracelet. "This doesn't exactly go with your seduction outfit.

You're wearing it for a purpose. Does this actually mean anything?"

When Tempest inhaled abruptly and looked down, Marcus ran with the first thought that leaped into his mind; he didn't question the potential psychic connection. "You're wearing it for protection. Against me? So that I—me, your lover, the only man you've touched with your naked hands—won't know what you're up to? So that you can block me from what you know? Why? What are you keeping from me?"

Tempest's head came up, her eyes wide, her lips parted in surprise; her startled expression proved that his guess had been correct. He lifted her wrist to inspect the bracelet closer and found an inscription, angular this time, a contrast to the flowing Celtic design. "Tell me what those characters mean."

"Child of Aisling," Tempest whispered slowly, unevenly. "When I was pasting myself back together and feeling guilty as hell for betraying my family and what we were, I needed an—"

"An amulet—for protection. I understand. You have your gloves, but you needed more, something for strength and good luck. Does it say anything else?" he asked again, trying to understand the intricate details and life of the woman he would protect with his life.

Tempest nodded and searched his face as if seeking disgust. "It also says, Child of the Viking Thorgood. This is the second bracelet—I added Thorgood from the dreams that Mother has been having, and now Leona. Leona didn't want a bracelet to protect her. She wants nothing to do with our heritage, though she's been pushing to help Claire and me. However, she will wear the brooch because she knows it makes us feel better. Claire is too sensitive to wear this. Her protection is in her mind's focus and now her bond with her husband, Neil."

Marcus shook his head; understanding Tempest and her family might take a lifetime. "It's difficult, but I'm with whatever you say, Tempest. I'll protect you. And Francesca is nothing more than a friend."

Francesca's name hadn't left his lips when Tempest's eyes turned to that angry gold. "She was your father's lover, and you wanted to wave your—manly conquest in his face. What did it get you?"

Marcus pounced on that fact. "What do you mean, she was my 'father's lover'? He wanted her, but Francesca detested him."

"Oh, great," Tempest stated in disgust as she placed her hands on her hips. "Now see what you've made me do."

"Okay, we've stepped into this now, so tell me what you're holding." His hand was on her throat, pinning her to the wall again. "Answer me."

Tempest held her hands at her side, but her expression changed to concern. "I only *think* they were involved. I *think* a lot of things. I just get mad, I'm impulsive, and I say things. Forget I said anything, Marcus."

Even as his emotions stormed inside him, Marcus was careful not to hurt her, his thumb caressing her soft cheek. "You're holding quite a bit, aren't you? Tell me about Opal. Why is she avoiding me? What do you 'think' about her?"

Tempest's gloved hands slid up his chest, resting against him, her expression that of sympathy. "I think she loved your mother. There are things she'd rather keep to herself, but I need them—they may lead to that driver. I'm so sorry. Oh, Marcus. I know how painful this is for you. I wasn't going to—"

"Of course, she loved my mother. They were—" He caught Tempest's sympathetic expression and shook his head. A stream of confusing memories slid by him. The way Opal had looked at his mother, the way she had fiercely protected Winona. That night, just before his mother had called Kenny, Opal had kissed Winona on the lips, trying to hold her, and had been fiercely pushed away.

Marcus closed his eyes and remembered Opal's cry, *I love you, Winona. You can't go without me. I won't let you.* . . . The memories led to Opal's jealousy of Jason, and perhaps himself. Suddenly, Marcus felt very old and tired; all those years had passed, and he hadn't known. He sat down on the bed and held his head. "Do you think Opal could be involved with killing my parents?"

Tempest sat beside him, her arm around his shoulders, her hand gripping his. "I don't know. I know she hated Jason."

His abrupt, hollow laughter ricocheted against the walls. "Most people did."

Marcus turned to Tempest and noted the tears in her eyes, the silvery trails down her cheeks. He framed her face with his hands, his thumbs wiping away the dampness. "Hey. . . ."

"I am so sorry, Marcus."

The need to hold her close, to let her into emotions he'd hidden for years, was too overwhelming. Marcus lifted her to his lap, and Tempest cuddled against him. Her face tucked against his throat, her arms around him, seemed to ease the past.

He kissed her cheek, and whispered, "If you need to 'feel' Whitcomb anywhere around, I want to be there, okay?"

It was only after they'd made love that Marcus remembered Tempest hadn't agreed.

But as he held her close, he had to ask: "Are you and I . . . bonded, like Claire and Neil?"

Her quiet answer shook the room and Marcus's senses. "We have a connection, but too much lies between us for a true bond."

A true bond. Marcus realized that in this moment, he wanted that more than anything else. He gathered her closer, aware of how not only their bodies fit but how much he needed her. "We'll have to change that, won't we?"

When she didn't answer again, her reluctance to share her secrets nettled.

What else was Tempest hiding from him?

Fifteen

MINUTES LATER, MARCUS JACKKNIFED INTO A SITTING POSI-
tion, his back and shoulders bunched with tension. He
shrugged away Tempest's soothing hand. Marcus
stood abruptly as if wanting to leave her touch—and
what she had discovered of the past.

He moved into the bathroom. The door clicked
shut, a silent message that he wanted to be alone.
Tempest lay still and held her breath, uncertain of
what disgusted Marcus—what she was, a psychic
"feeler," a woman with a shady past, or the person
who opened a door to a past that he'd rather not
know.

Minutes later, he dressed quickly in the shadows
and walked out of the bedroom door.

It was just five o'clock now, the living room bright
with sunlight reflected off the lake; it silhouetted his
tense body in the bedroom doorway. With a weary
sigh, Tempest acknowledged that Marcus had reason
to be disturbed; he'd just found out that Opal had
wanted his mother, and that Francesca had been his
father's lover.

And there was nothing Tempest could do to ease his
past, but she shouldn't have told him; it was an impul-

sive, reckless heartbeat that had torn apart the few good solid things in his life. She took a quick shower, then dressed in a black sweater and slacks. She added her bracelet, brooch, gloves, and Winona's locket; she needed every shield and good-luck amulet possible to face Marcus.

She found him standing on the front deck, staring out at the lake. He tensed when her hand rested on his shoulder, his dark mood reflected in his grim expression. "You're angry, aren't you? I am so sorry, Marcus."

"I don't need your pity, and that's what you did in bed, wasn't it? Taking a little psychic edge off the way I felt, softening me a bit? I've heard that empaths can do that, but you usually work only with your hands, not your body."

Tempest saw no reason to deny that she wanted to soothe Marcus. She met his hard, condemning stare. "I'm learning. I'm changing . . . with you. I'm very sensitive to you, and it's a woman's nature to comfort," she added softly. This woman's instinctive need was to comfort one special man.

Marcus's self-protection energy and his frustrated, angry emotions bristled all around her, his anger burning her slightly, causing her skin to prickle. She rubbed her bare arms with her gloves and braced herself for an explosion.

As his lover, her body still bore the warm, sensual stamp of his, but she ached to hold him now. A proud man too long without love, Marcus didn't know how to share his wounds. She couldn't say, *Oh, Marcus, if you could see yourself, your pain, would you blame me for trying to protect you from the truth?*

She reached to comfort him, but Marcus quickly shrugged her hand away. He stood staring at the lake, apparently absorbed in memories. "It all makes sense, doesn't it? I keep seeing Opal—how she acted around my mother. I'm going to see her. I want to know what else I've missed and overlooked."

"I'll come with you."

When he turned to Tempest, his eyes were icy, his lips flat and tight across his teeth. He was once more the cold predator, not the lover she had comforted in her arms earlier. "You've done enough. Stay out of this."

His rejection tore through her, taking away her breath and bringing tears to her eyes. She heard Marcus move quickly through the house; she watched the BMW speed away, gleaming like some black charger in the shadows. Marcus was tearing apart his past, wounded by it, yet determined to find his answers. Did she blame him?

Tempest hugged herself, aware that less than a half hour ago, they had been snuggled together as though nothing could pull them apart. She rubbed her chest, but the ache in her heart wouldn't ease. It was true; that in helping others, an empath sometimes absorbed their pain as if it were their own. Or was it simply because, as with any normal woman, Tempest loved Marcus?

The sob she heard was her own, torn from her. He'd cut her away so easily.

Her hand on her throat, Tempest smoothed his mother's locket. She might not be at his side when he learned more about Opal and Winona, but she could use the time well.

She could do anything, but sit and wait for Marcus to return—if he did. She had to act, and quickly.

She could return Brice's e-mail and arrange for a meeting. He still wanted what she could do. She might be able to bargain with him, get him to back out of the game and any harm he could do to Marcus.

Or she could move to protect Marcus from the worst secret of his life—that Kenneth Ragnar had been not only his lifelong friend and protector—but also his father.

Whatever she did, she had little time before Marcus would come looking.

In the marina building, Kenny didn't look away from the motor he'd been repairing even though Tempest's footsteps echoed on the concrete. On her way to him, Tempest crossed the big square of sunlight passing through the massive doors. She glanced back to the harbor outside, the boats bobbing on the waves; the water seemed to beckon to her. She held very still and waited, and then it came, that psychic tug meant just for her. It was still out there, waiting. . . . It would have to wait until she had finished, and then she intended to call it out.

In those few steps from the entranceway across the sunlit concrete, Tempest sensed she was crossing Marcus's lifetime and perhaps losing him. Still, if Kenny was involved with that hit-and-run, she had to know. "Hello, Kenny."

Bent over his work counter, Kenny took a rag from his coveralls back pocket and wiped it over his injured hand. He glanced at her throat where Winona's locket lay. Those eyes, so like Marcus's, darkened with anger. He looked up and scanned the marina building. "Where's Marcus?"

"On an errand."

"He usually stays close—maybe that's because he doesn't trust you, and he's not alone in that."

Marcus didn't trust her—and he had good reason; she was digging into his painful past and coming up with unpleasant answers.

Tempest looked up at the stored boats, the way the chains lifted and lowered the boats from their bays.

The mechanism was intricate, worthy of a man with an engineering background, such as Kenneth Ragnar. "Would you like this locket back, a little bit of Winona to cherish?"

He scowled at her. "What are you talking about?"

Tempest unclasped the necklace and let it pool on the dirty work counter. Instantly, as if it were too precious to lie amid the grime, Kenny's good hand scooped it up. He carefully brushed the locket against his coveralls over his chest, then gripped it in his fist. The gesture was that of a man who needed the touch to warm his lonely heart, even for a moment.

"I know who and what you are to Marcus," Tempest stated quietly and watched his face pale above the gray beard, that fearful flicker of his eyes. "Kenneth Ragnar, the man Jason Greystone needed to make his business plans work, the mechanic, the engineer, the practical, the talented, the experienced seaman . . . the silent partner."

Kenny's tall body seemed to straighten, pain in his eyes visible, his deep voice uneven. He withdrew a clean, neatly folded and ironed handkerchief from his pocket and carefully placed the locket on it; he straightened the chain with a loving touch. Then he turned to her. "Who are you really? I know you're different," he asked unevenly.

"Yes, I am. And you sensed that I was a danger to you. That's why you were so unfriendly, wanting me to leave. You were afraid I'd discover your secret." Embroidered with the initials K.R., the handkerchief could have been a gift from Winona. Kenny might have chosen to carry that with him as a reminder of the woman he still loved, even as he shielded his true identity.

For years, Tempest had also hidden what she was, the descendant of the seer Aisling and the Viking conqueror, but now she squared her shoulders. "I'm a psychic, Kenny. I don't see the future, I don't communicate with the dead, but I can feel an object and know its history. Sometimes I pick up the energies of the people who have held it. For that reason, Marcus brought me here to help find whoever murdered his parents. Don't you see, Kenny? He has to have closure, and I'm going to give it to him. You've been afraid of what will happen then."

"You can take that psychic stuff and—He wants you, that's all. He brought you here because he wants you in his bed. It's just that simple. You look as if you'd just made love—you have that soft woman look." His snarl bristled around her, a dark warning, the tone much the same as Marcus's earlier.

The feral sound spoke of anger, and of terror, like an animal backed into a corner and forced to fight for his life. She was alone with Kenny, and the waves seemed to have grown as angry as the man, battering the harbor's concrete walls, the boats riding the waves creaking with warning.

Tempest focused on her mission; Kenny had said "made love," not "had sex." "That's how you remember Winona, isn't it? 'That soft woman look' as you lay out there on the cruiser named for her, as you took her sailing on San Francisco Bay?"

Stunned, Kenny looked at her as if facing his own death. But deep into peeling away the layers of the past, Tempest plunged on. She quickly stripped away her glove and took his injured right hand.

Searing pain jarred her, zigzagging like the cut of a knife up her arm. She found the struggle, men fighting, holding Kenneth Ragnar down. Unable to take any more, she staggered as she forced her fingers free. She fought the residue of pain, her own hand tightening into the shape of his. Tempest focused on straightening her fingers, aware that he watched her.

She eased each bone, each joint into its former position; if she didn't reshape her hand, it might retain that claw shape forever.

Kenny instantly covered his injured hand with his good one. "What did you do?" he demanded unevenly. "You're shaking as if you'd just come through hell."

She answered with the truth. "I did, but it was your hell. I saw what they did to you, those thugs along the waterfront. They deliberately maimed you on Jason's orders, didn't they?"

Tears shimmered in Kenny's eyes, his tall body shaking as he stared down at her. "No. . . . You couldn't have. You guessed . . . someone told you?"

His good hand gripped her wrist painfully. "Tell me who. Who told you?"

Easily read now, his fear turned to panic, one secret torn away and revealed.

When Tempest braced herself and simply stared up into his eyes, Kenny shuddered, his deep voice uneven. "You're saying things that could get you in a lot of trouble."

"Like it got Winona in trouble? She wanted to leave Jason the day they were killed, didn't she? Or did she? She was staying because of—"

"The boy. She was staying because of the boy, to protect Marcus. Jason had already threatened to do the same to him." He looked down to the hand he had clamped to her wrist and uncurled his fingers as if reluctant to release a lifeline. Kenny shook his head as if just realizing that he'd opened a door he couldn't close.

"You can say it now, to me . . . your son, Marcus. Jason threatened to hurt your son if Winona left him, and if you didn't continue developing new projects for him. He knew people who would do his dirty work. You were the real brains behind Greystone Investments. You made it all happen. Winona loved you, Kenny Ragnar. I felt it on her locket."

"She truly did, and I loved her. Somehow I knew you'd be the one to find out, after all these years. I was so afraid. . . ."

Tempest watched the way Kenny seemed to straighten into the man he'd once been. "You said 'her eyes were blue as the clear sky on a summer day.' That's the way a man talks when he still loves someone, after all these years. Was she carrying your baby when she died?"

After years of carrying his heartbreaking grief, Kenny seemed to crumble, a big man holding his head in his hands. "God, yes. My baby, and she was leaving him—"

Tempest gripped his good hand with her naked one. A river of pain rippled through her, Kenneth Ragnar's pain, a man who loved a woman so much that he would stay on the edges of her life, waiting for her and his son. "And coming to you?"

He nodded, his good hand gripping hers now, tears flowing freely down his weathered skin, glistening in his gray beard. "We were going to meet. Winona finally had had enough, and she was coming—"

"To you. She knew enough of Jason's dealings to blackmail him—her freedom for her silence, and yours. You were going to make a new life together."

Kenny's sob echoed in the marina. "I didn't know she was going to face him down that day, out on the lake. She'd promised we'd do that together. Then she called me that night and asked me to come get our son, and I knew it was time. We'd already decided on a place to meet, and we were going to—Jason must have forced her to tell where the boy and I were. He must have forced her from the driver's seat."

Tempest focused on a myriad of scenes flowing through her mind. Two men, friends, working together, the excitement of a start-up company, and then the woman between them. "You built Greystone, didn't you? Not Jason. He had the business know-how, but you made it all work, didn't you? But no one expected you and Winona to fall in love?"

She held his hand fiercely, even as he seemed to fold into himself, the memories surging through him. Kenny leaned back against the wall as if needing the support, and a surge of his tender, loving energy wrapped around Tempest. She wanted to comfort him, but there was little time before Marcus would return to the house. She had to know, pushing through all the layers that Kenny had held so tightly within him for years. His grief clouded her probe, the images coming in bits, flashing, then escaping her grasp. "Jason was sterile, wasn't he? He needed the perfect picture, an heir, and Winona wanted a baby to fill her life? And you were there, and already in love with her."

"He just happened, a miracle. She was the most beautiful when she was pregnant with our son. I cried when he first kicked against my hand." Kenny's voice was soft and filled with the miracle of love. He picked up the locket, let it nestle in his palm as if it were the most precious thing in his lifetime. The necklace gleamed in his hand, a delicate link to the woman he loved. "A part of me died with her that day, but I knew I had to keep going for our son. Someone had to care for him, other than boarding schools and Jason's sister—that cold witch. I wanted to give him a part of what I was, what my father gave to me. I spent every minute I could with the boy."

"Kenny . . . Kenny, listen to me. I feel what happened, but I can make mistakes. Sometimes my own emotions can cloud what my hands tell me. I'm not that strong yet, and I don't know that I want to be. . . . I need to hear you say it. Tell me."

His harsh burst of breath, the words pounding after it came with tears that he'd held for years. "After I was hurt, Jason wanted me around as a reminder of what he could do. He wanted Winona to see what he could do to Marcus. He wanted her to be disgusted with how I looked, so that she'd never want my touch again. I didn't want her to see me. But Winona came after me, begged me to stay close to her and our son. Jason was gone so much, and those were our happiest times."

Kenny shook his head and wiped away his tears before continuing. "Winona was stronger than anyone knew. She almost killed Jason when she found out what he'd done to me. He woke up one night with a knife at his throat—only our son crying in his sleep kept her from killing him. I don't think Jason ever slept well after that, and I think he was afraid of her— but he would have hurt our son. She would have killed him for sure then. Time went on, and then another miracle—we made another baby—we were finally going to start a new life."

He stared at the locket and shuddered. "When I picked up Marcus, Winona promised to meet us after she'd finished up a few things at the house. And then I had to take the boy to identify his mother. I would have never let her face Jason alone—never!"

He shook his head. "Winona said she could move more quickly without Marcus. She was afraid he'd tip Jason somehow, and he'd be hurt. Marcus was so quiet when I picked him up. I should have known that they were arguing, that Winona had told Jason she was leaving. But it wasn't until a few hours later that

Marcus said they were really fighting—the boy kept things to himself—but I should have known."

His breath caught on a sob jerked from his soul. As much as Tempest wanted to hold him, she had to probe deeper, "Do you think Jason arranged for her death and got caught in his own trap?"

Kenny nodded slowly, a tear fell from his cheek to the locket. He smoothed it away with his thumb and rocked his body. "He knew people. One call, and he could do almost anything, except save Greystone from bankruptcy."

A sound in the shadows caused Tempest to turn. Marcus walked into the light, his expression hard and furious. "Well, that was an enchanting little story. Anything else you'd like to add, Kenny?"

As if his time had come to take his punishment, Kenny stood slowly and faced his son. Painfully, he tried to straighten, as though his hunched disguise had locked into his bones. His voice uneven with emotion, he simply stated, "I loved your mother."

Marcus's glance at Tempest held contempt, and then his fists balled at his sides as he faced Kenny. "You're saying that my mother—"

"Was my only love."

"You're saying that you're my real father. After all these years, and you said nothing? Did nothing? I don't believe you. You're lying."

Kenny's good hand reached out to grip Marcus's shirt. "Boy, I do not lie."

Fiercely emotional, the two men towered over Tempest. In another heartbeat, one wrong word could destroy them both. She reacted instantly and gripped Marcus's hand in hers. The psychic jolt hit him, and connected back to her. Marcus's fierce expression turned down to where their hands joined, hers pale and smaller within his. "What the hell are you doing now?"

In that instant, Tempest took the most dangerous chance of her life. She understood the risk: that her energy would never be the same—that she would never be the same, in fact, she could become nothing, her energy overwritten by the males'. She raised her free hand to her lips and used her teeth to peel away her glove. When her hand was free, she placed it over Kenny's, still locked to Marcus's shirt.

The living connection between the two men, father and son, Tempest focused on transmitting the men's memories and emotions; she became a river through which the exchange flowed. Kenny's callused hand slowly released Marcus and turned to hold hers. "I don't know how to do this," he whispered unevenly. "I don't know what you're doing, but I know what you want."

She glanced at Marcus, who stood rigid and pale, his stare locked on Kenny as if seeing him for the first time. A vein throbbed in his forehead and another along his jaw, down into his throat. "The same eyes—"

Pitting herself against the emotions of both men, the angular, bristling male energy whipping through her, Tempest braced herself for the reaction. "I don't know what I'm doing either. But both of you are going to stand there and take what comes."

Both men seemed riveted on each other, their eyes locking, their hands gripping hers. Sweat beaded Marcus's forehead; tears shimmered in Kenny's eyes. Her forehead dampened as she bit her lip, focusing on that river of emotions and memories. She caught some of the images as they passed through her, flipping, changing from one to another, like torn pieces that fit and yet did not match. Love coursed through her, that of a father for a son, and that of a lost boy needing a gentle, understanding hand. Love for a woman, each in a different way, the solid link between them.

Tempest pushed free of the images briefly, enough to whisper, "That's what Kenny was doing last night, when he couldn't be found. He was in the *Winona*, being with her."

Marcus's expression changed from shock to disbelief. He slowly took in Kenny's concealing beard, the width of shoulders he had straightened. "No. I don't believe this," he whispered raggedly, and pulled away from Tempest's touch.

He rubbed his hand as if trying to erase the sensations he'd felt from Kenny. "You're the anonymous 'friend of the family' who wanted to keep Greystone afloat until I came of age?"

"I'd managed funds that Jason didn't know about. Or maybe he did, then at the end. I'd told Winona that I had enough to—"

Marcus suddenly rounded on Tempest, furious with her. "You stay the hell out of my life."

"Boy—" Kenny began, as Tempest slid her hand from his.

As if cornered and fighting for his life, Marcus uttered a deep growl. "That's enough. I don't want to hear any more."

"Winona and Kenny protected you, Marcus," Tempest whispered. She understood his shock, a life lived in lies, years without the truth hitting him now. Marcus seemed frozen to the spot, staring at Kenny, as she continued, "It was what she wanted, not what he would have done. He gave her the locket with the initials of Winona Ragnar, because they were married—in their hearts. But she was terrified Jason would hurt you—or worse. She made Kenny promise—"

"It's true. She made me promise, to protect you, our son. I've been over it every hour, every minute of my life. I wondered what I could have done, should have done, and didn't. I should have taken you both, fought him."

Tempest eased her gloves on, her eyes blurred by tears. "She threatened never to see you again, or let you see your son, didn't she?"

"No." Marcus's one word denied the past. "I need time to think. Just leave me alone, the both of you."

Clearly shaken, he turned to Tempest, his expression stunned. Then he turned and walked out of the marina building.

Kenny slumped against the wall, as if he'd taken a body blow. He rubbed his hand across his face as if drained. "You paid hard today, whatever you did while holding both our hands. You love him, don't you? You love my son enough to put yourself in danger. I saw what it cost you."

Tempest nodded, her own tears sliding down her cheeks. She felt stripped of her life, of her future, an empty ache growing inside her. Marcus had been so stunned, so hurt.

"You look like you're hanging in air. Let me hold you." When Kenny reached for her, Tempest went easily into the shelter of his arms, the older man rocking her against him.

"I don't know how to help him now. I don't know what to say."

"If I hadn't been on the other side of this thing, I would have wanted you to do the same thing for my son. He'll come around to you. He's a good man, and he just needs time to deal with a lifetime that wasn't really his, with me. However he feels about me, he's not going to toss you away. You gave him the truth, and that is a precious gift. Now tell me about you. I've got some feeling that you're not just an ordinary girl. You were working magic somehow, holding both our hands, and now you're all wrung out, exhausted.

You're shaking like a little scared bird, but it was time."

Tempest nodded, her throat tight with emotion and concern for Marcus. She ignored the tears flowing down her cheeks. "I guess I do love him. Maybe. He's not an easy man."

"That he is not. He hasn't had an easy life. I'd change it all if I could, you know. He's going to need some cooling-down time anyway, before he comes around— to you at least. Tell me how it works, this touch of yours."

"Kenny, I need to know—that night I climbed up the marina's back stairway and was dangling above ground—were you standing and watching me?"

In his office, Marcus tossed back a shot of bourbon, and then another. The burn down his throat did little to place the fragments of the past in order. They ripped painfully through him, the impact even worse because now they made sense, the facts lining up too neatly. He stared at the photograph of him and his mother on the *Winona*; he couldn't believe that she'd actually led a secret double life, even to her son. The baby she carried when she died had been Kenneth Ragnar's. Ragnar, not Morrison, the locket's W.R. initials stood for Winona Ragnar, secret wife of the Greystone handyman, an engineer with degrees, fluent in several languages, once the young owner of a successful start-up sailboat business. Kenneth Ragnar had given up a lifetime to be with the woman and son he loved.

Marcus's hand trembled as he reached for the decanter of amber liquid again, and he thought of Kenny's hand, and rubbed his own.

Fragments of the psychic energy flowing through Tempest hit him, one after another. The actual pain would have been unbearable, a purposeful disfigurement, intended to brand a man forever, to disgust the woman he loved.

With the second baby coming, Winona had finally agreed to leave Jason and that night, she'd faced him alone . . . while "Kenny" waited with Marcus, keeping him safe and ready. They were finally going to be together, and they loved each other desperately.

Marcus stared at his reflection in the picture's glass. "The same eyes . . . the same nose."

Beneath the full gray beard the jaw would probably be the same, and when Kenny had painfully tried to straighten, squaring his shoulders, they were almost the same height—father and son.

Marcus held his head, pushing back the throbbing memories. After a terse, emotional exchange with Opal, he'd used the handheld tracking device to pinpoint Tempest at the marina. He hadn't intended to overhear Kenny and Tempest, but he'd paused outside the entranceway to study the waves hitting the docks and boats along the harbor. Without a ship's strong wake or a storm, the waves were unusually fierce, especially in front of the marina building.

As Marcus had stood watching the water hit the dock and the boats, without a natural cause, he'd heard Tempest say, "A little bit of Winona to cherish."

Marcus slapped his hands flat on his office desk and shook his head. He crushed a financial report in his fist. "And then I heard the rest."

He turned to study his mother's expression—vibrant, alive, and in love. In love with a lover, not a legal husband, but with a man named Kenneth Ragnar. "Kenneth Ragnar . . . just who is he?"

Marcus quickly sat and began running computer searches. Then he called a friend, Luke Jameson, a very good researcher who had dug up facts on the Blair Institute of Parapsychology and every person around at the time of the hit-and-run, anyone with a motive for murder.

Within half an hour, Marcus had skimmed material on a highly educated Kenneth Ragnar, and he'd found Kenny's young photograph. "A mirror image of myself. . . ."

Luke's call followed within minutes. "The guy spent some time in a hospital. A boating accident crushed his hand and forearm. Surgeries didn't help. He had to sell his company, and then he dropped out of sight the next year. That was thirty-five years ago."

Thirty-five years ago. . . . Marcus had been born thirty-five years ago.

When the call finished, Marcus stared out at the lake, but he was picking through the past in his mind.

"Kenny—Kenneth Ragnar—had unsuccessful surgeries to repair that hand. They would have taken some time. Then he started working for Jason . . . . She came after him. She needed him." Marcus stood and quickly crossed to a table filled with plans for the marina, hoists for each dry-storage bay, and designs for Greystone's fishing and pleasure boats, a freshwater cruiser that had been a top seller, and the modifications for a cruiser named *Winona*. Marcus skimmed the plans, noted the leftward slant of the letters, and compared them to Jason's right-handed signature. But then Kenny's left hand would have compensated for an injured right one, wouldn't it?

Marcus flipped through the plans to Greystone's early days. A sailboat design matched one of Ragnar's, but was labeled as a Greystone model. The signature at the bottom was Kenneth Ragnar, and it was that of a man with a good right hand.

He remembered Kenny tying sailor's knots and handling sailboat rigging, agilely compensating for his disfigured hand. He remembered Jason and Kenny's private sessions behind closed doors, the way Jason lit up, forging new contracts, making deals—after those sessions. And immediately a new Greystone project would take flight.

Kenny had kept the *Winona* in perfect shape, a shrine to the woman he loved. Marcus remembered his mother, so happy on the days when Kenny took them out on the cruiser, the way she looked at him—like a woman in love.

"The little bastard," Jason had called Marcus.

Marcus poured another shot of bourbon, but didn't drink. He held the squat glass and swirled the amber liquid. He'd brought Tempest to Port Salem for two reasons: First, because he wanted her, because he couldn't get the taste and feel of her out of his blood. Secondary, but also important, he wanted answers to a cold case.

He stared at his parents' bedroom door and nodded. He understood now why Tempest had seemed so shaken when she'd touched the bed. His mother and Kenneth, Jason and Francesca, Opal's unwelcomed desire for Winona. . . .

Marcus heard a steady stream of curses ricochet against his office's walls and realized that the raw, rough tones were his own.

He closed his eyes, and memory took him back to the night his mother died. Opal had tried to embrace his mother and Winona had held her away. He heard again Opal's cry, *I love you. . . . You can't leave me!*

Then he remembered his mother's dark, furious threat, *You know what I can do, Jason. . . . Not this one . . . not my son. . . .*

Not this one. . . . My son, not our son. . . .

Bastard, Jason had often called him. . . .

Marcus tapped the glass on his desk, a rhythm that matched his thoughts.

And every one of the facts lined up to form the truth.

Sixteen

"MARCUS NEEDS SOME SPACE AND THINKING ROOM, AND I have something I have to do. I may as well do it now." Tempest stood up from the office chair. She looked across the marina's office desk to Kenny, who sat studying his damaged hand. Since shortly after Marcus had left, they were silent, each locked in their own thoughts and fears about the man they both loved. Though Kenny had made tea for them, it had been a long half hour.

Still shaken by Marcus's explosive reaction to the man who was his biological father and had acted like one throughout his lifetime, Tempest brushed away a teardrop trailing down her cheek. Maybe Marcus hated her; maybe he hated everyone involved. Forcing a conversation with him now would not help; Tempest was too emotional and unable to fully settle. She decided to use the time and her stormy emotions to her advantage—by seeking out Brice Whitcomb. "I just need to tie up a loose end, and now is a perfect time."

Instantly concerned, Kenny frowned. "Want me to go with you?"

"No, you stay here in case Marcus decides to come back. It's important that you two talk. I need to finish something. And Kenny, I'd rather you didn't call him to tell him I've gone, okay?"

Kenny shook his head. "He's not going to like it, is he?"

"Probably not. See you later."

"My son picked a fast mover, and a woman who likes to get things done." He picked up the necklace and locket and tossed it to her. "Whatever you're doing, take this. My—my Winona would want you to have it. Good luck."

"Thanks." Tempest secured the necklace. "I'll take good care of it. You'll be all right?"

Kenny nodded slowly. His, "Do what you have to do," sounded like Marcus.

That psychic link with Marcus had given Tempest the name of the resort where Brice Whitcomb was staying. As she drove the ten miles north of Port Salem to the El Fandango, Tempest thought of Marcus's reaction, his disbelief, and then his shocked expression. She wiped away the tears that wouldn't stop flowing down her cheeks. If only he hadn't overheard, and there had been time to gently enter the past.

At the resort, Tempest moved swiftly through the atrium-style lobby of the El Fandango. She scanned the fountain area, surrounded by tropical plants, and the bar where several people were relaxing. Brice Whitcomb wasn't in sight. At seven-thirty in the evening, he would be holed up in his room, focusing on the next day's poker game.

She tugged up her gloves, a habit she'd developed lately, while preparing to use her "feeler" psychic skills. On the hunt and ready to face the man who had almost ruined her life, she couldn't afford to be sent off course by one accidental touch.

After living with Brice for two years, she knew his habits well.

A light meal, a little relaxation with music and tension-relieving yoga, and then he'd focus on the game and his opponents' weaknesses. He would have already studied Marcus, what he had to lose, and his touch points. At some point in the game, when the stakes were high, Brice would carefully mention some sensitive tidbit, perhaps about Marcus's parents, such as the hit-and-run, his struggle without parents, the way he rebuilt a sagging empire.

A predator whose instincts told him exactly how to play a vulnerable victim, or catch the right moment to distract an opponent, Brice wasn't to be underestimated. He was cunning and experienced, and ruthless.

She'd never touched him with her naked hands. Perhaps her instincts had warned her that his dark energy could shatter her. If he actually was the man who had held that handbag in Leona's vintage shop, if he was the man who held hatred and rage close, who needed revenge, Tempest would soon know.

While holding Marcus's and Kenneth's hands, the images and emotions flipping through her, she'd caught Brice Whitcomb's current image. He still wore his shirt opened too low, to show off a heavy gold necklace. It would match a sizeable ring, if he still had it after years of bad luck. The image reflected a fading overweight playboy, his features deeply lined and overtanned, his thinning hair carefully pushed into a spikier look. The style did not erase his years of hard living.

The sharp edge of guilt twisted within Tempest's belly; she'd been so susceptible to Brice's worldly charm, fascinated with him. But she wasn't that inexperienced girl any longer, and she wasn't his "little freak."

If Brice had anything to do with the dark events surrounding her family, if his touch equaled that evil one on the handbag—"If he's connected to the rage that hurt Claire, I swear I will fry him. I don't care what happens to me."

Tempest's angry threat echoed in her mind after she'd spoken; a powerful psychic could do damage, but she wasn't certain she could actually hurt Brice—at least mentally. She knew she could physically defend herself and toss him; she'd done that years ago. His image said he'd be in worse shape now.

As Tempest moved through the lush hallways to the room number 101, the fragment she'd caught from Marcus, she also moved through her thoughts. In reality, she didn't know what she would do, the threat impulsive. But then, she was impulsive, and when it came to protecting those she loved, Tempest held revenge close. She wasn't soft like Claire, and she wasn't cool-thinking like Leona; she was merely herself, closer to the rebellious, fighting Viking strain than to Aisling's gentle blood.

Tempest rubbed the wolf's-head brooch for good luck, another new habit. "Come on, Viking great-granddaddy, let Thor's hammer strike. I don't know what I can do, maybe not 'fry' him, but he is going to pay. I want to look him in the eye when I hold his hand. I'll do that for myself, make him understand that I know what he is—nothing at all to me. I want him to know just how low I know he is, and that I am wiping those two years with him away as if they never existed. I am a different woman now, stronger and wiser, and he can never hurt or influence me again. He needs to know all that—directly from me and my touch."

Tempest braced herself to meet her past and the man who almost destroyed her. If Brice was the man standing outside the marina calling her name, she'd know. "This 'little freak' intends pure payback, but if Brice is involved with harming my family, I can't promise anything. Especially if he has any bit of that same rage as Sean."

Tempest stopped and braced herself in front of Brice's room. Soft meditation music floated out to her, an indication that Brice was right on schedule, preparing for the next big day in which he planned to "take the suckers."

Locked in her purpose, Tempest rapped on the door. Brice might choose not to see her—until he was ready, but she was ready now. Tempest chose a less obvious method to make Brice open the door. "Delivery service."

A few heartbeats later, the door slowly opened.

Brice stood with a towel around his waist; it sagged beneath a bulging belly. Embedded in his gray chest hair, his trademark heavy gold chain was not the expensive one he'd worn years ago. Disgusted by his appearance, disgusted for herself for once adoring him, Tempest braced herself to smile. "Hello, Brice. Long time, no see."

A sudden trickle of danger ran up her nape, a forceful, bristling energy pulsed through her. Her heartbeat kicked up, she caught a familiar scent, and the heavy hand on her shoulder warned her that Marcus had arrived.

She didn't have time to react before Brice's lips parted, his eyes wide as he stared over her head. "Greystone?"

Marcus gently shoved Tempest into the hotel room and closed the door behind him. "That's right . . . *Marcus Greystone*. You've met Tempest—correction, Dominique, I believe."

His emphasis on "Marcus Greystone" seemed to bite into the air, a residue of the earlier traumatic scene. Tempest studied his cold, grim expression; the silver heat of his eyes locked meaningfully on her. In a dangerous mood, Marcus was in command, and he wasn't arguing the fine points, like his right to be at her side and to protect her.

Tempest fought her initial wave of anger, trying to push it back. If he spotted a weakness, Brice knew her well enough to use it. She eased her elbow back against Marcus's ribs, a warning to back off and let her handle Brice. Instead, he moved closer.

"The game is tomorrow, Greystone, and I'm not happy about getting chummy tonight," Brice managed as he backed away from Marcus and Tempest. "Give me a minute to get dressed."

When Brice hurried to the bathroom, Marcus glanced at Tempest. "I can always count on you, can't I? You just jump right into things and muck them up."

Like my life? he might have said. "This is for myself, Marcus, and my family. You have no right to barge in here and take over."

He leaned down to look directly into her eyes, his expression cold and furious, his voice too low and too soft. "You touch him with that hand—without your gloves, and you'll find just exactly what the hell I can do, honey. While you were doing your little interfering-transmitter act at the marina, I was soaking up a few things, too."

As intimidating as Marcus was now, Tempest refused to back down. In the aftermath of the emotional exchange between father and son, she felt like lightning that could strike anywhere—if she didn't crumble into a sobbing mess first. In an uncertain show of bravado, Tempest crossed her arms and stared up at him. "Oh, yeah? Like what?"

His lips drew back against his teeth, those gray eyes narrowed at her. "That's for me to know, right? No sense in sharing too much with you, is there, sweetheart?"

"What do you mean 'sharing too much'? Like what? And how did you know I was coming here?"

"Kenny called and said you'd taken off. You couldn't wait for me to handle Whitcomb. Oh, no. Not you. Did you ever think that you might endanger yourself? How the hell would I explain to your family that I couldn't take care of my hardheaded, very impulsive woman?"

"I can take care of myself—"

"That's debatable."

"I want to know how you knew I was here. Kenny didn't know." Tempest considered Marcus's unreadable expression. "And you're good at poker, I suppose."

"I am. Call it the result of a misspent youth."

"I do not believe you can sense where I am without some way to track me." She touched the locket Kenneth had wanted her to wear. Just that flicker of Marcus's smoke-colored eyes and she knew exactly how he had found her earlier. "You put something in this locket, didn't you? How could you?"

"You don't exactly leave an itinerary, and you've been threatened. With Whitcomb in the area, I had to know where you were every minute. I didn't want anything happening to you. It was for your own protection."

Tempest layered every bit of guilt into her next words, "It was your mother's, Marcus. Shame on you."

He looked uneasy with that reprimand, and Tempest was about to press her advantage when Brice chose that moment to reenter the room. Apparently shaken, he'd recovered enough to face them—since he didn't have a choice. He walked to the bar, and his hands shook as he poured a drink; he downed it quickly before turning to Marcus and Tempest. Tempest tried to shrug away Marcus's possessive hand on her shoulder; it stayed.

"So this is your new one, Tempest," Brice murmured

as he poured another drink. "Care for something to drink, Greystone? I'd offer Tempest one, but I know she doesn't drink. It upsets her little psychic-self."

"I believe I will have a drink, Brice. Thank you," she said, because her emotions were riding high and because it was true. She was impulsive and sometimes reckless. At the moment, she was feeling both. Tempest ignored Marcus's hand as it tightened warningly on her shoulder. She took the warning under consideration, then added, "Something with orange juice and ice cubes."

Behind her, Marcus's breath seemed to explode. Brice considered her a moment, shrugged, then turned to the bar and mixed a drink. When he walked to hand it to Tempest, he looked over her head. He spoke as if sharing a confidence with Marcus. "She gets that way. Just has to prove you wrong at times."

Tempest lifted the glass, touched it with Brice's in a show of bravado and anger, and then quickly downed the drink. "Yum. More, please."

Marcus's hand tightened again, his body tense behind her. A predator, and quick to collect any nuances that would benefit his purposes, Brice caught the play between them and smiled. "She's expressive, isn't she? Always easy to read. Okay, Tempest, why are you here? And by the way, Greystone, it isn't exactly cricket to turn up unannounced or uninvited to an opponent's room the night before the game. But maybe that's an insider-professional thing that guys like you might not understand. Or was there something you wanted to discuss prior to the game?"

"Tempest has something she needs to do. I thought I'd come along to see that everything goes okay," Marcus answered too softly.

"Like what?"

"She wants to hold your hand."

Brice blinked just that once, and then he laughed.

"You've got to be kidding. We were lovers for two years, Greystone. I touched her all right. She touched me back."

A storm of male energy, bristling with angry heat circled Tempest, and she pushed back against Marcus's taut body. Brice was deliberately taunting Marcus, trying to find just that "edge," the way to distract his opponent. "It doesn't matter. Don't."

Marcus's tone was too soft and loaded with a challenge. "It's a simple thing, Whitcomb. To let her hold your hand, isn't it? Or are you afraid of her? What she might do?"

The alcohol in Tempest's drink was starting to work; she was having trouble focusing, and her body was beginning to feel heavy. She couldn't afford that, not now, not with Brice near and a potential danger to her family, and to Marcus. She had to act quickly and pulled off her glove. She reached for Brice's hand.

Before she could connect, Marcus caught her wrist. "Not without me," he stated grimly.

Tempest closed her eyes, letting his energy flow and meld with hers. The combination was good and strong and clean, a fresh start; Marcus understood who she was, what she had to do. Marcus would fight for her, put himself in danger to protect her. He was her protector, her lover, despite everything else. The loving energy flowed between them, creamy rich and soft as satin, it wove into a braid, wrapping around her protectively. Yin and yang circled each other, fitting perfectly together.

As though sensing their tender connection and despising it, Brice suddenly took her other hand and slid away her glove. His hand gripped hers, the energy hurting and evil and dark, filled with narrow shadows and dangerous black ribbons, of raging red ones.

Tempest locked herself into the connection. She relied on Marcus's strong energy to support her as she wound through Brice's dark passages. Then Marcus tugged her hand away. "That's enough."

The sensations she'd discovered in Brice exploded from Tempest. "He doesn't know Sean. Brice is a liar, and he's a con man. He lacks a conscience, and he's lazy and hateful and jealous of you. But he isn't who I want."

"Who the hell is Sean? And who the hell do you think you are, you little freak?" Brice demanded.

As if something had snapped in Marcus, his fist shot out to catch the other man on the jaw. Brice staggered back, found his balance, and yelled, "You'll pay for that. I'll have you charged with assault. I'll sue the hell out of you!"

"Try," Marcus challenged as he picked up Tempest's gloves and handed them to her. Her hands shook as she replaced them.

"You wouldn't do anything. Because if you do, I'll tell everything I know about her, your little freak."

Marcus drew her close to him, his hand on her waist. "That's right. She is mine. See you tomorrow, Whitcomb. The game is still on. The stakes are big, and the players have the money to back them."

"Like who?"

Without answering the question, Marcus ushered Tempest out of the hotel room. Before he closed the door, he turned to Brice, and stated, "They're looking forward to it. I wouldn't disappoint them, if I were you. They have your name. It won't be worth manure if you don't show."

Wrapped in the moments that had just passed, Tempest did not protest Marcus's hustling her out of the El Fandango. She settled into his car and into replaying the sensations she'd just gotten. One glance at Marcus told her that he was in no mood to discuss anything—his real father, or her decision to meet Brice.

Tempest wanted to ignore the prickle rising up the

back of her neck, but when her cell phone rang clearly, Marcus glanced at her. "Which one is it?"

She looked at him as she answered, "Leona, I'm a little busy here. Stop laughing. It is not funny. Okay, I went to see Brice. I had to know if he was the man who was standing outside the marina building that night, watching me. He wasn't. He doesn't feel like the energy on that handbag. He doesn't match the description you gave me of the man in your shop. Brice is such a sleaze."

Tempest eased down into her seat. If she wasn't mistaken, Marcus's mood had just shifted slightly, a little lighter, and definitely cheerful. She turned her attention to Leona's call. "Marcus is full of himself now. I did not ask him to help me."

Leona's tone held her laughter. "He's a protector. What did you think he would do?"

"It was all so macho." Tempest ignored Marcus, but his tense body said he was definitely listening. He was going to get an earful. If he didn't want to talk to her, she'd talk to her sister. "I could have handled Brice by myself. Marcus doesn't understand."

"Do you think that Brice used that truck to push you and Marcus over that hill?"

"No. In the first place, he wouldn't know how to drive it. In the second place, he usually takes it easy before a big gig. In the third place, his energy wasn't of the active-man kind. It was more of having others do for him."

"So it's still out there, then. You're wearing your brooch, aren't you?"

Tempest caught Leona's quiet, pensive tone. "You've been dreaming again, haven't you?"

"Yes. I think what is happening with you, and that disturbing man in the shop, are all a mix that won't let me rest. I feel as if something is going to happen, Tempest Best, and I'm worried for you."

Tempest noted the familiar Greystone driveway. She ended the call as Marcus parked the car. He got out without speaking and stood waiting for her at the back deck. He reached for a small parcel resting on a bench, scanned the label, and then tossed it to her. "For you."

Tempest glanced at the return address and recognized it; her friend had worked very quickly on her special request. Tall and silent, Marcus followed her into the house, and then said, "I've got some business to take care of."

He was walling himself off again. Marcus was evidently still tightly wrapped in the discovery that Kenny was his biological father. Maybe it was better if Tempest opened the discussion and let Marcus share his thoughts. "I'd like to talk about earlier, at the marina," she stated.

In the kitchen, Marcus opened the refrigerator and scanned it. He took out a bottle of orange juice and drank from it. The gesture was pure male, a reminder of his actions earlier. Then he leveled an icy look at her as he capped the bottle and replaced it. "Today is finished. We both need to cool off. Take my advice, and don't try anything again tonight. It's almost midnight, and I'm not in a good mood."

Tempest placed the small package on the counter; she would open it later. Right now, she had a big, angry male on her hands, and she wasn't too certain about her own simmering temper. "It's always better to get things out."

"That's you. You're always right there. I'm not like that. Chitchat and replay are a waste of time. Call your sisters. Call your mother. You have the capability to drive me nuts."

He reached for her, and his lips fused to hers, the kiss hot and hard and shattering. Tempest was in the storm, responding, locking her body to Marcus's before she could think; she was a part of him, body and soul, loving him, soothing him.

And then suddenly, she was free, standing alone, her legs weak. Tempest grabbed the kitchen counter to steady herself as Marcus's glare heated her from head to foot and back again. His fierce look stripped away civilization and marked her as his possession. "Did you get that straight, Storm? Or do we need further discussion?" he demanded.

"I believe I understand." A kiss like that took little explanation. "Tell me what you got in the marina. You said—"

"While you were busy shoveling images and feelings back and forth between Kenny and me?" Marcus cupped her chin in his hand and lifted her face. "I got this: You love me. I'm perfect for you, and you think I'm sweet. You want to protect me and hold me and take away every pain I ever had. You can't do that. No one can. You scare me, Tempest. I know I scare you."

She couldn't deny how she felt about him. She'd just torn off the facade of his life. She wouldn't blame Marcus if he did not return the favor. "I scare most people, but you seem to handle it. Anything else?"

Marcus's steady stare and his silence told her he was chewing on one very big fact, and he wasn't certain he liked it.

"Anything else?" she prodded, a little desperate now because he was keeping something from her.

"Not that I'd like to talk about at this moment. I don't know how I feel about it. In fact, I don't know how you might feel about it."

"When then?"

For an answer, Marcus turned and walked into his office, closing the door behind him.

Tempest rubbed her gloved hands over her face. At the marina, she'd accidentally opened up his wound, a secret that perhaps he might never have known, but now he did—because of her. She needed to go to Marcus, to comfort him, to hold him safe in her arms and make his heartache disappear.

She glanced at the package and decided it would have to wait; dealing with Marcus now would take a thoughtful strategy. She wasn't experienced in handling bristling angry males, especially one who knew that she loved him.

What else had he gotten that he was hoarding from her? What could it be?

Seventeen

TWENTY MINUTES LATER, MARCUS STOOD IN HIS SHADOWY bedroom, flicking open the buttons of his shirt. He glanced at Tempest, who had come to stand in the doorway. "I couldn't concentrate on work. I've had enough for one day, and tomorrow is going to be a big one. I don't want to argue all night, or what's left of it."

Tempest leaned against the doorframe and crossed her arms, the small box held tightly in one hand. She ached for the pain Marcus was experiencing, his emotions written in bitter lines and shadows on his face; his body was tightly coiled, his movements abrupt, indicating his anger and frustration. The door to his past was almost fully open, and that inner room wasn't pretty; Marcus would be untangling the past in his emotions and mind for a long, long time.

But as his lover, and since he already knew she loved him, Tempest had certain rights. One of them was comforting him, but Marcus clearly was in no mood to be eased and cuddled, his life torn apart. He'd just discovered that his biological father wasn't his mother's legal husband. No one on earth would be able to accept that readily.

Tempest's second option was head-on and to-the-point confrontation; it wouldn't be sweet or endearing, but then it might serve to exorcise some of his savage mood now. In addition to any natural emotional pain Marcus would be suffering from that psychic link with Kenny, Marcus's psyche would be all torn, raw edges now. She'd experienced those sensations often enough to recognize them. If Marcus needed someone to battle him at this moment, to come down off that ragged peak, where he'd had his first taste of extrasensory perception and the reality of his life had been shattered, Tempest would try to help him.

The best way to get those wounds out in the open, and cleansed so that they could begin to heal, was to call him out. She gripped that small box tighter in her gloved hand and braced for his explosion. "Great. You don't want to talk. You want to forget what just happened. It's not going away, Marcus. Deal with it."

Even as the words left her lips, Tempest regretted their cut, but understood the necessity. She didn't want to hurt Marcus, but she wasn't going to watch him destroy himself, either. The more he brooded, the deeper the wound. Psychic wounds could rebound on themselves and worsen, let alone the natural emotional ones.

In one-half of a heartbeat, Marcus picked up her challenge. He rounded on her fiercely. "You knew all the time, didn't you? You knew, and you didn't say anything."

"I suspected, nothing more."

"Yeah . . . sure, tell me another one."

"She made him promise, Marcus. Kenny wanted to see Winona and his son, and be a part of their lives. She needed him for herself and for you. He kept that promise. It wouldn't have been easy, especially not with Jason taunting him and wringing him dry of ideas. Then, when Greystone Investments started to sink, Kenny stayed to protect both you and your mother—and her unborn baby."

Marcus tore off his belt, tossed it aside, and put his hands on his hips. "I don't know what you're talking about. No man would do that."

"Oh, no? They loved each other deeply, Marcus. They sacrificed for each other and for you. Is it so bad to be created out of love, rather than—"

He scowled at her. "Stop right there. I don't want to talk about it."

"Fine. Then I'm sleeping in the guest room. There is no reason for me to be with you when you're holding so much from me. You already know I love you, and that I'm here for you, Marcus. But I will not watch you torture yourself."

His scowl deepened, and he tore off his shirt, tossing it aside. "I don't believe any of that—what I felt. You could have been projecting some fairy tale to me. I've read about psychics distorting reads."

"So? It happens. The real, human part and natural emotions of a psychic can't be dismissed. What if I did alter the energies, the memories, toning them as I wanted? What if I admitted that? What would happen then? Some fast sex that solved nothing? And you'd still be wanting to tear life apart with your bare hands? I don't think so."

Tempest drew a deep, unsteady breath, her love for Marcus, the need to protect him, battled with another reality. "Marcus, if you don't face this now, work through it, you'll never know. It's not going away."

He rammed his hand through his hair and glared at her. "I just need some time, dammit. Back off."

"I can't do that. I care too much."

Silence shook the room as they stared at each other.

Then Marcus's voice vibrated with anger and frustration. "Boy, you're something. I can't even turn my back, before you're off and running to see Whitcomb."

"Oh? We're jealous now, are we?" At least he was talking now. Tempest tossed the box to him. "Maybe this will help that one little problem. I never touched Brice, except tonight, with you. I know how I felt at that moment. How did you?"

Marcus stared at the small box in his hands as he appeared to be considering that moment. "Lighter. I felt lighter."

"Okay, that was me, my energy. We flowed together, and you made me stronger, yin and yang. You made me feel safer and protected. That's what you are, a protector. Every instinct you have is to protect me. I feel the same toward you. That is why I am standing here now, arguing with you. If I didn't care, I wouldn't waste my time. Now open that box."

Marcus took a deep, resigned sigh, then removed the box's lid. "It's a bracelet."

"A man's silver bracelet. I had it made especially for you. I wish you'd been wearing it when we were at the marina. It might have helped you remember that you're not alone, that I love you. You said you'd felt that, right? Do you think I ever told Brice I loved him? No way. But I do love you, and you are going to wear that bracelet."

"Oh, boy. Just what I need after a day like today—jewelry."

Tempest ignored the sarcastic remark, attributing it to Marcus's unbelievable day. Whatever was lurking around the Aislings could have sensed Marcus's energy, maybe it was feeding off him now, and Tempest wanted to give him whatever small protection she could. "Put it on, and do not take it off."

Marcus was wrapped in his traumatic discovery, stunned by it. "Do you know that practically every person I've trusted in my entire life—people who took care of me—had a motive to murder my parents? Correction: To murder my mother and her husband? No wonder Jason called me a bastard. I really am."

Marcus suddenly sat on the bed, tossed the bracelet aside, and held his head in his hands. Then he looked at his right hand, as if comparing it to Kenny's damaged one, and he shuddered. " 'Not him, not this one,' my mother said. She meant that she knew what Jason had done to Kenny—to Kenneth Ragnar—or had caused done. I saw it—"

His right hand began to curl into that claw shape. Tempest hurried to Marcus, sitting beside him. She gripped his hand, forcing his fingers straight and apart.

"What are you doing?" Stunned, Marcus stared at his hand. "That's the shape of Kenny's hand. What's happening?"

"You're riding on the aftermath of an extrasensory experience, some of the remnants are still inside you. Don't let your fingers curl, Marcus, or they'll stay like that."

He looked at Tempest as if he'd never seen her before. "Is that what happens to you?"

"Residuals can be iffy and dangerous. I've had some unpleasant experiences, but I've learned a few things to protect myself. Let's not take a chance, shall we? Marcus, I want you to wear that bracelet for protection. Please," she said in earnest. When Marcus's hand relaxed into its normal shape, Tempest gripped it tightly. Marcus had to understand that what he couldn't physically see actually existed and had to be fought just as strongly, too. A partial belief could not protect him; that small bit of doubt could allow him to be harmed. "Too much has happened, and you could be in danger, too."

"Come on, Tempest. What could be worse than what I just went through today?"

She gripped his hand tighter, desperately willing him to understand. "No matter how you're feeling now, I want you to wear that bracelet. You were with me, out there in the fog, just like I was with my sister before this, in Montana. It followed me, or I took a part of it inside me that it can find and use. If it knows me, it could recognize your energy, too. Please?"

"Tell me about this residual stuff, what psychic high I'm coming off of."

"It can be nasty, and it can flip any which way, take your emotions swinging all over the place. Because you were wounded emotionally, you were more vulnerable in that link, and the residual went deeper." She ignored his disbelieving snort, but understood that right now Marcus was also fighting the emotional battle of his lifetime. Pile his first psychic experiences on top of that, and he needed every bit of help she could give. She reached for the bracelet and held it out to him. "I never really loved Brice. I do love you, you said you felt that. Put it on."

Marcus's gray eyes darkened as he studied her face. "Who was that hit-and-run driver? You know, don't you?"

She met his searching stare, and said, "I don't know, and that's the truth. But I will find out."

"Because of that damned brooch—you're making this all more difficult than it should be. That could be on its way to your mother. I've talked with your sister about this. There's no reason why you should feel you need to earn it. Not when your life and your psychic gift can be in danger. It's too risky." He checked his wristwatch. "It's past one now, a new day. She might have it today if you weren't so damned stubborn."

"Could we just take one thing at a time, like I really want you to wear this bracelet for good luck. And maybe I'd like you to think of me, the person who destroyed your life—"

"You didn't destroy my life. It was destroyed before you came into it. You're the best thing in it."

She bent her head then, unable to stop the tears flowing down her cheek. "If I hadn't gotten into your life, you could have gone on without ever knowing."

Marcus took her hand to his lips. "Maybe. Right now, I'd like to tear everything apart and put it back together the way it was, but with you in the picture. I don't think I believe it. It's probably all malarkey anyway. Right now, I want it to be."

"You'll have to work through that yourself, how you're going to handle it. That's for you to decide."

"You know that I'm going to have to follow every lead, no matter what I want to believe. Hell, Opal was right in the middle of that argument after they came back from the lake. Maybe Jason just wanted to get away from her."

Tempest took a deep breath and released another shocking tidbit that Marcus could believe or not. "Your mother was leaving them both. She'd had enough of everything. She had you and Kenny waiting for her. At the first chance she got, she sneaked out of the house, headed for her car—but Jason muscled her over, out of the passenger seat. Kenny only suspected it. But Opal actually saw it from her room."

Marcus stared at her, apparently stunned. He looked at the wall, as if it revealed those last scenes with his mother. He shook his head, closed his eyes, and sighed. "It's all mixed up. I always thought Opal was defending my mother. But that wasn't the case then. If she saw them leave, she could have gone after them, rammed them. Or she could have had someone do it for her."

Suddenly, as if needing a distraction, Marcus lifted the heavy link bracelet, a masculine design. He studied the engraving on the silver band. "Okay, I know enough to recognize Viking characters. What does it say?"

Tempest swallowed, her throat tense with emotions. "I don't want you to go out there tomorrow, not on the lake, please."

"I'm going to. What does it say?" Marcus insisted.

If that something, stronger near the water, recognized Marcus's energy, it could take him to his death. Her fear for Marcus danced inside Tempest as she managed unevenly, "It says Man of an Aisling woman who is descended from Thorgood the Viking."

"Thorgood. . . . You know that name for certain?"

Tempest took the bracelet and opened the clasp, closing it again when the bracelet circled Marcus's wrist. "Both clairvoyants, Mom and Leona, have dreamed of Thorgood, and yes, I believe that's his name."

"It's a lot to believe, Tempest. But I—I'm . . ." Words seemed to fail Marcus as he stared into her eyes. Suddenly, he stood and walked from the room.

Tempest wrapped her arms around herself. She could only wait for Marcus to sort through his traumatic emotions, and speak with her—if he ever did. She was the reason his life had been torn apart. Feeling very old and worn, Tempest slowly undressed. She slipped into their bed to hold his pillow tightly against her. The silence of the house ached, punctuated periodically by some small sound that indicated Marcus was pacing, dealing with his torment.

She gripped the sheets with her fists. On edge, torn apart, Marcus wanted to be alone to brood, to ache, to refuse the fragments of his life's truth.

She heard him moving through the house, and then silence. Unable to wait longer, Tempest rose and slipped on a T-shirt. She moved slowly; her body and mind felt as if she'd traveled through centuries, but she couldn't rest until Marcus did. She found him sitting in the dark living room, staring out at the night; his bare feet rested on the coffee table, a drink held on his stomach. The bracelet she'd given him gleamed softly on his wrist. Comforted that he still wore the gift, Tempest relaxed slightly.

"I want to be alone right now, Tempest."

Those quiet, deadly words hit her like a physical blow, and her hand covered her heart. "Do you hate me so much?"

When he turned to look at her, Marcus's face was in the shadows, those eyes just slits of silver. "I think we settled that—I love you. You did what I wanted. The question is: Which one of the three people I've trusted most in my life would hate either one of my parents enough to kill them? The next question is, will you be here when I come back tomorrow?"

"Of course, I will. But please don't go out on the lake tomorrow, Marcus. There is absolutely no need to do this silly revenge on my part. I don't need anyone to stand up for whatever honor you think was taken," Tempest finished abruptly. "I . . . love . . . you. Brice means nothing. He's all threats, and—"

But Marcus had turned back to staring out at the night and shutting her out.

Tempest stood in the shadows for a long time, aching for him, for the memories that hadn't made sense as a child but were now falling into place.

"Marcus has the *Winona* out now, picking up Whitcomb at the resort's dock." Kenny glanced at his neatly folded clothing, arranged on his bed beside his open suitcase. "He wants me out of here. . . . There's the check he wrote for the money I put into Greystone Investments to keep it afloat."

After yesterday and a long, hard night, Marcus had finally come to lie beside her. His lovemaking had been tender and slow. Tempest had purposefully absorbed whatever nettling psychic residue she could as she rested near him. Exhausted, she'd slept overlong that morning, awakening to find Marcus already gone. He hadn't answered his cell phone, but she'd hoped to find him at the marina building, talking sensibly to Kenny. With that thought, Tempest had rushed out into the morning.

Kenny wasn't at the marina building. She hurried to his home, where she'd found him packing. He'd shaved and, without that full beard, his features mirrored his son's. "You can't go, Kenny."

He picked up the photograph album and ran his fingers across it, as if the photographs were the most precious things in his life, memories of the only woman he loved, the mother of his son. "That's what my son wants. He'll be okay. He loves you. Things will work out."

"They can't if you don't stay and let him work through what happened. Did he actually say he wanted you gone?"

Kenny lifted a questioning eyebrow, the expression so much like Marcus's. "He sent a check over, full payment for the money I put into Greystone when it was going down. I'd say that was a tip-off that he wants to be clear of anything to do with me. I tore up the check, but I got the message. I can't blame him if he never wants to see me again."

"Marcus is just wading through so much now. Give him a chance to put everything into perspective. Please don't leave before talking with him. I'm just so afraid for him, that something will happen out there on the lake. I need you to stay—for me, Kenny. Please."

"He said you were afraid of the water, that a sailboat accident when you were young had terrified you of big water. He said it had changed you and your sisters."

"It's more than that, but right now I'm worried about Marcus."

Tempest quickly informed Kenny of the real reason for the poker game. The older man smiled and nodded sadly. "He's right to call Whitcomb out. Marcus is protecting his woman. Any honorable man would do the same. I should have done the same."

Tempest wrapped her arms around herself, fighting off the chilling premonition that this day would be one of the worst in her lifetime. "I know what you mean. What a man has to do, and all that. It's silly, antiquated, macho bull. But Kenny, you did what you had to do to protect your love and your son. And you acted as Winona wanted, too."

"Maybe. He's always been a proud man, an honorable one. Let him do his job."

"It's going to be a long day. I don't think I can face it without you," she whispered. "I love him, you know."

"I'll be here, honey . . . until Marcus is back, anyway."

By late afternoon, the *Winona* was anchored offshore, near Marcus's house. Tempest had called her family, who had warned her to stay away from the lake, and she'd answered angry calls from both Opal and Francesca.

Opal had been first: "I knew you were trouble from the moment I laid eyes on you. Now Kenny is leaving with no reason. He called last night. Both of us worked ourselves to the bone, keeping that house and the marina going. I borrowed money and put my life savings on the line. Now Marcus is accusing me of—of wanting his mother? It's because of you, you little tramp. He says he doesn't want me back in the house, but that I can live here. Here, in a rented condo, when I had a real home and everything in it was mine. That is my house, and I want you out of it, no matter what he says."

On a clear day with a slight wind, the streamlined cruiser lay majestically upon the lake. Tempest used her binoculars but saw no one on the deck. "Opal, you never said if you knew Winona had taken a lover—"

"You'd dirty the name of Marcus's mother?" Opal had screamed. "I'll see you in hell."

"Well, I won't see you in this house, will I?" Tempest had answered smoothly.

The catty remark was designed to score, to hit its mark and bring out the truth. Opal's voice had risen angrily. "I knew Winona had someone. She'd come back from one of their rendezvous all lit up and rosy. That was only while the Greystones were here—they lived in other places, and I have no idea what happened while they were away."

Opal might have wanted to kill Winona for her "defection." Tempest had to test what Opal knew of Kenny's love for Winona. "Who was he?"

"I never knew, but if I did, I wouldn't tell you," Opal had stated before she hung up.

An hour later, Francesca's usually smooth tone had crackled angrily over the telephone lines. "Everything was fine, until you came. You know you don't fit into Marcus's life. He's fired Kenny, a longtime friend and almost like his father. Kenny has given his life to the Greystones, and he wouldn't leave unless Marcus fired him. You come into Marcus's life, and suddenly he's cutting ties with everyone. Marcus told me that he was going to marry you. You! I tried to talk reason to him, but he's already cut off Kenny, and Opal—"

Momentarily stunned by Marcus's mention of marriage, Tempest had tried to hold her focus. Marcus was probably upset, rash in his words. But who had told

Francesca that Opal and Kenny had been cut off? The information source was Opal. Were Opal and Francesca involved with that deadly hit-and-run? Both of them would have had motives.

Francesca's next curt words had confirmed Tempest's thoughts. "Opal told me that he came over and told her off. Oh, she'll be supported and have a place to live, but he doesn't want her back in the house again. She's tended that house like she would a baby, and she's destroyed. Poor old woman, tossed away just like Kenny. Marcus won't ever marry you. I'll make him see how freaky you are, how you don't fit in, how—"

"How he owes you? What's the matter, Francesca, isn't he as easy to deal with as Jason?"

The taunt was intended to set Francesca over the edge, but instead she had asked quietly, "Who told you that? Opal? Kenny? It was Kenny, wasn't it? He never liked sharing Marcus with me. I could tell. He's never been friendly, and he's a freak, just like you, that awful hand. Why Marcus put up with him, I'll never know."

Tempest knew. The father-son bond had been there for years, even if it hadn't been recognized.

"And if you mean so much to Marcus," Francesca had continued, "why didn't he ask you to make his guests comfortable, instead of me? That's what a woman does for her man, isn't it? Helps him entertain, helps him with business?"

Tempest tried not to think of the lake and the potential danger to Marcus; she tried not to think how badly she needed to hold him and know that he was safe. And what had he felt during that psychic transference that he wouldn't tell her? That they were both, or he was, going to die? Was it possible that in that transparent, glimmering spiderweb of connections, Marcus understood some danger that he didn't want her to know?

What had he seen? What secret did he hold? So much had happened, everything so quickly, one trauma on top of another, her past, his life. . . . Tempest gripped her brooch and her body shook. Amid the fast-moving storm of intrigue and danger, her fear of the water and the fog, and their passion, she'd forgotten to tell him that Brice always carried a small handgun. . . .Had Marcus seen his own death? Or Brice's?

When the call ended, Tempest tried to call Marcus one more time. When he didn't answer, she took one look at the *Winona* and knew what she had to do. Live or die, it would be with Marcus, the man she loved.

In the *Winona*'s salon, Marcus glanced out at the small white sailboat, headed straight for the cruiser.

With Whitcomb sitting across from him and watching for any kind of an indication of Marcus's poker hand, he couldn't afford to be distracted. The other two players were brothers and friends of Marcus's, who understood this was actually a private match and a vendetta; all men were only using first names. At seven o'clock in the evening, the game was just getting interesting; Marcus saw that Whitcomb was an excellent player and read his partners and the cards well.

Tom Stanfield, an Australian, looked out of the stateroom's window to a small sailboat. "She's having a rough time. Looks like whoever is out there is inexperienced, and there's a squall coming up."

Jake Stanfield followed his brother's stare. "Some girl out there, mate. Maybe we'd better help. . . . It looks like she's about to capsize."

Whitcomb's eyes met Marcus's. "That's her problem. If the lake is that rough, she shouldn't be on the water. Let's play."

Tom stood up and went to the window. "Wouldn't you know it? Cracky. A redhead. She doesn't know what she's doing."

A redhead ... Tempest! Marcus stiffened and caught Whitcomb's eyes; they'd just flickered with satisfaction. Of course, he would have known that Tempest wouldn't stay out of this match—that she'd have to come after Marcus.

According to the base rules they'd established before the game, the first player to leave the game, or the cruiser, was a loser. And nothing mattered but Tempest's life. . . . "Let me introduce you to Tom and Jake Stanfield, sons of Lewis Stanfield, a man you fleeced out of his life savings. Boys, you may want to take away that handgun he's got strapped to his ankle—just so he doesn't hurt himself. Gentlemen, excuse me. That redhead may be mine."

Whitcomb leaped to his feet, but Marcus's hard slap knocked him backward, and the brothers were on him. "Like I said, 'Excuse me,'" Marcus said as he hurried out to the main deck.

"Tempest?"

The whisper chilled her more than the icy water splashing over her. Treading water away from the capsized sailboat, she could feel the sucking at her feet, as if actual hands were pulling her down. While sunset skimmed the water, the evil darkness waited below. The energy was the same as in the fog, but now it was stronger.

"This is all in my mind," she repeated for the third time, as another wave crashed over her. The swells looked like mountains, moving endlessly, ominously toward her. Icy cold, she couldn't last long. . . .

Tempest struggled to the surface, fighting with all her strength, but the waves were too strong, cresting and falling upon her. "Tempest?" the voice whispered again, the tone seductive. "I've been waiting for you. You know that, don't you? That I've been waiting?"

She shook her head, fighting the voice. It was just inside her head. It wasn't real. She was more vulnerable now, because she was frightened and she was in a major lake. She was exhausted, mentally and physically. Everything was just in her extrasensory perception, not in her reality. She couldn't believe, or she would die.

Tempest spit out a mouthful of water, aware that the chilling temperature was taking its toll on her body, and in a few moments—She was only having a flashback, her terror overriding her logic. None of this was real; it was only in her mind. Somehow, the energy had connected with her, settling deep in her mind. Now it slithered out and wrapped her in fear. She had to push free and repeated the protective mantra she'd learned as a child. "Stop . . . focus . . . think. . . ."

Another wave crashed over her, and she fought to the surface again. She was losing the fight to live, and Marcus might die because she hadn't told him about Brice's handgun.

"Tempest!" This time the voice wasn't in her head; it was louder and desperate.

She saw him swimming toward her, just as her father had done. But this time it was Marcus, and he could die.

The dark energy bristled around her, angry at the interference. Or was she just imagining? Just in case reality and the unreal had blended into one truth, Tempest yelled, "He's wearing the mark of a daughter born of Aisling and Thorgood. We're bonded, and together we are strong."

"Damn right we are," Marcus stated harshly as he appeared at her side. "Hold on."

Marcus supported her body as they worked back the few yards to the *Winona* 's dinghy. He hefted her over the side, and then himself. He quickly mopped the water away from Tempest's face. "Are you okay?"

Crying, Tempest clung to him, afraid that it had just been a dream, and that somehow he wasn't real. "Come on, honey," Marcus urged as he rubbed her arms, trying to warm her. "We've got to get you to shore."

He started the small outboard motor, headed the boat toward his house, and turned briefly to wave to the three men standing on the *Winona*'s deck. Moments later, he had pulled the dinghy onto the beach and was carrying Tempest up the embankment to his house. "We've got to get you warm. And quick."

Inside, Marcus quickly stripped her clothing away and wrapped a blanket around her. "You could have died out there. What the hell were you thinking?" he asked as he rubbed warmth back into her shivering body.

"That I love you? That you love me?" In view of the past danger, her answer seemed feeble, but it was true.

Marcus stared at her, and then tugged her into his arms; he kissed her face, warming it with his breath. "If I lost you, I don't know what I'd do."

"It was out there, Marcus. I felt it. The same energy as in the fog, the same rage, the same need for revenge."

When he stilled, his face against hers, Tempest knew—"You felt it, too, didn't you?"

His answer was cautious. "I knew that if I didn't get to you, we'd both be dead—in one way or another."

Marcus frowned as he slowly bent to pick up her wet sweater and study it. "You're not wearing it? Your pin?"

Tempest ran her gloved hand over the place where her brooch had been. "It's gone. I was wearing it."

"It doesn't matter. You can make another one. But we're getting the real one to your mother. Then we'll know how to stop this."

Tempest stripped away her wet gloves and cradled his face in her hands, willing him to be safe. She let his strength, their silky, flowing bond wrap warmly around her. "It's true then, you are my protector."

"Uh-huh. Neil said you'd come to realize that. Now all I need is a sword and a shield," he whispered against her lips. But Tempest understood that his tease covered the tumultuous emotions he was feeling now, his fear of losing her. He rotated his shoulders as though settling into a very comfortable sweater. "It feels nice, all this yin-yang stuff."

Forty-five minutes later, after they had taken a hot shower, and Tempest was curled on the couch, Marcus hung up the telephone. "They've hauled the sailboat into port. There was nothing wrong with it, only the inexperienced person using it. When you're up to it, we could go down there and you could see if you could catch anything—any 'residuals' off the boat."

"I only think something was out there. Okay, I'm pretty certain that someone was broadcasting to me, talking to me. I think . . . I think when I touched those games and Sean's computer, I picked up a residual, and it fed on my fear of the lake. Psychic power can boomerang. It can lie in wait until the time for it to spring. It came out when I was most afraid, like in the fog, and that means he's really getting stronger. Or I'm getting weaker, more susceptible."

"You're anything but weak." But Marcus's mind was elsewhere as he watched the *Winona* glide away out of sight.

"They're not going to hurt Brice, are they? Those brothers?"

"Not if he behaves himself. He took your pride and your life for two years. Just now, you almost died, and he knew you were in trouble and never so much as blinked. And you're worried about him?"

Marcus shook his head. "No, they won't hurt him. But they'll be 'entertaining' him for a while, and he'll be making some apologies. I don't think he'll like working at their isolated sheep ranch in Australia, going with them out to the bush, and they'll be keeping close tabs on him after that."

"You feel left out—you wanted to ruin him."

"I wanted to do more than that, and I still may. All bets are off if he tries to contact you again."

"He won't. He doesn't like to be exposed for what he is. . . . Marcus, you have a whole life waiting for you. Kenny—"

Marcus stood suddenly and walked to the window overlooking Lake Michigan. He crossed his arms and braced his legs, and Tempest understood that he was turning over what he had learned in the marina.

The second week of July's sunset laid a fiery strip over the lake's dark swells, seagulls pale and hovering in the distance. Boats were pulling into the harbor, a party cruiser just pulling out onto the lake. "Ragnar," he said quietly. "That's Scandinavian, isn't it?"

"Yes, it is." Tempest moved to stand near him, her bare hand on his back. If Marcus was trying to work through his life, Tempest wanted to give him her strength. He shrugged her hand away. She understood: Marcus was taking his time unraveling the snippets of his life, trying to weave them back together into a logical path.

"Ragnar . . . Viking?"

"Probably."

"I'm probably descended from Vikings. I have that blood, right? The same as you?"

Marcus was neatly arranging and understanding the bond made centuries ago. "I'd say you were probably certified class-A Viking beefcake. You probably took to boats before you could walk. You probably lived on the water when you could." Like father, like son.

"I spent most of my childhood on the water. . . . Ragnar," he repeated, as though testing it on his tongue and settling it in his mind.

Tempest ached for him; he'd lived a life as Greystone, but he was Kenneth Ragnar's son. "You could have tests done."

"I'd rather not." Marcus inhaled abruptly, held his breath, and then released it. He lifted his arm and studied the engraved bracelet. "How do you know your line traces back to this Aisling and Thorgood? Some genealogy chart?"

"Nothing so realistic. But from dreams of my mother and her mother before her, and so on . . . dreams that Leona has, all separate and yet too much alike." The dreams that had driven Tempest's grandmother mad, because she fought what she was.

Marcus turned to study her. "Claire's husband, Neil Olafson, is probably of Viking descent, too, right? And he's called Claire's protector, like I am called yours? So this 'protector' business is no joke?"

"It's no joke. Think of how many times you've saved me just in the space of a few days."

Marcus shook his head. "You're saying that what we have, this Viking connection thing goes back centuries to Aisling and Thorgood? That it runs parallel? That this Thorgood captured a psychic Celt woman and they bonded—fell in love?"

"Truly, that's the way of it. So far as we know, all of their female descendants looked somewhat alike, with Aisling's red hair, green eyes, and pale skin."

"I bet that was a hell of a fight if you're ⟨...⟩ go by." He began to smile. "Then, if all that is ⟨...⟩ really didn't have a chance, did I?"

"No, probably not." And this time, Tempest smiled as she placed her hand on his arm.

Marcus shook his head and moved away from her touch. "Oh, no. I know what's going on behind those green eyes. I am not ready to talk with Kenny. Where are we with finding my mother's killer? Do you think we're any closer?"

"I think we're very close."

Eighteen

"IT'S TEN O'CLOCK AT NIGHT, AND I DON'T KNOW HOW I LET
you talk me into this," Marcus stated. "Kenny isn't at
his house, and he's probably already left town. He's
got no reason to come back to the marina. I don't know
what else needs to be said. You just missed getting
killed, and we should call it a night."

He stared at the marina building's side door, and
then down at Tempest, whose gloved hand rested on
his arm. He was busy replaying her earlier arguments
and warring with his unsteady emotions.

Marcus glanced at the harbor's waves, then back
down at Tempest's concerned expression. Those wide
green eyes pleaded with him to understand Kenny's
actions. That might take forever. "Anything? You feel
anything coming from the lake?"

She shook her head. "I'm fine. I just want to see
Kenny and explain to him what a hardhead you
are."

"Okay, back to that. I told you I needed more time,
but oh no, you just had to see him tonight. I wasn't
letting you go anywhere alone, and here we are. . . .
What did you mean, he tore up my check? It's good. It
doesn't make sense not to cash that check."

"It's called pride, Marcus. And he has money. He's a good businessman, too. He didn't spend his lifetime working here with you and nurturing you—yes, that's what a real father does, if you'd stop and think—because he wanted repayment. You weren't his investment to be repaid, you are his son, and your mother was the only woman he loved."

But Marcus was listening to the sounds inside the building. Someone had just revved the forklift. He punched in the security code and eased Tempest behind him as he opened the side door.

In the dim light from the office windows, he saw Kenny sprawled on the floor, and the forklift maneuvering around the supply shelves, set on a course to him. Evidently an expert at handling the forklift around narrow aisles, the driver's face was in the shadow of a ball cap.

Tempest was already in action, running toward Kenny. Marcus cursed as he looked at her and the approaching forklift, which could kill them both. He quickly moved up into the boat-storage racks; he worked his way across them as he tracked the forklift below.

In position above the machine, Marcus poised to leap. He glanced at Tempest, who was struggling to haul the unconscious man into the office. The forklift was headed straight for them. "She'll never make it. They'll both be killed."

Marcus tensed and held his breath. He had one chance to land on the driver and stop Tempest and Kenny from being crushed. He gripped the support of the pleasure boat's storage bay and focused entirely on the driver. And then he leaped. . . .

In just that instant, Francesca stared up at him. She leaned to one side to avoid getting hit by his body, and suddenly, she was tumbling down.

Marcus felt the hard bump as the forklift ran ove
Francesca. He quickly settled into the controls and
swung the machine away from its head-on course
toward Tempest and Kenny. Marcus killed the engine
and leaped over the side; he glanced at Tempest, who
was crouched beside Kenny.

She stared at Francesca's crushed body, her coverall
stained with blood. Tempest's face was too pale as she
whispered, "Go to her, Marcus. I'll call for help."

As she lay on the concrete floor, Francesca looked a
Marcus when he bent to her. He took her hand gently
"Hold on, Francesca. The ambulance will be here soon."

"How do I look?" she whispered raggedly, the ques
tion at odds with her condition, her body crushed. "Fi
my hair, will you, honey?"

Marcus removed the ball cap and arranged her hai
around her face. She was dying, her body chilling
Those bright blue eyes were starting to dim, bu
Marcus had to know. "Now would be the right time
Francesca, to do the right thing."

"It doesn't hurt, not now." The rattle in her throa
said she didn't have long. "Sure, it was me. I did it.
drove that tulip truck and the city gravel truck. . . .
knew what you were doing with her up there. . . . Afte
years of waiting for him, all the promises to marry me
Jason said he wasn't ever going to let Winona go. . .
After all I'd done for him, stuck by him. You were
doing the same thing."

She coughed, shuddered, and closed her eyes. He
voice was weaker, slipping away to the shadows as she
continued, "It was all Kenny's fault. . . . I heard him tel
Jason that I wasn't fit to touch Winona's shoes. Me. . .
I sacrificed everything for Jason. But Jason wouldn'
have me because Kenny said I was cheap."

An ambulance siren whined, coming closer, a
Marcus asked, "How did you know they'd be out there
on that road that night?"

Francesca coughed and struggled to continue. "Not hey—her. I knew Winona would have to take that road to get to where Kenny was keeping you . . . I followed him after he picked you up. . . . Winona had made some traveling purchases in town, including a slinky nightie—and she sure wouldn't be wearing that for Jason. They hadn't had sex since before you were born. She was all lit up, and I knew she was taking off. But I'm glad Jason died, too. Scumbag. . . . I wasted my life on him . . . and my eyes are brown, but he liked blue."

"How did you know the exact time?" Marcus pressed.

Francesca's breath came slowly now, her words faint and fading. "I was in the parking lot that night. Kenny was all excited, and he went inside the marina. He left his car trunk open. . . . I saw some suitcases—and a woman's overnight case. It was Winona's. He had some groceries, and a bouquet of roses. . . . I knew the deal—that they loved each other. . . . You could see it in their eyes, the way they moved around each other. They were going to make a break for it that night. He was going to pick you up, so that meant she would follow. I waited. . . . So long, kid."

Marcus held Francesca's hand for moments after she was gone and the medics had arrived. He felt Tempest's hand on his shoulder and stood slowly to find her supporting Kenny.

"Kenny needs attention. She hit his head," Tempest said unevenly. "Marcus?"

Hollow and drained, Marcus felt as if he were sleepwalking in a nightmare. Mac approached them, the marina building lit now and filled with people, the medics and the police. A paramedic came to sit Kenny up and work on him, but Marcus couldn't look away from Francesca.

Tempest wrapped her arm around his waist. Strange,

Marcus thought distantly, how such a small woman could have such strength when all of his had just drained out of him.

"Okay, here's what happened," Tempest spoke to Mac. He took notes as she described how Francesca had tried to kill Kenny.

Mac scowled at Tempest. "Lady, you're keeping our medical examiner busy. We've got a dead woman on our hands, a kid just killed himself in my jail, and things just don't make sense with you around. . . . And it seems like wherever you are, things happen. You've been here, what? Five–six days? You've made my life a living hell . . . I hate paperwork. Where's the *Winona*, Marcus? I heard you left it to rescue Miss Trouble-maker here. Hey! Someone call the M.E.'s Office," he yelled to his men.

Francesca had driven the tulip truck . . . she had killed his parents . . . all this time, Marcus had thought she was a friend. . . . "I loaned the *Winona* to a couple of friends," Marcus stated in a hollow tone.

"I'll need details, names, addresses, contact numbers."

At his side, Tempest tensed and looked at Kenny, who had come to stand beside them. He was hunched, holding a concealing rag to his jaw and in his characteristic slump. He looked at Marcus and lied slowly, carefully, "Francesca and I had a thing. . . . She didn't want me talking about it. I finally decided that if I wasn't good enough for her to show off, then we were finished, no more sneaking around. She didn't like me turning her down much, I guess."

Mac grunted and studied Kenny from head to toe. "You sure? I mean, she was a fine-looking woman. And you—well, you'd be lucky to get her to tell the truth."

Kenny shrugged, and added, "She's been known to have a bad temper, Mac."

"True. She drove a car right through a dealer's window when she thought he'd screwed her on a deal. Her father was a hard-drinking, tough old son of a gun. He had her on heavy-duty equipment when she was just a kid. I guess she'd know how to drive anything."

"Including that city gravel truck last night. Before she hit me, Francesca said she just got mad when she saw Marcus and Tempest together. She said she was drunk, and something just clicked in her. She went crazy, wanting to have what they had and never getting what she wanted. She was sorry afterward because she did like Marcus."

"Makes sense. I saw her old man snap like that once. Too bad." Mac snapped his notebook closed and studied Marcus, Tempest, and Kenny. "Looks like a bad night. The medical examiner will want to go over this place, so the marina is closed for business, got it? And we'll have our regular morning tea party down at the station first thing tomorrow, okay? Now, why don't you all go get some rest?"

Outside, in the marina parking lot, the red lights of the police cars cycled in the night. Marcus gripped Tempest's gloved hand and started to hurry toward his car.

She drew back, and when he turned to her, Tempest stated firmly, "Not without Kenny. He's coming with us."

Kenny shook his head. "I don't think so."

Tempest took his hand and started drawing both men to the car. "We're in this together. You two are staying together until I'm satisfied, and Kenny just took a hard blow to the head. He needs someone to watch him tonight."

Marcus's hard, forbidding stare didn't stop Tempest. "Oh, yes. Or else I'm staying with him . . . at his house."

Marcus glanced at Kenny, who was shaking his head. He fingered the bandage the medics had placed over the contusion at the back of his head. "I'm going to be okay."

Tempest locked her stare with Marcus's. "His house or yours."

Kenny placed the ice pack Tempest had given him on the back of his head. At midnight, as he watched Marcus prowl around in front of the living-room windows, Kenny's ache for his son clearly visible. "I was picking up a few tools my father gave to me, packing up to leave, when Francesca came in. She was furious with me—with you, Tempest—because he loves you and wants to marry you. In her skewed mind, she couldn't take a second round of being put aside, poor woman. I caught her here, at the house, trying to create little accidents—to make me look responsible, I guess. She was jealous of me, wanting me out of Marcus's life, and she'd overheard what I'd said to Jason about her. She thought I'd ruined her life."

"Like the railing," Tempest murmured as she curled on an opposite couch, wrapped in an afghan, despite the warm July temperatures flowing through the open door. With everything that had happened, she still hadn't overcome the lake's chill and the fear of what could have happened in the water—or to Kenny.

Kenny nodded, his face pale where the beard had been, weathered above it, his features clearly resembling his son's. Then he looked around the living room and tears shimmered in his gray eyes. "When Jason was gone, and Opal, too, this was heaven—here or out on the *Winona*. I will love that woman until I die."

He glanced at Marcus's unforgiving broad back, the way he braced his legs, and slowly, painfully stood. "I'd better be going. I'll be around to see that they believe me, and then, I'm moving on."

"You're not going anywhere," Marcus stated slowly as he turned and walked to stand in front of Kenny. Then he added slowly, "Kenneth Ragnar."

Sensing tension, Tempest stood, the two tall men towering over her. Father and son stared at each other for what seemed like an eternity as Tempest held her breath.

"Take it easy, boy. You're all wound up and ready to fire," Kenny warned softly. "Not in front of the lady."

Marcus stared at Kenny for a long time, as if seeing through the years, sorting out the moments and lining them up into some kind of sense. When Tempest came to stand beside him, fearing what he would do, Marcus drew her close to his side. "She's trouble," he said curtly.

Kenny nodded slowly, cautiously. "That she is."

"A redhead, and you know how they are."

Kenny's lips curved as if he understood. "Uh-huh."

"Wait a minute," Tempest interrupted. "Now is no time to start in on my hair color—"

"This one is a psychic, which makes it even worse. Her whole family is loaded with extrasensory perceptions. Probably every child they have is going to be into things, climbing all over the place, nothing but trouble, every minute."

This time Kenny smiled, his eyes twinkling. "You'll have your hands full."

"How am I going to get their mother away for a little R and R?"

Tempest placed her hand on his chest; she'd lost the thread of the conversation somehow. Why would Marcus want to take Greer on vacation? "What are you two talking about?"

Marcus and Kenny ignored her. "When's her family coming in?" Kenny asked.

Tempest pushed away from Marcus. "My family?

Here? I don't think so. A whole houseful of us? C
you have no idea—"

But the men continued looking at each other, ignori
her. "How many chances does a man get to meet a hous
ful of psychics, Kenny?" Marcus asked. "You're invitec

"Now that's an offer that's too good to pass up
might just stick around for that."

Tempest gripped the front of each man's shirt in h
fists. "I'm tired, and nothing is making sense. I'm goi
to bed. Whatever is fine with me. Work it out. I'll s
you in the morning."

She tapped Kenny's chest with her finger. "You. I
find you anywhere you go, so just don't try it."

When she turned to Marcus, he wrapped her ha
in his and brought it to his lips. His eyes held promis
that took away her breath; Tempest saw herself
those gray eyes with their bronze flecks. "What d
you feel when I held your hand and Kenny's? What
you know that I don't?" she whispered.

While he didn't answer, the lingering tender bru
of his lips spoke of promises Marcus intended
keep.

Four days later, Tempest lay dozing with her arr
around Marcus's pillow. The scent of morning coff
and the rumble of the men's voices had made her
too comfortable. Add the residual effect of Marcu
loving during the night, and she was truly relaxe
The cup of tea waiting on the bedside table caused h
to smile, and she sat up to enjoy it.

Marcus, Kenny, and Tempest had attend
Francesca's funeral, but Marcus had said little, I
brooding silence an indication of his dark emotior
Francesca had been his friend and had murdered h
parents. That betrayal would leave a wound th
would lessen with time. Still, it was the final chapt
in his search for the hit-and-run driver. His emotio

bout Kenny would take time to work through, but
he sturdy lifetime friendship wasn't damaged, and it
vould grow.

The men's voices moved from the kitchen, past Mar-
us's bedroom, and into the living room. "Ragnar"
lowed amid Kenny's description of his parents, and
hey were looking at the duplicate pictures he'd put
nto an album for his son.

Last night, all three of them had walked along the
each, and she'd sensed nothing but mist and calm
nd incredible peace . . . and Marcus, ready to draw
er to safety. She'd considered waves, and that light
oving warmth in her heart. If her father had been out
here, he was at rest now.

Marcus suddenly swung open the bedroom door,
nd said, "Hey, sleepyhead. Someone sent you a pres-
nt. Get up. And no, I'm not bringing it to you."

Tempest dabbed at the tea she'd just spilled when
urprised. "Okay, okay. Give me a minute."

She dressed quickly and hurried to the living room,
vhere Marcus and Kenny sat. Marcus tossed a pack-
ge to her and she quickly opened it to find a tiny
ongship, a perfect replica of a Viking model. Tempest
nrolled the red silk square, finished with Claire's del-
cate hand stitches. "Red, the color of blood, to make
heir enemies afraid," she whispered.

Tears came to her eyes; her sister had known the
erfect way for the closure that Tempest had needed
or years. She looked at Marcus, who had instantly
ome to his feet, his arm around her protectively. "Let's
o down to the lake."

The morning was calm and bright, perfect as the
ittle ship with the red sails floated out on the lake.
'lames began to lick at the red sail. "Rest now, Dad,"
'empest whispered, and instantly felt much lighter,
er childhood guilt disappearing.

"We've got company," Marcus stated, as an older

woman with shining red hair, touched by a streak (
gray, came down the pathway to the beach.

Greer Aisling smiled at Marcus and held her daugh
ter's hand as they traced that little longship with th
burning red sails.

"Daniel would have liked that," Tempest's mothe
said softly, tears filling her eyes. "It's just what h
needed."

It was just what Tempest had needed, too.

"The gathering of the clan," Marcus stated that evening
as Claire and Neil Olafson, Leona Chablis, and Gree
Aisling sat in his living room. Tempest sat beside him

By being absent from this particular family gathe
ing, Kenny was missing quite a sight. The soft ligh
brought out the fiery highlights of the women's hai
their slanted cheekbones. and mysterious earth-gree
eyes. While the unique Aisling women resembled eac
other, their temperaments were definitely quite diffe
ent. More animated and impulsive than the othe
three, Tempest was clearly nervous throughout th
family dinner. Marcus liked that word, "family";
curled warmly around him, taking away the years (
loneliness.

With her long, sleeveless, black lounging gow
Tempest wore her cuff bracelet and Winona's locke
Claire wore an embroidered cream blouse wit
flowing sleeves and loose black slacks, her single lor
braid a dark red brand over her shoulder. When sh
had arrived with Neil, she'd merely walked up t
Marcus and studied him. She'd taken his hands i
hers and smiled softly. Gentle waves enfolded an
soothed him, Claire's empathic psyche at worl
"Hello, Marcus," she'd said as though they'd bee
friends forever. "You'll be fine. All you need is tim
to work through it all."

Leona had merely hugged and studied him, as if she already knew he would heal. For this special evening, she had chosen a dark green lounging gown with long sleeves, and both women wore one of the wolf's-head brooches at their shoulders. Lean and tall, both women exuded class and grace and total control.

Greer had dressed simply for the evening, a dark blue tunic and slacks, with a woven, homespun-looking shawl around her shoulders, held in place by the family brooch. She lifted her glass in a toast to Marcus. He sensed that she understood the dark, brooding passages of his life and how he needed time to heal.

Marcus studied the night outside the windows. The sound of the waves and the wind seemed in harmony. The psychics seemed at ease—at least their extra senses seemed not to be picking up anything dangerous. Tonight, another tension ran beneath the quiet layers of the women. Neil's usually easygoing manner was overlaid by his evident concern for Claire.

Marcus thought of Sean's "Later," and how Tempest had wondered if that rage could be transferred to someone else, someone who could harm the Aisling women in the future. That was no small worry.

At times, the women sometimes didn't speak, but communicated with a look, a touch. But now their voices weaved softly around him.

Then Leona lifted her wineglass to study the dregs and calmly dropped a verbal bomb into the peace. "Mother thinks that we have a psychic vampire on our hands."

"I was going to introduce the idea a little bit gentler, Leona." Greer had tensed and faced her daughters. "But yes, I do. Leona's sense of being crushed matches my own."

"My husband was killed in an avalanche . . . it's

natural I would feel that way. She's saying that some
one else is in our game, and he, or she, isn't nice,"
Leona stated flatly. She appeared to study the glass as
if uninterested in the topic. "He, she or it, is feeding of
the weaker and becoming stronger."

"Strong enough to block me," Greer admitted.

"A vampire, but it's not after blood. It's after what we
are. It's a psychic vampire, isn't it?" Claire whispered
ominously. "Someone, something that can make you do
things you don't want, who sucks your strength. It came
after me, I felt that way, like it wanted me. It wanted me
to pay. I still don't know why it wanted revenge."

"Neither do I." Tempest clasped Marcus's hand
tightly. "It can make you do things, think things you
normally wouldn't. I think that's what it did to me.
When I touched things it had connected with, I picked
up its energy. It actually took hold of me, enough for
me to imagine I heard voices."

"It started with Claire." Greer adjusted her shawl as
if chilled, though the second week of July evening was
warm. "She would be the most vulnerable, an empath
who can sense emotions and the physical well-being
of others. I think it began with her, testing her. Then
her bond with Neil made her stronger, and now Tem
pest has Marcus."

"Both are of Viking heritage. Both protectors. I
didn't have a chance. Now, logically, by the process of
elimination, it wants me," Leona said. "But I'm not
living near a large body of water. The only time I've
been near any is with Mother or my sisters. We're
stronger together. We always have been."

"Love is the bond," Greer murmured softly.

Marcus stood and left the room. He returned mo
ments later to place a familiar box in Tempest's hands.
"Let's do it, honey. You've earned it. You've paid the
price you thought you owed your family."

When the original brooch lay on its dark cloth, cra

dled in Tempest's gloved hands, she whispered, "You had it sent here?"

"No, I had it all the time."

To bring the brooch to her mother's keeping had driven her, and now Tempest stared helplessly at it, her eyes brimming with tears. She'd felt she'd betrayed her family, that to her ease her guilt, she had to deliver the brooch into Greer's hands, to protect them all. And now she could.

Marcus kissed her forehead. "Go on, sweetheart. Take it to her. You've earned it."

Greer accepted the brooch with elegance and formality. "You've done what you wanted. You owe nothing to us, do you understand? Nothing to Daniel, or to me, or to your sisters. You only owe yourself, and Marcus, the happiness you deserve. You're free."

Her moment had come, and filled with emotion, free of guilt, Tempest could nod and return to sit beside Marcus.

Greer carefully studied the large rectangular brooch, closed her eyes, and ran her fingers over the inscriptions. "Marcus never touched it, but his residual is here, because of Tempest . . . Tempest's bare hands, the collector, and the antiquities hunter. . . ."

Tempest's arm around Marcus's shoulder tightened as she leaned forward. Claire and Leona were pinned to the sight of Greer's fingers sliding over the inscription. "There is a curse lying over it, the same as in Leona's and my dreams. Violence . . . killing, savagery. I . . . I'm getting the inscription, but there are waves of hatred surrounding it. The curse is like a cloth over the meaning."

She shuddered and gripped the brooch as if diving into another realm. Her fingertip traced the angular inscriptions surrounding the wolf's head. "It says, House of the Wolf, Thorgood the Great, whose mighty hand holds his people safe, who will kill those who defy him. His line will be long and powerful, reigning after him, for he who holds the wolf, holds the power. . . ."

"But that's not the curse. That's only the inscription," Leona whispered, straining to follow Greer's fingertips.

Suddenly, Greer's body jerked, and she touched the brooch to her forehead. "It's an old line, as old as ours. The curse is on the line of Thorgood and Aisling. He's sworn vengeance when the time is right . . . when he is strong enough. That would mean that his line has found the right descendant, one with enough power to take us on. But first he has to end the line."

"That's us. He kills all of us, and he gets the brooch and all the power. He gets revenge," Leona whispered. Her sleek, shoulder-length hair shifted as she bent her head, concealing her face.

"He's been testing us, trying to break the birth and psychic bond between us. If one goes down, the others weaken. He brings us down, he gets the brooch, he gets the power, he gets revenge. For what?" Tempest asked. "Why?"

Leona looked out at the lake. "Simple. He didn't get the girl. The good guy won. He won everything. The bad guy didn't like it. It's an old story. He didn't curse the brooch, he cursed the family, the line. She's picking up what happened when they fought. He was Viking, too, and not a happy camper."

Greer nodded. "It's true. We needed the brooch to put it all together. Leona and I had the same dream."

"It's usually the future. But not this dream. It's the same," Leona whispered unevenly.

"Let's go get this guy. What do we do?" Tempest asked.

Leona wrapped her arms around herself as if chilled. "That's the question, isn't it? But I will not let fear rule my life."

"Be smart and take care, Leona Fiona."

"Will do, Tempest Best."

Epilogue

THE LAST WEEK OF JULY SPREAD A SOFT MIST OVER THE
Lake Michigan night.

Tempest stood on the shoreline, watching the filtered moonlight ride the swells. The waves played at
her bare feet, the sand sliding beneath her soles. She
waited for the first trickling warning of danger, but no
soft beckoning came, no whisper of her name.

The mist had dampened Marcus's shirt, and the
wind pushed the edges against her bare thighs. She
drew it around her, snuggling down into his scents,
the man she loved. Could she really stay in one place,
really become the woman, the life mate Marcus should
have? Was all that possible after her years of wander-
ing, of those layers of guilt, recently shed?

The mist's dampness tingled on her skin, on her
bare legs as she thought of the man sleeping heavily in
their bed, struggling hourly, daily, to put the past
behind him. How could she, a psychic who used her
hands, possibly fit into Marcus's life?

Tempest smoothed his mother's locket with her bare
fingertip, as she had many times before. Winona, the
picture-perfect wife to the wrong man, had given her
heart and soul to another, a lifetime of happiness captured in tiny, sporadic, precious moments.

The mist circled Tempest, and she held out her bare hands to it, and waited. The damp tingle came naturally from the mist, nothing more—no eerie, silent presence. Then another tingle ran up her nape, and she turned—

A tall man walked toward her, the mist swirling around him. She couldn't see his face. . . . Tempest held her breath. Maybe it wasn't over, the darkness haunting her family.

"You're not going anywhere without me." Marcus's deep, uneven tone curled around her.

She saw him clearly now, the harsh planes of his face, the wind tugging at his hair. A slip of moonlight caught his eyes, silvery in the shadows.

"What would you do? Hunt me down?" she asked lightly as she stretched out her hand to his.

"Always." His fingers slid between hers, his palm broad and hard against her own. The bracelet claiming him as her own, intended to keep him safe, slid along her skin. Love, strength, endurance, the emotions still unsettled about his mother and father, but there was understanding, too—all flowed up her arm and nestled warmly in her heart.

"What do you know that I don't?" she asked, as Marcus tugged her against him, and she fisted his hair with her bare hands. Tempest loved touching him, exploring every texture, free of fear. He was her lover, her heart.

But Marcus needed the words. "First, tell me if we have that true bond, like Neil and Claire?"

She angled her head, studying him. "I'm never going to make life easy for you, you know. Yes, it is a true bond."

Marcus drew her close to rest against his chest, where she could feel the steady beat of his heart. "Tell me the secret."

"Your family didn't stay long."

"They can't stay too close to each other for very long. Neil has settled Claire's senses, balancing them. She's not as sensitive as she was to the thoughts and feelings and physical well-being of the rest of us. But as for the rest, as a triplet and a psychic, we merge too easily into each other's senses. We'll need to live apart."

"Claire with Neil. . . . You said he balances her?"

"Uh-huh. Yin and yang." She nuzzled his chest, inhaling the familiar scents and textures. "I'll always have to wear gloves, Marcus. But I'm less impulsive, and I could stay like this forever. You're avoiding telling me the secret you're holding. Tell me."

"Well, that true bond makes it a lot easier for the kids we're going to have."

She leaned back in his arms and blinked up at him. "Huh?"

Marcus took her face in his hands. "Mm. How to explain this. . . . You let a part of yourself flow through the images and sensations, like you love me."

"You already told me that."

"Feel for yourself."

Tempest immediately gripped his shoulders, closed her eyes, and focused; she dived into the different layers. Yin and yang circled each other, spinning. . . . She waded through the strength and love, Marcus's honor, the natural macho bristling stuff of a male, searching the layers for what she had missed. The harsh memories had softened a bit, a love for his father growing stronger. . . .

In a distant dark corner, something quivered, and Tempest dived for it. She wrapped a psychic fist around it and held tight. The quivering nugget fluttered and connected with something inside Tempest, and she knew she had it. It ticked, counting down minutes.

When she opened her eyes, Marcus had that predator, got-you-now expression. He didn't have long to wait for her reaction: "It's a biological clock. I didn't know," she whispered. "I haven't even thought about it."

She'd been so concerned about Marcus unraveling his past and his relationship with Kenneth Ragnar that she hadn't consciously worked her way through any future other than her love for Marcus and being with him forever.

"Forever" had a lot of connotations for the average woman in love. It usually meant giving the man she loved a child or children. How often had she looked at Marcus while he slept beside her and wondered what he would have been like as a child? Lately, she'd been watching the children on the beach and thinking how cute they were and how she would like to cuddle them.

She felt the tiny ticking again, almost like a tiny heartbeat that would share her body in the future. Somewhere deep in her psyche, unrecognized by her conscious mind, she'd wanted a child with Marcus, to fill his life and her own with love.

That ticking was there all along, a biological clock in her future, like any other woman's, and she hadn't known!

"That's what you felt? That someday, I'd want—"

"Well, now you know. I can't have you running all over the place with that thing starting to tick and me not around, can I?"

Marcus was actually asking for something else, but Tempest understood. "No, you're absolutely right. But Marcus, I'm not the mother type. I've never—"

"Oh, you can do anything. Think of it as climbing a building and feeling your way along."

A V O N

MEG CABOT

...he went all the way

978-0-06-134024-6

Leslie Carroll

Choosing Sophie

978-0-06-087137-6

i want candy

KIM WONG KELTNER

978-0-06-084798-2

This Is How It Happened

JO

978-0-06-124110-9

Lisa London

GOOD MAN HUNTING

978-0-06-134039-0

LITTLE PINK RAINCOAT

GIGI ANDERS

978-0-06-111886-9

Visit www.AuthorTracker.com for exclusive
information on your favorite HarperCollins authors.

Available wherever books are sold, or call 1-800-331-3761 to order.

ATP 0408

Avon Romantic Treasures

Unforgettable, enthralling love stories, sparkling with passion and adventure from Romance's bestselling authors